She's lost her memory—
but her body still remembers!

Amnesia

THREE LITTLE MIRACLES
by
Rebecca Winters

THE SECOND MRS ADAMS
by
Sandra Marton

A HUSBAND'S REVENGE
by
Lee Wilkinson

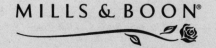

MILLS & BOON®

*MILLS & BOON and MILLS & BOON with the Rose Device
are registered trademarks of the publisher.*
*Harlequin Mills & Boon Limited,
Eton House, 18-24 Paradise Road, Richmond, Surrey, TW9 1SR*

AMNESIA
© by Harlequin Enterprises II B.V., 2000

Three Little Miracles, The Second Mrs Adams and *A Husband's
Revenge* were first published in Great Britain by
Harlequin Mills & Boon Limited in separate, single volumes.

Three Little Miracles © Rebecca Winters 1996
The Second Mrs Adams © Sandra Myles 1996
A Husband's Revenge © Lee Wilkinson 1996

ISBN 0 263 82415 2

05-0005

*Printed and bound in Spain
by Litografia Rosés S.A., Barcelona*

Rebecca Winters, an American writer and mother of four, is excited about the new millennium because it means another new beginning. Having said goodbye to the classroom where she taught French and Spanish, she is now free to spend more time with her family, to travel and to write the Mills & Boon® novels she loves so dearly.

THREE LITTLE MIRACLES

by
REBECCA WINTERS

To Rhonda,
whose baby twins provided the
inspiration for this book!

CHAPTER ONE

"GOOD morning, Tracey. How's our miracle patient today?"

Tracey paused in her writing to look up at her doctor. "Good morning, Louise."

"I'm glad to hear you call me by my first name."

The corners of Tracey's sculpted mouth turned up in a faint smile. "It seems an impertinence."

"Nonsense." Louise's keen eyes made a cursory examination. "You look good."

"I feel good. So good, in fact, that I'd like to go outside."

"All in due time," Louise murmured as she examined the latest entry in Tracey's journal. "Excellent. Your writing is as lucid and logical as I'm certain it was before your accident. You deserve a treat."

"I love treats."

"Good. Then you'll get one, but first, I'd like you to draw another picture for me."

Tracey stirred restlessly in the chair. "I'd rather play a card game or checkers with you."

"This is like a game."

"What do I have to draw?"

"You're still experiencing disturbing dreams about

5

some kind of animal that terrifies you. I'm curious to see what it looks like,'' she said, her eyes radiating compassion.

Tracey shook her head in denial and shrank from her.

''Come on, Tracey. You can do it. It's important. Maybe if I show you some pictures, you can tell me if any of them are the kind you keep talking about in your sleep.''

Louise opened a book and flipped the pages slowly, urging Tracey to look. In spite of her fear, Tracey was fascinated by the dozens of animal pictures, everything from bighorn sheep in the wilds of the Yukon to gazelles roaming the darkest depths of Africa. When the last one appeared, Tracey lifted her head. ''None of them looks like it.''

Louise put paper and pencil in front of her. ''I didn't think so. Therefore, I want you to draw what you continue to see in your mind. Remember, it can't possibly hurt you because it's only a picture on a piece of paper.''

Tracey thought about it for a long time, trying to get up the courage. ''If I do it this once, then will you let me go outside and walk on the grounds?''

''Tracey—I'm trying to get you well enough that you can walk out of here free to resume a full, productive life. But if you're so terrified of this animal, how can I let you go out of doors where animals live when a fear like yours is still unresolved?''

Letting out a tortured sigh, Tracey agreed, "You can't." After another long hesitation, she said, "All right. I—I'll do it. But I hate it." Her voice trembled.

With a less than steady hand, she began to draw the image of the horrifying creature that kept menacing her every time she closed her eyes and went to sleep.

No matter what she did, she couldn't hide from it. The only way to make it go away was to force herself to wake up. When she did, she found herself screaming and panting, completely exhausted. She'd discover that her body glistened with perspiration, that her pillow was drenched.

"There!"

She pushed the offensive drawing away. Louise picked it up without looking at it, then pulled out a wrapped chocolate bar and handed it to her. The red foil with the gold printing caused Tracey to pause before she opened it.

"*La Maison Chappelle,*" she read the words aloud. "*Fabrique en Suisse.*"

"Chappelle House," Louise explained quietly. "Have you eaten that brand of chocolate before?"

"Yes, I have," she said with certainty. Her finely arched brows furrowed. "That name, Chappelle…"

"Your father was the U.S. representative for Chappelle House until his death."

Tracey's head flew back and she stared at the other woman. "That's the second time you've mentioned my father."

"Do you remember him at all?"

Tracey shook her head, then rubbed her thumb over the gold embossing on the label. "But I do seem to remember *something* connected with the Chappelle name."

The older woman darted her a shrewd regard. "Maybe that's because it's the most famous name for fine chocolate in the world. Chappelle House is well over a hundred years old. It's a very prestigious company, very established among confection connoisseurs. Go ahead, have a bite."

With a feeling of déjà vu, Tracey undid the wrapper and ate one of the thin squares. "Umm...hazelnut, my favorite. How did you know?"

Louise winked. "I'm psychic. Are you familiar with that word?"

"Yes." Tracey smiled. "So tell me my other favorite kind."

"Hmm... Let me see. White chocolate with little nuts."

Tracey sat back in shock. "You really are psychic."

"No." The other woman shook her head. "A lucky guess. I happen to love nuts, that's all. I'll bring you some next time."

She stood up, considering Tracey for a long moment. "And now I have another surprise for you. There's a lady outside who's anxious to talk to you. But if you don't feel ready to see anyone yet, then just say the word."

Curious, Tracey also got to her feet. "Have I met her before?"

"Yes, about two months ago, but it made no impression on you then. She keeps in constant touch and loves you very much. Here's a picture of her." Louise held out a photograph, which Tracey plucked from her fingers.

At first glance, the picture of the elegant woman staring back meant little to Tracey. But upon closer inspection, the facial features began to be familiar and her throat started to work. "*A-Aunt Rose!*" she finally cried out in recognition.

The doctor beamed. "That's right. Soon you're going to get *all* your memory back. That woman is your Aunt Rose Harris. You were living with her when the accident happened. Do you remember?"

"No. Not a thing. But I know this face."

Eagerly Tracey touched the image that bore a startling resemblance to Tracey's own mother's lovely countenance. Suddenly her father's handsome face flashed in her mind.

"*Daddy!*" she whispered as one tear started, then another, unleashing a myriad of memories from her youth, of a sister and loving parents, of halcyon days of summer surrounded by hillsides of wild narcissus and luscious fruit orchards.

Some of the memories were so poignant and had been dammed up for so long, they came rushing in faster than she could assimilate them. Yet overriding them all was a sudden deep, piercing sadness, too indescribable for words.

Trying to shake it off, she cried, "I want to see Aunt Rose. I *have* to see her," she said, her voice throbbing. "Let me walk out with you," Tracey begged, feeling a sudden compulsion to communicate with the aunt who had taken her and Isabelle in after their parents had died in a plane accident.

"She's in the lounge."

Louise held the door open for her to pass. These days, Tracey could walk normally without a cane and had the run of the floor.

"*Aunt Rose!*"

"*Tracey, darling!*" her aunt called out as they rounded the corner of the hallway.

Tracey flew into her outstretched arms and clung to her, saying her name over and over again.

"Finally you know who I am. I've been waiting ages for you to remember." Rose wept.

"Louise showed me your picture just now and I recognized you."

They both let go of each other long enough to wipe their eyes, then Rose grabbed Tracey's hands. "Four months ago, the doctors said there was no hope, yet here you are alive, amazingly healthy and more beautiful than ever. A miracle has happened."

"At the rate her memory is coming back, she's almost ready to go home," Louise interjected. "Now I'll leave the two of you to your reunion."

"Thank you," Rose murmured to the doctor while Tracey studied her aunt's face, wondering why she hadn't been able to recognize her until today.

The sixty-year-old woman looked a lot like Tracey's mother and sister with her chestnut brown hair. However, where the two older women had blue-green eyes, Isabelle's were brown, like their father's.

As for Tracey, her eyes were a translucent green, darkly lashed, and set in an oval face with high cheekbones and classic features framed by ash blond hair, the odd Saxon throwback her sandy-haired father used to tease her.

"Let's go to your room where we can be private, darling. We have four months of catching up to do."

"Tell me about Isabelle. How is she? How are Bruce and Alex? I just realized I have a sister with a family. Why didn't she come with you?" Tracey asked one question after another as they walked arm in arm down the hall.

Her aunt sobered. "Which question do you want me to answer first?"

They entered her room and shut the door.

"All of them," Tracey cried, so delighted to see her aunt, she felt euphoric. "Come and sit down over here by me," she insisted, patting the couch. The furnishings reminded Tracey more of an elegant hotel suite than a hospital room, a fact her aunt commented on, as well. "Now tell me everything."

"Well..." Rose nervously tucked a loose strand of

hair into the back of her chignon. "Your sister would be here, but she's a little under the weather right now."

"Is it serious?"

Rose seemed to ponder her question before saying, "No. Not at all."

"Aunt Rose—I know that look. Something's wrong with Isabelle. Please don't be afraid to tell me. I'm fine and getting stronger every day."

"I can see that, darling, and I thank God for your remarkable recovery. The truth is—" she eyed Tracey uneasily "—Isabelle is expecting another baby and she has dreadful morning sickness."

"Oh, dear. She suffered from that with Alex, too. But how wonderful to be pregnant, to be a mother at all." Her voice ached with longing for things she felt would always elude her, like a family of her own.

In her turmoil, she was scarcely aware of Rose's hands twisting convulsively in her long strand of pearls, or the fact that she'd averted her eyes.

"Is Bruce excited?"

"I—I'm afraid he's too busy thinking of ways to bankrupt them to realize what's happening. I hope he wakes up before it's too late."

Tracey nodded. "So do I." On a burst of energy, she jumped to her feet. "Just as soon as I'm released, let's drive over to Sausalito and surprise them! I can't wait to hold Alex again. While he was having his second birthday party, I was in that coma. To be honest,

I can't wait to get out of this place." She cast a guilty glance at her aunt.

"I don't mean to sound ungrateful. Everyone here keeps telling me I'm a living miracle and I believe them. They've been absolutely wonderful to me. But I feel like my whole life has been spent inside these walls. I—I'm starting to get claustrophobia."

"Of course you are. Anyone would feel the same way." Rose got to her feet and put an arm around Tracey's shoulders, commiserating with her. "The doctors only plan to keep you here a little longer."

Tracey sighed. "I wish I could leave with you right now. To be so near the ocean, yet not see or smell anything... Oh, Aunt Rose, I can't wait to go out on the Bay. It will be heaven to sail under the bridge and feel the wind in my face again." When her aunt didn't say anything, Tracey turned to her. "Aunt Rose? Something's the matter. You're acting different... strange..." Tears stung her eyes. "A-am I a freak of nature or something? Did the doctors tell you I'm not quite all there anymore?"

"Oh, no, darling. Anything but."

Suddenly Tracey was enfolded and allowed to cry out her tears against her aunt's soft cashmere sweater that carried the unforgettable scent of roses, her signature for as long as Tracey could remember.

"I thought you would realize that you're in Switzerland, not San Francisco."

Tracey blinked. *Not in San Francisco?*

When Rose's words registered, Tracey pulled away, appalled by the revelation because she should have figured it out long before now.

She shook her head in consternation. "I'm really a mental case, aren't I?"

"Of course you're not!"

Groaning, Tracey clasped her arms to her waist. "No wonder Louise won't let me out of here yet. I'm like a newborn baby who doesn't know anything." Fresh tears spilled down her cheeks. "Maybe I'll never be well enough to leave here."

"Hush, darling. Don't talk that way. You've lived through an ordeal not many humans have ever survived. And don't forget. French comes as easily to you as English because you've been bilingual since you were a little girl."

Tracey moistened her dry lips. "You don't have to make excuses for me."

"*Excuses*? You've been busy healing, getting your memory back. You've done it so fast, you've astounded the entire medical staff here! Of course you're not completely oriented yet. You haven't had time to make a connection with the outside world. But, darling, none of it matters."

"Of course it matters," Tracey lashed out in self-deprecation. "I should have caught on immediately. Look at the ornate furniture in this room. And the food I've been eating! *Escalope de veau* is hardly California's Jack in the Box style, is it? Where am I, exactly?"

"You're in Lausanne."

"*Lausanne*?"

"Yes."

Tracey let out an angry laugh. "The place where they have all the famous clinics for the most serious maladies afflicting mankind. The place where you have to be a wealthy movie star or a Greek shipping tycoon to even begin to afford it.

"Is that where I am, Aunt Rose? In one of those fantastically expensive facilities that has used up all of the inheritance Father left Isabelle and me as well as your modest retirement income?"

Rose walked over to her and cupped the side of her hot cheek with her hand. "You're in a hospital for recovering head injury patients, getting the help you need. That's all that's important."

"Not if *you've* been left with nothing to live on! I couldn't bear that, not after your sacrifice," Tracey agonized. "You could have married again if it hadn't been for us."

"That's not true, Tracey. I didn't want to marry Lawrence. We were just good friends."

Tracey shook her head. "I don't believe that, and I want to see the horrendous bill I've been running up to this point in time. Then I'm going to pack my bags and fly to San Francisco where I'll get an apartment and a job so I can start paying you back."

"That's exactly what you're not going to do," her aunt said in a surprisingly firm tone.

"I know you'd do anything to protect me, Aunt Rose. But I'm a big girl now. My doctor told me I couldn't leave here until I was ready to function in the real world again." She paused for a fortifying breath. "Paying one's own way is part of living in the real world. After four months of being reliant on you, of keeping you separated from Lawrence, it's time I justified my own existence."

"Tracey...I never could bring myself to marry Lawrence, not after what your uncle and I shared. Besides, Lawrence died three months ago of a heart attack."

"Oh, Aunt Rose," Tracey moaned and hugged her again. "I'm so sorry."

"Don't be. He's with his wife now. What's important is *you*."

The note of strain and agitation in her aunt's voice checked Tracey's movements. "You sound so serious. What's wrong?"

"There's nothing wrong. That's why I hate to see you excite yourself needlessly over money. A-all along someone else has been responsible for the bills, so you're not to worry about that."

Someone else?

Since her accident, there were many things Tracey still had to relearn, but no one had to teach her about the soaring of hospital costs in the nineties. Her treatment had to be in the hundreds-of-thousands-of-dollars range by now, if not more.

"Aunt Rose, what person do you know who would have that kind of money, let alone be willing to pay for *my* medical bills?"

"I can answer that," said a deep, velvety male voice directly behind Tracey.

Seized by inexplicable fear, she broke out in a cold sweat, unable to turn around and face whoever it was because she'd heard that voice over and over in her nightmares.

"Julien!" her aunt cried out in alarm, making gestures for him to leave.

Julien Chappelle...

Like a rock thrown at a plate glass mirror, the sound of his name on her aunt's lips made something burst inside Tracey, shattering the shell of her fragile defense system into infinitesimal pieces, leaving her core exposed and bleeding....

She didn't have to turn around and look at him to remember. His jet black hair and eyes, his tall, lean body, those aquiline features so full of character, so incredibly male and breathtaking were indelibly inscribed on her mind and heart forever.

He made every man she'd ever met or dreamed of fade into insignificance beside him. No man could ever be his equal, not in any way. It simply wasn't possible. Tracey loved him more than life itself.

But it was a forbidden love.

Suddenly every atom of her body was filled with that soul-destroying pain she'd lived with for months before the accident. A pain only the coma could camouflage. But even that cocoon of unreality hadn't lasted long. Now the pain was back, more fiery, more unendurable than ever....

"*Dear God...*" she groaned in agony.

That awful sickness welled up in her throat and she barely made it to the bathroom in time.

"Tracey," he murmured anxiously in that low, husky tone she loved so much, having followed her inside the Italian-tiled room to steady her from behind while she retched over and over again.

Don't touch me, she screamed from within when she felt him slide his hands familiarly around her upper arms like he used to do on their honeymoon as a prelude to making love. They couldn't bear to be apart from each other, not even for short periods of time.

Every time he touched her, it was like the first time. But right now she was too violently sick, too weak from the shock of being in his presence again to say a single word.

"If you don't mind, Monsieur Chappelle, I'll take over now," she heard Gerard, one of the nurses, say with an underlying trace of command.

"I do mind," he ground out. "She's my *wife*!"

Tracey almost collapsed from the ring of love and fierce possession in his voice. She couldn't allow this to continue another second.

"*Julien*. Please!" This from Aunt Rose. "We'll wait in the lounge."

Tracey felt the tremor that passed through Julien's powerful body, witness to his tremendous struggle before he finally relinquished his hold of her, leaving her more devastated than ever.

"I'll be back, *mignonne*," he vowed in a hoarse whisper she felt to every tiny hair follicle of her skin.

When she heard their footsteps fade, she slumped heavily against Gerard, who assisted her to walk from the bathroom to her bed.

"Don't let him come back in, Gerard," she begged as he helped her to sit and started taking her vital signs. "He's not my husband anymore. Keep him away from me. Please. I don't want to see him!"

Her relief was exquisite when he said, "Until the doctor says otherwise, no one's going to be allowed in here except the staff. Get ready for bed. Louise is on her way."

"Yes. I need Louise. I need her now!" she cried in panic.

After Gerard left the room, Tracey hurried over to the dresser and changed into a nightgown. Being sick to her stomach had depleted her strength. All she wanted to do was lie down and pray for oblivion.

No sooner had she climbed in bed and drawn the covers over her than Louise strode in, her lab coat flapping. The two women eyed each other as the doctor pulled up a chair next to Tracey and sat down.

"You've had quite a day. You've also made some major breakthroughs that we need to talk about before you go to sleep."

Tracey squirmed to a sitting position, unconsciously drawing the edge of the sheet to her mouth with her hands. "I'll never be able to rest knowing *he's* just down the hall, able to walk in at any time. He's determined to see me." Her voice quaked in fear.

"He's already left the hospital with your aunt. I asked them to leave and watched them drive off."

"Thank heaven." She couldn't have faced him again.

"When he realized that his presence brought on your sick spell, he didn't need anyone to tell him to go. You have to understand that he's spent every night with you for the past three months, trying to soothe you during your nightmares. His devotion has been phenomenal."

Tracey's heart was pierced anew. *Forgive me for doing this to you, Julien, but it's the only way things can be from here on out.*

"Tell me about your husband."

Tracey's fingers locked in a death grip. "He's not my husband."

"Because you don't want him to be?"

The question drove her to explain, "We're divorced."

"He's paying your hospital bills."

Hot tears trickled down her cheeks. "I know. My aunt told me. It's her fault."

"That he's paying the bills?"

"No. That he found out where I was hiding. She's to blame. He broke her down and got the truth out of her b-because she's always thought he was the most wonderful man who ever lived, which of course he is," she said, her voice wobbling precariously.

"I see. So his wealth wouldn't have tempted her to ask for a financial favor?"

"No. Never. My hus—Julien would have insisted on paying for everything. He's always been like that."

"Always? How long were you married?"

"Two months, but our families had been friends for many years before that. The fact is, h-he's the most honorable man alive. His goodness, his decency to people is well known. He's exceptional," she murmured in an aching voice. "That's the problem.

"E-even though we're divorced, I'm afraid he'll always feel a sense of obligation and duty where I'm concerned because that's the way he's made. It would be useless to tell him I want to pay for everything myself now that I'm on my own. H-he wouldn't let me."

"Let me see if I'm understanding you correctly. You think he's the most wonderful man alive and you're not afraid of him. You simply don't want to live with him anymore."

"*Yes*!" She grasped at Louise's summation as if it were a lifeline.

"He's still desperately in love with you."

"I know." Tracey lowered her head. "If you don't

mind, I don't want to talk about this anymore. I don't want to be in this place anymore. I'm thankful for everything you've done for me. Obviously I wouldn't be alive without your help. But now I'm well. You told me that yourself just this morning.''

"That's true. Physically, you're in amazingly good health."

"I want to go home, Louise. I want to go home tonight!''

Louise lounged back in the chair, her arms folded. "Where is home?''

"San Francisco.''

"How will you get there?''

"I have enough cash in my purse to take a taxi to the airport in Geneva. I'll phone my sister collect and have her prepay an airline ticket for me. When I get to San Francisco, she can pick me up at the airport and take me home with her. In a few days, I'll get a job and an apartment, and I'll start making my own way.''

"In theory, that all sounds fine. Except that you can't check yourself out of the hospital.''

Angry flags of color tinted her cheeks. "What do you mean, *I can't*?''

"Your husband admitted you. He's the only one who can say when you leave.''

"But I've already told you. He's not my husband! I divorced him.''

"That may be true for you, but he never signed those divorce papers. *Legally, you're still his wife.*''

CHAPTER TWO

TRACEY gasped for breath. "You're *lying*!"

"No." Louise shook her head. "I've never lied to you. I never will. By the time your attorney had served his attorney with papers, you had already been hit by that car and were lying in a coma. According to your Aunt Rose, your husband refused to do anything about your marital status because he was too beside himself with grief."

Tracey's hands flew to her mouth. "Then I'm still Tracey Chappelle?"

"Yes."

No! "I—I can't bear it."

Louise leaned forward, compassion shining from her eyes. "I'm sorry this has come as such a terrible shock to you."

"Why didn't you tell me sooner?" Tracey whispered.

"Because it's best when recovering head injury patients remember the past on their own, when it comes back naturally, when the mind is ready to accept new information.

"So far, that's exactly how your case has progressed. That's why you're in such excellent shape. But tonight your husband changed the rules when he insisted on making his presence known. It was a risk, and now I've had to give you some information you weren't ready for. I'm sorry about that. I didn't want to do it, Tracey. I wanted you to remember on your own, but your husband has been in pain too long. When he saw that you recognized your Aunt Rose, he couldn't hold back any longer.''

Tracey dashed away her tears. ''How much more is there that I don't know about?''

After a brief pause, ''I won't lie to you. There's more, but as your doctor, I don't feel that now is the time to tell you. You've suffered enough shocks for one night.''

''So what you're saying is, I'll have to stay in here until *all* of my memory comes back on my own, and even then, I'll still be a prisoner until Julien sees fit to release me?'' she cried in despair.

''No. I'm not saying that. You've regained most of your memory, an amazing amount. But there's no way to predict if you're going to have total recall or not. Only time will tell.

''Tracey, speaking as your doctor, I have no problem with your leaving the hospital tomorrow. Naturally I'd like to be able to say good-bye to you knowing that you'd dealt with your recurring nightmares. But your release is not contingent on that. The only thing stopping you from walking out of here now is your husband.''

"What if I get an attorney?"

Louise's brows met in concentration. "You could. But do you have the kind of money it would take to hire counsel as good as your husband's?"

Tracey already knew the answer to that question. Her shoulders shook in defeat, and once again she was convulsed. "I need to be alone, Louise."

"All right. I'll come back tomorrow and we'll talk."

A paroxysm of tears wracking Tracey's body made her speech jerky, almost incomprehensible, as she said, "G-give m-e s-some-th-ing t-to s-slee-p, p-plea-se—"

"You no longer need medication. Your demon has finally surfaced. Confront it head-on. Then your dreams won't be disturbed and your sleep will be even more beneficial. Good night."

For the first time since she could remember, Tracey felt violently angry with Louise and kept shouting at her to come back and help her, even after the other woman had turned out the light and shut the door.

"Tracey?"

She jumped at the sound of Gerard's voice. For a fraction of a moment, she'd thought— With the hall light shining behind him, his tall body was a mere silhouette in the doorway of her darkened hospital room, reminding her of—of...

He turned on the light. "Have you changed your mind about dinner?"

"No!" she answered with uncharacteristic rudeness.

"How about a cold fruit drink?"

"No. I need a sleeping pill."

"The doctor didn't write orders for that. Sometimes a little *lait chaud* does the trick."

"No, thanks. I've never liked hot milk."

"Then I'll say good-night. If you need me, press the button."

"I'll never get to sleep!"

"Then turn on the television."

"I hate television. Why can't I go outside? I'll walk till I'm tired. You don't know how caged up I feel."

"Dr. Simoness will be on duty in the morning. When he comes in for his morning rounds, tell him how you feel."

"*I can't wait until tomorrow*! H-has Louise gone?"

"I don't know."

"Will you find out, please? Tell her—tell her I need to talk to her again." Tracey felt as if she was going to jump out of her skin if she didn't get some relief.

"I'll see if I can find her."

A few minutes later, Tracey was still pacing the floor when Louise reentered the room and shut the door.

"Gerard tells me you're more agitated than he's ever seen you before. We both know the reason why, don't we, Tracey?"

Tracey's chin lifted and she stared at her doctor through swollen lids. "Louise…" she began. "I've got to get out of here, out of Switzerland. What am I going to do?"

''I know what I'd do,'' the older woman murmured quietly, but Tracey heard her.

''*What*?''

''You'd have to be strong.''

Tracey bristled. ''I am strong.''

''Strong enough to tell your husband that you no longer want to live with him?'' Her brows arched. ''That's what he's waiting for, you know. To see you look him in the eye and tell him to his face that it's over. After all, you *did* tell me he's the most wonderful man alive.''

Tracey bit her lip hard. ''Yes, I did, because he is.''

''Then he deserves that much from you, Tracey. By your own admission, and his, he has never broken his marriage vows, has never done anything to jeopardize the bond between you. *You* were the one who ran away from him without explanation, who never let him know where you were, and then ultimately served him with divorce papers.''

''I know,'' she said in a barely audible voice, crushed by the pain she'd inflicted on Julien.

''*I* happen to believe that he's every bit as wonderful as you say he is. And I firmly believe that if you go to him in complete sincerity, then he'll agree to your release from the hospital, and he'll grant you that divorce.

''He won't like it, of course. How could he? He's madly in love with you. But because his love is so unselfish, he'll put your happiness above his own and you can walk away with your secret still intact."

Tracey's head flew up. "*Secret*?"

"Tracey, I've worked with you far too long not to know when you're holding something back from me. It's all right, you know. Anyone is entitled to his or her own secrets. I suppose the trick will be to keep it from him, but as I said, you'll have to be strong."

Tracey averted her eyes. Louise understood everything, and she was right! *The only way out of here was to face Julien.* The time had come.

Please, God, help me find the strength, the words.

Before she lost her courage she said, "W-would you call him tonight and tell him to come over?"

"I could. But if you're really ready to do this, then the phone call should come from you. If he sees a woman who is in complete control of her faculties, who is able to function like a normal human being again, then you'll be twice as convincing." There was a short silence. "I'm on your side, Tracey."

"I know, and I'll never be able to thank you enough." Tracey reached out and embraced her doctor.

"You've come such a long way. You're almost home. I'll pray for you." Louise gave her a pat, then added, "Gerard will bring a phone in here so you can talk to your husband in complete privacy."

"Thank you, Louise."

"*Bonne chance.*"

Good luck. Tracey was going to need much more

than that to face Julien. She stood where the older woman left her, watching as Gerard came in with an auxiliary phone and plugged it into the outlet.

For several minutes after he went out, she hovered near the writing desk, trying to gird up her courage.

There was no doubt in her mind that Louise had been honest with her. The only way out of the hospital was through Julien. *Tracey would have to put on the greatest performance of her life.*

Her hand shaking, she picked up the receiver and punched in the château's number, which she knew by heart. Solange answered the phone.

Dear Solange…the housekeeper who'd been with the Chappelles long before Tracey's family had started visiting them two months out of the year for business and pleasure. Tracey had only been nine years old when she'd first started traveling to Switzerland, to Julien's world…

"Ma chère Tracey," Solange cried out the second she recognized the younger woman's voice. After effusive tears that warmed Tracey's heart, Solange told her that after Julien had deposited Rose at the front doors of the château, he'd driven off as if pursued by demons. Did Tracey wish to speak to her aunt?

Tracey couldn't handle a conversation with Rose right now and told Solange she'd call her later. After ringing off, she followed her hunch and punched in Julien's private number at work. He often went to his office when something was disturbing him.

She glanced at her watch. It was 10:45 p.m. If he had driven there, he'd be alone....

After six rings, "*Oui*?" came the terse response.

Suddenly Tracey couldn't talk and tried to swallow to get some moisture back into her mouth. Finally she said his name and heard his sharp intake of breath.

"*Mon Dieu—Tracey*?"

Her fingers tortured the phone cord. Her heart was racing so fast she felt slightly sick to her stomach.

"Y-yes. It's me."

"Do you have any idea how long I've been waiting for this moment?" His voice shook with love and need and so many other emotions, she didn't know how she was going to follow through with her plan. "It is you, isn't it, *mignonne*? I'm not hallucinating?"

Hot tears trickled down her cheeks. *No, darling. You're not hallucinating.*

"No. I—I'm sorry to have been sick in front of you earlier. Louise said that the shock of remembering sometimes upsets your stomach."

"Does this mea—"

"Julien," she interrupted because she could hear the joy, the hope in his voice, and wanted to stop him before things went any further. "We have to talk."

"I'm on my way."

"No!" she blurted in panic. "N-not tonight."

I can't see you tonight. I thought I could, but I can't! I need the rest of the night to prepare myself.

"After all these months of praying for you to say

my name, praying that you'd remember me—you're asking me to *wait*?'' he demanded in such a pained voice, she wished she'd never started this.

''I'm sorry. It's just that I'm very tired and was hoping you would come in the morning.''

''I can't do that,'' he groaned. ''For months I've watched you lying there, your eyes and mind closed to me,'' he said in thick tones. ''At least when you wake up tomorrow, you'll know who I am and can say my name. I'm coming now, but I swear I won't disturb you if you're asleep. I just want to be in the same room with you. Is that too much to ask, *mon amour*?''

Yes. It's too much to ask. But what choice do I have?

''No. I-it's all right.''

''*À tout à l'heure, petite.*''

Oh, dear God, what have I done?

Tracey dropped the receiver on the hook. She'd never get to sleep now, not with him in the room watching her. She couldn't trust him not to try to hold her, kiss her, not when his emotions and feelings were running so high.

Whether she liked it or not, she was going to have to face him in the next little while, which meant she needed to be dressed and ready for him in the public lounge where there were no doors he could close to shut out the world.

Quickly she dashed to the bathroom for a shower. There wasn't a moment to lose. This time of night, the traffic was light. In his Ferrari, it wouldn't take him long to get to the hospital, which she had learned was on the outskirts of Lausanne.

Since he'd always preferred her hair long, she deliberately pulled it back in a chignon like her aunt's, and put on her most tailored blouse and skirt with a conservative navy blazer to look as businesslike as possible.

She would wear no perfume and left off her makeup to de-emphasize her features. It was important that she appear confident and look well enough to leave the hospital, yet draw as little attention to herself as possible.

Wearing her medium leather pumps, she left her room and walked to the nursing station opposite the lounge. "Gerard?"

When he heard his name, he lifted his head from a chart he was reading and stared at her in stunned surprise. "What have you done to yourself? I hardly recognize you."

She could tell that he didn't know what to make of her. That was good. "I'm expecting my husband. I'll just wait here in the lounge."

"Would you like some tea?"

"Maybe when he comes?"

"*Bien sûr.*"

She murmured her thanks and sat down on one of several upholstered chairs placed next to a love seat. On the coffee table were some travel magazines. Desperately needing something to do with her hands, she reached for one and started thumbing through it without seeing the pictures or reading the words.

Whenever she heard footsteps in the hall, her heart would start to pound and she'd look up nervously, only to find a staff member or one of the patients passing by.

"*Mignonne*?"

A slight gasp escaped her throat when Julien suddenly appeared calling her his darling. He'd made no sound to warn her of his coming. She knew she had to look at him, that she couldn't flinch or turn away. Staying seated, she raised her eyes, bracing herself to take a closer look at him.

There were changes that wounded her heart. Lines that hadn't been there before darkened his aquiline features. His black hair was longer than she remembered his wearing it. He was leaner, harder somehow. His black eyes had a hunted look. But for all that, in a dark gray business suit, the kind he wore to work, his male appeal was more disturbing, more attractive than ever, making her moan inwardly.

She could tell he was waiting for her to get up and run into his arms. In the past, that had always been her way. Julien evoked such love and passion, she could never get enough and could never hide how she felt, even with other people present.

In as steady a voice as she could manage, she said,

"It's good to see you, Julien. Sit down. Gerard said he'd bring us some tea as soon as you came."

He remained in place, his body taut, his features wooden. She noticed his hands making fists at his sides. "That's all you have to say to me after twelve months of pure, unadulterated hell?" he asked in an agonized whisper.

"I thought I was being perfectly civil. Today was a day of surprises. Not only did I find out that you were the one responsible for putting me in here, for paying the bills, but I learned that our divorce had never gone through because you never signed the papers."

All the time she was speaking, she watched the blood slowly drain from his face and prayed for this cruelty to end as soon as possible.

"That's why I called you. I want a divorce. It's all there in the papers my attorney sent you. I haven't asked for anything from you. Just my freedom."

His chest rose and fell as if he were fighting for breath.

"*On what grounds*?" His words came out more like a hiss.

This was it. This was the moment she'd been dreading. But when she remembered what had to be done, a great calm came over her.

"I won't lie to you, Julien. You and I both know I have no grounds."

His head reared back as if she'd just struck him because he hadn't expected that kind of bald honesty.

Rising to her feet, she walked over to him and tipped her head to look directly into eyes that were black pools of pain.

Hardening herself against the impact of his suffering, she said, "I love you, Julien. I'll never love anyone else. Never doubt that for a moment. But I found out I don't want to be married. I'd like to go back to San Francisco and get on with my life."

Like a man driven over the edge, his hands shot out and gripped her shoulders, bringing her close to his hard body. "Why?" he demanded with a ferocity that would have defeated her under any other circumstances.

Still keeping eye contact with him, she said, "I wish I could explain it, but I can't. When we returned from our honeymoon, I realized I wanted my freedom back and took the coward's way out by running away."

His fingers tightened on her arms, revealing the depth of his agony.

"It was wrong of me, and I'll always regret the pain I caused you by disappearing. You would never be as cruel to me, which should tell you something about the *real* me. I'm not the woman you want to be married to for the rest of your life." *I can't be.*

His piercing eyes searched her face relentlessly, trying to come to grips with this new reality, trying to find some sign of weakness but finding none.

"I left the way I did because I knew you'd ask me

why I wanted a divorce, and I wouldn't be able to give you an answer that would satisfy you."

"You're right," he bit out in fury, shaking her. "After what we shared on our honeymoon, nothing you've said or done since makes any sense."

"That's your answer, Julien. What we had in Tahiti defies description. We experienced something out of the ordinary, something no one can ever take away from us."

Because it happened before the veil was so cruelly torn from my eyes.

"What we shared couldn't ever be duplicated because life isn't like that. Now we're back to reality and I want to go my own way. *Alone.*"

He shook his head in total incredulity. "I don't believe you." In the next breath, his mouth descended, crushing hers, trying to evoke the response that in the past had always been his for the taking because she was so deeply and totally in love with him.

But certain information had changed her world forever, and though the flesh was weak, her soul knew this was wrong, wrong enough that Julien could sense a change in her.

When he finally tore his lips from hers and raised his head, her heart broke all over again to see the mixture of pained confusion and anger coming from the depths of his beautiful eyes. Slowly his hands slid down her arms as if he were still feeling, still testing her for any sign of vulnerability.

Standing her ground, she said, "I understand you're the one who must give permission for me to leave the hospital. I'd like to go in the morning."

He stood absolutely motionless, his ashen countenance adding years to his age. Eventually he said in a lifeless voice, "You haven't recovered all of your memory yet."

"I know. Louise told me I might never get the missing pieces back, but I'm still well enough to be released. It looks like my fate is in y-your hands," she said, her voice faltering for the first time. "After the way I hurt you by running away, you now have the perfect opportunity to hurt me back by refusing the divorce and forcing me to remain in here until I remember everything, which might or might not ever happen."

His body gave a great shudder and his mouth had thinned to a dark line. "You think I'm such a monster that I'd shut you away in here out of some perverted form of revenge?"

"No," she whispered in anguish. "But a lesser man might do it, and with much less reason than you. I hurt you, Julien, when I never wanted to. You didn't deserve it and I wouldn't dream of asking your forgiveness when I know there can be none."

Julien said nothing, only continued to eye her strangely until she started to grow uneasy because she couldn't tell what he was thinking.

"If this has something to do with Jacques, rest assured he'll never be allowed to come near you."

She shook her head. "Jacques has nothing to do with anything."

Jacques, Julien's younger brother, had wanted her long before she'd met Julien, who'd been away studying at Cambridge in England. But once Julien returned to Lausanne and Jacques could sense Tracey's interest in his elder brother, he'd gotten her alone and had tried to force himself on Tracey. Before things went too far, a fiercely angry Julien had intervened, warning his younger brother off for good.

After that night, Julien, ten years her senior, had kept a proprietorial eye on Tracey, picking her up from school every day, giving her a job at his office where she could stay busy and do her homework undisturbed. Tracey, who'd always been intrigued by the enigmatic Julien, fell hopelessly in love with him. The forever kind of love.

An unholy love.

Throughout the long, painful silence, Julien was weighing every word, every nuance of meaning in her denial, trying to find the flaw.

Finally, "I'll sign the release papers tonight on one condition," he grated. She drew in a shaky breath that he couldn't fail to notice. "That you come back to the château to live for one month and give our marriage a chance to work. If at the end of that time you still want the divorce, then I'll agree to it."

Dear God. No!

Julien bit out a strangled epithet. "*Mon Dieu*, your face has gone as white as the walls. I'm not suggesting we sleep in the same bed!"

"I *couldn't*."

"You think I don't know that?" he scathed.

"Then why d—"

"I want *proof* that you'd rather live alone," he cut her off brutally. "You were only a bride in my home for four days before you bolted. Surely after the year of hell you've put me through, you could give me, give us, a thirty-day trial."

Now *her* body was shivering. "But it wouldn't be fair to you, Julien."

"You're in no position to judge what's fair to me," he retorted harshly. "Other components make up a marriage besides conjugal love."

"But if that isn't right, then nothing else works," she said, panicking, sensing that she was losing this battle.

"As you said yourself, those two months in Tahiti speak for the kind of passion we shared. Whatever problem you have, it has nothing to do with the way we communicate in bed. Something much more fundamental is going on here.

"You *owe* me a month's time to explore it. If at the end of that period, you still feel the same way you feel right now, *then* I'll set you free."

Julien had laid down his terms.

Louise had asked Tracey if she was strong enough. It looked like she was going to *have* to be. Julien was fighting for his life.

But then again, *so was she.*

"All right. You can pick me up in the morning after Dr. Simoness has made his rounds. I need to pack and say good-bye to everyone who has been so good to me."

If he was surprised at her capitulation, he didn't show it. "I'll be here at nine."

"Julien…I'd like to pay for part of my hospital bill with whatever money Father left me."

"I'm still your husband," he reminded her savagely. "While you're married to me, I intend to be responsible for you. I took a vow to love, cherish and protect you, to keep you in sickness and in health, to bestow my worldly goods on you. *I intend to keep that vow, Tracey.*"

I know you do, darling. I know you do, her heart cried out as he wheeled away from her and disappeared down the corridor. *But it isn't possible.*

CHAPTER THREE

To TRACEY, the familiar smell of Lake Geneva seemed even more pronounced in the brisk fall air as Julien maneuvered the Ferrari down the tree-lined drive to the front gates of the hospital grounds.

With that effortless masculine grace she remembered so well, he shifted gears and accelerated onto the main road. His car performed brilliantly, eating up the kilometers with a speed that told Tracey he couldn't whisk her away from the clinic and all its attendant memories of grief and pain fast enough.

Since his arrival at the hospital on the dot of nine to check her out, there'd been an underlying possessiveness in his every word and action that alarmed Tracey because Julien could be a terrifying adversary when provoked. He would fight in ways she hadn't even conceived to break her down, but what he didn't know was that she could *not* be broken down, and he would *not* be successful. The knowledge gave her no joy.

Sitting at an angle so she couldn't see him out of her peripheral vision, she let her hungry eyes take in the quiet elegance of the charming residential streets. As they drove, her ears listened to the myriad of Sunday morning church bells pealing throughout the city.

Lausanne had always represented paradise to her. A civilized, gracious paradise in which the exciting man of her teenage dreams had first made his appearance. He was at her side right now. All she had to do was reach out and touch him to feel his warm, solid flesh. But she could never do that again.

She could never think of him in that way again.

When they reached the Gothic cathedral overlooking the city, he unexpectedly headed north away from town. She grew anxious and blurted, "W-we're going the wrong way to the château!"

"I'm taking you to breakfast first."

"Please don't bother. I'm not hungry."

"For the first time in a year, I find that *I* am," he murmured in a voice of unmistakable authority. "I've made arrangements for us to eat at the Chalet Des Enfants. You were always partial to its view of the mountains, and the food."

That was true. Long before their marriage, they would usually end their boat rides or long walks at the quaint little inn high above Lac Léman, where they could see the tips of the French Alps across the mirrorlike lake.

In a gentle, teasing mood, Julien would ply her with the most delicious croissants and honey, followed by steaming cups of sweet cocoa. They'd talk for hours about anything and everything. No time with him was long enough. She never wanted any of it to end.

She still didn't!

Unable to bear this kind of pain much longer, she was on the verge of telling him he would have to eat by himself, that she'd stay in the car, when Louise's warning came back to haunt her.

The only way he'll let you go is to convince him you're fully recovered, that you're physically and emotionally strong enough to handle being on your own.

Thirty days to carry off this charade...

Tracey closed her eyes. This was only day *one*, and already the torture was almost beyond enduring.

The sound of the Ferrari gearing down jerked her from this new waking nightmare and she discovered Julien had pulled into the private drive of the chalet, where he levered himself from the driver's seat to help her. But not before his dark eyes took in her pronounced pallor, causing his lips to twist in a painful grimace that spelled unbearable grief and frustration.

Guilt smote Tracey anew because she and she alone had the power to satisfy his curiosity by telling him the truth. But then another door of pain would open, one so much worse, and Julien would never recover.

She'd had many months to weigh her decision and decided that remaining silent was still the only course to follow. No matter how unacceptable her rejection of him might be right now, in time he would come to accept what happened and rally enough to love again.

Julien had a tremendous capacity to love, and when he finally allowed her to disappear from his life for good, there would be other women to fill the void, women eager to become the next Mrs. Julien Chappelle, women who had the *right* to be his wife and give him the family he longed for. If he never learned the soul-destroying truth from Tracey, he'd be free to pursue a new direction in life.

As for Tracey, there was no possibility of her marrying again. Julien had ruined her for all other men a long time ago. Her only solution was to devote her life to a career that would take her around the world and keep her so busy she wouldn't have time to look back or dwell on forbidden memories.

Frantic to keep her distance from him, she jumped from the car—just out of reach of his hands—and hurried inside the timbered hideaway that had always reminded her more of a dining hall in a monastery than a restaurant.

With a sense of déjà vu, she drew close to the warmth from the grate fire that staved off the chill. On this Sunday morning, she only saw one other couple, but was glad for even that small amount of company.

She seated herself at a nearby table without Julien's help, an action he noted with a distinct frown. Yet nothing marred his striking features, she observed with a pang.

In the shadowy interior, his naturally olive skin took on a darker sheen, as did his hair and brows. The firelight flickered in the blackness of his eyes and emphasized the strong bones of his male beauty.

As he sat down opposite her, his broad shoulders

blotted out part of the view from the picture windows. She quickly averted her head to school her instinctive reaction to his masculine appeal. The chemistry between them had always been overpowering, and a year's separation had only increased his potent charisma.

But certain facts had changed the way she was permitted to think of Julien. From now on, whenever she looked at him, it would have to be with the detachment she might feel for a close family friend, nothing more.

No sooner had they sat down than the *patronne* of the inn appeared at their table, greeting Julien like an old friend. He gave their order without consulting Tracey. Certain habits could never be broken, and one of them was the fact that Julien had always taken care of her because he knew her tastes and could anticipate her needs without any words passing their lips.

The incredible harmony between them was still there and always would be, she moaned to herself, clutching her hands together in a death grip beneath the table.

When the owner hurried off to the kitchen, Julien didn't speak right away. Instead, he lounged indolently in the chair and watched Tracey. She moistened her lips in a nervous gesture and began the speech she'd been preparing throughout the endless night at the hospital.

"I—I don't think you can imagine how long and empty my days at the clinic have been."

"They couldn't have been any longer or emptier

than mine,'' he grated in raw pain, giving her a further glimpse into his suffering.

Clearing her throat, she said, ''Please don't get me wrong. Everyone was wonderful to me and I'll always be grateful to them, a-and to you. Without your intervention, I might never have made a full recovery.''

''Thank God you did,'' he murmured in thick tones, tearing at her emotions even more.

''But the thing is, I'm not used to such inactivity and the thought of staying at the château with nothing to do for hours on end is anathema to me. If I'm to survive this next month, I'd like a job at your office. I know I can be an asset.''

There was a sharp intake of breath before he sat forward in the chair, eyeing her with that sobering intensity she could feel to her bones though she didn't look at him directly.

''Your value to the company has never been in question, but the fact is, I'm taking the month off from work to be home with you. We're going to do everything together, and I can assure you, you won't be bored.''

Mingled with that undeniable certainty was an assertive note of determination that said he had no intention of letting her out of his sight, let alone his life.

''*No!*''

Her terrified cry reverberated in the hollow room, briefly drawing the other diners' attention. Julien's dark brows lifted a trifle mockingly. Too late she realized her mistake in letting him see how frightened the prospect of being in his company day and night had made her.

He'd been waiting for her first sign of vulnerability, and she'd just allowed him a glimpse of it.

Summoning every bit of courage within her, she lifted her head and stared straight into his eyes. "Louise told me how you've put your life on hold for the past year because of me. I can't live with that guilt, Julien.

"Please allow me to do something constructive part of each day so that you can deal with your business. Because of me, you've been unable to give your full attention to matters far too long as it is! I'm begging you. Let me make up for that in some small way. After I received my language degree in California, I only worked for your company a short time be-before—"

"Before we were married," he broke in determinedly. "A marriage we both wanted from the first day we met, but I had to wait for you to grow up, so don't insult my intelligence by denying it."

I won't, darling. I won't.

For a moment, she felt dizzy and clung to the edge of the table. "A-all I'm asking is that you let me prove to you that your faith in hiring me in the first place wasn't misguided."

His expression grew remote. He gazed back at her through narrowed lids. "If I never stepped inside my office again, the company would survive. The only thing of importance to me is my marriage. I'll move heaven and earth to make it work."

Another moan escaped. This was so much worse than she would ever have imagined.

Swallowing hard, she said, "I've already told you tha—"

"I know it by heart, Tracey," he broke in coldly. "Thirty days is all I have to convince you that you want to live your life with me and be my wife in the Biblical sense. You gave your word."

"I did, but I had no idea you would put your empire in jeopardy for me when it isn't necessary. We can work together at Chappelle House. It will be like old times." She tried to feign a lightness in her voice, but failed.

"Hardly," he bit out with brutal candor, forcing her to remember the rapture of their honeymoon in Tahiti, a honeymoon she now knew should never have taken place. "Up until Rose informed me of your accident, you've had everything your own way, *mignonne*. Now I'm laying the ground rules." His eyes bored holes into her, making her tremble. "We do this my way, or you go back to the clinic. The choice is yours."

A palpable tension hovered between them. "I couldn't go back there again." *I need to get away from you. Away from your life. Forever.*

A gleam of satisfaction kindled the depths of his eyes. She knew that look and shuddered as he murmured, "*Bien*. Then let's enjoy our food. *D'accord*?"

Thankful that the owner had returned with their order, Tracey made no comment. Instead, she forced herself to eat the large breakfast so that Julien wouldn't attribute her lack of appetite to the fact that she hadn't been totally honest with him.

He knew there was a reason why she didn't want to continue in the marriage, a reason she patently refused to divulge. But being Julien, he couldn't and wouldn't accept what she'd told him. He believed that time would reveal the truth and he'd get his wife back.

Somehow, someway, she'd have to convince him that she'd meant what she'd said, that she didn't want to be married anymore.

Tracey had been making it a matter of prayer. Now that they were together again, she'd have to pray even harder for the strength and inspiration to carry this off.

Judging by the way he reached for another helping of croissants, Julien was obviously pleased at the way things were going. Finishing a second cup of coffee, he eyed her broodingly over the rim. "Whatever the reason that sent you rowing down the lake and out of my life, how did you manage to stay lost so long before making contact with Rose?"

She'd been waiting for that question. If their positions were reversed and he had been the one to have disappeared, she would have been so wild with pain she would have riddled him with a hundred different questions upon finding him again. She wouldn't have been able to rest until she'd obtained the right answers.

Under such precarious circumstances, Tracey couldn't help but admire his forbearance and realized that he deserved an explanation.

"I had enough money to get to London. My intention was to find a good job, but without references I was turned down by everyone except a couple who needed a temporary nanny while their permanent one was in hospital. When she came back to her job, I had no choice but to contact Aunt Rose."

At that admission, his features became an expressionless mask. He put his coffee cup on the saucer. "Since you didn't go back to work at Chappelle House in San Francisco, what did you do to fill the hours, aside from hiring an attorney to serve me papers?"

His question pained her all over again. "I—I don't honestly remember. My last memory is of getting on a plane at Gatwick Airport. Apparently Aunt Rose found some place for me to stay wh-where no one would find me."

"You mean where *I* couldn't possibly get to you," he interjected bleakly. "Not even your sister knew where you were."

Everything he said compounded her guilt. Tracey put fingers to her forehead where she could feel the beginnings of a headache. "All I know is that Rose told me I was hit by a car while crossing a street, but my mind is totally blank for that portion of my life. It wasn't until yesterday that Louise informed me I was still married, that our divorce hadn't gone through."

Julien assimilated what she said, then rose slowly to his feet. In Tracey's eyes, he looked larger than life as he mercilessly gazed down at her. "If you really thought I would agree to a divorce under the circumstances in which you ran away from me, then you never knew me at all. But we're going to rectify that," he vowed with shocking ferocity, tossing his napkin on the table. "Are you ready to go home?"

Home.

Julien's château could never be home to her now, but she nodded her assent and got up from the table before he reached her. Leaving him to deal with the check, she rushed outside and sucked in deep drafts of the pure autumn air, which was even cooler up on the forested mountainside.

Her sweater dress with its matching blue wool jacket, an outfit she'd purchased in San Francisco several years before, felt good against the elements. She put up the collar of the loose-fitting garment against her cheeks while she waited for Julien to appear and unlock the car.

Since coming out of that coma, all her clothes were too big for her, but Dr. Simoness had promised her that within three months she'd be back to her normal weight, provided she ate proper meals and exercised regularly.

Right now, exercise was exactly what she needed. It felt so stimulating to be out in the fresh air, she wanted to run through the woods until she dropped from exhaustion. But Julien's presence prevented her from giving in to that impulse.

She didn't dare be alone with him any longer.

"Let's take a walk, shall we?" Julien's low voice broke in on her tortured thoughts. When he cupped her elbow in that familiar way, which was always a prelude to something much more intimate, she thought she'd lose her mind. But somehow she managed not to pull away from him.

Floundering for the right response, she said in a quiet tone, "I thought that was what I wanted, too. But oddly enough, I feel very tired, probably because I didn't sleep well last night. Dr. Simoness warned me not to overdo it for the first few days. If you don't mind, Julien, I'd like to get back to the château and rest for a little while."

A stillness came over him. She could feel the dichotomy of emotions warring inside his hard, taut frame.

Just when she thought he might insist on having his way, his hand dropped, and she thought she heard a muffled imprecation. It made her realize just how much control he was exercising not to pick her up in his arms and kiss them both into oblivion.

Several times throughout their meal, she'd seen that burning look of desire in his eyes, the look that used to turn her body molten with longing. But that was a lifetime ago when she was innocent of certain knowledge. Now everything was different. *Now that look crucified her.*

By tacit agreement, they moved to the car. Hoping the crunch of leaves beneath their feet camouflaged the sick hammering of her heart, she held herself rigid as he put her inside. She didn't take another breath until he was behind the wheel and had switched on the ignition.

Before he pulled out onto the mountain road, she heard him mutter, "*Mon Dieu.* You've lost every bit of color. Why didn't you tell me you weren't feeling well?"

Beneath his angry demand, she detected an underlying note of anxiety. In the past he'd always been solicitous of her needs, had always put her welfare before his own. That deep concern was in evidence now, even stronger than before, *if* such a thing was possible.

Suddenly it came to her that the situation couldn't be allowed to continue. Thirty more days of this would destroy them completely. Already the past two hours in his company had turned both their lives into disaster.

Since he couldn't know the truth, there was only one thing to do. Before the week was out, she'd find a way to escape and check into a religious retreat where no questions were asked. She knew of such a place high in the Jura Mountains. The nuns welcomed troubled, destitute people who arrived on their doorstep needing to sort out their lives.

Julien would never think to look for her there. All

she had to do was bide her time and wait for a day when a delivery truck came from town. She could hitch a ride, or even hide in the back, anything to be long gone from the château, from Julien. But with one fundamental difference.

This time, she'd disappear forever.

"You can forget what you're planning, Tracey." Julien read her mind with stunning accuracy. "We made a bargain and you're sticking to it, even if it means suffering my company twenty-four hours a day. Forget any ideas you've been entertaining about running away. It won't happen again."

Feeling trapped and helpless, she cried, "I need my privacy, Julien."

Those long, lean fingers she could easily imagine around her neck tightened on the steering wheel. "I've already given my word that I won't invade your bed. But be warned, that's as far as my magnanimity extends."

He might as well have sworn an oath.

Immediately Tracey realized her mistake in leaving the clinic. What a fool she'd been to think she was emotionally strong enough to spend even one second in Julien's company when a secret of such devastating proportions was tearing both of them apart.

They'd been too close, shared too much. In time he'd break her down, and once he knew the truth, not only Julien, but both their families, would be destroyed forever.

The only choice left to her was to starve herself until Julien was forced to put her back in the hospital. She'd heard Dr. Simoness, the head of the medical staff at the clinic, explaining to Julien how important it was that Tracey gain weight. Julien might do everything in his power to keep her at the château, but he'd never prevent her from getting medical help if she needed it.

Once she was back at the clinic, she'd stay there until she found a way to escape. Several people on the housekeeping staff had become her friends. She'd work on one of them to help her.

With her mind made up, she was able to relax somewhat for the rest of the drive, and even made a few conversational observations about the beauty of the grounds as they entered his estate.

But she wasn't prepared for the emotional impact of pulling up in front of his home. For a moment, she was taken back to her youth, to that breathtaking time when she'd first caught sight of the fairy-tale-like château. Such a vision had to include a handsome prince, she'd confided to her sister, Isabelle, who was ten on that trip, only a year older than Tracey.

Isabelle agreed, having been raised on the same *Grimm's Fairy Tales*. With a sense of awe and wonder, the two girls followed their parents inside the structure, which was as magnificent and enchanting as Sleeping Beauty's castle, though on a smaller scale, of course. Walking backward half the time, Tracey and her sister gazed in fascination at the paintings and period furniture.

While Henri Chappelle, the tall, attractive, dark blond man with intimidating brown eyes welcomed the girls to Lausanne and introduced them to his wife, Celeste, Tracey saw some photographs on his desk. Within seconds, she fixated on the center one of Julien, and lost her heart completely.

Through bits and pieces of conversation, she learned that he was the eldest out of Jacques and Angelique and was in his first year of university in Paris. As far as she was concerned, Julien Chappelle, with his dark, fascinating looks, was the personification of a prince come to life.

Isabelle noticed his picture at the same time and was as smitten as Tracey. Over the years and the thousands of miles that separated them from Lausanne each time their family returned to the States after their two month stay, the girls continued to weave fantasies about him.

Then came a day after Tracey had turned seventeen when her prince unexpectedly appeared at the château in the flesh.... Tracey groaned aloud at the disturbing memories, afraid they would always haunt her.

Mortified because Julien had probably heard her, she shook her head to clear it. But if he noticed anything, he didn't comment on it. In fact, he seemed curiously detached as he came around her side and helped her from the car. She had the impression he wasn't worried about her escaping his world again.

This time, she didn't flinch when he grasped her elbow to assist her up the steps. She was feeling so shaky, she secretly welcomed his support and was anxious to get settled in.

"Will it be all right if I stay in the same guest room I once used?"

"I'm afraid it's occupied," he told her briefly.

Maybe he had installed Rose in Tracey's old room. Maybe there were business associates of his staying at the château right now. Tracey hoped as much. Anything to divert Julien's attention away from her.

Perhaps like his father, Julien preferred to negotiate the most important contracts and business transactions at home where the atmosphere was congenial, where he could ply his guests with fine food and after-dinner liqueurs.

"For the time being," he continued in a level tone, "you'll be on the third floor, in the room adjoining mine."

Her first instinct was to scream aloud her refusal. But judging by Julien's mood, he wouldn't care if she alerted his guests and entire staff to their precarious situation. In fact, he'd probably welcome it because it would prove that she wasn't as in control as she pretended to be.

The second they stepped through the massive doors, Solange, Julien's plump, redheaded housekeeper, appeared in the vaulted hallway with its tapestried walls and threw her arms around Tracey, warming her heart.

The older woman's raisin eyes didn't miss a detail. No doubt she was comparing Tracey to the way she looked a year ago.

"*Grâce à Dieu*," she cried aloud her welcome. "Thank goodness you're home at last, even if you look so fragile, *mon petit choux*. But *n'inquiéte pas*! Cook and I will have you fattened up in no time. Already she has made your favorite *galette au vin* for you."

Pierced by guilt because of what she was planning to do—knowing it would hurt the staff when she refused the meals they would meticulously prepare in her honor—Tracey hurriedly thanked Solange for everything, then turned to Julien to tell him she needed to go to her room.

But he'd already anticipated her comment, and before she could countenance it, he'd swept her into his arms as if she were light as air, and started up the ancient-looking stone staircase.

"Put me down!" she begged in a low voice so Solange couldn't hear, keeping her head averted so their faces wouldn't touch.

"If I do, I have the feeling your legs will collapse beneath you. Relax, *mignonne*. You're home now and I'm going to take care of you, so don't try to fight me or you'll expend the little strength you have left."

He was right. Her body felt like mush.

To counteract the feelings such intimacy aroused—memories of his carrying her up the stairs almost exactly this way upon their return from Tahiti, except that their mouths had been fused in passion—Tracey's only weapon was to slump against his chest and pretend to fall into an exhausted sleep.

In truth, it wasn't difficult to do. Since the night before, when Julien's deep, distinctive voice had broken through the barrier to bring her back to stark reality, she'd been so emotionally drained, she craved her bed.

Once they'd entered the elegant suite adjoining his, he laid her down on smooth, silk sheets.

"All I want you to do is sleep, *petite*," he murmured, his lips brushing her forehead with a tenderness that was almost her undoing.

Except for the feel of his hands as they removed her jacket and shoes, she remembered nothing else but the cool of the pillow against her hot cheek and the delicious warmth of the covers Julien drew over her inert body.

CHAPTER FOUR

WHEN next Tracey came awake, the angle of the sun's rays through the mullioned windows alerted her that she'd slept hours. Her watch said 4:36.

Shocked to have been asleep so long, and even more shocked not to find Julien sitting in the love seat guarding her, she threw back the covers of the canopied bed and slid off the mattress, noticing that her bags had been brought up and her things put away while she was unaware.

After padding over the oriental rug into the en suite bathroom, she took a quick shower, then rummaged in the seventeenth century armoire for a pair of jeans and a blouse, her uniform at the clinic once she'd been able to start dressing herself.

Using a navy chiffon scarf to tie back her ash blond hair, which was longer than shoulder length by now, she slipped into loafers and left the room to find Rose. No doubt her aunt occupied one of the rooms on the second floor since the Chappelles reserved the third floor for members of their immediate family.

Tracey had a lot of questions only her aunt could answer. She particularly wanted to know why her mother's sister had felt such an abiding loyalty to Julien that she'd overridden Tracey's wishes, landing her in the untenable situation she found herself in now.

Though she hadn't been inside Julien's home for a year, she knew it by heart, having explored its architectural wonders many times over with Julien's brother and sister. Every corridor running past the various rooms of the spacious château led to the central staircase that wound to the common rooms of the ground floor.

She could make her way blindfolded to the second floor and hurried down the stairs to join Rose, who was probably having tea in her room, her habit this time of day.

But when she heard a baby crying, her steps slowed, and she looked all around, wondering which room housed the sound, trying to imagine who of Julien's acquaintances would be staying at the château with an infant.

It didn't sound like a newborn, but its cry was far too young to be her nephew, Alex. In any event, Julien would have told her if Isabelle and Bruce had come.

To Tracey's knowledge his sister, Angelique, hadn't had a baby yet, so it couldn't be her child unless something had happened in the past year Tracey knew nothing about.

Puzzled, she made her way down the corridor toward the room where she could hear the baby's vigorous voice building to a crescendo. Then came a woman's voice, speaking French in cajoling tones, attempting to hush the child's tears to no avail.

Driven by an instinct she didn't understand or question, Tracey knocked gently on the door that led to Isabelle's old room and was told by an unfamiliar female voice to enter.

Obeying the woman's bidding, Tracey turned the knob, but the sight that greeted her eyes sent her into shock. No longer a guest room, it had been completely transformed into a nursery whose colors reminded her of sunshine.

What was going on here?

What did it mean?

Whose baby was so important that Julien would transform a room of the château into a nursery with every convenience imaginable?

The fortyish-looking stranger, dressed like one of the staff at the clinic, held a squirming baby girl of five or six months against her shoulder. She greeted Tracey cordially enough, but was too occupied with her charge to engage her in conversation.

In a total daze, Tracey swung her gaze to the jet black curls framing a perfectly oval face. Her rounded cheeks were wet and flushed from her crying spell. To Tracey's mind, the baby was the most adorable little thing she'd ever laid eyes on in her life.

She wore a tiny white undershirt and a disposable diaper, displaying sturdy limbs and the kind of cuddly body Tracey loved to squeeze.

Whether the baby had just awakened from a nap, or was refusing to be put down for one, it appeared she wouldn't be comforted.

Obeying blind impulse, Tracey crossed the expanse to get a closer look. But what she saw sent a stabbing pain to her heart.

The dark, finely arched brows that were wrinkled in a frown, the set of the firm little chin wobbling from repeated outbursts, looked increasingly familiar.

As she studied the baby's olive complexion—the shape of the long fingers with their half-moon nails curled into fists of frustration—Tracey was put in mind of the man she loved beyond description.

Julien.

Tracey gasped.

Like pure revelation, she knew this was *Julien's* child. Genes didn't lie. No one but his own flesh and blood would be given such a place of honor in the family home and showered with every worldly possession.

This was his love child.

Obviously he'd turned to another woman after Tracey had disappeared. *Who*? Someone Tracey knew?

Again, stabbing pain tore her to pieces, this time from jealousy, an emotion she'd never had any reason to experience until now.

What was he doing fighting the divorce when there was a woman out there who loved him enough to bear his child and let him raise it as a Chappelle?

Clutching at the nearest support that happened to be the crib, she wondered what kind of insanity drove him to force Tracey to live with him for the next month when it was perfectly obvious he had another woman just waiting in the wings.

But she already knew the answer to that question. Julien was an honorable man and brutally honest. One who, when he discovered that Tracey had awakened from the coma, would give her this last chance to change her mind about remaining his wife before he signed those divorce papers.

Unable to look at the child who should have been, could have been theirs if certain knowledge hadn't come to light, she wheeled around in despair and raced for the door.

Since their own love was forbidden, maybe in time she'd thank providence that he'd been able to turn to another woman for comfort and now had a child of his own to love.

But right now she was in too much agony to bear it and fled from the room, only to career into Julien standing at the threshold with an enigmatic expression darkening his arresting features.

He put out his hands to steady her, but she as quickly backed away from him, unable to bear his touch when it still burned her skin with its fire.

''You've been busy while I was gone,'' she said in a ragged whisper, using English so that hopefully the nanny wouldn't be able to understand them. She didn't want to sound accusing. She didn't have the right, but she knew she sounded like an insanely jealous woman who'd just been confronted with the naked truth of her husband's perfidy.

"You could say that," he drawled in kind, not acting the least bit uncomfortable or guilty. While she stood there grappling with the indisputable proof of his extramarital affair, he switched to French and asked the woman named Clair to bring him the baby before she went on break.

Clair looked relieved as she placed the howling infant in his arms and disappeared out the door.

The baby soon quieted down and nestled against Julien's shoulder as if to rest against that treasured spot and be loved by her father was what she'd been waiting for all the while.

The light in Julien's eyes left Tracey in no doubt that he adored his little girl. Love was evident in the way his hand roamed over her pliant back, the way his lips grazed her dark curls and neck with kisses until she started to croon in response.

Unable to repress her emotions, Tracey blurted, "Who is she, Julien?"

His black eyes searched hers for an overly long moment. "Her name is Valentine," he said in a low, husky voice. "She was born on the fourteenth of February."

A muffled cry escaped Tracey's throat. "I don't mean the baby. I mean her mother."

After a tension-filled silence, "Who do you think she is?"

His comment brought her up short. "I have no idea," she replied, her voice shaking.

For a split second, she saw a glint of pain in those dark recesses before they became shuttered and he said, "She's the most beautiful woman alive, the only woman I'll ever love."

Tracey lowered her head, cut to the quick by his cruelty. Why in heaven's name would he want to hang on to her, Tracey, when he had just admitted his love for this ravishing creature who'd borne him a daughter?

Unable to stop her mind from wandering, Tracey's imagination conjured up pictures of several women he knew socially and at the office. Too many of them classified as great beauties. But which one had he turned to in his need?

"Take a closer look at Valentine, especially her green eyes and rosebud mouth, then you'll recognize her mother."

Tracey blinked in confusion. *Green eyes? Rosebud mouth*?

But according to Julien, those were Tracey's own characteristics....

Her head flew back and she stared at him, uncomprehending.

His expression grew bleak. "When Louise showed you a picture of Rose, you finally recognized your aunt.

I was praying that when you saw Valentine, you would realize she's *our* daughter, Tracey. Yours and mine.''

''*Our* baby?'' she half groaned the question and staggered on her feet so that he was forced to help her to a chair.

''*Oui, mignonne.* Ours and no one else's. Valentine is six months old. If you work out the time frame, she had to have been conceived on our honeymoon.''

''B-but that's im-impossible,'' she whispered in shock.

''Nevertheless, the impossible happened,'' he insisted quietly. ''Feel free to call Hillview Hospital in San Francisco. She was delivered by Dr. Benjamin Learned. Examine her closely and you'll see yourself in her smile, in her translucent eyes, which are identical to yours.''

He got down on his haunches and placed the baby in her arms, still allowing Valentine's fingers to cling to one of his so she wouldn't cry.

Though Tracey shook her head in disbelief, she felt compelled to obey his suggestion. With fear and trembling, she took a long, hard look at the beautiful baby cradled in her lap. A miracle of creation.

Slowly one sob, then another, shook her body as she recognized various family traits that could only belong to the Marshes and the Chappelles, branding Valentine *her* child. And Julien's...

''No!'' she cried out as the ramifications of what this

meant hit her with full force. "No..." she whispered
in agony, needing to get out of the room.

Her tormented state communicated itself to
Valentine, who didn't like being relinquished to her
father so quickly and broke into tears immediately,
clutching at Julien's neck with all her force.

"Tracey—*Mon Dieu*—come back here!" Julien
called in an anxious voice. But she flew out the door
and within seconds reached the safety of her own bathroom on the third floor, where she could turn the lock
and examine herself in a mirror.

The accident that had put her in a coma had caused
several lacerations on her arms and legs, so she hadn't
given any thought to the scars below her navel.

"Good heavens!" she cried to herself when saw the
fading pink lines that had been made by a doctor's
scalpel and were still healing.

She had to have delivered before her accident!

But how could she have given birth to Valentine and
not have known it, not remembered it? *How was that
possible*?

At the clinic, when Louise had told her there was
still more of her past to recall—that it would be best
if she remembered it on her own—Tracey had had no
idea. No idea at all...

"Tracey?" Julien called to her from the bedroom.
The next thing she knew he was knocking on the door.
"Tracey...I know this has come as a tremendous shock
to you. Let me in. We have to talk."

No wonder Julien had made that bargain with her.

He knew her child was waiting for her back at the château. A child who should never have been born.

A child who most likely would have defects and problems she couldn't bear to think about.

Tears ravaged her cheeks. She buried her face in a towel to stifle the sound. "Go away, Julien," she begged, sobbing hysterically.

"I can't, *mon amour*. Now that you've met Valentine, you need to know everything so there won't be any more shocks."

She lifted her head. "W-what do you mean, more? How could there be a-any more?"

"Open the door and find out."

Traumatized by the revelation that she and Julien had brought a child into the world, Tracey couldn't bring herself to turn the lock. She slumped against the door in an effort to stay upright.

That's when her ears picked up the unmistakable sound of Valentine's voice. But she thought she heard the noise of another baby, as well. Maybe she was hallucinating, so she listened more intently as Julien spoke in gentle, soothing tones, his tenderness reaching her soul.

"We're not going to go away until you come out, Tracey. Open the door. Raoul and Jules have been wanting to say hello to their *maman* for a very long time."

Jules? Raoul?

The names reverberated in her head and suddenly another dam broke, releasing the last torrent of suppressed memories: the sounds of her babies all crying at once as she entered the hospital's preemie unit. Three babies, born a month early.

Babies she'd named without Julien's knowledge, thinking he would never know, never find out. Babies who might never be normal.

"Tracey!"

Under ordinary circumstances, the alarm in Julien's voice would have made her reach out to release the lock. But for the life of her, she couldn't move because another memory had intruded on her consciousness, paralyzing her.

Like a flash of lightning that illuminated everything, she had total recall. Her flight from England, the shocking news that she was expecting triplets, her months of seclusion in the California summer home of a friend of Rose's, the complicated delivery of her three children and the aftermath, the days and nights she'd spent holding them, feeding them, memorizing each perfect feature and the differences in personality.

She remembered many long hours in the darkness of night when she'd kept an anxious vigil in the preemie nursery, loving them, feeding them, changing their diapers, planning how she was going to take care of them and raise them without Julien's help.

My babies, she groaned as an overwhelming wave of love and longing for them swept through her. *Five months* she'd been separated from her precious children—five months that someone else had been a mother to them.

But they hadn't gone without love. Julien had been there for them from the beginning, had bonded with them, showering them with the kind of attention only he, their marvelous father, could provide, while she—

The taxi!

She remembered the day she was set to take the babies home from the hospital, remembered her anger and frustration against Rose before getting out of the car. They'd been arguing violently because Rose was on Julien's side and didn't approve of Tracey asking him for a divorce without telling him about his children.

She remembered slamming the car door and running into the path of an orange taxi unexpectedly coming at her from the right. Then everything went black.

The same kind of blackness enveloping her now...

"*Louise*!"

"*Bonjour*, Tracey."

When Tracey realized it wasn't Julien, she sat up higher against the pillows, trying to pull herself together. First Dr. Simoness, now Louise.

When Tracey had refused to see or talk to Julien after the head of the clinic had examined Tracey last evening, Julien must have sent for Louise, knowing how close Tracey felt to her.

The older woman came into the bedroom and shut

the door. Without asking Tracey's permission, she pulled one of the matching damask chairs next to the bed and sat down.

"W-what are you doing here?" Though Tracey already knew the answer, she was so frantic she'd said the first thing to enter her head.

"Locking the bathroom door gave your husband quite a fright," the doctor replied in mild chastisement. "As I understand it, he had to break it down to get to you, fearing your faint might have sent you into another coma."

Tracey shivered as a fresh attack of pain and remorse almost incapacitated her.

"When Dr. Simoness arrived at the château in response to his phone call around dinnertime, he said your husband was in as bad a mental state as you are."

Lowering her head to avoid Louise's probing gaze, Tracey's anxiety over Julien finally forced her to ask, "I-is he all right now?"

"What do you think?"

A dreadful silence prevailed before she blurted, "I can't stay here any longer, Louise! Julien let me out of the clinic on the condition that I live under the same roof with him for thirty days, and if at the end of that time I still wanted a divorce, then he'd give it to me. I thought I could do it, but—"

"But you never wanted children because you're not the marrying type, and now that you've found out you're the mother of triplets, you're repulsed by the idea.''

''*No*!'' Tracey cried in horror at Louise's misconception of the situation.

Instead of looking surprised, her doctor actually seemed gratified by Tracey's outburst. Too late it dawned on her that the other woman had tricked her into revealing her true feelings.

''That's what your husband is beginning to believe, you know. He tells me you've refused to look at your sons, even to acknowledge them.''

Louise knew exactly what to say to reach Tracey, who threw back the covers and got out of bed. The view of the lake was particularly beautiful from her window, but all she could see was Julien's tormented expression when she'd come out of her faint. His agony, coupled with her own, had finally brought her to the breaking point.

Wiping the moisture from her cheeks, she wheeled around to face Louise.

''I'm *a-afraid* to look at them,'' she admitted shakily, remembering the strong Chappelle characteristics she saw in Valentine.

''Because they're replicas of your husband and you don't want to live with him anymore?''

''*No*!'' Her denial resounded in the room. Louise said nothing, but her eyes invited Tracey to unburden herself. After another tension-fraught pause, Tracey found herself saying, ''I—I can't bear to look at them—f-for fear I'll see Julien's *father* in their features.''

''But that would only be natural, wouldn't it, seeing he's the grandfather?''

''No! You don't understand.'' Tracey groaned. ''Henri Chappelle is *my* father, too.''

''*Ahh...*''

There was a wealth of understanding in that one word. Tracey could sense Louise studying her through new eyes, her mind obviously computing this latest revelation with all its damning ramifications.

''Tell me something, Tracey. Was Henri Chappelle a tall man with an imposing countenance and dark, piercing eyes?''

Tracey's head whipped around. ''Yes. He's *exactly* like that. How did you know? Have you seen a picture of him? Do my sons resemble him that much?'' she asked, her voice throbbing in agony.

''I've never seen your children, but I do have a picture of your father-in-law in my possession. It's the one you drew for me day before yesterday,'' she said softly.

''*What*?''

Louise nodded. ''That wasn't an animal you sketched. It was a man in the shape of a bird of prey, an eagle to be exact. You've just provided me the missing piece of the puzzle. *He* was the cause of your terrible nightmares.''

Tears poured down Tracey's cheeks.

''The second I saw the drawing, I knew it couldn't

be your husband, and it certainly wasn't your father, because your aunt had already shown me pictures of your family.''

"Except that Daddy's not my daddy," Tracey whispered in a stricken tone.

Louise's hands went to the pockets of her suit jacket. "I presume it was Henri Chappelle himself who told you his terrible secret after you and your husband returned from your honeymoon."

"Yes."

"That explains your precipitous flight."

"Yes."

"Deathbed repentance on his part?"

Tracey nodded as more tears dripped down her face. "He could barely get the words out about his affair with Mother before Monseigneur Louvel came in to perform the last rites."

On her feet now, Louise approached Tracey. *"Ma chère*...I can't tell you how sorry I am. I wish there were some magic words to make the pain stop."

"I wish I were dead."

"I can understand why you would feel that way," Louise commiserated. "After living as man and wife, to be asked to treat your beloved Julien like a brother is asking *too* much.

"Now we know why your mind suppressed all memory of your pregnancy and delivery for such a long time. It makes perfect sense. That, and the guilt, because you're incapable of viewing Julien in any other light than your lover."

"Yes." Tracey broke down sobbing and felt the older woman's arms go around her. Louise understood everything.

"But no matter how much pain you're in, you have two handsome sons and a beautiful daughter to consider. Three infants who need their mother. You must live for *them*, Tracey."

Tracey's shoulders shook and it took a few minutes to recover her composure before she moved out of Louise's arms. "I know."

"Naturally you're afraid that because you and your husband are half brother and sister, your children will have abnormalities, which might or might not be the case. Check with the pediatrician right away and put your fears to rest."

"I—I'd already planned to do that this morning."

"Good for you. But please remember. Whatever you learn and have to deal with, it will be better than the agony you've suffered since returning from your honeymoon."

"I—I came to that conclusion last night," Tracey concurred in a piteous voice.

"There's something else." Louise eyed her shrewdly. "You're going to have to break the silence and tell your husband, Tracey."

CHAPTER FIVE

"*I COULDN'T possibly*!" Tracey cried out, shaking her head.

"Every day is a new nightmare for him," the doctor reasoned. "He doesn't deserve it."

"But the truth will destroy him. It will change the way he feels about his entire world! Nothing will ever be the same for him again," she retorted despairingly.

"Nothing has been the same for him since you disappeared. Don't you know that *you* are his entire world, you and the children?"

"Please don't say that," Tracey appealed to her. "People get divorced every day and survive it."

"Not people who love as profoundly as you and your husband have loved each other."

Tracey couldn't stand to listen to any more. "In time he'll find someone else to love and it won't be forbidden."

"He has the right to know, Tracey, and you don't have the right to keep it from him. Look at the damage done because your mother and Henri Chappelle lived all these years holding on to their guilty secret."

Tracey felt like she was in some sort of trance, hardly aware of speaking her thoughts aloud. "It's no wonder I wasn't invited back to the château."

"Tell me about that portion of your life. We could never talk about it before because of your memory loss."

Tracey needed little encouragement. Now that Louise knew the truth, it was easy to fill in the missing portions of her life for her.

"...so I guess when Mother and Henri could see what was happening between Julien and me, they separated us and the family visits ended for good. Only Isabelle was allowed to stay with Angelique for a few weeks at a time out of the year, while I—" her voice caught "—was never invited back." Her heart ached with resurging sadness. "I wonder if Daddy knew."

"If he did, it obviously never changed the way he felt about you. Not only that, he must have loved your mother enough to forgive her," Louise commented at last. "Otherwise it doesn't make sense that he remained her husband and stayed with Chappelle House until his death."

Tracey passed a trembling hand over her eyes. "I'm sure you're right. When I think about it, I never really believed that Celeste's failing health was the reason our family had to remain in San Francisco. She'd always been fragile, so it didn't make any sense to me that she suddenly couldn't cope with guests. Henri always had plenty of staff to see to her needs.

"I never did come right out and ask Julien about it, but I'm positive he didn't believe it, either. He probably thought the permanent separation had something to do with Jacques and me. That must be why he insisted on our marriage taking place in private without either family's knowledge. I doubt he told anyone about our wedding plans when he left Switzerland on business.''

Louise cocked her head. ''So now it's time for the whole truth to come out. If you keep this from your husband, you'll not only hurt him irreparably, but you'll be compounding your parents' sin in a way that could one day rebound on the heads of your children.''

Her words terrified Tracey.

''Louise, this doesn't affect just Julien and me. There's our brothers and sisters to consider. News of such a scandalous nature would rock close family members and friends on both sides of the Atlantic.

''Right now, I'm the only one who knows the truth except for you. I—I can't risk it.'' She bit her lower lip so hard it bled. ''Julien will be in pain for a while, but he'll eventually get over it and carry on with his life.''

Louise shook her head. ''You know that's not true. He won't get over it, Tracey. I watched him at your bedside every night for months, attempting to comfort you during your nightmares, willing you to recover. His love for you transcends everything else.''

She pressed Tracey's arm gently. ''If you truly love him, you'll tell him everything. Both sets of parents are dead now, so they can't hurt or be hurt anymore. Scandals die, you know. But the truth is the only way to free your husband. Then, and only then, will he be able to find someone else to love, *if* that is his choice. Don't you see that otherwise you'll be condemning him to a prison he didn't make?''

Tracey stiffened. ''If Henri had thought Julien could handle it, he would have told him the truth instead of me.''

''Nonsense,'' Louise came back firmly. ''I've learned enough from what you've just told me to know that Henri Chappelle went selfishly to his grave, content that his elder son still worshiped him.

''It was easy enough to rid his conscience with you since your mother had already passed away and he no longer required her permission to act. He also knew your character well enough to count on your loyalty, knowing you'd keep his secret rather than destroy the family.

''*Think about it*! The second he slipped from life, you disappeared on cue. Don't you understand that he manipulated you and is still continuing to do so?''

Twisting her hands together, Tracey blurted, ''I can't do it, Louise. Julien and his father were very close. I couldn't bear to damage that. Promise me you'll never tell a living soul.''

''I made that promise when I became a doctor, Tracey. Whatever you've told me remains confidential, but I'm warning you. You'll keep this secret to your own peril.'' Heaving a sigh, she said, ''I'm going to leave now. You know where to find me if you wish to talk about it further. Just remember one thing. I'm on your side. Always on your side.''

''Thank you, Louise.''

After following the older woman to the door, Tracey hurried into the shower, her mind racing ahead.

Maybe the pediatrician would see her before the day was out. She needed to be dressed and ready in case she was told to come in at her earliest convenience.

There had to be tests Tracey could arrange to determine if there'd been any genetic damage to the babies.

Julien wouldn't think it strange that she wanted to see the children's doctor. Any woman who truly loved her children and had been separated from them this long would do as much. In fact, he would be more than pleased that she was taking so much interest in their welfare. No doubt he would view her actions as a positive sign that she was coming around to the idea of being a mother. *And a wife. Darling Julien. If only you knew…*

Hurriedly she put on the same outfit she'd worn home from the hospital, then rushed out of the room. But her flight was short-lived because Julien came striding toward her with purpose in every step.

Quickly she averted her eyes, but not soon enough to blot out the devastatingly attractive picture he made. In a navy polo shirt and khaki trousers that molded his powerful body, his casual attire reminded her of their honeymoon.

Julien hadn't taken any formal clothes to Tahiti. The

two of them were much like children of the sea, playing and loving anywhere they felt like it, often without the benefit of clothes.

On the rare occasion when they went to the nearby village for dinner, they dressed informally, with her wearing a native wraparound he'd bought for her, and Julien sporting the kind of outfit he was wearing now.

Those memories went soul deep. *How was she ever going to erase them*?

"Louise's visit must have done you some good. Your color is back." His low, velvety voice broke in on the heavy tension between them.

"Yes," she responded, her breathing shallow. "W-we've been talking about the babies."

"Tracey," he said on a ragged whisper, "I should have told you about the children last night before I left the clinic. But because you didn't recognize me until I spoke to you, I assumed the same miracle might happen again when you heard our children crying or saw them in my arms."

"I-it did happen. Your plan worked. There are no more memory gaps. I remember everything, even the color of the taxi that hit me."

At the mention of the accident, his face blanched. "But at what cost?" he bit out in self-denigration.

"It was better this way, Julien. Your instincts are rarely wrong. I'm glad to know the whole truth. That's why I was coming to find you, to tell you that I'm all right now. You don't need to worry about my having a relapse or any such thing.''

He stood with his strong legs slightly apart, those dark winged brows forming a skeptical frown as he rubbed the back of his neck in an unconscious gesture she'd seen before. It meant that he patently didn't believe her.

''Actually, I feel good enough to visit the children's doctor,'' she assured him. ''Today, if possible.''

He blinked, obviously puzzled. ''Why? If you're worried about them, you don't need to be. I can promise you they're in perfect health.''

His comment was reassuring enough on the surface, but she wanted to know a great deal more than that.

One black brow dipped in concern. ''*Mignonne*, if you're suffering over Raoul, then don't. It's true that before the accident, he was the one who had the most difficulty breathing on his own, but that problem cleared up after a couple of weeks.''

''Thank heavens for that,'' she murmured in heartfelt gratitude. ''Look, Julien. I believe you.'' Her hands twisted together nervously. ''But it's just that I've missed so much of the past five months, I want to know all there is to know about their medical histories and development before I get reacquainted with my precious babies.''

Searching for any plausible excuse, she continued, ''I—I want to see their growth charts and what they've eaten and liked and disliked. You know.'' Tears welled in her eyes. "All the little things a mother normally knows about her children."

Whatever he'd been expecting her to say, her words caught him off guard. Judging by the way the hard muscles of his body appeared to relax, she knew she'd pleased him.

"Having been deprived of them this long, naturally you have questions," he concurred with a gentleness that was too piercingly sweet. "I'll arrange it with Dr. Chappuis right now, *mignonne*."

Stop calling me that, her heart cried out. Somehow, someway, she was going to have to school herself not to react every time he used one of his special endearments for her. "I realize he probably has a full schedule so—"

"If he's not at the hospital, I'll make certain he sees us this morning," Julien murmured, making it sound like an avowal.

Not *us*, she moaned inwardly. But that was another thing she was going to have to get used to. Julien meant what he said when he told her they would be doing everything together for the next month.

"Where are the children now?"

"Out for a walk in their prams. It's a beautiful autumn day." What he didn't say with words, his eyes were telling her. That it was the kind of glorious morning the two of them used to relish.

Julien, don't get your hopes up. Please, darling.

"Well—" she cleared her throat "—if you don't

mind calling the doctor, I'll run to the kitchen for some breakfast.''

Without waiting for a response, she hurried down the corridor to the stairs, praying Julien wouldn't follow her.

To her intense relief, he wasn't behind her as she entered the kitchen and interrupted Solange, who was delighted to see her and began plying her with hot chocolate and melt-in-your-mouth brioches dripping with butter and conserves.

Under the circumstances, the idea of starving herself to get away from her husband was not only absurd, but criminal. Her babies needed her. The last thing she wanted was another separation from them because of poor health she'd purposely brought on.

If anything, remembering that she had three children gave her the impetus to put on the weight she'd lost as quickly as possible so she could take care of them without help.

Of course, Julien couldn't have managed without full-time nannies, but now that she was back, things had to change. She didn't want anyone else raising her babies. If Julien was demanding that she stay with him for a month, then she could make demands, too.

Her first request would be to let the nannies go. Julien said the children were in perfect health. Certainly if necessity made it difficult for Tracey to cope on her own, there were enough maids employed at the château to lend an occasional hand.

Not only did Tracey want her babies to herself, she needed to stay so busy that it would keep Julien at a distance until the thirty days were up. Beyond that, she could scarcely think. Since Julien would never let his children go, maybe she could get an apartment near the château so that they could share them on a daily basis.

She would watch over them during the day, and Julien could take care of them after he left his office, if that was what he wanted. Sort of a joint custody situation that would give him the space he needed to build a new life with someone else. It could work. *She'd make it work*.

Gone were her plans of a career and travel. She was a mother now, something she'd always wanted to be. There was no question in her mind that Julien would provide for her so that she could give their children all the love in her.

It would be her mission to raise them. To bathe and cuddle them, to play with them and read them her favorite stories. To teach them how to talk and sing and pray, how to love and give love, how to be perfect little ladies and gentlemen their daddy would be proud of.

She couldn't wait to immerse them with love. What better outlet to sublimate her love for Julien than by devoting her life to their children.

"Tracey?"

Her head swerved in Julien's direction. She'd been so deep in thought, she hadn't heard him enter the kitchen.

"Dr. Chappuis's nurse said he's still at the hospital doing rounds, but he's expected back shortly. We're to come as soon as we can get there and she'll fit us in."

Frightened, yet relieved that she'd have answers shortly, Tracey finished swallowing the last of her roll before she said, "Thank you for arranging it, Julien. Give me a minute to run upstairs and get my purse."

"I brought it down with me to save you a trip."

Julien thought of everything and was always five steps ahead of her. Not only that, he'd accomplished a minor miracle. Most pediatricians' offices were so overbooked with sick children, getting in to see the doctor on an unscheduled visit was close to impossible.

When he handed her the tan leather purse she'd brought from the hospital, the touch of his fingers felt like the lick of brush fire against her skin. She quickly pulled away.

His sudden grimace let her know he was aware of her reaction, and his terse "Shall we go?" didn't bode well for the rest of the day as she thanked Solange and followed him out to the Ferrari parked at the rear of the château.

The second she stepped into the warm sunshine, she was reminded of other such beautiful fall mornings when the mist on the lake had already dissipated. With a pang of longing, she remembered the two of them stealing away from the house so they could enjoy a few hours alone together, whether it be on a boat ride to visit a castle, or a picnic in the mountains, surrounded by fields of wild narcissus.

Unlike now, however, there had been this incredible harmony between them and an almost sick sense of excitement on her part because she was going to have him all to herself.

Once alone, she'd do everything in her power to get him to kiss her, but he always stayed in control, never giving in to the passion she felt sure he was capable of.

He never showed the sensual side of his nature until he unexpectedly attended her graduation from college. That night, he kissed her for the first time. A kiss that went on and on and transformed her world forever. When he finally released her, he told her they were getting married the next time he came to San Francisco, but she was to tell no one their plans.

She'd been so happy then. *So happy…*

"Tracey?"

The sound of her name brought her back to the present. "Yes?" she whispered guiltily.

"Valentine has your exact profile. She's perfect. Do you have any idea how incredible it is to look at her and see *you* every time she opens her eyes and smiles?"

Don't.

"She has your hair and fingernails, Julien."

He flashed her an all-encompassing glance, reminding her too late of her mistake. The fact that she'd been looking for resemblances of him in their daughter proved that she wasn't indifferent to him no matter how much she tried to pretend otherwise.

"It's her beautiful face I'm talking about," Julien added in a quiet voice. "Clair continually scolds me because I dote on her more than the boys. Poor Clair. I don't suppose she's ever known a love like ours, so she couldn't possibly understand."

"Julien," Tracey blurted, anxious to get off such a dangerous subject, "about Clair and the other nannies—I realize you couldn't possibly have gotten along without them. But now that Dr. Simoness has given me a clean bill of health, I want to take care of the children myself."

His long, well-shaped fingers suddenly tightened on the steering wheel so the knuckles stood out white, an indication of the depth of emotion he was experiencing.

"I'd hoped you'd feel that way," he said in thick tones. "We'll ask them to join us for dinner this evening, then tell them their services are no longer required."

On that note, he double-clutched the Ferrari, causing it to fairly leap onto the main road while Tracey craned her head for some sight of the children.

Always a step ahead of her, Julien murmured, "They took the path to the lake. If it's this warm tomorrow, we'll ask Cook to prepare a picnic and we'll take our children on a boat ride."

"That would be wonderful," she burst out excitedly

before realizing her mistake. To cover her tracks, she quickly added, "But we'd have to buy some little life preservers first."

"I took care of that a long time ago in anticipation of this day."

Julien sounded happy. *Too happy*. It broke Tracey's heart all over again.

"After our visit to Dr. Chappuis, we'll go to La Fermière for lunch. It's been a long time since you enjoyed raclette."

Raclette. Their favorite potato dish, covered with cheese fondue flavored with the cherry brandy called kirsch. There was nothing quite like it, but that was probably because she'd always eaten it with Julien. He made every experience magical.

The problem was, it would do no good to tell him she didn't want to have lunch or dinner or anything else with him. Along with his desire to see her gain back the weight she'd lost, his determination to be a real family—to make their marriage work within the thirty-day time period—was a fact of life she had to accept.

The only thing to do was go along with him and treat him like a good friend.

A good friend was all he could be to her now.

"That sounds nice," she said, trying to keep her voice level.

Though he said nothing, she felt his rapier glance,

which penetrated the surface to the troubled woman beneath the facade.

Her body shrank from that look because it meant that Julien intended to do everything possible to break her down. He'd let nothing stop him, but he was up against something beyond his power to fix.

Within the month, he'd realize she was incapable of passion. Then, and only then, would he be forced to let her go....

"Dr. Chappuis is back from the hospital and will see you now."

With trepidation, Tracey turned to her husband, not liking what she had to do. But there was no other way.

"Julien, if you don't mind, I'd like to go in alone. Up until now, you've been doing everything for me, treating me as if I'm an invalid or something. I—I want to feel like I'm a viable person again, independent," she murmured. "You *do* understand what I'm trying to say?"

A devastating bleakness extinguished the light from his eyes.

Another wound. One of many she would be inflicting over the next twenty-eight days.

With an almost imperceptible nod of his dark head, he granted his consent, standing immobile while she followed the nurse from the reception area on legs that felt as insubstantial as water. Thankful when she could no longer feel his gaze on her retreating back, she hurried toward the pediatrician's private office.

Dr. Chappuis looked to be in his sixties, a short, smiling, gentle man who put her at ease and seemed genuinely happy to meet the recovered coma victim and lovely mother of the famous Chappelle triplets.

Before she could ask any questions, he'd shown her to a seat opposite his desk, then proceeded to assure her that her babies were in perfect health and progressing beautifully.

Since Julien had told her as much, the doctor's words came as no surprise. Still, the wonderful news was like a balm to her soul.

After he'd finished going over each of the children's charts with her, he assumed she was satisfied and rose to his feet, obviously assuming their visit was over.

That's when Tracey found the courage to look up at him and tell him the truth of the situation. After swearing him to secrecy, she explained the reason why she'd run away from Julien in the first place, the reason for her temporary amnesia, *and* the reason why she was here now—because she needed to know the triplets' prognosis and be prepared for future medical problems.

In an instant, Dr. Chappuis's beaming face was replaced by a shocked, pained expression. Slowly he sat back down, staring at her with the same kind of compassion she'd felt from Louise.

"In a case like yours," he began after clearing his throat, "there really aren't any tests to be run, not for chromosome damage. We'll simply have to wait and watch for mental retardation, which, *if* it's going to show up, probably won't be evident for several more years.'' After a pause, he added, ''If it's any consolation, to this point in their development, your children have progressed within the normal limits.''

So far they were all right. That was something to be thankful for!

Tracey's eyes closed tightly. From here on out, she'd live one day at a time caring for her dear babies and be grateful. The future she would leave to God.

Another fierce rush of longing to hold them in her arms had her practically leaping from the chair. Proffering her thanks for everything he'd done for the children, she left Dr. Chappuis's office.

As she rounded the corner to the reception area, she almost ran into Julien. It took every ounce of willpower not to fling herself in his arms.

He caught her hands, rubbing her wrists with his thumbs. ''What's wrong, *mignonne*?'' His dark eyes made a clinical appraisal of her features. ''Your pulse is racing too fast to be healthy.''

Because of you, Julien. All because of you.

''After talking to the doctor, I'm so anxious to get back to the children I don't want to waste another second,'' she assured him not untruthfully and eased her hands away. ''Can we go to La Fermière another day?''

His eyes narrowed as if he was still looking for that

elusive something. Tracey's limbs trembled because Julien possessed uncanny powers of perception and she didn't know how long she could keep up this facade.

"I only suggested it in case you weren't quite ready to undertake the strenuous task of mothering three children at once," he murmured.

"I'm more than ready."

For the moment, her unequivocal statement seemed to satisfy him. "Then we'll go straight home."

Armed with a lot of new information provided by the doctor, she found it easy enough to keep the conversation focused on the children as Julien drove them back to the château. Anyone listening would have thought they were the typical married couple, discussing the ups and downs of raising their offspring.

But every once in a while she would cast a furtive glance at Julien because she couldn't help herself. Then she would remember how *un*typical they were, and she'd feel crucified all over again because *she still wanted him with every breath in her body*.

Terrified of her feelings for Julien that, to her chagrin, seemed to be growing stronger instead of the other way around, she jumped from the car the second he pulled up in front of the château. He hadn't even shut off the engine before she let herself in the front doors.

One of the maids greeted her as she bounded up the curving staircase. Tracey called back to her but didn't pause in stride as she raced toward the children's bedrooms on the second floor.

Not used to the exertion, she entered the first door on her right out of breath, surprising one of the nannies who was in the process of changing a diaper. "Madame Chappelle!" the older woman muttered in surprise.

Tracey barely registered the astonishment on the woman's face because her attention was focused on the baby lying in the crib. He had light blond hair, his inheritance from Henri Chappelle. *But she wouldn't think about that now*.

"Which one is he?" she asked in an awestruck whisper.

"It's Raoul." Her husband's deep voice spoke from behind, startling her. "*Bon après-midi*, Jeanette."

The kind-faced woman flashed Julien a welcoming smile as she lifted the baby off the mattress so Tracey could have a better look. "He's the quieter of your two sons, *madame*, except when he's hungry. I believe he's a great thinker, and reminds me the most of your husband."

Her words caught Tracey off guard. For five out of the six months, this woman had been Raoul's mother. Naturally she would notice everything. The knowledge filled Tracey with a terrible envy.

"*Raoul!*"

CHAPTER SIX

THE name of her baby had barely passed her lips before she reached for him, hardly able to believe that this robust, chunky, pink-cheeked son had been the one at risk, the one she'd almost lost.

Raoul's struggle for breath during the first few weeks of his life had bonded her to him in a very special way. Tracey remembered the hours she'd spent in the pree-mie unit hovering over him, willing him to start breathing on his own.

"My little sweetheart," she crooned, her voice catching as she drew him into her arms.

Tracey lost count of the next few minutes as she alternately kissed and squeezed him, then examined every inch of his roly-poly body.

Miraculously the baby let her pour out her affection without trying to wriggle away. But his black eyes, which mirrored Julien's and now were studying her face with that keen attentiveness so characteristic of her husband's, made Tracey gasp.

As the inevitable sobs welled up, she tried to stifle them against Raoul's shirt-clad tummy. That's when he started to cry, no doubt because she'd frightened him.

In an effort to repair the damage, she propped him

against her shoulder and rocked him back and forth, shaping her hand against his head to memorize the sweet feel of him. "Forgive me, Raoul. Mommy's sorry. It's just that I love you so much," she whispered over and over again, but he wouldn't be comforted.

"Before you picked him up, he was hungry for his lunch," Jeanette interjected. "I think he's like a lot of men who get a little grumpy before they're fed."

Her comment plus the twinkle in her eye made Tracey feel better. Still, it was hard to relinquish Raoul to the older woman's care.

Julien kissed the top of his blond head before he said, "While you attempt to satisfy that insatiable appetite, *mon fils*, your mother and I are going to see what our firstborn has to say for himself."

Though Julien hadn't been there in the beginning, he seemed to know everything about their children, about the precarious circumstances of her delivery, even the order in which the children had been born, with Valentine in the middle.

After the complicated procedure, Dr. Learned had explained to Tracey that because Raoul had come out last, he may have been the one with the least amount of room in her womb, which could have accounted for his underdeveloped lungs.

But he was certainly making up for them now. Tracey could hear his wails the second she followed Julien from the nursery. After all that attention focused on him, he must have felt abandoned.

Tracey didn't envy Jeanette, who had to try to calm him down before she could feed him. Naturally Tracey wanted to be the one to do everything for her precious baby, but until she held her other son in her arms, she wouldn't know any peace.

Avoiding Julien's eyes because all her emotions were spilling over right now, she ran ahead of him and opened the next door along the corridor.

When she entered the nursery, the nanny, whom Julien addressed as Lise, looked up in surprise and greeted them. But all Tracey's attention centered on her other son, who was being fed in his swing.

Though he, too, had inherited blond hair that was somewhat darker than Raoul's, his olive complexion and physical likeness to Julien shouted at her. Here was the son who with his leaner body and long limbs would look the most like his father when he grew to maturity.

Without stopping to consider the consequences, Tracey raced over to him and got down on her knees, anxious to see the color of his eyes, which were a definite hazel and heavily lashed, much like her own. Apparently he'd been eating squash and plums because traces of both remained on his upper lip.

"Oh, Jules!" Tears pooled in Tracey's eyes. "How adorable you are." Unable to resist, she cupped his handsome face in her hands and began kissing him, food and all.

But Jules wasn't having any of it and burst into tears,

reaching for Julien, who quickly extricated him from the swing and quieted him down.

The baby kept hiding his face in Julien's neck, obviously a familiar position, holding on to his father for dear life. Tracey circled them and tried to get her son's attention, but he jerked his head the other way as if he were terrified she'd try to hold him.

On an intellectual level, Tracey understood his reaction. The problem was, she was too full of feelings— too eager to make up for the past half year—to view his behavior as anything but rejection.

Julien knew exactly what she was experiencing because he murmured, "While I calm him down, why not go see if Valentine has finished her lunch?"

Tracey didn't want to leave, but what choice did she have? If she stayed in the room, Jules would refuse to look at her or finish his food. This was hardly the way she expected their first reunion to go.

After nodding to Julien, she left in search of their daughter, thankful that Raoul hadn't turned away from her at first sight, or she probably wouldn't have been able to handle it.

When she entered Valentine's room, she discovered Clair fitting her dark-haired baby girl into a pink velour sleeper outfit with feet.

After the experience with Jules, Tracey approached her daughter cautiously. "Has she had her lunch?" she whispered to Clair. Like radar, Valentine's tiny shell ears picked up on it and she turned her head in Tracey's direction.

Clair nodded. "She ate half her lamb and all her apricots. Now she's ready for bed and a bottle. Would you like to give it to her?"

"If she'll let me," Tracey murmured in a shaky voice.

"Let's find out. Sit down."

After Tracey did her bidding, the nanny handed her the baby. At first, Valentine squirmed a little and made a few sounds of protest. But the second Tracey took the bottle from Clair and put the nipple in the baby's mouth, she settled down and started drinking.

"Valentine, darling," she crooned to her daughter.

All the while the baby sucked and made loud breathing noises, her green eyes stared into Tracey's as if she recognized their color and could see beneath the surface.

Was it possible Valentine remembered the sound of her mother's voice, her fragrance?

For the whole month of her hospital stay, Tracey had held all three babies exactly like this. Could *that* be the reason why Valentine unexpectedly relaxed against her?

The beautiful oval face looking up at her so trustingly would have thrilled any mother, but no one more than Tracey, who hugged this child to her heart.

Suddenly Valentine wasn't enough. Tracey needed to be with all her children.

Responding to a mother's instinct, she got up from the chair and left the room with Valentine still cuddled in her arms. She headed directly for Raoul's room and upon entering was glad to see he hadn't finished his bottle or fallen asleep.

"Jeanette?" she called to the nanny who was cleaning up the lunch mess. "Would you please ask one of the maids to get a big comforter from off one of the beds and bring it in here?"

Though the older woman looked puzzled by the request she said, "Of course," and immediately left the room. While Tracey waited, she went over to Raoul's crib and cupped his rounded cheek with her free hand.

In response, his mouth let go of the nipple and his left hand reached up to touch her fingers. She put out her pinky and he clung to it, trying to put it in his mouth.

"*Voilà, madame.*"

"Would you mind putting it on the chair, Jeanette? Then you and Clair are free to do whatever you'd like for the rest of the day." Tracey sensed the nanny's surprise and felt forced to explain, "I need time with my children."

"Very well, *madame*. But we won't be far in case you get too tired."

It was difficult for Tracey to tell if Jeanette's reluctance to leave her post stemmed from her attachment to the baby, or her concern for Tracey's health. Perhaps it was a little of both.

Certainly if Tracey had been the one caring for Raoul all this time, she would have loved him so much that when the moment came, she wouldn't have been able to give him up.

More than ever, Tracey was determined that the nannies be relieved of their jobs and allowed to find work elsewhere. She had the grace to feel sorry for them because she knew they'd never be employed by anyone as kind and as fair as Julien.

Relieved when the door closed, Tracey went over to the crib and placed Valentine inside next to Raoul. For a few minutes, she smiled down at her two children, whose eyes never left her face while they held their own bottles and finished drinking.

Taking advantage of the quiet, she reached for the comforter and spread it near the crib on top of the wall-to-wall carpeting Julien had had installed, probably to make the upstairs rooms warmer.

When that was accomplished, she took off her shoes and jacket, left them on the chair, then lifted Raoul from the crib and laid him on the quilt, tummy-side down. She did the same with Valentine, then assumed the identical position on the quilt so she could watch and touch them both without having to move.

The next few minutes felt like pure bliss to Tracey, who continually kissed them, rubbed their backs and talked to them about her plans for their future.

"Well, well, Jules," came a low, familiar voice from the doorway, quickening Tracey's senses so her heart began its painful hammering. "It looks like my family is having a caucus. Shall we join them and find out what's going on?"

Before she could countenance it, Julien had plopped Jules on his stomach between Valentine and Raoul, then extended his own masculine length next to Tracey so the five of them were in touching distance of each other.

Julien could have no idea how his nearness affected her. As for Jules, he wasn't happy about the situation, either, but his misery stemmed from being separated from his father.

Out of a sense of preservation and the desire to comfort her son, Tracey inched her way forward and started playing with Jules's long fingers whose square-shaped ends were exactly like his father's. He didn't want to accept her ministrations, but Tracey kept speaking in soothing tones to him and he finally stopped his fussing.

Her head was close enough for her other babies to pull the ash blond strands of her hair and try to put them in their mouths. Yet while that part felt so right, her body could sense the warmth radiating from Julien, who lay far too close to her. The male tang from his body combined with the scent of the soap he used in the shower teased her nostrils and nearly drove her mad.

To cover her emotions, she reached for Jules, then turned on her back so she could play with him by lifting him in the air and kissing his tummy. The other two children still held on to her hair, not seeming in the least upset she was paying attention to their brother.

But as soon as she made Jules laugh out loud, she realized her mistake because by now Julien had turned on his side to watch her.

Tracey recognized the stillness that had come over him. She didn't have to see into his eyes to know the fires that blazed beneath those shuttered lids.

Though he did nothing overt—nothing she could accuse him of—his desire reached out for her like a living thing, intensifying the danger of being this close to him.

His mere presence triggered such an overwhelming response in Tracey, she was forced to turn on her side, away from temptation.

Using Jules as a human shield, she cuddled her baby against her trembling body and began singing a lullaby. Perhaps it was the music that calmed him because he let her kiss and love him, just like her other babies.

The bittersweet moment caused hot tears of joy and pain to trickle from the corners of her eyes. Joy because her fulfillment as a mother was so great. But it came at a price that brought nothing but soul-destroying pain. Lying next to her was the man she loved more than her own life. The one man denied to her from birth, *if* she had but known it.

She knew it now.

Still, a part of her rebelled against this ghastly new

knowledge that had literally torn her world to pieces. Part of her wanted to ignore everything and go on loving Julien as if Henri Chappelle had never spoken.

But God knew her terrible secret, and He knew that *she* knew it. There was no hiding place, no limbo where she and Julien could go to live out the rest of their days.

Indescribable sadness pierced her breast as she pressed her wet face against Jules's sweet-smelling nape. From here on out, her children would have to be her only comfort, her *raison d'être*.

"*Mignonne*?"

No. Please. No. Don't talk. Don't say anything.

But it was too late. He *had* spoken. Tracey groaned because there was no mistaking the urgency or the huskiness in her husband's voice as he called softly to her.

"Months ago, when things looked their darkest, I used to dream about moments like this...ensconced in my own home, surrounded by my children, my wife....

"How is it possible you can lie here next to me and our babies and not feel what I'm feeling? Not want this to go on forever?

"Tell me, *mon amour*—if you can. Convince me that you don't belong in my arms, that you don't hunger for the kind of rapture we shared up until the very second you disappeared from my life," he entreated, his voice throbbing. "*Tracey...*"

Everything he was feeling, everything she

couldn't—wouldn't—allow him to say, was alive in
that one pleading word of endearment.

Her soul felt murdered all over again. Out of self-
preservation, the only thing to do was lie there and
feign sleep.

Oh, to be one of her babies, all of whom had drifted
into slumber and had no worries.

Each moment that passed now was pure agony because Tracey knew that Julien was waiting for the
slightest sign that she'd heard him, that she wanted and
needed him as much as he wanted and needed her.

She couldn't possibly respond and found herself
praying harder than she'd ever prayed in her life. To
her immense relief, her body finally started to relax
until she knew no more.

When next she became cognizant of her surroundings, she felt a weight across her hips. In her somnolent
state, she assumed Jules had somehow climbed over
her. Without conscious thought, she felt for him, wanting to touch his silky hair with her palm and assure
herself that he was really there.

But she knew something was wrong the instant her
hand came in contact with the head nestled against her
breast. The features were too prominent, the hair too
vibrant and crisp to be Jules.

Her eyes flew open and she had to bite her lip to
keep from crying out.

Somehow during her nap, she'd let go of Jules, who

was still sleeping as soundly as her other babies, and had turned toward Julien, who had also drifted off.

What wasn't possible when she was conscious, had happened while they'd slept. Instinctively she and Julien had reached for each other. His arm had caught her around the hip in a possessive hold, while her arms had enfolded his head and shoulders just as greedily.

While Tracey was still trying to recover, never mind figure out a way to get up without disturbing her husband, Clair chose that moment to peek inside the room. But just as quickly she went away again, obviously realizing she'd interrupted something very intimate and personal between husband and wife.

Tracey could imagine what construction the nanny would put on what she thought she saw. No doubt she'd tell the others.

When Tracey looked down, she saw that her blouse was badly wrinkled and that it had come loose from the waistband of her skirt. Not only that, Julien's arm had made the material ride up her legs, exposing more than was decent of her silk-clad thighs.

Embarrassment consumed Tracey along with a scorching sense of guilt. White-hot heat filled her cheeks.

This should never have happened, could never be allowed to happen again.

Twenty-seven more torturous days to get through and already one of her worst fears had come to fruition.

In absolute panic, she backed away from him, hoping he wouldn't wake up. But she'd forgotten Jules, who was in her path and didn't like the sudden jostling his mother's backside gave him. He let out a loud cry of distress that brought everyone awake. Almost instantly the other two joined in the ruckus.

Full of remorse, Tracey got to her feet as fast as she could, but not fast enough to escape Julien, whose eyes opened the moment he felt her slip from his embrace. The triumphant message in those dark depths told her he knew exactly what had happened while they'd been asleep.

He'd been waiting for such a sign. Now she'd given it to him and there was no denying it.

Knowing how Julien's mind worked filled her with terror. Armed with this new knowledge, he'd use it until he broke her down completely.

In a frantic move, she swept Raoul in her arms. Oddly enough *he* was crying the hardest, so she carried him over to his crib to change his diaper. She found his pacifier and inserted it in his mouth, crooning softly to him. It seemed to do the trick and his tears stopped.

By now the noise had abated because Julien had picked up the other two. As he went out the door, she heard him say, "Let's give your mother some time with your brother. Soon it will be your turn. She's home to stay, *mes enfants*, and we'll have the rest of our lives to be together."

No, Julien. We won't. Not the way you mean.

*   *   *

"The children have always liked drives in the car, but I believe they're enjoying the boat more. What do you think?"

Clever Julien, sticking to the children as the topic of conversation, never once touching on anything personal, never referring to that scene in Raoul's bedroom yesterday when she'd been caught holding her husband in her arms.

"Since this is all so new to me, I have no way of knowing such a thing, but they do seem content."

All three infants lay propped in their carryalls on the floor behind Julien, who handled the controls of the sleek twenty-one-foot ski boat. Avoiding even a glance in his direction, Tracey watched her babies play with their hands and bite on a few rattles Julien had brought along from their toy bin.

Besides their life preservers and stretchy suits with feet, they wore sky blue cotton sweaters. Tracey pulled up the hoods to cover their ears and head. Only their precious faces were exposed to the warm afternoon sun that took the fall nip out of the air.

When she wasn't feeding them or changing their diapers, she'd reach for them one at a time and cuddle them. As they cruised around the placid lake, she'd point out a famous landmark like the medieval Château de Chillon or the water jet in Geneva's harbor.

At one place near the shoreline at the Château de Clarens, an old fossil of a fortress, Julien cut the engine to get himself something to eat from the cooler. The cook had prepared mouth-watering quiches, *tartes aux framboises*, and she'd supplied them with Grapillon, a grape drink Tracey adored.

While her eyes scanned the hillsides teeming with vineyards full of ripe grapes ready to be harvested, he fixed a plate for Tracey, then himself, and they ate in what must have looked like companionable silence. But inside, she was a seething mass of nerves.

In an effort to break the tension, she said, "You were very generous to the nannies last night when you told them that we were letting them go. I'm sure they're grateful, Julien."

He swallowed another tart before replying, "There's not enough money in this world to recompense them for mothering the children until you could take over. But I have to admit that for their sakes, I'm glad they've been forced to move on. Jeanette, particularly, was too attached to Raoul."

Tracey nodded. "I sensed as much yesterday. He's so sweet." Her voice choked up and her eyes filled as she looked at her children. "They're all so sweet."

"They're perfect, and today I feel as if I'm the luckiest man alive," he murmured with gut-wrenching emotion.

"Julien," she blurted, anxious to cut him off before he led them into deeper waters, "I—I hope you won't mind that I called Isabelle early this morning and—"

"Why in heaven's name would I mind?" he bit out unexpectedly, revealing that he wasn't as in control as she had imagined. "This is your home now, and she's your sister after all."

Clutching her hands together, she said, "You didn't let me finish. I haven't seen her or Alex in half a year and I'm afraid he'll forget me, s-so I've invited them to come and stay at the château with us for a while."

Not by the twitch of a facial muscle did Julien reveal his true feelings on the matter. Instead, he bit into his quiche, then asked in a bland voice, "Do you think that's wise after what Rose told us at dinner last night?"

Tracey sucked in her breath. "You're talking about Bruce."

"Tracey—" Julien frowned "—he doesn't know the meaning of work. Being a guest at the château will only set him back further."

"I know," she whispered. "That's why my invitation didn't include him. Rose and I talked after we put the babies to bed. She agrees with me that maybe it's depression over Bruce, rather than morning sickness, that is getting her down. Maybe a few weeks here, playing with the babies and getting out of herself by spending time with Angelique, will be good therapy. Isabelle needs to be with family right now," she added not untruthfully.

But her real reason for inviting her sister to Lausanne was to widen the gulf between herself and Julien, and he knew it.

"How soon would you like her to come?"

"As soon as arrangements can be made."

"Then I'll see to her airline tickets when we get back from boating."

"No, Julien." At her rejection of his offer, his head reared back and she knew she'd angered him. "I—I mean, she'll take care of that herself."

"How?" he demanded a trifle aggressively.

"She still has some savings."

"Then she needs to hold on to them."

"Daddy left that money for her. I told her to use it. Bruce needs a rude awakening, or he'll end up destroying their marriage."

The minute the words left her mouth, she knew she'd said the wrong thing and wanted to die. In the damning silence that followed, the color drained out of Julien's face, leaving it an expressionless mask.

"Would it be all right if I took the boat back to Lausanne?" she asked, trying to change the subject to cover her pain. "I know it's been a long time, but since there's no wind, I think I can handle it."

"There was never any doubt of that, *mignonne*," he replied in a deceptively mild voice. "But since the children and I aren't ready to go home yet, why don't you head for Évian?" Inherent in his seemingly innocent question was a command, one she had to obey without remonstration or she'd give herself away.

Tracey's heart sank to her feet. Évian was on the French side of the lake. It suited Julien to be gone several more hours, hours in which she would have to think up new ways to keep her emotional distance from him.

After yesterday, she didn't dare show him how vulnerable she was and had to comply with his wishes. But her hands were unsteady on the gears as she raised the anchor and started up the motor.

"Better switch to the other tank," he reminded her because she'd forgotten. "We'll fill up again when we reach the opposite shore."

Except for the humming sound of the engine, nothing else broke the silence as they skimmed across the pale blue water. It appeared they had the lake to themselves. Not even the occasional wake from another boat made so much as a ripple on top of the glasslike surface.

Looking back over the years, she recalled there'd been other days much like today—before Henri Chappelle's confession—when Tracey had come out in the boat with Julien and found inestimable joy just by being in his company, by getting close to him.

She fought tears because she had an idea that Julien was remembering those heavenly times, too. But such moments of innocence were gone forever, could never be repeated. She felt crucified all over again at the cruel reality of their situation.

Julien had insisted she stay with him for a month in order to prove that she wanted out of her marriage. But she was fast coming to the conclusion that she'd break before the thirty days were up. If Isabelle's visit didn't produce the desired results, Tracey didn't know what she was going to do.

Telling Julien the bald truth might change him beyond recognition. Tracey realized the disillusionment and pain wouldn't kill him—he was too strong a character for that—but something inside him would shrivel up and die. He'd no longer be the same Julien everyone admired and loved.

No, no matter how many times she went over it in her mind, she always came back to her original conclusion—that he should not be told the truth. Much better that he suffer from a broken heart rather than try to function with a murdered soul.

So deep were her black thoughts, it wasn't until Julien moved her aside with firm hands and physically took over the handling of the boat that she realized he'd been trying to get her attention.

Shivering from his touch, which she felt through her windbreaker, she hurried back to the children.

"If we pull in over there," he called over his broad shoulder, pointing to a dock in the distance, "they'll gas up the boat while we go inside the restaurant. It has a new owner and they prepare the best white fish along the lake."

"But the babies—" Tracey gasped quietly, attempting to drum up any excuse that would prevent her from being alone with him much longer.

"They'll have infant chairs."

"Julien—"

"Humor me, *mignonne*. I've waited long enough for the day when I could take my family out to dinner," he murmured in a faraway voice. "That day is here, and I intend to celebrate it."

CHAPTER SEVEN

IN THIS kind of mood, Julien was invincible. She had no choice but to go along with his wishes.

Once they'd tied up to the dock, he gave instructions to the man running the gas concession, then turned to Tracey. "If you'll carry Valentine, I'll bring the boys." Assisting her out of the boat, he handed her the baby, sans carryall or life preserver.

Within seconds, he'd joined her, his strong arms around Raoul and Jules. Together, they walked the length of the dock to the shoreside restaurant.

Evening was fast approaching. The outdoor section of the sloping terrace looked particularly inviting with tables set beneath its lighted torches.

As far as Tracey could tell, most of the diners were dressed in stylish evening clothes. She felt totally out of place wearing Levi's and tennis shoes. As for Julien, he looked magnificent in anything he wore, particularly the white turtleneck layered with a navy pullover over khakis.

Wherever they went, her husband always drew attention, especially from women. But now that they were carrying three babies who were obviously triplets, every head in the place turned and people started clapping.

Out of deference to the children, the headwaiter showed them to a table inside the restaurant where they'd be warm. He snapped his fingers to the other waiters, who hustled to find infant seats. Before Tracey could sit down, dozens of people had approached her to comment on their adorable babies.

If she'd known about Julien's surprise plans, she would have done something with her hair rather than leaving it tied back with a scarf at the nape.

Casting a furtive glance at Julien, she was awed by the smile of pride and satisfaction on his handsome face, the light radiating from his eyes. He was happy, eager to show off his family to people who recognized him and couldn't seem to keep from touching the children and asking questions.

The Chappelle name was an institution in Europe and Julien was its dynamic head, but few people knew him the way Tracey did. Being with his family on an outing meant more to him than all the accolades heaped upon him by the corporate world.

That's why she couldn't tell him the truth about his father! *Their* father. Joy would go out of him. The light in his eyes would dim and his smile would fade forever. She couldn't do that to him!

Suddenly Julien's gaze locked with Tracey's, a dark, brooding look she couldn't escape. Helping her to be seated, he rasped, ''I know your feelings about being married to me, but for the children's sake, pretend to enjoy this evening, *petite*.''

She heard so many things in his voice—pain, rage, abject frustration. *It was killing her as surely as it was him.*

The rest of the evening passed by in a kind of blur. Tracey put up the best front she could and ate her food though her appetite had deserted her. But by the time their dessert had been brought to the table, the babies had started to fuss. After receiving a surfeit of attention, it was apparent they needed their beds. As far as Tracey was concerned, it was a miracle they'd been good this long.

Julien must have come to the same conclusion. In a quiet aside, he murmured, ''I think we'll have to enjoy our *galette au chocolat* another time. Shall we go?''

Relief filled her system and she nodded. For the past hour, she'd felt like she'd been caught in a trap with all eyes upon her, upon them. At least in the boat it would be dark and Julien would have to drive, leaving her free to deal with the children and her fears.

The night air was decidedly cold now that the sun was gone. Clouds she hadn't noticed before obscured the stars. No conversation passed their lips as she followed a remote Julien from the restaurant to the dock. Once they'd settled the children in the boat, he reached for the top. By tacit agreement, she helped him snap everything in place to make the interior warm and snug for the cruise home.

Some workers on the dock who'd been discussing

an approaching storm helped them cast off. Julien drove out of the harbor at an almost wakeless speed.

"Ready?"

Tracey shivered at his clipped tone. "One second." She'd decided to hold Jules because he cried every time she started to put him in his carryall. The minute she settled him on her lap he quieted down. "All right. You can go now."

With a change of gears, the boat leaped forward and flew across the water. A wind had sprung up out of nowhere, causing the waves to buffet them somewhat. But with Julien at the helm, Tracey didn't give it a thought. In fact, the steady slam of the hull breaking each wave seemed to put the children to sleep.

They might have traveled another five minutes before she felt the boat lose speed and start to turn around.

"What's happening?" she called out, forgetting her vow to leave him alone.

"The storm is building in intensity. By the time we reach the middle of the lake, it will feel like a hurricane. If we didn't have the children, I'd keep going. But I refuse to put my family at risk so we're going to head back to shore and wait it out."

No! Tracey's heart cried. But she'd known Julien for too many years. Once he'd made up his mind about something, that was it. Besides, he'd lived by the lake all his life and she trusted his judgment completely. If he thought their predicament could be in the least life threatening, then she didn't dare argue with him. The babies were his first priority.

How she loved him for the kind of man he was. No other man of her acquaintance could touch him. No man ever would....

Pressing her lips to Jules's blond head, she listened to the rain hitting the windshield like spatter paint. Soon it was coming down in sheets and Julien had to use every bit of his considerable strength to keep the boat under control.

But since he thrived on challenge, no one kept a cooler head or a steadier hand. She would always be able to count on him, especially in a crisis. Anyone else would be panicked by now, but not her darling Julien.

"He'll find us a safe place," she whispered to Jules, who was still awake but had stopped crying. No doubt the noise of the storm had become more interesting to him than the sound of his own voice.

While she rocked him back and forth, her eyes sought Valentine's and Raoul's sleeping forms in the darkness. Tracey envied them because they were as blissfully unaware of the elements as they were of the tragedy created by their grandparents' lies of omission.

Like a never-ending stream, tears coursed down Tracey's cheeks. For the thousandth time, she asked herself why Henri hadn't died before she and Julien returned from their honeymoon. A few days would have made all the difference to their lives. She and Julien

could have enjoyed their marriage without ever knowing the circumstances that now forced them apart.

How could Henri have done this to them? Why
hadn't her mother ever said one word? Why had she
never raised a cry of warning to her daughter when she
could see that Tracey had fallen under Julien's spell?

What possessed their parents to continue forcing the
two families together for all those years when they
were party to a secret that if revealed, threatened the
very fabric of both families' existence?

"It doesn't make sense," she found herself moaning
aloud.

"Tracey?"

She heard real anxiety in Julien's voice and her head
flew back. "Yes?" she said, frantically dashing at the
tears with her arm.

"Are you all right?"

No. I'm not. I'll never be again.

"I—I'm fine," came her tremulous response.
"H-how are you?"

He didn't say anything right away, making her uneasy. The tension between them was much worse than
the elements playing havoc with the boat. When he
finally spoke, it was in a grating voice and her heart
started to thud.

"Do you realize that's the first personal question
you've asked me since you awakened from your
coma?"

Tracey could feel his pain, but was incapable of responding for fear she'd give in to the impulse to tell him everything. Then it would all be over and Julien's life would change forever.

He started to say something else, then bit out an unintelligible epithet because the hull suddenly grated against a sandbar, bringing the boat to a lurching stop.

Tracey practically slid off the seat, but caught herself in time. Unfortunately, Jules started to cry at being jostled so rudely. As for Raoul, his carryall tipped on its side.

Though he landed on a padded quilt Julien had placed there in the event of such an occurrence—so they couldn't get hurt—the baby cried out in fright. This immediately awakened Valentine and within seconds all three children were crying.

While Julien climbed out the side of the boat to pull it higher up on the beach, Tracey got down on the floor to right Raoul's carryall and put Jules in his. After kissing each little flushed face, she rummaged in the cooler for their bottles.

Thank heavens for baby bottles that could go anywhere and live through anything, she mused. By the time Julien had secured the boat with ropes and had returned, the children were noisily drinking. Tracey sat in the midst of them and let them hold on to her hands with their tiny fingers, thereby reassuring them that she hadn't left them alone in the darkness.

"Do you think the hull was damaged?" she asked

Julien while he made up beds for them from the padded seats running down both sides of the boat.

"Possibly to the paint, but nothing structural."

"Where are we?"

"A half mile south of the restaurant on someone's private stretch of beach. We'll be safe here until the storm passes."

If only their lives could be as simple.

"*Mon Dieu.* This is hardly the way I planned this evening to end."

"You can't order the elements around as easily as your employees," she teased so he wouldn't be so hard on himself.

"Obviously not," came the dry retort, reminiscent of other conversations in the past when there had been no threat to their happiness. "Tracey—" the longing she heard when he said her name always made her pulse race " —I'll take over with the children now. After this ordeal, you should lie down and get some rest."

"No, Julien," she stated in a firm voice. "You're the one who needs the respite. For months you've had the responsibility for the whole family on your shoulders. You deserve a night off. Let me watch over them while *you* sleep. I need to bond with them so they won't miss their nannies too much. I want them to love me," she said, her voice catching.

Although he was lying down with his head near the steering wheel, she heard his quick intake of breath. "You bonded with them during their first month, the most crucial time of all. They got the start they needed. As for loving you, could you be in any doubt after the way they clung to you tonight at the restaurant?''

They *had* clung to her. But because her thoughts were so tied up with Julien, she hadn't stopped to analyze the children's behavior at dinner. They'd reached for her as much as for Julien when strangers put their faces too close or wanted to hold them.

''Thank you for those words.'' Her voice choked up. ''You've been so wonderful,'' she admitted, hiding her burning cheeks against Raoul's tummy.

''You can still say that when I'm holding you hostage until your thirty days are up?''

In an instant, the bitterness was back. What frightened Tracey was to hear his pain, except that it was more than pain now. Rage was growing alongside it, the one destructive emotion she hadn't thought him capable of. She couldn't bear to see what was happening to him.

''Julien—''

''I thought you were giving me the night off,'' he interrupted brutally. ''I've decided to hold you to your word.''

On that acid note he turned away, bringing an abrupt end to their conversation. She should have been relieved. She *was* relieved that he would let her take care of the children while he caught up on some much needed sleep. But she knew her continued silence over the reason for wanting a divorce was tearing him apart.

Which hell was preferable? The one he was living in now, or the new one her confession would create? Was Louise right? Would not knowing the truth drive Julien over the edge?

Throughout the rest of the night, long after the storm had passed over leaving everything as peaceful as before, Tracey sat with her arms around her babies, debating what to do. When morning came, she was still in agony and no closer to reaching a decision.

Upon awakening, Julien took one look at the dark shadows beneath her eyes and assumed she'd had a hard night of it with the babies. In a gravelly tone, he announced they were returning to the château with all possible haste. Once there, she was going straight to bed.

Tracey decided not to argue with him. There'd be time enough for that after she'd showered and changed into clean clothes.

What Julien didn't know was that she planned to do a little remodeling of his house. She wanted her children closer together. Remembering how much fun it had been to share a room with Isabelle while growing up, she felt her babies should enjoy the same experience.

If she put all three beds in one nursery, that would leave the middle room free for their toys and swings and the like. The third nursery could be used for Alex during her sister's stay. One of the playpens with padding would make an acceptable bed for him.

As for the empty guest room across the hall from the nurseries, Tracey planned to move into it so she could listen for the children. Only a mother should have to sleep next to so many little bodies and voices.

Isabelle needed rest and quiet and could be ensured of a good sleep in the room next to Aunt Rose on the third floor. Julien had put her at the opposite end of the hall from their suite for the very reason that he didn't want the children disturbing her.

Tracey hoped Julien wouldn't mind the changes. Surely he realized that she'd never run away again, not now that she had her memory back and intended to devote her life to the children.

Full of plans and ideas that helped keep her mind from dwelling on the pain, she returned to the château with Julien and went straight to her room. She didn't fight him when he said that he'd bathe the babies and see to their breakfast.

If she gave in to him now, he'd eventually go to his study to do some work while the children were napping. Then would be the time she could start carrying out her schemes.

Once Solange knew the plan, she'd heartily approve and direct the maids to help with the moving. Everything could be taken care of before Julien looked in on the babies again and discovered her fait accompli.

Julien had told her this was her home. He'd given her permission to treat it as such and probably wouldn't mind the changes where the babies were concerned, particularly since the rooms were so large.

Of course, he might remain adamant that she stay in the bedroom adjoining his and offer to sleep across the hall from the babies *himself*. That would be something he'd do. But she'd just have to chance it. Hopefully when the time came, she could reason with him by virtue of the fact that she'd lost five months with the children. What better way to make up for the loss than by sleeping close to them?

The rearrangement of the rooms would bring her a measure of peace where her babies were concerned.

A voice deep inside reminded her that sleeping away from *him* would make life a little more bearable while she waited for her divorce.

Two hours later, after an invigorating shower and a fattening breakfast in the kitchen, Tracey went in search of Solange, who was busy dusting.

The second she told the housekeeper her plans, Solange clapped her hands and agreed that it was time to turn the house into a home. Always the talker, she confided to Tracey that she was glad the nannies had gone.

She threw up her hands by way of demonstration that she hadn't exactly approved of them, though she had to admit that they did take "adequate" care of *les petits enfants*.

But no one could ever take the place of their *chère maman*, and now that Tracey was back where she belonged, the house could return to normal and everyone could be happy again.

Tracey could see where this conversation was leading. Solange's loyalty to Henri and Celeste Chappelle had never been in question, but Julien was her favorite person in the world. No way did she approve of Tracey sleeping apart from him.

Which was why Tracey decided to say nothing about the change in her own sleeping arrangements. Solange would find out soon enough, and though she wouldn't like it, there wouldn't be anything she could do about it.

One of the maids enlisted to check on Julien's whereabouts returned to the kitchen to tell Solange that after putting the babies to sleep, he had gone down to the private dock with the estate manager to check out the damage to the boat.

Armed with that information, Tracey and Solange set about their tasks with a camaraderie built over many years' association because of their mutual love of one man.

As they worked side by side, Tracey tried to imagine the impact on Solange if she ever learned the truth about Julien and Tracey. Somehow she suspected it would be devastating to the family retainer.

Solange was a good Catholic. To discover that her esteemed employer had had an affair with Tracey's mother would constitute the ultimate betrayal.

The truth would bring about too much sadness for

everyone involved. Tracey couldn't bear to be the one to impart it.

"Good night, my little darlings," she whispered to her children a few hours later. "Sleep well. Mommy loves you."

Tracey had held each of them to give them their bottles. Now they were snug in their sleepers and ready for bed.

She breathed a sigh of satisfaction at seeing all of them together in the same bedroom. Even with three cribs and dressers, there was still plenty of room to spare.

Their bright eyes followed her movements as she covered them with a light blanket. Every smile, every baby sound tugged at her heartstrings. She still had a hard time believing she'd given birth to all three at the same time.

They were so perfect! Of course, she had her husband to thank for their beautiful bodies and features.

"We do excellent work, don't we?"

Julien had come into the nursery without her noticing. She had no idea how long he'd been watching, but judging by his remark, his thoughts were on the same wavelength as hers.

That's the way it had always been with them. They could read each other's mind without a word passing between them. This was one of those magical times.

Holding her breath, she asked, "Do you mind my putting them together? I thought I'd try an experiment, but I can always ask the maids to help me change everything back tomorrow. It's just tha—''

''Perhaps if my parents had put Jacques and Angelique in the same room with me when we were babies,'' Julien broke in quietly, ''the three of us would have been much closer. The château is large, and the rooms are too isolated from each other.''

''That's what I was thinking.'' Encouraged by his acceptance of her logic, she explained what she'd planned to do with the other two nurseries.

He watched her through narrowed eyes, seeming to concentrate on her mouth as she spoke. She had the impression that he was no longer listening and her heart started to pound out of rhythm.

''The thing is,'' she said in a breathless voice, avoiding his unnerving gaze, ''n-now that the nannies are gone, I need to be closer to the children, so—''

''We'll *both* move down to this floor,'' he inserted smoothly. ''You choose which room across the hall you want, I'll take the other.''

''But, Julien—'' She panicked. This wasn't going the way it was supposed to. She'd hoped to put distance between them. Instead, they would be having more interaction than ever.

''Our children are a joint responsibility, *mignonne*. I intend to help you in every way that I can, which means we'll take turns getting up in the night when necessary.'' He wandered over to the doorway and flipped off the light switch. ''Now that the children are in bed," he said in a low, silken tone, "why don't we start to move into our new rooms? We can help each other."

Heat crept up her face and neck. "A-actually, I've already put my things in the room across from this one."

Something flickered in the black recesses of his eyes. Once again, she'd plunged a dagger deep into his heart. Another wound that would never heal.

"Then I'll gather a few things and move into the one next to yours. Come with me and we can plan another outing for tomorrow. I thought a drive to the narcissus fields might appeal."

Stop it, Julien.

"Isabelle will be here day after tomorrow," he continued. "Since she's not a nature lover like you, we should take advantage of this time. A picnic among the flowers will be the perfect place for the children."

Don't say any more. Don't be so loving, so considerate. I know what you're trying to do, but you'll only end up with a greater heartache.

To hide their trembling, Tracey slid her hands into the pockets of her jeans. She moved farther into the hall, tortured by his nearness. "Why don't we wait until tomorrow before we make any definitive plans? If you don't mind, I'm more tired than I realized and would like to go to bed."

"That's not surprising," he murmured. "You were

up all last night with our children while I slept. Tonight it will be my turn. *Bonne nuit, mon amour.*''

He opened the door to her room. Of necessity she had to step past him.

It was a mistake.

The action of her arm brushing against his chest aroused the passion that had enflamed them both on their honeymoon. Terrified that he could sense how easily his touch had turned her into a throbbing mass of need, she walked over to the phone on the bedside table and picked up the receiver.

She pretended not to know that Julien was still standing there while she dialed her sister in San Francisco. Ten o'clock Swiss time meant it was seven in the morning over there.

The second Isabelle answered, Tracey greeted her with feigned enthusiasm and burst into an excited account about the children and the arrangements she'd made for Alex once the two of them arrived.

It seemed a long time before Tracey heard the click that sounded a death knell in her heart. Julien had gone. She'd shut him out on purpose and wondered how much more he would let pass by before retaliating. Worse, she feared the form it would take. Under the circumstances, she didn't dare accompany him on that mountain picnic tomorrow.

Children or no children, anything could happen while they basked under a warm sun among the flowers. At this point, to go anywhere alone with Julien was courting disaster. It was unthinkable.

CHAPTER EIGHT

TRACEY got ready for bed and slid under the covers, wishing her sister were here right now. Haunted by the hunger she'd glimpsed in Julien's eyes, it was impossible to fall asleep. She spent the greater part of the night figuring out how to put him off. As far as she was concerned, Isabelle couldn't come soon enough.

But as it turned out, Tracey needn't have worried. At daybreak she got dressed in a skirt and blouse and hurried into the nursery to check on the children.

To her astonishment, she found Julien in his robe, his hair attractively disheveled, walking the floor with Raoul, who was running a temperature. He'd been the fussy one on their boating trip and now she knew why.

"Let me take over," she insisted, and plucked the baby from his arms. The fact that Julien allowed her to take Raoul proved just how tired he was. Yet the fatigue lines around his eyes and mouth, the shadowy rasp along his jaw, made him more appealing than ever. Tracey quickly looked away before he could discover she'd been staring at him.

Rubbing the back of his neck, he said, "A half hour ago I gave him some liquid aspirin to bring down his fever, but I'm not sure it's working."

"If his temp stays up, I'll call Dr. Chappuis's office. Why don't you go to bed? I promise to let you know if he doesn't improve."

He shook his head. "Valentine and Jules will be awake in a minute."

"Julien, millions of women around the world take care of larger families than ours every day of their lives. I'll manage just fine."

He straightened to his full, imposing height. "You're barely out of hospital and need waiting on yourself."

Darling Julien. "I'm stronger than I look, and according to my bathroom scales, I've already gained two pounds. It's true," she avowed when she saw the skepticism in his expression. "Being at the clinic gave me claustrophobia and I had no appetite. But now that I'm out, food tastes good again."

He couldn't very well refute her, not when he'd watched her consume everything on her plate at the shoreside resort.

While she stood there patting Raoul's back to comfort him, she could sense Julien's ambivalence. He was relieved about her weight gain, but hesitant to leave her with all the work.

She was prompted to say, "If you don't take care of yourself, you'll probably come down with Raoul's cold, so—"

"If he has a cold, then I've already been infected," Julien broke in dryly, "so this won't matter." Following that comment, he kissed Raoul's head, then brushed her unsuspecting mouth with his own before leaving the nursery.

Tracey reeled in shock.

It was only the briefest of contact, but she felt it to her bones and was appalled because she should never have put herself in a position where such a thing could happen. *She could never let it happen again.*

Julien's sole purpose in keeping her at the château was to find her vulnerable spot and attack. How could she have forgotten that for one instant? But as she looked into Raoul's feverish face, she realized that her worry over him had made her careless.

Hardening her resolve, she determined to take steps to ensure that the situation wouldn't be repeated before she left Julien at the end of the month.

Much as she disliked any of the children being sick, Raoul's condition had thwarted his father's plans for a mountain picnic later in the day. If she didn't miss her guess, Valentine and Jules would probably come down with the same thing before long. There'd be no outings for a while and then Isabelle would arrive, frustrating Julien's attempt to undermine her resolve to leave him, whatever the reason.

And if he knew the real reason, what then? Would he be able to turn off his feelings and see her only as a half sister? Treat her with kindness rather than passion for the rest of their days?

But Tracey already knew the answer to that. She'd

lived a year with the knowledge that he was her half brother, and *nothing* had changed for her.

If anything, her desire for him was even greater than before. *Never* would she be able to think of Julien without wanting to lie in his arms and know his possession.

It would be no different for him.

That was why there was no point in telling him about their parents' affair.

She'd come back to the château to prove to him that she was no longer capable of being his wife. That was where it had to start, *and end*—even if it meant being cruel....

Tracey took one look at Isabelle and asked, "Are you tired, Iz? There's a bench up ahead. Want to sit down?"

"Maybe for a minute. But I don't know how long Alex will last."

Tracey's gaze darted to the children in their double strollers. For some reason, her nephew doted on Valentine and insisted on riding with her. Being an active two-year-old, the minute they'd pause to look at the ducks or the paddleboats on the lake, he'd want to climb out and run around. He didn't seem to understand that Valentine was too little to run around with him.

"If he gets too restless, I'll walk him to the car and we'll come for you and the babies. How's that?"

"That sounds good." Isabelle sat down with a heavy

sigh. She was only four months pregnant, but to Tracey, she looked six. "Who would have dreamed when our school used to take afternoon walks along this promenade, that one day you and I would be here with our own children?"

"I know," Tracey murmured with bittersweet emotion. "Remember that poor tree over there with the damaged bark? The one Indra ran into with Jacques's car?"

Isabelle started to laugh. "And we had to take up a collection from everyone to get it fixed so he never found out? Where is Jacques anyway? I've been here two weeks and he's never shown his face."

"I haven't seen him, either, but I believe he's out of the country on business for the company."

"On Julien's orders, I presume. Ever since Jacques made a play for you, there's been a rift between them. Angelique says it's worse than ever."

"That was over a long time ago, Iz," Tracey defended, but suffered another guilty pang. Was it possible that Julien was purposely keeping Jacques away, thinking that he might have something to do with Tracey's desire for a divorce?

"Hey, Trace? Now that we're on the subject of Julien, how about coming clean with me? I know you're leaving him at the end of the month, but for the life of me, I can't figure out why."

"I've told you before. I don't want to be married."

Isabelle cocked her dark head, perplexed. "Are you

insane? Julien worships the ground you walk on. He never saw anyone but you. I ought to know because I tried everything in my power to make him pay attention to me. He just treated me as if I were invisible. It's embarrassing to have to admit that there was a time when I hated you for your power over him.''

Tracey's head swerved around and she stared at her sister in stunned surprise. ''You don't mean that.''

''Yes, I'm afraid I was very jealous of you in those days. So jealous I probably married Bruce right off the bat because when he met the two of us at that party in San Francisco, it was *me* he wanted, not you.''

''Iz…'' Tracey whispered. ''I didn't know.''

''Hey, that was over a long time ago—'' Isabelle flashed her a reassuring smile ''—and whatever his faults, I love my husband. Being separated from him has made me realize just how much. Look, Trace, the only reason I brought any of it up is because it's obvious you're tearing your husband apart. It kills me to watch. I adore Julien. Good grief, how can you ignore him the way you do? How can you stay out of his bed? That's what I want to know.''

Tracey's eyes closed tightly. ''I've told you. Our marriage is over and I want my freedom.''

''Why? Angelique thinks maybe you're secretly afraid of getting pregnant again. But there are ways to ensure you don't have to worry about that.''

''Look, I don't mean to be cruel, but it's no one else's business. Julien and I are through.''

"Say that to anyone but me. As I recall, you could never get enough of him and practically had a nervous breakdown when you found out our trips to Switzerland had been called off permanently."

"That's because I was besotted. But I grew up, Iz."

She shook her head. "I don't buy it. Not for one second. You're lying, Trace, and though Julien hasn't said as much, he knows you're lying, too."

Miraculously, Alex chose that moment to climb out of his seat, forcing Tracey to jump up and grab him before he ran into the street. After giving him a kiss and a squeeze, she said, "I think your little guy has had enough. As for my babies, they need a diaper change and some dinner. Let's get back to the car."

"I'm not finished with you yet, Trace."

"Yes, you are, Iz," she muttered angrily. "*Tu comprends*?"

"Get as mad as you want, but I can see through you and I'm not about to let this go."

Tracey wheeled around, hot-faced. "Have I ever once interfered in your marital problems?"

"No," Isabelle retorted. "And heaven knows Bruce and I've got them. I think that's why I've felt so sick. Fortunately, Julien has given me some sound advice." It didn't surprise Tracey. He had always been able to get through to Isabelle when no one else could. "I'm going to try it out on Bruce when I go home tomorrow."

"That's good, but I have to confess I'm not ready to let you go yet," Tracey cried in a plaintive voice.

"I don't want to leave you, either, but last night Bruce sounded like he really missed me."

"I'm sure he does. Forgive me for being selfish. He's crazy about you and I love him for it."

"So if I were to suddenly ask Bruce for a divorce, are you telling me that you wouldn't want to know the reason why? That you wouldn't hound me for the truth?"

Though she could feel it slipping away from her, Tracey stood her ground and said, "Yes. Your marriage is your own business. I would give you credit for knowing exactly what you were doing, and I'd never presume to tell you how to run your life."

"I'm not trying to tell you anything, Trace. All I'm asking for here is a little honesty. Mom and Dad are gone. Since you refuse to confide in Aunt Rose, then use *me*. Let me help. Please." Her voice shook with emotion.

Tracey was touched by her sister's sincerity. In ways, they were closer than ever, probably because they'd both become mothers and shared common interests now. It was going to be a real wrench when she left.

But much worse, Tracey and Julien would be alone again. The thought absolutely terrified her.

She took a shallow breath. "I've told you the truth, but like Julien, you refuse to accept it. That's why I ran away the first time, because I knew he couldn't handle it. Apparently you can't, either," she said in a dull voice. "I'm sorry."

"You couldn't be as sorry as I am. What you're doing to Julien is wrong, Trace. One day you'll find out just how wrong."

Isabelle was starting to sound like Louise. Tracey couldn't deal with it anymore and took off for the car at a brisk pace, preventing further conversation.

Jules and Raoul had been asleep in the stroller, but at their mother's speedy departure, they awoke with a start and began to whimper. It couldn't be helped. Tracey didn't want Isabelle to catch up with her.

She had no desire to continue their soul-destroying confrontation, the kind only sisters who knew each other so well—who'd shared the good and the bad over a lifetime—could get involved in.

It was draining enough trying to figure out how she was going to stay away from Julien another seven days before she walked away from him for good.

As if the fates were against her, chaos developed when they arrived back at the château and Alex threw a temper tantrum because he had to be separated from Valentine.

As Isabelle carried her kicking, screaming, out-of-control son into the château, Julien emerged to help Tracey with the children. He reached for his sons, kissing them on their blond heads while Tracey plucked her daughter from the stroller.

"What's the problem?" he murmured, locking gazes with her.

"I think Valentine has become my nephew's obsession."

The minute the words left her lips, she felt as if someone had just walked over her grave.

Dear God. Was history starting to repeat itself?

Could Alex's preoccupation with his beautiful little dark-haired cousin be the beginning of a serious attachment?

Julien's eyes glowed like banked fires. "I'm not at all surprised. She takes after her mother."

His low aside produced more panic inside Tracey. If the two cousins were allowed to grow up together, would it result in a full-fledged love affair? Another family secret? Another lie with disastrous consequences?

Horrified at the prospect, Tracey unconsciously tightened her hold on her daughter until Valentine squirmed. Immediately contrite, she kissed her baby's cheek, vowing that she'd never let that happen to Valentine or the boys.

In a few more months Isabelle would deliver another son or daughter. In time both Angelique and Jacques would probably have children. Over the years there would be family get-togethers, vacations...

Tracey would have to start right now to distance her children from their relatives. She'd heard too many true accounts about first and second cousins falling in love.

Suddenly she was glad Isabelle was leaving. Much as she adored Alex, there was no way she would let him get close to Valentine.

Her tortured thoughts shot ahead. She prayed her sister's new baby wouldn't be a girl with a fatal predilection for men named Chappelle. Somehow Tracey would have to take steps to make certain that never happened!

"*Mignonne*?" Julien's anxious voice brought her back to the present. "You've gone pale. What's wrong?"

He saw too much! "Nothing that a good dinner won't fix," she rushed to assure him and started for the door.

"Somehow I don't believe you." He followed her inside the foyer. "It's because Isabelle's leaving tomorrow. Maybe what I have planned will help cheer you up."

Tracey paused on the first step and turned her head toward him. "What do you mean?"

A faint smile broke the corner of his compelling mouth. "This evening you and I are giving a going-away party in Isabelle's honor. Solange has set up everything in the main dining room."

"W-who's coming?"

"Angelique helped me draw up a list to include mutual friends. You haven't laughed or been carefree for a long, long time. I'm hoping tonight will rectify the situation, if only for a few hours."

A huge lump lodged in her throat so she could hardly swallow. Julien was a giver. He always thought of others before himself. He certainly couldn't have planned anything calculated to please Isabelle more.

But except for the joy she found in her children, there could be no laughter in Tracey's life. One day soon, Julien would realize that his marriage was a lost cause and he'd stop wishing for the impossible.

Unfortunately, she still had tonight to get through. In a small voice, she asked, ''What time will our guests be arriving?''

''You have an hour to pamper yourself. Tell Isabelle to do the same. I've already instructed the maids to deal with the children and put them to bed.''

''Then I'd better hurry.''

Without waiting for a response, she dashed up the stairs with Valentine.

To her chagrin, instead of being able to distance herself from her husband, he'd once again put her in a position where she'd be forced to work hand in hand with him.

He knew exactly what he was doing when he told her that her only job was to get dressed up and play hostess to Angelique and a dozen of their close school friends from the past. They'd be eating in the *grande salle à manger* generally reserved for important business associates.

Tracey knew Julien's tactics better than anyone alive. He was fighting for their marriage and had deliberately placed her in a situation from which she couldn't talk or wiggle her way out without hurting her sister irreparably.

The next few hours passed in a kind of blur for Tracey, who had no choice but to be cordial to their guests and appear lighthearted. The absence of Aunt Rose, who'd gone to dinner and the ballet with friends, was no coincidence.

To everyone assembled, Tracey must have looked like the perfect chatelaine of the Chappelle manor, dressed in simple black silk for the occasion.

Though the initial conversation had to do with all the girls' teenage school memories, it eventually centered on the adorable triplets and Tracey's marriage to Julien.

At one time or other, every female in the room had had a crush on Angelique's older brother and freely admitted it. Each of the girls had some story to tell about Tracey and how in love she'd been with him, how she'd carried his picture in her wallet long before he'd come home from Cambridge.

But the coup de grace was delivered by Isabelle, who revealed Tracey's deepest secret.

"Do you know what Tracey told me after she blew out all eighteen candles on her birthday cake?" Isabelle confided to Julien so the whole table could hear. "She said she was going to marry you and live here forever. If I recall correctly, she mentioned something about having six handsome sons who would look just like you, *mon cher frère.*"

"You've got a good start," Angelique teased while everyone else at the table laughed wholeheartedly.

None of them had any idea of the suffering they caused Tracey, the pain. Averting her eyes, she refused to look at Julien. She could tell by the way his mocking gaze never left her face that he was loving every minute of her sister's candid revelations.

While he allowed the girls to regale him with more tidbits about Tracey's huge crush on him, his calculated silence invited them to go on and on and do their worst damage where she was concerned.

Through the din of excited chatter, she could hear his mind saying to her, *Everyone knows that you've always loved me, that you always will. There's no way I'm letting you give up on our marriage, mon amour.*

All of a sudden, Tracey couldn't stand it any longer. She found herself remembering other meals at this very table with both families present.

How could her mother and Henri have allowed such a thing to happen? Why didn't they intervene before it was too late?

Overwhelmed by intense pain, Tracey proffered the excuse that she needed to use the rest room, then hurried out of the dining hall.

It was just as well she did because when she dashed upstairs to check on the children, she discovered that Valentine was giving the maid problems. One look at her tiny flushed face and Tracey guessed it was her daughter's turn to be sick now that the boys had recovered.

Though she would never wish illness on anyone, least of all her own precious babies, Tracey was relieved that Valentine's condition made it impossible for her to go back downstairs.

It wasn't long before Julien—formally dressed in a midnight blue suit that made him look so handsome it took Tracey's breath—came into the nursery. His long strides shortened the distance in a hurry. "What in the hell is going on, Tracey?"

He so rarely swore, Tracey knew he was really angry. Even Valentine sensed it and clung to Tracey's neck.

"As you can see," she said in a low voice, "Valentine's not well. I thought she looked a little flushed before the party started so I came up to check on her."

Which wasn't altogether a lie, but Tracey had assumed that the crisp fall air had had something to do with the roses in her daughter's cheeks earlier.

Grim-faced, he put a hand on Valentine's forehead. *"Mon Dieu!* She's burning up." One look at his miserable daughter and his black expression turned to one of frustration and concern.

Tracey could read his mind. He'd orchestrated the evening to his advantage, but Valentine's unexpected sickness fell outside his machinations.

Without looking her husband in the eye, Tracey relished telling him, "I'm going to have to get her fever down. Go back to our guests and spend the rest of the evening with them. Please tell them I'm sorry, but Valentine needs me."

In the pregnant pause that followed, she could feel Julien's white-hot tension. "Our daughter may be ill, but she's not the reason you bolted a few minutes ago."

"Please, Julien, you're upsetting her."

He bit out an epithet. "You won't always have the children to wear like a shield against me. This night isn't over yet," he warned fiercely.

She held her breath until he turned on his heel and strode swiftly from the nursery.

The second he was gone, Tracey went limp and clung to her daughter. When she got some of her strength back, she gave the baby liquid aspirin to bring down her temperature, then took her to her room across the hall.

The double bed was big enough to hold both of them comfortably. That way, Valentine wouldn't disturb the boys and Tracey could nurse her daughter without having to keep getting up to check on her.

More than anything else, Tracey needed the comfort of Valentine's warm little body, someone on whom she could lavish her love without it being wrong or forbidden.

Feeling her mother's arms around her must have given Valentine the security she craved. After draining half a bottle of apple juice, she and Tracey both fell asleep.

When Tracey awakened the next morning, she discovered herself alone. Since none of the maids would have disturbed her, it meant that at some point during the night, Julien had come into her bedroom.

She knew exactly why he'd come.

For the past three weeks he'd kept his word and hadn't once tried to make love to her. But tonight had precipitated a situation that was fast growing out of control. Julien was on the verge of snapping.

Even from opposite ends of the huge banquet table, whenever she'd dared look at him, she'd caught glimpses of raw hunger in his eyes. To her horror, her body had leaped in response to that pulsating desire and he knew it!

Tracey hid her face in her hands.

She had the strongest conviction that Julien had come to her in the night because he couldn't help himself.

Thank heavens she'd been asleep!

Thank heavens he'd found Valentine cuddled next to her mother!

But what about the next time, when the children were all well and sleeping soundly in the nursery? When he knew Tracey would be alone?

She shot straight up in bed. *There couldn't be a next time.*

Since Isabelle was leaving on the afternoon plane,

Tracey would use Valentine's illness as the excuse to say good-bye at the house.

While Julien ran Isabelle to the airport, Tracey would slip away during the children's naps and get a hotel in town.

Her promise to stay the full month with Julien was no longer important. She had to get out of his house *today*.

CHAPTER NINE

AT LAST all three babies were asleep. Valentine had fussed the most because of her cold, but she'd finally succumbed.

Tracey glanced at her watch. Ten after four. Julien and Rose would be halfway to Geneva with Isabelle and Alex right now. The perfect time for Tracey to go down to the kitchen and enjoy tea with Solange.

When the housekeeper wasn't watching, Tracey would grab for the wallet she'd hidden in one of the drawers and disappear out the back door. By the time anyone discovered she was missing, she'd be safely ensconced in a hotel room with a lock. From there she'd phone the château and enlist Solange's help with the babies until Julien returned.

After one more fleeting glance at her children, Tracey tiptoed across the nursery floor. But she never left the room because she came up against something rock hard that prevented her from going anywhere.

"Julien!"

She staggered from the impact but he locked her against his virile body, defeating her.

Her shocked gaze flew to his and what she saw in those black depths caused her body to tremble violently. "W-what are you doing here?"

The wintry smile didn't reach his eyes. "I decided to let Rose drive your sister to the airport so you and I could spend the rest of the afternoon and evening together undisturbed."

Dear God. He knew!

"But Valentine—"

"She's sleeping soundly and the maids are close by."

Tracey's mouth had gone so dry she could hardly make a sound. "I don't think she should be left alone, Julien."

"Really." His lips thinned to a white line of anger. "Then how do you explain *this*?" He reached inside the breast pocket of his shirt and held up her wallet. "I watched you plant it in the kitchen drawer this morning when you thought I was in my study. I know exactly what you're up to, *petite*."

His eyes glittered with rage. "Now that I have proof you've broken the promise you made to me at the clinic, there's no longer any contract between us. After a year's abstinence, I intend to make love to my wife and there isn't a thing you can do about it."

"*No!*" she screamed, but Julien wasn't listening. In a lightning move, he picked her up in his arms. Holding her cruelly tight, he lowered his dark head and covered her mouth with smothering force, reducing her cries to pathetic little moans. Then he started down the hall toward the stairs and Tracey felt the last avenue of escape close over her head.

Julien was a physically powerful man who'd always kept his emotions under control. The only time she'd seen him lose his sangfroid was the night he'd threatened Jacques if he so much as looked at Tracey again. A terrified Jacques had backed off and had never come near her since.

But over the past year, too much damage had been done to Julien and she'd finally unleashed the savage in him. Louise had warned her she could only drive him so far....

By the time they'd reached his suite on the third floor, Tracey had fought him so hard she'd reached the point of exhaustion.

When she felt the mattress against her back, every bit of fight seemed to go out of her. Julien's body all but covered hers so he knew the exact moment she gave up the struggle. That's when he started making love to her in earnest, overwhelming her with his need, pouring out the driving passion he'd had to suppress for so long.

"Stop, Julien!" she screamed when he left her mouth alone long enough to kiss her throat. He'd finally sent her over the edge and there was no going back. "What we're doing is a *sin*!"

For a brief interval, he kept on kissing her perfumed skin, then after a deep chuckle she felt to her toes, he whispered huskily, "We're married, *mon amour*. The only thing sinful about this is how wonderful it feels to be loving again. Is that why you ran away from me?

Because you're ashamed of losing yourself in my arms? Are you afraid to admit that this is the place you'd rather be than anywhere else in the world?''

He cupped her hot face in his hands and willed her to answer him.

''Tell me the truth, *mignonne*. No more lies. In some ways, your father had a puritanical outlook on life. Did he teach you that it was sinful for a man and a woman to enjoy each other the way we do?'' He shook her gently. ''Is that what happened?''

''No...'' she groaned aloud, moving her head back and forth as hot tears gushed from her eyes. ''He wasn't *my* father, Julien.''

Julien went still, then his brows formed into one black slash of consternation. ''What are you saying?''

Tracey took a fortifying breath. ''Henri Chappelle was my father, too. Yours *and* mine.''

Such was Julien's enamored state, he couldn't comprehend what she was telling him. Blinking in confusion he grasped her tighter, though she was certain he was unconscious of his great strength.

Oh, dear God, help me. ''You're my half brother, darling,'' she whispered in a tortured voice. ''I'm your half sister. Your father made his confession to me before the priest gave him the last rites.''

A wild look crossed Julien's face, creating the illusion that he was part jungle predator. His expression was more terrifying than all her nightmares put together.

"You're lying," he grated through locked teeth, his eyes devoid of light.

"No." She cupped his rigid jaw with her hand, afraid his face had been forever transformed into a cold, lifeless facsimile of itself, just as she'd feared. "He and Mother had an affair after you and Jacques a-and Isabelle were born." Swallowing a sob, she said, "I always wondered where my blond hair came from."

Julien's taut body didn't move. All the while she'd been talking, he'd been trying to grasp everything, tearing it apart then putting it back together to find an acceptable answer when there was none—exactly the way she'd been doing for so many months.

His chest heaved in tangible agony. "Do you swear before God you're telling me the truth?"

"Yes, darling. You know I love you more than life itself. I could never lie to you." Trying to stifle her sobs, she said, "Why do you think I ran away? I couldn't bear it."

She saw his throat working. Like an incurable disease, the pain was eating him alive. "Would you swear it before Monseigneur Louvel?"

"Yes."

"*Mon Dieu.*"

His muttered imprecation sounded as if it had come from the lips of a dying man.

For endless minutes, his incredible black eyes probed her soul trying to come up with any other answer than the one she'd just given him.

With tears running down her cheeks and over his hands, she cried, "I wanted to spare you. I'd hoped to run away where you could never find me so that in time you'd learn to hate me and love someone else.

"But when I found out I was pregnant, I had to turn to Rose for help. You know the rest.... Louise told me I suppressed most of my memories to stave off the pain as long as possible."

She heard her name cried on a mournful sound before he crushed her in his arms. They clung to each other in desperation, then came the inevitable silence and the convulsive heaves of his body.

Needing to be strong for him, Tracey absorbed each shudder, recognizing the layers his mind was being forced to wade through before he could accept this new reality.

When he could find words, his voice was barely recognizable. "I know you're not lying, *mignonne*, but I refuse to accept what you've told me until we've spoken to the monseigneur."

"That was the first thing I thought of doing, but then I remembered the confidentiality between a confessor and his priest. The monseigneur would never break his vows, not even if your fa—Henri bared his soul to him."

"He'll tell me," Julien vowed with a violence that made Tracey's heart bleed all over again. "When he understands the gravity of Father's confession to you, the far-reaching consequences to both our families and our children, he'll be forced to reveal what he knows. I'll remind him that his responsibility is to the *living*, not the dead.''

His hands slid to her shoulders, unconsciously squeezing them until she almost moaned from the pressure.

''I don't want to wait to talk to him. We'll drive over to the church *now*.''

When he was in this mood, Tracey knew better than to argue with him or suggest that he call to see if this was a convenient time for the priest to receive visitors.

''Maybe we'd better check on the chil—''

''The children will be fine,'' he broke in with that authoritative tone she'd only ever heard him use with Jacques, or the people at his work when there was a real crisis. ''Solange guards them like a mother hen and would never let anything happen to them.''

She nodded and would have gotten up from the bed but his hands still held her. Their faces were only centimeters apart, their mouths a mere breath away. She knew he wanted to make love to her and never stop. God knew she wanted him in the same way. Nothing had changed for either of them. It never would.

But now Julien had second sight. Together they were forced to share this new burden of knowledge that their religious and cultural values wouldn't allow them to ignore.

At the very last second, another tremendous shudder wracked his powerful body and he checked himself.

With a groan she could feel, he got to his feet and raked his hands through his hair, visibly tormented.

Tracey avoided looking at him and almost made it to the door before his arms came around her from behind, dragging her against him. She gasped from the familiar feel of the masculine physique she loved so well.

He buried his face in her hair. "Tell me none of this is true, *mon amour*," he begged with tears in his deep voice. "Tell me we can come back here tonight and love each other the way we did in Tahiti."

His whole soul was reaching out to her now. She had no defense to counteract his kind of pain.

"Julien, don't you think I want to love you in every possible way for the rest of our lives?" she cried. "If it weren't for the children, I'm not sure I could go on living."

Arms of steel bound her even closer to him. "Don't ever say that, *mon amour*," he commanded her in the fiercest tone she'd ever heard. "I have to believe there has been a mistake. You could have misunderstood Father. He had few lucid moments during his last hours. The priest will clear it up and end this torture. Let's go." Cupping her elbow, he ushered her from the bedroom and down the hall.

Don't let your hopes blind you, darling. But Tracey knew from past experience that all the wishing in the world wouldn't change his determination. He was a fighter. If by any chance she had misinterpreted Henri's last words, Julien wouldn't sleep until he'd learned the real truth for himself.

With a brief word to Solange, they left the château through the back entrance and got into the Ferrari.

While they'd been in Julien's room, it had grown dark out. Switching on the headlights, he headed for the main road. But he was too intent on his destination to be cautious. Rose had just turned the Mercedes onto the grounds of the estate and he had to slam on his brakes to avoid crashing into her.

Muttering a curse, he lowered the window and called out an apology to her but kept on going without waiting for a response.

Tracey had it in her heart to feel sorry for her aunt, who was probably aghast at the speed Julien was traveling. Not only that, she must have wondered why Tracey was in the car when she was supposed to be home nursing Valentine.

Julien's turmoil was such that they didn't talk during the short ride to town. By the time they'd arrived at the rectory next to the cathedral, Tracey's anxiety had reached its peak. Her husband's certainty that there'd been a mistake had started infecting her.

She found herself offering a fervent prayer that Julien was right, that the priest would have another answer for them, one that would free them from their prison and allow them to continue on in the sanctity of marriage.

"*Je regrette*, Monsieur Chappelle," the caretaker responded after they'd alighted from the car and tugged on the bellpull. "The monseigneur is away in Neuchâtel. If he stays the night, he will phone. All I can do is tell him that you came by and are most anxious to speak to him."

Julien's frustration was so great he almost crushed her hand in his grip. Tracey didn't cry out. In fact, as they turned away and walked back to the car, she welcomed the pain, wishing it could blot out the agony wracking their souls.

The tires screeched against the cobblestones as Julien backed out of the drive and raced through the narrow side street bordering the cathedral.

"Julien," she ventured in a tremulous voice, "after we make certain the children are all right, I think it would be best if I checked into a hotel tonight."

"You're not going anywhere," he ground out, the violence of his tone stunning her into silence. "Aside from what the priest has to say, there are DNA tests we'll have run on ourselves and the children to verify whether or not the same blood flows in our veins.

"But until we know for an absolute certainty that you and I were fathered by the same man, you'll share my bed."

"I can't do that, Julien," she whispered heartbrokenly. "You weren't there to hear your father."

"That's right," he bit out in fury. "More and more I'm finding it inconceivable that he would wait until death's door to keep something so damning from everyone in the family but *you*, or that your father and mother never once hinted at their liaison.''

Tracey was listening intently. She'd thought those same thoughts—rehearsed those same arguments—so many times, she'd almost gone insane.

''My father was a cold man, not given to a lot of emotion, but I never knew him to be intentionally cruel. The night Jacques and I almost came to blows, I told Father how I felt about you, that one day I intended to marry you. He had his opportunity to tell me the truth then, *mignonne*, but he never said a word.''

''Oh, Julien...'' Her voice rang with joy. *Maybe Henri really had been too far gone to make sense.*

''I suppose it's possible he could have been unfaithful to Mother,'' Julien continued in the same vein. ''She was ill for many years, but I always sensed that she was happy in her marriage. She never alluded to a possible affair between him and another woman, let alone your mother.''

He shook his head. ''After considering every aspect, I have to believe the heavy painkillers caused his rambling, that he didn't have any idea what he was saying.''

''That's because you *want* to believe it!'' she cried in renewed fear because his logic was too convincing and she could feel herself weakening.

His dark head whipped around and he impaled her with his eyes. ''Don't *you, mon amour*?''

Tracey couldn't lie to him or withstand his laserlike

glance. She looked out the window before tearfully confessing, "More than anything."

"Then there's nothing else to discuss. *Mon Dieu*, it's a miracle you're alive and well. Tonight we're going to celebrate your return to life, to me." Another groan escaped. "Do you have any idea how much I need to hold you again, to feel you in my arms all night long?"

By this time they'd reached the private estate road, but before she was even cognizant of it, he'd pulled the car to the side and had reached for her.

"Tracey..." he murmured against her trembling mouth. "I can't wait any longer for this." Then he was igniting passions that turned her body liquid and had her straining toward him in spite of the gearshift being in the way.

Like a starving person who had finally come home to feast, she let go of her reservations and gave herself up to Julien's kiss, unable to fight her love or the clamoring of her senses for the assuagement only her husband could give.

Losing track of time, she sought the exquisite rapture of his mouth and hands, anticipating the intimacy she would share with him once they returned to the house. But they were so on fire for each other, they couldn't break apart long enough for Julien to start up the car. A year's deprivation had rendered them frenzied in their desire to show their love.

When headlights of another car unexpectedly flashed through the rear window, illuminating the interior of the Ferrari, Julien tore his lips from Tracey, cursing the person who dared intrude on his private property this late.

Struggling for breath, Tracey looked around in time to see a black limousine with its official church insignia pull up alongside them.

"*Mon Dieu!*" Julien's voice dropped like rocks. "It's Monseigneur Louvel."

Julien stepped out of the car and the two men held a short conversation. Before she knew it, her husband was back.

"We're going to follow him to the rectory. Under the circumstances, it's just as well no one at the château knows about this meeting."

"I agree. D-did you tell him why we wanted to meet with him?"

"No."

With that one word she had to be satisfied since Julien showed no inclination to talk. She couldn't blame him, not after what had transpired before the priest came on the scene.

Fortunately, the short drive gave her enough time to comb her hair and put on a little makeup. But nothing could restore the ecstasy she'd felt before the priest arrived.

By the time they reached the church grounds and were shown inside the *salon*, Tracey was petrified at what they might learn. Fresh guilt assailed her for having given in to her emotions, no matter how briefly.

Julien darted her a private glance that told her to stop torturing herself. They had nothing to fear.

I pray you're right, darling.

Once the monseigneur asked them why they'd come, Julien started in without preamble, then invited Tracey to tell the priest exactly what Henri had said to her moments before he died.

After she'd finished, Julien demanded, "Did my father confess the same thing to you, Father? We've been through a living hell and it's still not over. You are privy to certain information that will affect our lives forever."

While Tracey held her breath, Monseigneur Louvel clapped his hands on his knees and looked Julien straight in the eye. "I commiserate with your pain, and pray God's blessings upon both of you. But a confession is for God and no one else."

Julien sucked in his breath. "Our marriage is sacred!"

The priest nodded. "Yes. And for that reason, there is something I can tell you, but be careful lest you interpret it the wrong way."

His amber eyes switched to Tracey and looked on her with a compassion that struck new terror in her heart.

"Once, years ago, a woman who resembles you strongly came into the chapel to pray. She looked so sad. When I asked if I could be of help, she told me she wasn't a Catholic, but hoped it was all right if she stayed there a while because she felt the need for more spirituality in her life.

"I asked if she wanted to talk to someone. She said it wouldn't help, not if her husband couldn't forgive her. Then she left. I didn't see her again until years later when she accompanied the Chappelle family to mass for Angelique's first communion." He spread his hands. "That is all I know. I'm sorry." He made the sign of the cross and left them alone to talk.

In the ghastly silence that followed, Tracey rose to her feet, traumatized by the priest's words. She didn't need to look at Julien to feel his shocked reaction. What the monseigneur had just told them was as damning as Henri's confession.

The room started to reel. Out of nowhere, Julien was there to save her from falling. With his arm biting into her waist, he helped her out of the rectory to the car. Before closing the passenger door, he cupped her chin in his hand, forcing her to look at him.

"Don't forget the priest's admonition. He warned us not to put the wrong interpretation on his words."

"Stop it, Julien," she cried in anguish. "We have our answer."

His jaw tightened. "I don't think so. I think he was trying to help us without breaking his vows as a priest."

"You're only saying that b-because you don't want to face the truth. I was that way in the beginning. But I've finally come to terms with it."

His eyes glittered dangerously. "You *never* came to terms with it, *mon amour*. Otherwise you wouldn't have let me kiss you senseless tonight."

"What we did was wrong. I wish to God it had never happened." She tried to turn her head away, but his hand kept her from moving.

"You know you don't mean that," he grated.

Tears poured from her eyes. "Please take me home. We left a sick daughter."

After another tension-fraught moment, Julien released her and went around to the driver's side. For the second time that night, he maneuvered the Ferrari back to the château with a speed that took her breath. "Tomorrow we'll make arrangements to go in for DNA tests."

"There's no point, Julien."

"That's what the doctors in San Francisco said when I told them I was having you moved to the specialized head injury clinic here in Lausanne."

Humbled by his faith and that indomitable will of his, she whispered, "I had no idea. You've been too wonderful to me."

"Are you telling me that if our roles had been reversed, you wouldn't have done everything conceivable to bring me out of that coma?" His hand reached out to squeeze her thigh gently. "Tracey?" he prodded in a husky tone.

"You already know the answer to that."

"Then we understand each other."

"I hope so."

She felt his body tauten once more. "What is that supposed to mean?"

Moistening her lips nervously, she said, "Until we know the results of the tests, I'm going to move to an apartment."

"There's no need for that. I swear I won't touch you."

"I made the same promise to myself when I agreed to come home with you for a month. But tonight I broke that promise. It could happen again, only this time it would be with the almost certain knowledge that we're brother and sister. The thought sickens me, Julien. Please. Don't make me despise myself more than I already do."

There was a deadly silence for the rest of the drive home. Once he'd shut off the motor, Tracey tried to get out, but he'd set the lock, making escape impossible.

"Are you telling me that if we find out we have the same father, you're going to live apart from me?"

"Julien, we'll have to get divorced. There's no other solution!" she cried out in torment. "I'll find a place in Chamblandes. That's only two minutes away from you. We can share in the raising of the children so they'll see both of us as much as possible. I'll take care of them while you're at work, and you can come for them whenever you're through. In time, you'll meet s-someone else and be able to—"

"*Mon Dieu*," he cut in abruptly, "I don't believe what I'm hearing."

"That's because you're still in shock. You need sleep."

"After today, that would be impossible."

"Don't..." she begged him in a tortured whisper.

"Be warned, Tracey. Whatever you're thinking, I didn't spend a year of my life getting you back only to let you go again!"

"We'll still be friends, Julien."

"*Friends*?" His angry laugh filled the car's interior.

"Yes, darling. For our children's sake. They say time heals all wounds. I-it's possible you'll want to marry again one day."

"If you can say that to me, then you never knew me." His frigid voice was crucifying her.

"I had months before my accident to face reality."

"Months to have met another man, you mean," he accused hotly and bolted from the car. "Is that why you're flinging marriage in my face, because there's someone else waiting to warm your bed?"

Tracey had never seen Julien this out of control in her life. Everything she'd feared where he was concerned was coming to fruition.

Slowly she got out of the passenger seat. "The children are my one and only priority," she replied quietly. "If you'll support me in that endeavor, that's all I'll ever desire or need."

In the moonlight, his ravaged, gray face chilled her to the bone. Panic-stricken, she hurried into the house.

What a cruel, bitter irony that an accident of birth would forever deny them the comfort of each other's love, the only thing they ever truly wanted out of life.

CHAPTER TEN

"TRACEY? I think I've found the wallpaper for you.
Come in the living room and look at this."

"We'll be there in a minute, Aunt Rose. Won't we,
my little sweetheart?" Tracey kissed Jules's tummy
until he was convulsed with laughter. First came the
baby powder, then a clean diaper and a fresh change
of T-shirt and overalls.

Finally all three babies were ready for their father to
pick up for the weekend. Since that disastrous night
three weeks ago when the priest had confirmed Tracey's worst fears, she'd been living in a sort of limbo,
with Julien dropping off the children on his way to
work and picking them up at the end of the day.

They'd decided to trade off the babies every weekend. This time it was her turn to let the children go.
She dreaded it, dreaded the loneliness of her third-floor
apartment when the children weren't there. Getting
through Friday evening to Monday morning without
her darlings was turning out to be the major achieve-
ment of her existence.

Rose knew how difficult this time had been for Tracey and had agreed to come over and spend the night
to keep her company. She was the one who had sug-

gested that some redecorating would help Tracey feel
more at home in the gracious three-bedroom apartment
Julien had found for her.

Only three minutes from the château, the security
and privacy were rivaled only by the charm of the
rooms facing the lake. Tracey didn't care that they
needed refurbishing, but recognized that Rose wanted
to feel useful.

So far there'd been no word about the results of the
DNA tests done on the five of them. The doctor said
it might be another couple of weeks before they heard
anything. Tracey tried not to think about it since they'd
only confirm what she already knew.

No matter how devastating this time had been for
them, she was thankful Julien hadn't fought the separation. At least a routine of sorts had been established.
Soon the children would come to view both the apartment and the château as home.

Neither she nor Julien wanted anyone on either side
of the family to know the real reason they'd separated,
not even Rose. There'd been enough pain to last a lifetime. One careless word could harm their children
someday, something they'd fight to avoid.

By tacit agreement, they kept their conversation limited to talk of the babies. They never discussed how he
spent the hours away from her, or what she did to pass
the time when her day wasn't full of feedings and
baths.

Out of a sense of self-preservation, she never looked

into her husband's eyes. To any passerby, she and Julien probably appeared to be old acquaintances who
were civil and polite to each other, nothing more.

It killed Tracey to see the new remoteness in Julien
these days. He'd grown a hard veneer that changed him
into an emotionless replica of his former self. Only
when he responded to the children did she detect traces
of the vital man she loved with her whole soul.

She didn't even want to think what their lives would
be like if they didn't have their precious babies who
were fast growing into little people with minds and
personalities all their own.

Julien was probably on his way over right now, anxious to cuddle Valentine and play with the boys. Tracey
yearned to get right into the thick of it with them.
Every time she found herself daydreaming, she chas-
tised herself for losing control and tried to concentrate
on something else. But it was a futile exercise when
she was so madly in love with him.

"Who was on the phone?" she asked her aunt as
she walked into the living room carrying Jules. She'd
heard it ring but knew Rose would answer it.

"Julien. He's going to be late."

Tracey bit her lip as a dichotomy of emotions at-
tacked her. Though relieved because she'd have the
children a little longer, she lived for his visits, no matter how brief.

"Did he say why?"

"A business dinner, I believe."

"At the house?"

"No. The Château D'Ouchy."

"I see." Tracey tried to keep her voice level, but failed miserably and her aunt knew it. When Julien left the house for the evening, that meant there would be women as well as men in his dining party.

Tracey had never thought of herself as a jealous person, but that was before Julien had become forbidden to her. From here on out he was fair game to any female in sight. One too many times a beautiful woman would make a play for him on an evening not unlike this, and he'd respond....

Just the thought of it ripped Tracey's heart out.

"Dear?" Rose called to her in a worried voice. "Are you all right?"

"Yes. Of course," Tracey hastened to assure her aunt. "I was thinking that the babies' sweaters are too hot. I'll take them off until he comes."

After relieving the other two of their outer garments, she put all three tots together in the playpen, then crawled around on the floor playing peekaboo with them through the mesh.

One by one, the children laughed belly laughs that were so contagious, Rose had to wipe the tears from her eyes.

"Oh, Tracey. You're a natural mother. They absolutely adore you."

"I hope so, because they're my whole life."

Rose's expression sobered. "Why can't you include Julien in that statement?"

One mention of her husband and the happiness Tracey had been feeling as she cavorted with her children shriveled up.

"We've been over that ground before, Rose. Why don't we change the subject? Have you heard from Iz?"

"Not since you have. Julien suggested they consult a good financial adviser and I think she's talked Bruce into it. It's a start in the right direction. Maybe the day will come when she'll begin to concentrate on being the kind of mother you are."

"I thought she handled Alex extremely well for being four months pregnant," Tracey defended.

"But it doesn't come naturally to her. She needs to watch you."

Tracey frowned. "You're serious, aren't you?"

"Perfectly. She treats him like an expensive toy that has to be handled carefully. She picks him up and puts him down, but she doesn't get into a mad scramble with him as we used to say when I was a young woman. She doesn't get physical with him the way you do with your children. Your father used to play with you like that. That's probably where you learned it."

"*Daddy*?"

Rose blinked. "Of course. The first thing he'd do when he came home from work was make a beeline for you. You'd both get down on the floor and play hard until your mother called him to dinner.''

"What about Iz?"

"I'm afraid she was your mother's girl."

Tracey shook her head. "That's terrible. There should never be a mommy's girl and a daddy's girl. Each child should feel loved in the same way."

"You see, darling? You have a true mother's instincts, but some parents aren't blessed in the same way." A shadow of pain crossed her aunt's face, one that haunted Tracey. "And sometimes, circumstances change the nature of things."

There was such sadness in Rose's remark, Tracey felt her aunt was trying to tell her something. She broke out in a cold sweat.

Did Rose knew the truth?

Tracey stared at her aunt. "You're not talking in generalities, are you?"

"No. I'm talking about your parents because they're not here to defend themselves and I'm afraid my reminiscing about the past has given you some wrong impressions."

"You mean about my parents showing their preferences for me and Iz?"

"Exactly."

Tracey's heart bled to think of the man she'd always thought of as her father trying so hard to love another man's child. Without stopping to think, Tracey blurted, "I already know the reason why, Aunt Rose."

The older woman let out a quiet gasp but Tracey heard her.

"How long have you known?" she asked in a shocked voice.

"A year."

"Who told you?"

"My father."

"But he said he wasn't going to tell you until you were married and had a child of your own."

"That's exactly what he did do, except that neither he, nor I, knew that I was pregnant at the time."

"Tracey—you're not making sense. Your parents were killed in that plane crash long before you married Julien."

Totally confused, Tracey said, "Now you're the one not making sense since we both know Henri Chappelle is my biological father."

"Oh, no, Tracey. No!" Rose cried and leaped to her feet in agitation. "Whatever gave you that idea?"

Tracey started to shake and couldn't stop. "I went in to see Henri for a few minutes on the day he died. H-he told me about his affair with mother, how they decided that she and Daddy would raise the baby so no one would ever know the truth. He begged me not to tell Julien because it would hurt him. Then he wept and reached for my hand, murmuring that he loved me like a daughter. I thought I heard him say something about forgiving him, but his words became garbled. I was in a state of shock when I left the room."

"Oh, no," Rose whispered, shaking her head. "You thought that baby was *you*! *That's* why you ran away, why you fought so hard to end your marriage. Oh, my dearest girl. Don't you know he was talking about Isabelle?"

Tracey felt the blood drain out of her face. "*Isabelle*?"

"Yes, Tracey. Yes. Isabelle is Henri's daughter, not you. If you'll think about it, she has Henri's eyes and bone structure. I'm surprised you never noticed. Your sister was conceived during a time when your parents were estranged."

"*What*?" Tracey was too staggered to respond.

"Soon after their marriage, your mother suffered a miscarriage. Your father was so upset by her depression, he didn't want to try for another baby in case history repeated itself. She interpreted it that he didn't love her anymore.

"On one of their trips to Lausanne, she got too close to Henri because he and Celeste were having problems. Her arthritis unintentionally caused her to shut him out, making him vulnerable. Your mother told me they were only together one time, but Isabelle was the result."

"This is all so unbelievable," Tracey cried out, aghast.

"It was very sad. Your mother confessed everything to your father and he forgave her because he knew he hadn't been attentive to her when she needed him. But he insisted on raising Isabelle as his own daughter to prevent a scandal. He agreed they should tell her one day after she married. And though he tried, he could never love her the way he loved you.''

''Did Celeste know?''

''Yes, and guilt made her feel partly responsible.''

''How horrible for everyone.''

''Yes,'' Rose murmured pensively. ''After that, your father unconsciously lavished most of his attention on you. To compensate, your mother doted on Isabelle. But when Jacques made your life so miserable, your father's bitterness flared up and he put an end to the family trips, with the exception that he allowed Isabelle to visit Angelique for a few weeks each year out of compassion for Henri.''

''So *Daddy* was the reason…. It's all making sense. Does Isabelle know the truth now?''

''No. Not yet. One day I'll tell her when the time is right.''

''Then I don't understand why Henri said those things to me.''

''He assumed your parents had already told you about Isabelle. Henri was asking for your forgiveness because he was aware of your love for Julien and knew it had broken your heart to be parted from him. He was afraid you blamed him for the separation.''

I did, her heart moaned with remembered pain.

''Oh, Aunt Rose…'' Tracey's whole body trembled. ''What you've just told me has made me the happiest woman on earth. *Julien and I aren't related!*" she shouted for joy, bringing the children's heads around.

Her beloved little offsprings stared at her as if she was a complete oddity, making her want to laugh and cry all at the same time.

Their perfect children. Hers and Julien's. Able to grow up with the expectation of normal lives.

Rose grinned. "Oh, yes, you are related, but only by your own marriage, *which* your husband refused to give up on. Of that, I am living proof! Honestly, Tracey, I never saw a man so in love with a woman in my life."

Tracey's euphoria made her feel she was going to burst. "I—I've got to go to him! I've got to find him right now! I've got to tell him! Aunt Rose—"

"I'm planning on tending the babies through the weekend," she said, anticipating her niece's request with the greatest of joy. "Put on that beautiful violet dress he bought to complement your lovely hair. But don't keep him waiting too long! After the agony he has suffered, another minute would be too cruel.

"Oh, Tracey dear, how I'd love to see the look in his eyes when you join him at dinner and release him from that terrible prison...."

Tracey was living for that moment herself.

The next hour flew by. While Rose called the Château D'Ouchy to ascertain that Julien was still there with his dinner guests, Tracey showered and washed her hair in record time.

Fastening her amethyst-jeweled earrings, she slipped

into high heels with matching jewels on the straps, then pronounced herself ready to meet her husband. After a kiss to her babies' rounded cheeks and a huge hug to her aunt, Tracey dashed down to the waiting taxi Rose had called for her.

She was so excited and jittery she couldn't have driven a car and was thankful to be chauffeured to the elegant château-hotel located in the lakeside suburb of Ouchy.

Judging by her hot cheeks, Tracey knew she was glowing when she entered the hotel and asked directions for the Chappelle party. The *maître d'hotel* couldn't help but hear her heart thudding out of control.

Unaware of heads turning, she wound her way through the main floor dining area, her gilt hair falling from a side part as it swayed freely about her shoulders.

She felt seventeen again and hopelessly, painfully in love with the handsome man she spied seated at the head table in the private dining room.

Julien looked marvelous in anything he wore, but never more spectacular than when he was turned out in full dress tux. Tonight the black of his jacket accented his olive complexion and emphasized his striking male features in a way that made her breath catch.

Even at the tender age of seventeen, the chemistry between them had been potent. Six years later and Tracey was still reacting the same way. She always would.

For a brief moment, she hung back to savor her joy. After twelve months of pain, she could drink her fill of her husband without any accompanying guilt. The freedom to love him completely was a gift beyond comprehension.

He hadn't seen her yet. Paul Loti, the comptroller of Chappelle House, held Julien's attention with something of vital import. Their two heads were bent together in concentration, one carrot red, the other a familiar black. Almost jumping out of her skin with anticipation, Tracey advanced toward her husband.

Suddenly the room grew quiet. One by one Julien's employees and their spouses recognized her and stopped talking to smile at her and nod a welcoming greeting. On some level, Julien must have detected a change in the room's ambience because his head lifted abruptly and swerved around.

The second his intelligent eyes caught sight of her chiffon-clad figure, the way the material swished around her long, slender legs, he leaped to his feet and started toward her.

Paul had the foresight to catch his chair, which would surely have crashed to the parquetry flooring, but her husband never noticed.

A mixture of emotions played across his unforgettable face, robbing his complexion of color. As he drew closer, she saw shock, because never once since she'd come out of her coma had she sought him out, or initiated a visit to his office.

Only a few feet away now, she divined fear. After everything she'd done to make certain they stayed apart, he had to assume that her unprecedented appearance at his company dinner meant something must be seriously wrong with one of the children, or perhaps all of them.

Yet underlying his surprise and anxiety was a look of incredulity. She knew he was seeing the *old* Tracey. His bride. The starry-eyed lover of those warm Tahitian nights who'd given him her body, her heart, her soul…

"*Tracey…*"

There was a tentativeness in his low, husky voice as he whispered her name. For the first time since she'd known him, he sounded unsure of himself. The fear that this might be some fantastic dream from which he would awaken more desolate than before, seemed to rob him of the decisiveness she'd always associated with his character. For Julien to be uncertain of anything was a revelation to her.

With a compulsion too strong to be denied, she reached for him.

In that one act, she conveyed something more powerful than words. She conjured up the magic that unlocked the door of his prison.

When he intercepted her hand midair and clung to it, Tracey knew he'd divined the truth. Explanations could come later.

Like a miracle, his taut body relaxed. She felt him let go of the anger and pain, felt him shed the layers of unbridled grief as if they'd never been.

A brilliant smile illuminated her countenance, turning her eyes into orbs of green fire. They stared into the stunning blackness of his with pure, unadulterated joy, savoring the glory of this moment, the promise of future glories.

Then, with the confidence born of a woman who knew she was loved, who knew that she and she alone had the right and privilege to claim this one perfect man for her own, she turned to face their captive audience.

"Chers amis—" her voice caught a little *"—*please forgive the interruption, but I have something of vital importance to discuss with my husband in private.

"B-because of me, he's been under a tremendous strain this past year. Through it all, I'm well aware of how supportive and patient you've been. Thank you for helping Julien handle an impossible situation.

"As my repayment, I'll make you a promise that from here on out, everything is going to be different. If you'll give us a few days to enjoy a second honeymoon, I'll send him back a new man."

At first there was complete silence. Then Paul started to clap. He was followed by the people at the head table. Soon everyone in the room was standing and applauding.

"Make that a few weeks," Julien amended wickedly before pulling a flushed Tracey toward the exit. To the delight of his staff, she almost had to run to keep up with him. No one could be in any doubt that the head of Chappelle House had other thoughts on his mind than business.

Tracey assumed Julien was headed for the exit to the parking lot. She didn't understand when he stopped at the front desk with his arm clamped around her waist. "We would like a room, please. Preferably the bridal suite."

The correct-looking concierge flashed them a subtle smile. "*Certainement*, Monsieur Chappelle. With our compliments."

Tracey hid her face in her husband's broad shoulder. "The château is only a few minutes away. There's no nee—"

"There's every need," he contradicted her, brushing his lips against the adorable rosebud mouth lifted to him with unknowing provocation. "You've put me in such a condition, I'm not capable of moving a meter, let alone the distance to the car. *Tu comprends, mon amour*?"

The concierge must have heard Julien because when he handed him the key, he murmured, "Your elevator is the one you can see on your right. Do you require assistance?"

"Only my wife's." He chuckled. With his arm still hugging her against him, they crossed the lobby to their own private elevator, one of the best features of the hotel. The second the door closed, he cupped her face in his hands, pressing kisses to her hair, eyes, nose, cheeks and throat. "I feel like I'm dreaming. Tell me, *mignonne,*" he said, his voice shaking, "did the doctor call with the results of the DNA tests?"

"No," she whispered, chasing his lips until she found them. "I was given something much better. My source is infallible."

He sucked in his breath. "Does that mean Monseigneur Louvel broke his silence?"

"No, darling. *Aunt Rose.* She verified that your father and my mother had an affair. But it's Isabelle who's your half sister."

"*Isabelle*?" he said her name as the doors opened. He seemed to stagger for a moment. Tracey clung to him, offering him her strength.

"Yes, darling. Now that I know the truth, I understand even better why you've always been able to reach Iz when no one else could."

Julien shook his head, dazed. Slowly they entered the living room. He sank into the nearest couch, pulling Tracey onto his lap. They wrapped their arms around each other in that old, familiar way with Julien burying his face in her hair.

It was like coming home after being lost for years and years in a dark wilderness.

His deep voice murmured, "Monseigneur Louvel warned us there could be another explanation."

"Yes." Tears filled her eyes. "You were right. In his own way, he tried to give us hope."

Julien pulled her closer. "Tell me everything, *mon amour.* Don't leave anything out."

Tracey didn't need her husband's prompting. The desire to share their parents' secret had her pouring out one revelation after another. For an emotion-packed half hour, she supplied him with the sad facts surrounding Isabelle's conception.

"When I think how hard I've been on Jacques…" Julien whispered in a tormented voice.

"No more than I on your father. Before Aunt Rose said anything, I always had this feeling he didn't like me. I was so hurt when he allowed Isabelle to go back to Lausanne for visits."

Julien's hands twisted convulsively in her hair. "Neither of us realized your father was the one responsible. He always seemed to distance himself from me. That was why I never allowed my relationship with you to get physical."

Tracey shot straight up. "You mean Daddy was the reason you never kissed me?"

"That's right, *petite*. I meant to marry you and refused to do anything to jeopardize my plans. When he questioned my motives in picking you up from school every day and taking you to my office, I told him I had appointed myself your guardian against Jacques, which was true. Just not the whole truth. I gave him my word that he could trust me to treat you like a cherished sister."

"Julien…" She hid her face.

"You *should* be blushing," he teased softly. "Never has any man had to withstand more temptation than I."

"Oh, darling—" Tracey burrowed closer "—when I think how I threw myself at you."

"You did." He kissed her neck. "You were shameless and I adored you. And as long as your love kept growing, as long as those incredible green eyes kept making me feel immortal, I vowed I could be patient long enough for your father to accept me as a son-in-law. Unfortunately, he died before I could talk to him, but now that I know the truth, I doubt he would have given me his blessing."

"Yes, he would have," Tracey returned fervently. "He was very much aware you were—are my *raison d'être*. He knew what a wonderful man you were or he would never have entrusted me to your care. Daddy and I were very close. I *know* he wouldn't have stood in the way of my happiness."

Julien embraced her more fully. "Perhaps not, but I would always have been a reminder of his pain. Father betrayed your father's trust in a way that no man could forgive. I suppose he paid the price for that moment of weakness all the days of his life."

"I'm sure Mother did, too. But it's over now."

"Not quite. Isabelle has to be told."

"Aunt Rose wants to tell her when the time is right. I think she should be the one. She and Mother were extremely close. She'll be able to explain things in a way that Iz will understand and accept." Tracey outlined his mouth with her finger. "When she learns that you're her half brother, she'll love you more than ever. You were always her favorite person, too."

Julien grasped her hand and kissed the palm. "After we go back to the château, I'll phone Jacques in Brussels and ask him to come home. We'll invite Angelique over and break the news to them together. It's time we were a family again."

"I want that more than anything. The pain we've all had to endure because of our parents' affair should have been buried with them. Thank heaven the truth is out at last."

"Thank heaven you lived through that accident," Julien cried in a shaken voice. "*Mon Dieu*, when I think how close I came to losing you…"

Tracey kissed the tears from his cheeks. "There was no chance of that. Not with you watching over me and our babies. I'm the most blessed woman alive, Julien Chappelle," she spoke the words against his mouth. "Thank you for never giving up. Thank you for being the kind of man you are, for being father and mother to the children during such a traumatic period in our lives.

"Now it's my turn to take care of you. For the rest of the time granted to us, I'm planning to spend every minute, every second showing you exactly what you mean to me. I love you so much I can't contain it any longer.

"Julien," she cried in an anxious voice, "do you think a person could die from feeling too much love?"

"There's only one way to find out," came his impassioned response as he carried her into the bedroom. "At least if we go up in flames, it will be together, *mon amour*. One thing I can promise you. Wherever our love takes us, *we've only just begun.*"

Sandra Marton wrote her first story when she was seven years old and began to dream of becoming a writer. Today, Sandra is the author of more than 40 romance novels. Readers around the world love her strong, passionate heroes and determined, spirited heroines. When she's not busy writing, Sandra likes to hike, read, explore out-of-the-way restaurants and travel to far-away places. The mother of two grown sons, Sandra lives with her husband in a sun-filled house in a quiet corner of Connecticut where she alternates between extravagant bouts of gourmet cooking and take-out pizza.

THE SECOND
MRS ADAMS
by
SANDRA MARTON

CHAPTER ONE

THE siren was loud.

Painfully, agonizingly loud.

The sound was a live thing, burrowing deep into her skull, tunneling into the marrow of her bones.

Make it stop, she thought, oh please, make it stop.

But even when it did, the silence didn't take the pain away.

"My head," she whispered. "My head."

No one was listening. Or perhaps no one could hear her. Was she really saying anything or was she only thinking the words?

People were crowded around, faces looking down at her, some white with concern, others sweaty with curiosity. Hands were moving over her now, very gently, and then they were lifting her; oh, God, it hurt!

"Easy," somebody said, and then she was inside a…a what? A truck? No. It was an ambulance. And now the doors closed and the ambulance began to move and the sound, that awful sound, began again and they were flying through the streets.

Terror constricted her throat.

What's happened to me? she thought desperately.

She tried to gasp out the words but she couldn't form them. She was trapped in silence and in pain as they raced through the city.

Had there been an accident? A picture formed in her mind of wet, glistening pavement, a curb, a taxi hurtling toward her. She heard again the bleat of a horn and the squeal of tires seeking a purchase that was not to be found…

No. No! she thought, and then she screamed her denial

5

but the scream rose to mingle with the wail of the siren as she tumbled down into velvet darkness.

She lay on her back and drifted in the blue waters of a dream. There was a bright yellow light overhead.

Was it the sun?

There were voices... Disembodied voices, floating on the air. Sentence fragments that made no sense, falling around her with the coldness of snow.

"...five more CC's..."

"...blood pressure not stabilized yet..."

"...wait for a CAT scan before..."

The voices droned on. It wasn't anything to do with her, she decided drowsily, and fell back into the darkness.

The next time she awoke, the voices were still talking.

"...no prognosis, at this stage..."

"...touch and go for a while, but..."

They *were* talking about her. But why? What was wrong with her? She wanted to ask, she wanted to tell them to stop discussing her as if she weren't there because she *was* there, it was just that she couldn't get her eyes to open because the lids were so heavy.

She groaned and a hand closed over hers, the fingers gripping hers reassuringly.

"Joanna?"

Who?

"Joanna, can you hear me?"

Joanna? Was that who she was? Was that her name?

"...head injuries are often unpredictable..."

The hand tightened on hers. "Dammit, stop talking about her as if she weren't here!"

The voice was as masculine as the touch, blunt with anger and command. Blessedly, the buzz of words ceased. Joanna tried to move her fingers, to press them against the ones that clasped hers and let the man know she was grateful for what he'd done, but she couldn't. Though her mind willed it, her hand wouldn't respond. It felt like the rest of her, as lifeless as a lump of lead. She could only lie there unmoving, her fingers caught within those of the stranger's.

"It's all right, Joanna," he murmured. "I'm here."

His voice soothed her but his words sent fear coursing through her blood. Who? she thought wildly, who was here?

Without warning, the blackness opened beneath her and sucked her down.

When she awoke next, it was to silence.

She knew at once that she was alone. There were no voices, no hand holding hers. And though she felt as if she were floating, her mind felt clear.

Would she be able to open her eyes this time? The possibility that she couldn't terrified her. Was she paralyzed? No. Her toes moved, and her fingers. Her hands, her legs…

All right, then.

Joanna took a breath, held it, then slowly let it out. Then she raised eyelids that felt as if they had been coated with cement.

The sudden rush of light was almost blinding. She blinked against it and looked around her.

She was in a hospital room. There was no mistaking it for anything else. The high ceiling and the bottle suspended beside the bed, dripping something pale and colorless into her vein, confirmed it.

The room was not unpleasant. It was large, drenched in bright sunlight and filled with baskets of fruit and vases of flowers.

Was all that for her? It had to be; hers was the only bed in the room.

What had happened to her? She had seen no cast on her legs or her arms; nothing ached in her body or her limbs. Except for the slender plastic tubing snaking into her arm, she might have awakened from a nap.

Was there a bell to ring? She lifted her head from the pillow. Surely there was a way to call some…

"Ahh!"

Pain lanced through her skull with the keenness of a knife. She fell back and shut her eyes against it.

"Mrs. Adams?"

Joanna's breath hissed from between her teeth.

"Mrs. Adams, do you hear me? Open your eyes, please, Mrs. Adams, and look at me."

It hurt, God, it hurt, but she managed to look up into a stern female face that was instantly softened by a smile.

"That's the way, Mrs. Adams. Good girl. How do you feel?"

Joanna opened her mouth but nothing came out. The nurse nodded sympathetically.

"Wait a moment. Let me moisten your lips with some ice chips. There, how's that?"

"My head hurts," Joanna said in a cracked whisper.

The nurse's smile broadened, as if something wonderful had happened.

"Of course it does, dear. I'm sure the doctor will give you something for it as soon as he's seen you. I'll just go and get him…"

Joanna's hand shot out. She caught the edge of the woman's crisp white sleeve.

"Please," she said, "what happened to me?"

"Doctor Corbett will explain everything, Mrs. Adams."

"Was I in an accident? I don't remember. A car. A taxi…"

"Hush now, dear." The woman extricated herself gently from Joanna's grasp and made her way toward the door. "Just lie back and relax, Mrs. Adams. I'll only be a moment."

"Wait!"

The single word stopped the nurse with its urgency. She paused in the doorway and swung around.

"What is it, Mrs. Adams?"

Joanna stared at the round, kindly face. She felt the seconds flying away from her with every pounding beat of her heart.

"You keep calling me...you keep saying, 'Mrs. Adams...'"

She saw the sudden twist in the nurse's mouth, the dawning of sympathetic realization in the woman's eyes.

"Can you tell me," Joanna said in a broken whisper, "can you tell me who... What I mean is, could you tell me, please, who I am?"

The doctor came. Two doctors, actually, one a pleasant young man with a gentle touch and another, an older man with a patrician air and a way of looking at her as if she weren't really there while he poked and prodded but that was OK because Joanna felt as if she wasn't really there, surely not here in this bed, in this room, without any idea in the world of who she was.

"Mrs. Adams" they all called her, and like some well-trained dog, she learned within moments to answer to the name, to extend her arm and let them take out the tubing, to say "Yes?" when one of them addressed her by the name, but who was Mrs. Adams?

Joanna only knew that she was here, in this room, and that to all intents and purposes, her life had begun an hour before.

She asked questions, the kind she'd never heard anywhere but in a bad movie and even when she thought that, it amazed her that she'd know there was such a thing as a bad movie.

But the doctor, the young one, said that was what amnesia was like, that you remembered some things and not others, that it wasn't as if your brain had been wiped clean of everything, and Joanna thought thank goodness for that or she would lie here like a giant turnip. She said as much to the young doctor and he laughed and she laughed, even though it hurt her head when she did, and then, without any warning, she wasn't laughing at all, she was sobbing as if her heart were going to break, and a needle slid into her arm and she fell into oblivion.

It was nighttime when she woke next.

The room was dark, except for the light seeping in from the hushed silence of the corridor just outside the partly open door. The blackness beyond the windowpane was broken by the glow of lights from what surely had to be a city.

Joanna stirred restlessly. "Nurse?" she whispered.

"Joanna."

She knew the voice. It was the same masculine one that she'd heard an eternity ago when she'd surfaced from unconsciousness.

"Yes," she said.

She heard the soft creak of leather and a shape rose from the chair beside her bed. Slowly, carefully, she turned her head on the pillow.

His figure was shrouded in shadow, his face indistinct. She could see only that he was big and broad of shoulder, that he seemed powerful, almost mystical in the darkness.

"Joanna," he said again, his voice gruff as she'd remembered it yet tinged now with a husky softness. His hand closed over hers and this time she had no difficulty flexing her fingers and threading them through his, clasping his hand and holding on as if to a lifeline. "Welcome back," he said, and she could hear the smile and the relief in the words.

Joanna swallowed hard. There was so much she wanted to ask, but it seemed so stupid to say, "who am I?" or "who are you?" or "where am I?" or "how did I get here?"

"You probably have a lot of questions," he said, and she almost sobbed with relief.

"Yes," she murmured.

He nodded. "Ask them, then—or shall I get the nurse first? Do you need anything? Want anything? Water, or some cracked ice, or perhaps you need to go to the bathroom?"

"Answers," Joanna said urgently, her hand tightening on his, "I need answers."

"Of course. Shall I turn up the light?"

"No," she said quickly. If he turned up the light, this would all become real. And it wasn't real. It couldn't be. "No, it's fine this way, thank you."

"Very well, then." The bed sighed as he sat down beside her. His hip brushed against hers, and she could feel the heat of him, the strength and the power. "Ask away, and I'll do my best to answer."

Joanna licked her lips. "What—what happened? I mean, how did I get here? Was there an accident?"

He sighed. "Yes."

"I seem to remember... I don't know. It was raining, I think."

"Yes," he said again. His hand tightened on hers. "It was."

"I stepped off the curb. The light was with me, I'd checked because...because..." She frowned. There was a reason, she knew there was, and it had something to do with him, but how could it when she didn't...when she had no idea who he...

Joanna whimpered, and the man bent down and clasped her shoulders.

"It's all right," he said, "it's all right, Joanna."

It wasn't, though. The touch of his hands on her was gentle but she could feel the tightly leashed rage in him, smell its hot, masculine scent on the carefully filtered hospital air.

"The taxi..."

"Yes."

"It—it came flying through the intersection..."

"Hush."

"I saw it, but by the time I did it was too late..."

Her voice quavered, then broke. The man cursed softly and his hands slid beneath her back and he lifted her toward him, cradling her against his chest.

Pain bloomed like an evil, white-hot flower behind her eyes. A cry rose in her throat and burst from her lips. Instantly, he lay her back against the pillows.

"Hell," he said. "I'm sorry, Joanna. I shouldn't have moved you."

Strangely, the instant of pain had been a small price to pay for the comfort she'd felt in his arms. His strength had seemed to flow into her body; his heartbeat had seemed to give determination to hers.

She wanted to tell him that, but how did you say such things to a stranger?

"Joanna? Are you all right?"

She nodded. "I'm fine. I just—I have so many questions…"

He brushed the back of his hand along her cheek in a wordless gesture.

"I need to know." She took a breath. "Tell me the rest, please. The taxi hit me, didn't it?"

"Yes."

"And an ambulance brought me to… What is this place?"

"You're in Manhattan Hospital."

"Am I…am I badly hurt?" He hesitated, and she swallowed hard. "Please, tell me the truth. What kind of injuries do I have?"

"Some bruises. A cut above your eye…they had to put in stitches—"

"Why can't I remember anything? Do I have amnesia?"

She asked it matter-of-factly, as if she'd been inquiring about nothing more devastating than a common cold, but he wasn't a fool, she knew he could sense the panic that she fought to keep from her voice because the hands that still clasped her shoulders tightened again.

"The taxi only brushed you," he said. "But when you fell, you hit your head against the curb."

"My mind is like a—a blackboard that's been wiped clean. You keep calling me 'Joanna' but the name has no meaning to me. I don't know who 'Joanna' is."

Her eyes had grown accustomed to the shadowy darkness;
she could almost see him clearly now. He had a hard face
with strong features: a straight blade of a nose, a slash of a
mouth, hair that looked to be thick and dark and perhaps a
bit overlong.

"And me?" His voice had fallen to a whisper; she had
to strain to hear it. "Do you know who I am, Joanna?"

She took a deep, shuddering breath. Should she remember
him? Should she at least know his name?

"No," she said. "No. I don't."

There was a long, almost palpable silence. She felt the
quick bite of his fingers into her flesh and then he lifted his
hands away, carefully, slowly, as if she were a delicate glass
figurine he'd just returned to its cabinet for fear a swift
movement would make it shatter.

He rose slowly to his feet and now she could see that he
was tall, that the broad shoulders were matched by a powerful chest that tapered to a narrow waist, slim hips and long,
well-proportioned legs. He stood beside the bed looking
down at her, and then he nodded and thrust his fingers
through his hair in a gesture instinct told her was as familiar
to her as it was habitual to him.

"The doctors told me to expect this," he said, "but..."

He shrugged so helplessly, despite the obvious power of
his silhouette, that Joanna's heart felt his frustration.

"I'm sorry," she murmured. "I'm terribly, terribly
sorry."

His smile was bittersweet. He sat down beside her again
and took her hand in his. She had a fleeting memory, one
that was gone before she could make sense of it. She saw
his dark head bent over a woman's hand, saw his lips
pressed to the palm...

Was the woman her? Was he going to bring her hand to
his mouth and kiss it?

Anticipation, bright as the promise of a new day and
sweet as the nectar of a flower, made her pulse-beat quicken.

But all he did was lay her hand down again and pat it lightly with his.

"It isn't your fault, Joanna. There's nothing to apologize for."

She had the feeling that there was, that she owed him many apologies for many things, but that was silly. How could she owe anything to a man she didn't know?

"Please," she said softly, "tell me your name."

His mouth twisted. Then he rose to his feet, walked to the window and stared out into the night. An eternity seemed to pass before he turned and looked at her again.

"Of course." There was a difference in him now, in his tone and in the way he held himself, and it frightened her. "My name is David. David Adams."

Joanna hesitated. The black pit that had swallowed her so many times since the accident seemed to loom at her feet.

"David Adams," she murmured, turning the name over in her mind, trying—failing—to find in it some hint of familiarity. "We—we have the same last name."

He laughed, though there was no levity to it.

"I can see you haven't lost your talent for understatement, Joanna. Yes, we have the same last name."

"Are we related, then?"

His mouth twisted again, this time with a wry smile. "Indeed, we are, my love. You see, Joanna, I'm your husband."

CHAPTER TWO

THE nurses all knew him by name, but after ten days there was nothing surprising in that.

What was surprising, David thought as his driver competently snaked the Bentley through the crowded streets of midtown Manhattan, was that he'd become something of a celebrity in the hospital.

Morgana, his P.A., had laughed when he'd first expressed amazement and then annoyance at his star status.

"I'm not Richard Gere, for heaven's sake," he'd told her irritably after he'd been stopped half a dozen times for his autograph en route to Joanna's room. "What in hell do they want with the signature of a stodgy Wall Street banker?"

Morgana had pointed out that he wasn't just a Wall Street banker, he was the man both the President of the World Bank and the President of the United States turned to for financial advice, even though his politics were not known by either.

As for stodgy... Morgana reminded him that *CityLife* magazine had only last month named him to its list of New York's Ten Sexiest Men.

David, who'd been embarrassed enough by the designation so he'd done an admirable job of all but forgetting it, had flushed.

"Absurd of them to even have mentioned my name in that stupid article," he'd muttered, and Morgana, honest as always, had agreed.

The media thought otherwise. In a rare week of no news, an accident involving the beautiful young wife of New York's Sexiest Stockbroker was a four-star event.

The ghouls had arrived at the Emergency Room damned

near as fast as he had so that when he'd jumped from his
taxi he'd found himself in a sea of microphones and cameras
and shouted questions, some so personal he wouldn't have
asked them of a close friend. David had clenched his jaw,
ignored them all and shoved his way through the avaricious
mob without pausing.

That first encounter had taught him a lesson. Now, he
came and went by limousine even though he hated the for-
mality and pretentiousness of the oversize car he never used
but for the most formal business occasions. Joanna had liked
it, though. She loved the luxury of the plush passenger com-
partment with its built-in bar, TV and stereo.

David's mouth twisted. What irony, that the car he disliked and his wife loved should have become his vehicle of
choice, since the accident.

It had nothing to do with the bar or the TV. It was just
that he'd quickly learned that the reporters who still hung
around outside the hospital pounced on taxis like hyenas on
wounded wildebeests. Arriving by limo avoided the problem. The car simply pulled up at the physicians' entrance,
David stepped out, waved to the security man as if he'd been
doing it every day of his life and walked straight in. The
reporters had yet to catch on, though it wouldn't matter, after
tonight. This would be his last visit to the hospital.

By this time tomorrow, Joanna would be installed in a
comfortable suite at Bright Meadows Rehabilitation Center.
The place had an excellent reputation, both for helping its
patients recover and for keeping them safe from unwelcome
visitors. Bright Meadows was accustomed to catering to
high-profile guests. No one whose name hadn't been placed
on an approved list would get past the high stone walls and
there was even a helicopter pad on the grounds, if a phalanx
of reporters decided to gather at the gates.

Hollister pulled up to the private entrance as usual and
David waved to the guard as he walked briskly through the
door and into a waiting elevator. He was on the verge of
breathing a sigh of relief when a bottle blonde with a tri-

umphant smile on her face and a microphone clutched in her hand sprang out of the shadows and into the elevator. She jammed her finger on the Stop button and turned up the wattage on her smile.

"Mr. Adams," she said, "millions of interested *Sun* readers want to know how Mrs. Adams is doing."

"She's doing very well, thank you," David said politely.

"Is she really?" Her voice dropped to a whisper that oozed compassion the same way a crocodile shed tears. "You can tell *Sun* readers the truth, David. What's the real extent of your wife's injuries?"

"Would you take your finger off that button, please, miss?"

The blonde edged nearer. "Is it true she's in a coma?"

"Step back, please, and let go of that button."

"David." The blond leaned forward, her heavily kohled eyes, her cleavage and her microphone all aimed straight at him. "We heard that your wife's accident occurred while she was en route to the airport for your second honeymoon in the Caribbean. Can you confirm that for our readers?"

David's jaw tightened. He could sure as hell wipe that look of phony sympathy from the blonde's face, he thought grimly. All he had to do was tell her the truth, that Joanna had been on her way to the airport, all right, and then to the Caribbean—and to the swift, civilized divorce they had agreed upon.

But the last thing he'd ever do was feed tabloid gossip. His life was private. Besides, ending the marriage was out of the question now. He and Joanna were husband and wife, by license if not by choice. He would stand by her, provide the best care possible until she was well again...

"Mr. Adams?"

The blonde wasn't going to give up easily. She had rearranged her face so that her expression had gone from compassion to sincere inquiry. He thought of telling her that the last time he'd seen that look it had been on the face of a shark that had a sincere interest in one or more of his limbs while he'd been diving off the Mexican coast.

"I only want to help you share your problems with our readers," she said. "Sharing makes grief so much easier to bear, don't you agree?"

David smiled. "Well, Miss…"

"Washbourne." She smiled back, triumphant. "Mona Washbourne, but you can call me Mona."

"Well, Mona, I'll be happy to share this much." David's smile vanished as quickly as it had appeared. He raised his arm, shot back the cuff of his dark blue suit jacket, and looked at his watch. "Get that mike out of my face and your finger off that button in the next ten seconds or you're going to regret it."

"Is that a threat, Mr. Adams?"

"Your word, Mona, not mine."

"Because it certainly sounded like one. And I've got every word, right here, on my tape rec—"

"I never make threats, I only make promises. Anyone who's had any dealings with me can tell you that." His eyes met hers. "You're down to four seconds, and still counting."

Whatever Mona Washbourne saw in that cold, steady gaze made her jerk her finger from the Stop button and step out of the elevator.

"Didn't you ever hear of freedom of the press? You can't go around bullying reporters."

"Is that what you are?" David said politely. He punched the button for Joanna's floor and the doors began to shut. "A member of the press? Damn. And here I was, thinking you were a…"

The doors snapped closed. Just as well, he thought wearily, and leaned back against the wall. Insulting the Mona Washbournes of the world only made them more vicious, and what was the point? He was accustomed to pressure, it was part of the way he earned his living.

OK, so the last week and a half had been rough. Personally rough. He didn't love Joanna anymore, hell, he wasn't even sure if he had ever loved her to begin with, but that didn't mean he hadn't almost gone crazy with fear when the call had come, notifying him of the accident. He wasn't heartless. What man wouldn't react to the news that the woman he was married to had been hurt?

And, as it had turned out, "hurt" was a wild word to describe what had happened to Jo. David's mouth thinned. She'd lost her memory. She didn't remember anything. Not her name, not their marriage...

Not him.

The elevator doors opened. The nurse on duty looked up, frowning, an automatic reminder that it was past visiting hours on her lips, but then her stern features softened into a girlish smile.

"Oh, it's you, Mr. Adams. We thought you might not be stopping by this evening."

"I'm afraid I got tied up in a meeting, Miss Howell."

"Well, certainly, sir. That's what I told Mrs. Adams, that you were probably running late."

"How is my wife this evening?"

"Very well, sir." The nurse's smile broadened. "She's had her hair done. Her makeup, too. I suspect you'll find her looking more and more like her old self."

"Ah." David nodded. "Yes, well, that's good news."

He told himself that it was as he headed down the hall toward Joanna's room. She hadn't looked at all like herself since the accident.

"Why are you looking at me like that?" she'd asked him, just last evening, and when he hadn't answered, her hand had shot to her forehead, clamping over the livid, half-moon scar that marred her perfect skin. "It's ugly, isn't it?"

David had stood there, wanting to tell her that what he'd been staring at was the sight of a Joanna he'd all but forgotten, one who lent grace and beauty even to an undistinguished white hospital gown, who wore her dark hair loose in a curling, silken cloud, whose dark-lashed violet eyes were not just free of makeup but wide and vulnerable, whose full mouth was the pink of roses.

He hadn't said any of that, of course, partly because it was just sentimental slop and partly because he knew she wouldn't want to hear it. That Joanna had disappeared months after their wedding and the Joanna who'd replaced her was always careful about presenting an impeccably groomed self to him and to the world. So he'd muttered something about the scar being not at all bad and then he'd changed the subject, but he hadn't forgotten the moment.

It had left a funny feeling in his gut, seeing Joanna that way, as if a gust of wind had blown across a calendar and turned the pages backward. He'd mentioned it to Morgana in passing, not the clutch in his belly but how different Joanna looked and his Personal Assistant, with the clever, understanding instincts of one woman for another, had cluck-clucked.

"The poor girl," she'd said, "of course she looks different! Think what she's gone through, David. She probably dreads looking at herself in the mirror. Her cosmetic case and a visit from her hairdresser will go a long way toward cheering her spirits. Shall I make the arrangements?"

David had hesitated, though he couldn't imagine the reason. Then he'd said yes, of course, that he'd have done it himself, if he'd thought of it, and Morgana had smiled and said that the less men knew about women's desires to make themselves beautiful, the better.

So Morgana had made the necessary calls, and he'd seen to it that Joanna's own robes, nightgowns and slippers were packed by her maid and delivered to the hospital first thing this morning, and now, as he knocked and then opened the door of her room, he was not surprised to find the Joanna he knew waiting for him.

She was standing at the window, her back to him. She was dressed in a pale blue cashmere robe, her hair drawn back from her face and secured at the nape in an elegant knot. Her posture was straight and proud—or was there a curve to her shoulders and a tremble to them, as well?

He stepped inside the room and let the door swing shut behind him.

"Joanna?"

She turned at the sound of his voice and he saw that everything about her had gone back to normal. The vulnerability had left her eyes; they'd been done up in some way he didn't pretend to understand so that they were somehow less huge and far more sophisticated. The bright color had been toned down in her cheeks and her mouth, while still full and beautiful, was no longer the color of a rose but of the artificial blossoms only found in a lipstick tube.

The girl he had once called his Gypsy was gone. The stunning Manhattan sophisticate was back and it was stupid to feel a twinge of loss because he'd lost his Gypsy a long, long time ago.

"David," Joanna said. "I didn't expect you."

"I was stuck in a meeting... Joanna? Have you been crying?"

"No," she said quickly, "no, of course not. I just—I have a bit of a headache, that's all." She swallowed; he could see the movement of muscle in her long, pale throat. "Thank you for the clothes you sent over."

"Don't be silly. I should have thought of having your own things delivered to you days ago."

The tip of her tongue snaked across her lips. She looked down at her robe, then back at him.

"You mean...I selected these things myself?"

He nodded. "Of course. Ellen packed them straight from your closet."

"Ellen?"

"Your maid."

"My..." She gave a little laugh, walked to the bed and sat down on the edge of the mattress. "I have a maid?" David nodded. "Well, thank her for me, too, please. Oh, and thank you for arranging for me to have my hair and my makeup done.''

''It isn't necessary to thank me, Joanna. But you're welcome.''

He spoke as politely as she did, even though he had the sudden urge to tell her that he'd liked her better with her hair wild and free, with color in her cheeks that didn't come from a makeup box and her eyes dark and sparkling with laughter.

She was beautiful now but she'd been twice as beautiful before.

David frowned. The pressure of the past ten days was definitely getting to him. There was no point in remembering the past when the past had never been real.

''So,'' he said briskly, ''are you looking forward to getting sprung from this place tomorrow?''

Joanna stared at him. She knew what she was supposed to say. And the prospect of getting out of the hospital had been exciting...until she'd begun to think about what awaited her outside these walls.

By now, she knew she and David lived in a town house near Central Park but she couldn't begin to imagine what sort of life they led. David was rich, that much was obvious, and yet she had the feeling she didn't know what it meant to lead the life of a wealthy woman.

Which was, of course, crazy, because she didn't know what it meant to lead any sort of life, especially one as this stranger's wife.

He was so handsome, this man she couldn't remember. So unabashedly male, and here she'd been lying around looking like something the cat had dragged in, dressed in a shapeless hospital gown with no makeup at all on her face and her hair wild as a whirlwind, and then her clothes and her hairdresser and her makeup had arrived and she'd realized that her husband preferred her to look chic and sophisticated.

No wonder he'd looked at her as if he'd never seen her before just last evening.

Maybe things would improve between them now. The nurses all talked about how lucky she was to be Mrs. David Adams. He was gorgeous, they giggled, so sexy...

So polite, and so cold.

The nurses didn't know that, but Joanna did. Was that how he'd always treated her? As if they were strangers who'd just met, always careful to do and say the right thing? Or was it the accident that had changed things between them? Was he so removed, so proper, because he knew she couldn't remember him or their marriage?

Joanna wanted to ask, but how could you ask such intimate things of a man you didn't know?

"Joanna, what's the matter?" She blinked and looked up at David. His green eyes were narrowed with concern as they met hers. "Have the doctors changed their minds about releasing you?"

Joanna forced a smile to her lips. "No, no, the cell door's still scheduled to open at ten in the morning. I was just thinking about...about how it's going to be to go...to go..." Home, she thought. She couldn't bring herself to say the word, but then, she didn't have to. She wasn't going home tomorrow, she was going to a rehab center. More white-tiled walls, more high ceilings, more brightly smiling nurses... "Where is Big Meadows, anyway?"

"Bright Meadows," David said, with a smile. "It's about an hour's drive from here. You'll like the place, Jo. Lots of trees, rolling hills, an Olympic-size swimming pool and there's even an exercise room. Nothing as high-tech as your club, I don't think, but even so—"

"My club?"

Damn, David thought, damn! The doctors had warned him against jogging her memory until she was ready, until she began asking questions on her own.

"Sorry. I didn't mean to—"

"Do I belong to an exercise club?"

"Well, yeah."

"You mean, one of those places where you dress up in a silly Spandex suit so you can climb on a treadmill to work up a sweat?"

David grinned. It was his unspoken description of the Power Place, to a tee.

"I think the Power Place would be offended to hear itself described in quite that way but I can't argue with it, either."

Joanna laughed. "I can't even imagine doing that. I had the TV on this morning and there was this roomful of people jumping up and down…they looked so silly, and now you're telling me that I do the same thing?"

"The Power Place," David said solemnly, "would definitely not like to hear you say that."

"Why don't I run outdoors? Or walk? Didn't you say I—we—live near Central Park?"

His smile tilted. It was as if she was talking about another person instead of herself.

"Yes. We live less than a block away. And I don't know why you didn't run there. I do, every morning."

"Without me?" she said.

"Yes. Without you."

"Didn't we ever run together?"

He stared at her. They had; he'd almost forgotten. She'd run right along with him the first few weeks after their marriage. They'd even gone running one warm, drizzly morning and had the path almost all to themselves. They'd been jogging along in silence when she'd suddenly yelled out a challenge and sped away from him. He'd let her think she was going to beat him for thirty or forty yards and then he'd put on some speed, come up behind her, snatched her into his arms and tumbled them both off the path and into the grass. He'd kissed her until she'd stopped laughing and gone soft with desire in his arms, and then they'd flagged a cab to take them the short block back home…

He frowned, turned away and strode to the closet. "You said you preferred to join the club," he said brusquely, "that it was where all your friends went and that it was a lot more pleasant and a lot safer to run on an indoor track than in the park. Have you decided what you're going to wear tomorrow?''

''But how could it be safer? If you and I ran together, I was safe enough, wasn't I?''

''It was better that way, Joanna. We both agreed that it was. My schedule's become more and more erratic. I have to devote a lot of hours to business. You know that. I mean, you don't know it, not anymore, but...''

''That's OK, you don't have to explain.'' Joanna smiled tightly. ''You're a very busy man. And a famous one. The nurses all keep telling me how lucky I am to be married to you.''

David's hand closed around the mauve silk suit hanging in the closet.

''They ought to mind their business,'' he said gruffly.

''Don't be angry with them, David. They mean well.''

''Everybody ought to mind their damned business,'' he said, fighting against the rage he felt suddenly, inexplicably, rising within him. ''The nurses, the reporters—''

''Reporters?''

For the second time that night, David cursed himself. He could hear the sudden panic in Joanna's voice and he turned and looked at her.

''Don't worry about them. I won't let them get near you.''

''But why...'' She stopped, then puffed out her breath. ''Of course. They want to know about the accident, about me, because I'm Mrs. David Adams.''

''They won't bother you, Joanna. Once I get you to Bright Meadows...''

''The doctors say I'll have therapy at Bright Meadows.''

''Yes.''

''What kind of therapy?''

''I don't know exactly. They have to evaluate you first.''

''Evaluate me?'' she said with a quick smile.

"Look, the place is known throughout the country. The staff, the facilities, are all highly rated."

Joanna ran the tip of her tongue across her lips. "I don't need therapy," she said brightly. "I just need to remember."

"The therapy will help you do that."

"How?" She tilted her head up. Her smile was brilliant, though he could see it wobble just a little. "There's nothing wrong with me physically, David. Or mentally. I don't need to go for walks on the arm of an aide or learn basket-weaving or—or lie on a couch while some doctor asks me silly questions about a childhood I can't remember."

David's frown deepened. She was saying the same things he'd said when Bright Meadows had been recommended to him.

"Joanna's not crazy," he'd said bluntly, "and she's not crippled."

The doctors had agreed, but they'd pointed out that there really wasn't anywhere else to send a woman with amnesia…unless, of course, Mr. Adams wished to take his wife home? She needed peaceful, stress-free surroundings and, at least temporarily, someone to watch out for her. Could a man who put in twelve-hour days provide that?

No, David had said, he could not. He had to devote himself to his career. He had a high-powered Wall Street firm to run and clients to deal with. Besides, though he didn't say so to the doctors, he knew that he and Joanna could never endure too much time alone together.

There was no question but that Bright Meadows was the right place for Joanna. The doctors, and David, had agreed.

Had Joanna agreed, too? He was damned if he could re-member.

"David?"

He looked at Joanna. She was smiling tremulously.

"Couldn't I just…isn't there someplace I could go that isn't a hospital? A place I could stay, I mean, where maybe the things around me would jog my memory?"

"You need peace and quiet, Joanna. Our town house isn't—"

She nodded and turned away, but not before he'd seen the glitter of tears in her eyes. She was crying. Quietly, with great dignity, but she was crying all the same.

"Joanna," he said gently, "don't."

"I'm sorry." She rose quickly and hurried to the window where she stood with her back to him. "Go on home, please, David. It's late, and you've had a long day. The last thing you need on your hands is a woman who's feeling sorry for herself."

Had she always been so slight? His mental image of his wife was of a slender, tall woman with a straight back and straight shoulders, but the woman he saw at the window seemed small and painfully defenseless.

"Jo," he said, and he started slowly toward her, "listen, everything's going to be OK. I promise."

She nodded. "Sure," she said in a choked whisper.

He was standing just behind her now, close enough so that he could see the reddish glints in her black hair, so that he could almost convince himself he smelled the delicate scent of gardenia that had always risen from her skin until she'd changed to some more sophisticated scent.

"Joanna, if you don't like Bright Meadows, we'll find another place and—"

She spun toward him, her eyes bright with tears and with something else. Anger?

"Dammit, don't talk to me as if I were a child!"

"I'm not. I'm just trying to reassure you. I'll see to it you have the best of care. You know that."

"I don't know anything," she said, her voice trembling not with self-pity but yes, definitely, with anger. "You just don't understand, do you? You think, if you have them fix my hair and my face, and ship me my clothes and make me look like Joanna Adams, I'll turn into Joanna Adams."

"No," David said quickly. "I mean, yes, in a way. I'm trying to help you be who you are."

Joanna lifted her clenched fist and slammed it against his chest. David stumbled back, not from the blow which he'd hardly felt, but from shock. He couldn't remember Joanna raising her voice, let alone her hand. Well, yes, there'd been that time after they were first married, when he'd been caught late at a dinner meeting and he hadn't telephoned and she'd been frantic with worry by the time he came in at two in the morning…

"Damn you, David! I don't know who I am! I don't know this Joanna person." She raised her hand again, this time to punctuate each of her next words with a finger poked into his chest. "And I certainly don't know you!"

"What do you want to know? Ask and I'll tell you."

She took a deep, shuddering breath. "For starters, I'd like to know why I'm expected to believe I'm really your wife!"

David started to laugh, then stopped. She wasn't joking. One look into her eyes was proof of that. They had gone from violet to a color that was almost black. Her hands were on her hips, her posture hostile. She looked furious, defiant…and incredibly beautiful.

"What are you talking about?"

"What do you mean, what am I talking about? I said it clearly enough, didn't I? You say I'm your wife, but I don't remember you. So why should I let you run my life?"

"Joanna, for heaven's sake—"

"Can you *prove* that we're married?"

David threw up his hands. "I don't believe this!"

"Can you prove it, David?"

"Of course I can prove it! What would you like to see? Our marriage license? The cards we both signed and mailed out last Christmas? Dammit, of course we're married. Why would I lie about such a thing?"

He wouldn't. She knew that, deep down inside, but that had nothing to do with this. She was angry. She was furious. Let *him* try waking up in a hospital bed without knowing who he was, let *him* try having a stranger walk in and announce that as of that moment, all the important decisions of your life were being taken out of your hands.

But most of all, let him deal with the uncomfortable feeling that the person you were married to had been a stranger for a long, long time, not just since you'd awakened with a lump on your head and a terrible blankness behind your eyes.

"Answer me, Joanna. Why in hell would I lie?"

"I don't know. I'm not even saying that you are. I'm just trying to point out that the only knowledge I have of my own identity is your word."

David caught hold of her shoulders. "My word is damned well all you need!"

It was, she knew it was. It wasn't just the things the nurses had said about how lucky she was to be the wife of such a wonderful man as David Adams. She'd managed to read a bit about him in a couple of old magazines she'd found in the lounge.

On the face of it, David Adams was Everywoman's Dream.

But she wasn't Everywoman. She was lost on a dark road without a light to guide her and the only thing she felt whenever she thought of herself as Mrs. David Adams was a dizzying sense of disaster mingled in with something else, something just as dizzying but also incredibly exciting.

It terrified her, almost as much as the lack of a past, yet instinct warned that she mustn't let him know that, that the best defense against whatever it was David made her feel when he got too close was a strong offense, and so instead of backing down under his furious glare, Joanna glared right back.

"No," she said, "your word isn't enough! I don't know anything about you. Not anything, what you eat for breakfast or—or what movies you like to see or who chooses those—those stodgy suits you wear or—"

"Stodgy?" he growled. "Stodgy?"

"You heard me."

David stared down at the stranger he held clasped by the shoulders. Stodgy? Hell, for Joanna to use that word to describe him was ludicrous. She was right, she didn't know the first thing about him; they were strangers.

What she couldn't know was that it had been that way for a long time.

But not always. No, not always, he thought while his anger grew, and before he could think too much about what he was about to do, he hauled Joanna into his arms and kissed her.

She gave a gasp of shock and struggled against the kiss. But he was remorseless, driven at first by pure male outrage and then by the taste of her, a taste he had not known in months. The feel of her in his arms, the softness of her breasts against his chest, the long length of her legs against his, made him hard with remembering.

He fisted one hand in her hair, holding her captive to his kiss, while the other swept down and cupped her bottom, lifting her into his embrace, bringing her so close to him that he felt the sudden quickened beat of her heart, heard the soft little moan that broke in her throat as his lips parted hers, and then her arms were around his neck and she was kissing him back as hungrily as he was kissing her…

"Oh, my, I'm terribly sorry. I'll come back a bit later, shall I?"

They sprang apart at the sound of the shocked female voice. Both of them looked at the door where the night nurse stood staring at them, her eyes wide.

"I thought Mrs. Adams might want some help getting ready for bed but I suppose…I mean, I can see…" The nurse blushed. "Has Mrs. Adams regained her memory?"

"Mrs. Adams is capable of being spoken to, not about," Joanna said sharply. Her cheeks colored but her gaze was steady. "And no, she has not regained her memory."

"No," David said grimly, "she has not." He stalked past the nurse and pushed open the door. "But she's going to," he said. "She can count on it."

CHAPTER THREE

ALL right. Ok. So he'd made an ass of himself last night.

David stood in his darkened kitchen at six o'clock in the morning and told himself it didn't take a genius to figure that much out.

Kissing Joanna, losing his temper…the whole thing had been stupid. It had been worse than stupid. Joanna wasn't supposed to get upset and he sure as hell had upset her.

So why hadn't he just gone home, phoned her room and apologized? Why couldn't he just mentally kick himself in the tail, then put what had happened out of his head?

They were all good questions. It was just too bad that he didn't have any good answers, and he'd already wasted half the night trying to come up with one.

He'd always prided himself on his ability to face a mistake squarely, learn from it, then put it behind him and move on.

That was the way he'd survived childhood in a series of foster homes, a double hitch in the Marines and then a four year scholarship at an Ivy League university where he'd felt as out of place as a wolf at a sheep convention.

So, why was he standing here, drinking a cup of the worst coffee he'd ever tasted in his life, replaying that kiss as if it were a videotape caught in a loop?

He made a face, dumped the contents of the pot and the cup into the sink, then washed them both and put them into the drainer. Mrs. Timmons, his cook cum housekeeper, would be putting in an appearance in half an hour.

Why should she have to clean up a mess that he'd made?

David opened the refrigerator, took out a pitcher of orange

juice and poured himself a glass. You made a mess, you cleaned it up...which brought him straight back to why he was standing around here in the first place.

The unvarnished truth was that if he'd divorced Joanna sooner, he wouldn't be in this situation. By the time she'd stepped off that curb, she'd have been out of his life.

He'd known almost two years ago that he wanted out of the marriage, that the woman he'd taken as his wife had been nothing but a figment of his imagination. Joanna hadn't been a sweet innocent whose heart he'd stolen. She'd been a cold-blooded schemer who'd set out to snare a rich husband, and she'd succeeded.

Because it had taken him so damned long to admit the truth, he was stuck in this sham of a marriage for God only knew how much longer.

David slammed the refrigerator door shut with far more force than the job needed, walked to the glass doors that opened onto the tiny patch of green that passed for a private garden in midtown Manhattan, and stared at the early morning sky.

Corbett and his team of white-coated witch doctors wouldn't say how long it would take her to recover. They wouldn't even guarantee there'd be a recovery. The only thing they'd say was that she needed time.

"These things can't be rushed," Corbett had said solemnly. "Your wife needs a lot of rest, Mr. Adams. No shocks. No unpleasant surprises. That's vital. You do understand that, don't you?"

David understood it, all right. There was no possibility of walking into Joanna's room and saying, "Good evening, Joanna, and by the way, did I mention that we were in the middle of a divorce when you got hit by that taxi?"

Not that he'd have done it anyway. He didn't feel anything for Joanna, one way or another. Emotionally, mentally, he'd put her out of his life. Still, he couldn't in good conscience turn his back on her when she didn't even remember her own name.

When she didn't even remember him, or that she was his wife.

It was crazy, but as the days passed, that had been the toughest thing to take. It was one thing to want a woman out of your life but quite another to have her look at you blankly, or speak to you as if you were a stranger, her tone proper and always polite.

Until last night, when she'd suddenly turned on him in anger. And then he'd felt an answering anger rise deep inside himself, one so intense it had blurred his brain. What in hell had possessed him to haul her into his arms and kiss her like that? He'd thought she was going to slug him. What he'd never expected was that she'd turn soft and warm in his arms and kiss him back.

For a minute he'd almost forgotten that he didn't love her anymore, that she had never loved him, that everything he'd thought lay between them had been built on the quicksand of lies and deceit.

He turned away from the garden.

Maybe he should have listened to his attorney instead of the doctors. Jack insisted it was stupid to let sentiment get in the way of reality.

"So she shouldn't have any shocks," he'd said, "so big deal, she shouldn't have played you for a sucker, either. You want to play the saint, David? OK, that's fine. Pay her medical bills. Put her into that fancy sanitarium and shell out the dough for however long it takes for her to remember who she is. Put a fancy settlement into her bank account—but before you do any of that, first do yourself a favor and divorce the broad."

David had puffed out his breath.

"I hear what you're saying, Jack. But her doctors say—"

"Forget her doctors. Listen, if you want I can come up with our own doctors who'll say she's *non compos mentis* or that she's faking it and you're more than entitled to divorce her, if that's what's worrying you."

"Nothing's worrying me," David had replied brusquely.

''I just want to be able to look at myself in the mirror. I survived four years being married to Joanna. I'll survive another couple of months.''

Brave words, and true ones. David put his empty glass into the dishwasher, switched off the kitchen light and headed through the silent house toward the staircase and his bedroom.

And survive he would. He understood Jack's concern but he wasn't letting Joanna back into his life, he was just doing what he could to ease her into a life of her own.

She didn't affect him anymore, not down deep where it mattered. The truth was that she never had. He'd tricked himself into thinking he'd loved her when actually the only part of his anatomy Joanna had ever reached was the part that had been getting men into trouble from the beginning of time…the part that had responded to her last night.

Well, there was no more danger of that. He wouldn't be seeing much of his wife after today. Once he'd driven her to Bright Meadows, that would be it. Except for paying the bills and a once-a-week visit, she'd be the problem of the Bright Meadows staff, not his.

Sooner or later, her memory would come back. And when it did, this pretense of a marriage would be over.

Joanna sat in the back of the chauffeured Bentley and wondered what Dr. Corbett would say if she told him she almost preferred being in the hospital to being in this car with her husband.

For that matter, what would her husband say?

She shot David a guarded look.

Not much, judging by his stony profile, folded arms and cold silence. From the looks of things, he wasn't any more pleased they were trapped inside this overstuffed living room on wheels than she was.

What a terrible marriage theirs must have been. Her throat constricted. Dr. Corbett had made a point of telling her that

you didn't lose your intellect when you lost your memory.
Well, you didn't lose your instincts, either, and every instinct
she possessed told her that the marriage of Joanna and David
Adams had not been a storybook love affair.

Was he like this with everyone, or only with her? He
never seemed to smile, to laugh, to show affection.

Maybe that was why what had happened last night had
been such a shock. That outburst of raw desire was the last
thing she'd expected. Had it been a rarity or was that the
way it had been between them before the accident, polite
tolerance interrupted by moments of rage that ended with
her clinging to David's shoulders, almost pleading for him
to take her, while the world spun out from beneath her feet?

She'd hardly slept last night. Even after she'd rung for
the nurse and asked for a sleeping pill, she'd lain staring
into the darkness, trying to imagine what would have happened if that passionate, incredible kiss hadn't been interrupted.

She liked to think she'd have regained her senses, pulled
out of David's arms and slapped him silly.

But a sly whisper inside her head said that maybe she
wouldn't have, that maybe, instead, they'd have ended up
on the bed and to hell with the fact that the man kissing her
was an absolute stranger.

Eventually, she'd tumbled into exhausted sleep only to
dream about David stripping away her robe and nightgown,
kissing her breasts and her belly and then taking her right
there, on that antiseptically white hospital bed with her legs
wrapped around his waist and her head thrown back and her
sobs of pleasure filling the room.

A flush rose into Joanna's cheeks.

Which only proved how little dreams had to do with reality. David had apologized for his behaviour and she'd accepted the apology, but if he so much as touched her again,
she'd—she'd—

"What's the matter?"

She turned and looked at him. He was frowning, though

that wasn't surprising. His face had been set in a scowl all morning.

"Nothing," she said brightly.

"I thought I heard you whimper."

"Whimper? Me?" She laughed, or hoped she did. "No, I didn't...well, maybe I did. I have a, ah, a bit of a head-ache."

"Well, why didn't you say so?" He leaned forward and opened the paneled bar that was built into the Bentley. "Corbett gave you some pills, didn't he?"

"Yes, but I don't need them."

"Dammit, must you argue with me about everything?"

"I don't argue about everything...do I?"

David looked at her. She didn't. Actually, she never had. It was just this mood he was in this morning.

He sighed and shook his head. "Sorry. I guess I'm just feeling irritable today. Look, it can't hurt to take a couple of whatever he gave you, can it?"

"No, I suppose not."

He smiled, a first for the day that she could recall, poured her a tumbler of iced Perrier and handed it to her.

"Here. Swallow them down with this."

Joanna shook two tablets out of the vial and did as he'd asked.

"There," she said politely. "Are you happy now?"

It was the wrong thing to say. His brow furrowed instantly and his mouth took on that narrowed look she was coming to recognize and dislike.

"Since when did worrying about what makes me happy ever convince you to do anything?"

The words were out before he could call them back. Damn, he thought, what was the matter with him? A couple of hours ago, he'd been congratulating himself on his deci-sion to play the role of supportive husband. Now, with at least half an hour's drive time to go, he was close to blowing the whole thing.

And whose fault was that? He'd walked into Joanna's

room this morning and she'd looked at him as if she expected him to turn into a monster.

"I'm sorry about last night," he'd said gruffly, and she'd made a gesture that made it clear that what had happened had no importance at all...but she'd jumped like a scared cat when he'd tried to help her into the back of the car and just a couple of minutes ago, after sitting like a marble statue for the past hour, he'd caught her shooting him the kind of nervous look he'd always figured people reserved for vicious dogs.

Oh, hell, he thought, and turned toward her.

"Listen," he said, "about what happened last night..."

"I don't want to talk about it."

"No, neither do I. I just want to assure you it won't happen again."

"No," she said. Her eyes met his. "It won't."

"We've both been under a lot of pressure. The accident, your loss of memory..."

"What about before the accident?"

"What do you mean?"

Joanna hesitated. "I get the feeling that we...that we didn't have a very happy marriage."

It was his turn to hesitate now, but he couldn't bring himself to lie.

"It was a marriage," he said finally. "I don't know how to quantify it."

Joanna nodded. What he meant was, no, they hadn't been happy. It wasn't a surprise. Her husband didn't like her very much and she...well, she didn't know him enough to like him or dislike him, but it was hard to imagine she could ever have been in love with a man like this.

"Did Dr. Corbett tell you not to discuss our relationship with me? Whether it was good or not, I mean?"

"No," he said, this time with all honesty. "I didn't discuss our marriage with Corbett. Why would I?"

"I don't know. I just thought..." She sighed and tugged at the hem of her skirt. Not that there was any reason to.

The hem fell well below her knees. "I just thought he might have asked you questions about—about us."

"I wouldn't have answered them," David said bluntly. "Corbett's a neurosurgeon, not a shrink."

"I know. I guess I've just got psychiatry on the brain this morning, considering where we're going."

"Bright Meadows? But I told you, it's a rehab center."

"Oh, I know that. I just can't get this weird picture out of my head. I don't know where it comes from but I keep seeing a flight of steps leading up to an old mansion with a nurse standing on top of the steps. She's wearing a white uniform and a cape, and she has—I know it's silly, but she has a mustache and buck teeth and a hump on her back."

David burst out laughing. "Cloris Leachman!"

"Who?"

"An actress. What you're remembering is a scene from an old movie with Mel Brooks called...I think it was *High Anxiety*. He played a shrink and she played—give me a minute—she played evil Nurse Diesel."

Joanna laughed. "Evil Nurse Diesel?"

"Uh-huh. We found the movie playing on cable late one night, not long after we met. We both said we didn't like Mel Brooks' stuff, slapstick comedy, but we watched for a few minutes and we got hooked. After a while, we were both laughing so hard we couldn't stop."

"Really?"

"Oh, yeah. We watched right to the end, and then I phoned around until I found an all-night place to order pizza and you popped a bottle of wine into the freezer to chill and then..." *And then I told you that I loved you and asked you to be my wife.*

"And then?"

David shrugged. "And then, we decided we'd give Mel Brooks' movies another chance." He cleared his throat. "It's got to be a good sign, that you remembered a movie."

She nodded. "A snippet of a movie, at least."

"Anyway, there's nothing to worry about." He reached

out and patted her hand. ''Believe me, you're not going to find anything like that waiting for you at Bright Meadows.''

She didn't.

There was no nurse with a mustache and too many teeth waiting at the top of the steps. There were no dreary corridors or spaced-out patients wandering the grounds.

Instead, there was an air of almost manic cheer about the place. The receptionist smiled, the admitting nurse bubbled, the attendant who led them to a private, sun-drenched room beamed with goodwill.

''I just know you're going to enjoy your stay with us, Mrs. Adams,'' the girl said.

She sounds as if she's welcoming me to a hotel, Joanna thought. But this isn't a hotel, it's a hospital, even if nobody calls it that, and I'm not sick. I just can't remember anything...

No. She couldn't think about that or the terror of it would rise up and she'd scream.

And she couldn't do that. She'd kept the fear under control until now, she hadn't let anyone see the panic that woke her in the night, heart pounding and pillow soaked with sweat.

Joanna turned toward the window and forced herself to take a deep, deep breath.

''Joanna?'' David looked at the straight, proud back. A few strands of dark hair had come loose; they hung down against his wife's neck. He knew Joanna would fix it if she knew, that she'd never tolerate such imperfection. Despite the straightness of her spine, the severity of her suit, the tumble of curls lent her a vulnerability. He thought of how she'd once been...of how she'd once seemed.

All right, he knew that what she'd seemed had been a lie, that she wasn't the sweet, loving wife he'd wanted, but even so, she was in a tough spot now. It couldn't be easy, losing your memory.

He crossed the room silently, put his hands on her shoulders. He felt her jump beneath his touch and when he turned her gently toward him and she looked up at him, he even thought he saw her mouth tremble.

"Joanna," he said, his voice softening, "look, if you don't like this place, I'm sure there are others that—"

"This is fine," she said briskly.

He blinked, looked at her again, and knew he'd let his imagination work overtime. Her lips were curved in a cool smile and her eyes were clear.

David's hands fell to his sides. Whatever he'd thought he'd seen in her a moment ago had been just another example of how easily he could still be taken in, if not by his wife then by his own imagination.

"I'm sure I'm going to like it here," she said. "Now, if you don't mind terribly, I really would like to take a nap."

"Of course. I'd forgotten what an exhausting day this must have been for you." He started for the door. Halfway there, he paused and swung toward her. "I, uh, I'm not quite certain when I'll be able to get to see you again."

"Don't worry about it, David. This is a long way to come after a day's work and besides, I'm sure I'll be so busy I won't have time for visitors."

"That's exactly what I was thinking."

Joanna smiled. "Safe trip home," she said.

She held the smile until the door snicked shut after him. Then it dropped from her lips and she buried her face in her hands and wept.

Until today, she'd thought nothing could be as awful as waking up and remembering nothing about your life.

Now, she knew that it was even more horrible to realize that you were part of a loveless marriage.

"Mr. Adams?"

David looked up. He'd had his nose buried in a pile of reports he'd dredged out of the briefcase he always kept near at hand until the voice of his chauffeur intruded over the intercom.

"What is it, Hollister?"

"Sorry to bother you, sir, but I just caught a report on the radio about an overturned tractor trailer near the tunnel approach to the city."

David sighed and ran his hand through his hair. It wasn't any bother at all. The truth was, he didn't have the foggiest idea what was in the papers spread out on the seat beside him. He'd tried his damnedest to concentrate but that split instant when he'd seen those wispy curls lying against Joanna's pale skin kept intruding.

"Did they say anything about the traffic?"

"It's tied up for miles. Would you want me to take the long way? We could detour to the Palisades Parkway and take the bridge."

"Yes, that's a good idea, Hollister. Take the next turnoff and..." David frowned, then leaned forward. "No, the hell with that. Just pull over."

"Sir?"

"I said, pull over. Up ahead, where the shoulder of the road widens."

"Is there a problem, Mr. Adams?"

A taut smile twisted across David's mouth.

"No," he said, as the big car glided to a stop. "I just want to change seats with you."

"Sir?" Hollister said again. There was a world of meaning in the single word.

David laughed and jerked open the car door.

"I feel like driving, Hollister. You can stay up front, if you like. Just slide across the seat and put your belt on because I'm in the mood to see if this car can do anything besides look good."

For the first time in memory, Hollister smiled.

"She can do a lot besides look good, sir. She's not your Jaguar by a long shot but if you put your foot right to the floor, I think she'll surprise you."

David grinned. He waited until his chauffeur had fastened his seat belt and then he did as the man had suggested, put

the car in gear and the pedal to the metal, and forgot everything but the road.

He called Joanna every evening, promptly at seven. Their
conversations were always the same.

How was she? he asked.

Fine, she answered.

And how was she getting along at Bright Meadows?

She said "fine" to that one, too.

Friday evening, when he phoned, he told her he had some
work to do Saturday but he'd see her on Sunday.

Only if he could fit it into his schedule, she said.

His teeth ground together at the polite distance in the
words. Evidently, she didn't need to remember the past to
know how she wanted to behave in the present.

"I'll be there," he said grimly, and hung up the phone.

Sunday morning, he went for his usual run. He showered,
put on a pair of time-worn jeans, a pair of sneakers and—
in deference to the warming Spring weather—a lightweight
blue sweatshirt. Then he got behind the wheel of the Jaguar
and drove upstate.

Halfway there, he realized that he was out of uniform.
Joanna didn't care for the casual look. She didn't care for
this car, either. She had, a long time ago. At least, she'd
pretended she had.

The hell with it. It was too late to worry about and besides, it was one thing to pretend they hadn't been about to
get divorced and quite another to redo his life. He'd done
that for damned near four years and that had been three years
and a handful of months too many.

The grounds of the rehab center were crowded with patients and visitors, but he spotted Joanna as soon as he drove
through the gates. She was sitting on a stone bench beside
a dogwood tree that was just coming into flower, the creamy
blossoms a counterpoint to her dark hair. She was reading
a book and oblivious to anything around her, which was
typical of her. It was how she'd dealt with him during so

much of the time they'd been married, as if she were living on a separate planet.

It made him furious, which was stupid, because he'd gotten over giving a damn about how she acted a long time ago. Still, after he'd parked the car and walked back to where she was sitting, he had to force himself to smile.

"Hi."

She looked up, her dark eyes wide with surprise.

"David!"

"Why so shocked?" He sat down beside her. "I told you I'd be here today."

"Well, I know what you said, but…"

But he hadn't cared enough to come up all week. Not that it mattered to her if she saw him or not…

"But?"

Joanna shut the book and put it on the bench beside her. "Nothing," she said. "I guess you just caught me by surprise."

He waited for her to say something more. When she didn't, he cleared his throat.

"So, how are things going? Have you settled in?"

"Oh, yes. Everyone's very nice."

"Good. And are they helping you?"

"Have I remembered, do you mean?" Joanna got to her feet and he rose, too. They began walking slowly along a path that wound behind the main building. "No, not a thing. Everyone tells me to be patient."

"But it's hard."

"Yes." She looked up at him. "For you, too."

He knew he was supposed to deny it, but he couldn't.

"Yes," he said quietly, "for me, too."

Joanna nodded. "I just can't help wondering…"

"What?"

She shook her head. She'd promised herself not to say anything; the words had just slipped out.

"Nothing."

"Come on, Joanna, you were going to ask me something. What is it?"

"Well, I know I'm not a doctor or anything, but—" She hesitated. "Wouldn't my memory come back faster if I were in familiar surroundings?" He looked at her, saying nothing, and she spoke more quickly. "You don't know what it's like, David, not to be able to picture your own house. The furniture, or the colors of the walls…"

"You want to come home," he said.

Joanna looked up at him. There was no mistaking the sudden flatness in his voice.

"I just want to get my memory back," she said softly. "It's what you want, too, isn't it?"

A muscle flickered in his jaw. "It wouldn't work," he said carefully. "You need peace and quiet, someone to look after you. I'm hardly ever home before ten at night and even when I am, the phone's forever ringing, and the fax is going…"

A cold hand seemed to clamp around her heart.

"I understand," she said.

"Who would take care of you? I could hire a nurse, yes, but—"

"I don't need anyone to take care of me." Her voice took on an edge. "I'm an amnesiac, not an invalid."

"Well, I know, but what about therapy?"

"What about it?" she said with sudden heat. "I don't see how learning to paint by numbers or weave baskets is going to help my memory."

David stopped and clasped her shoulders. He turned her toward him.

"You don't really weave baskets, do you?"

She sighed. "No, not really."

"Good." A grin twitched across his mouth. "For a minute there, I thought Nurse Diesel might be breathing down our necks."

Joanna's mouth curved. "Don't even mention that movie when you're here," she said in an exaggerated whisper.

"They've got no sense of humor when it comes to things like that."

He laughed. "You said something?"

"Sure. The first day, an aide came to call for me. She said she was taking me to physical therapy and we got into this old, creaky elevator and headed for the basement. 'So,' I said, when the doors finally wheezed open, 'is this where you guys keep the chains and cattle prods?'" Joanna's eyes lit with laughter. "I thought she was going to go bonkers. I got a five minute lecture on the strides that have been made in mental health, blah, blah, blah..."

"Thanks for the warning."

"My pleasure."

They smiled at each other and then David cleared his throat, took Joanna's elbow politely, and they began walking again.

"What kind of therapy are you getting?"

"Oh, this and that. You can paint or sculpt in clay, and there's an hour of exercise in the pool and then a workout in the gym under the eye of a physical therapist—"

"Yeah, but there's nothing wrong with you physically."

"It's just the way things are done here. There's a routine and you follow it. Up at six, breakfast at six-thirty. An hour of painting or working with clay and then an hour in the pool before your morning appointment with your shrink."

"You see a psychiatrist, too?"

"Yes."

"Why?"

She made a face. "So far, to talk about how I'm going to adapt to my loss of memory. It didn't go over so well when I said I didn't want to adapt, that I wanted to get my memory back." She laughed. "Now I think the doctor's trying to figure why I'm always so hostile."

"That's ridiculous."

"Well, I said so, too, but she said—"

"I'll speak to the Director, Joanna. Someone must have forgotten to read your chart. You're not here for psychiatric counseling or for physical therapy, you're here to regain your memory.''

"Don't waste your breath.'' Joanna stepped off the path. David watched her as she kicked off her shoes and sank down on the grass. "Mmm,'' she said, leaning back on her hands, tilting her face up and closing her eyes, "doesn't the sun feel wonderful?''

"Wonderful,'' he said, while he tried to figure out if he'd ever before seen her do anything so out of character. Did she know she was probably going to get grass stains on her yellow silk skirt? He kicked off his sneakers and sat down beside her. "What do you mean, don't waste my breath?''

"I already spoke to the Director. And he said since nobody knew much about amnesia and since I was here, the best thing I could do would be to put myself in their hands. I suppose it makes sense.''

David nodded. "I suppose.''

Joanna opened her eyes and smiled at him. "But I swear, if Nurse Diesel comes tripping into the room, I'll brain her with a raffia basket.''

It stayed with him as he made the drive home.

Nurse Diesel.

It was a joke. He knew that. Bright Meadows was state of the art. It was about as far from a snake pit as you could get. The staff was terrific, the food was good—Joanna had joked that she'd already gained a pound though he couldn't see where. And what was wrong with spending some quiet time talking to a psychiatrist? And for the pool and all the rest…for a woman who used to spend half her day sweating on the machines at a trendy east side gym, physical therapy was a cinch.

His hands tightened on the wheel of the Jag.

But what did any of that have to do with helping her recover from amnesia? And that was the bottom line because until Joanna got her memory back, his life was stuck on hold.

Wouldn't my memory come back faster in familiar surroundings?

Maybe. On the other hand, maybe not. The last thing he wanted was to move his wife back into his life again, even if it was only on a temporary basis.

Besides, what he'd said about the house in Manhattan was true. It was nothing like Bright Meadows, with its big lawn, its sun-dappled pond, its bright rooms...

The house in Connecticut had all that, the lawns, the pond, the big, bright rooms. It had peace and quiet, birds singing in the gardens, it had everything including things that might stimulate Joanna's memory. They'd spent the first months of their marriage there and the days had been filled with joy and laughter...

Forget that. It was a stupid thought. He couldn't commute to the office from there, it was too far, even if he'd wanted to give it a try, which he didn't. He hated that damned house.

Joanna was better off where she was.

David stepped down harder on the gas.

She was much better off, and if that last glimpse he'd had of her as he left stayed with him for a couple of hours, so what? It had just been a trick of the light that seemed to have put the glint of tears in her eyes as she'd waved goodbye.

Even if it wasn't the light, what did he care?

He drove faster.

What in bloody hell did he care?

He drove faster still, until the old Jag was damned near flying, and then he muttered a couple of words he hadn't used since his days in the Corps, swerved the car onto the grass, swung it into a hard U-turn and headed back to Bright Meadows to tell his wife to pack her things, dump them into the back of the car and climb into the seat next to him so he could take her home.

Home to New York, because there wasn't a way in the world he would ever again take the almost ex-Mrs. Adams to Connecticut.

Not in this lifetime.

CHAPTER FOUR

IT STARTED raining, not long after David drove away from Bright Meadows for the second time.

He turned on the windshield wipers and Joanna listened to them whisper into the silence. The sound of the rain on the canvas roof and the tires hissing on the wet roadway was almost enough to lull her into a false sense of security.

Home. David was taking her home.

It was the last thing she'd ever expected, considering his reaction each time she'd suggested it, but now it was happening.

She was going home.

It was hard to believe that she'd stood on the lawn at Bright Meadows only a couple of hours ago, staring after David's car as it sped out the gate, telling herself that it was stupid to cry and stupider still to think that it wasn't her recovery he'd been thinking about when he'd insisted she was better off at the rehab center as much as it was the desire to keep her out of his life.

Why would her husband want to do that?

Before she'd even thought of an answer, she'd seen his car coming back up the drive. He'd pulled over, told her in brusque tones that he'd reconsidered what she'd said and that he'd decided she was right, she might get her memory back a lot faster if she were in familiar surroundings.

Joanna had felt almost giddy with excitement, even though he'd made it sound as if the change in plans was little more than an updated medical prescription.

"You go and pack," he'd said briskly, "while I do whatever needs doing to check you out of this place."

Before she knew it, she was sitting beside him on the

worn leather seat of the aged sports car as it flew along the highway toward home.

Whatever that might be like.

A shudder went through her. David looked at her. Actually, he wasn't so much looking at her as he was glowering. Her stomach clenched. Was he already regretting his decision?

"Are you cold, Joanna?"

"No," she said quickly, "not a bit." She tried hard to sound bright and perky. "I'm just excited."

"Well, don't get too excited. Corbett wouldn't approve if your blood pressure shot up."

He smiled, to make it clear he was only joking. Joanna smiled back but then she locked her hands together in her lap.

"You don't have to worry," she said quietly. "I'm not going to be a burden to you."

"I never suggested you would be."

"Well, no, but I want to be sure we have this straight. I'm not sick, David."

"I know that."

"And I'm not an invalid. I'm perfectly capable of taking care of myself."

He sighed and shifted his long legs beneath the dash.

"Did I ever say you weren't?"

"I just want to be sure you understand that you're not going to have to play nursemaid."

"I'm not concerned about it," he said patiently. "Besides, there'll be plenty of people to look after you."

"I don't need looking after." She heard the faint edge in her words and she took a deep breath and told herself to calm down. "You won't have to hire a nurse or a companion or whatever."

"Well, we'll try it and see how it goes."

"It'll go just fine. I'm looking forward to doing things for myself."

"As long as you don't push too hard," he said. "I want you to promise to take it easy for a week or two."

"I will." Joanna looked down at her folded hands. "Thank you," she said softly.

"For what?"

"For changing your mind and agreeing to take me...to take me home."

He shrugged his shoulders. "There's no need to thank me. The more I thought about it, the more sensible it seemed. Anyway, I knew it was what you wanted."

But not what he wanted. The unspoken words hung in the air between them. After a moment, Joanna sighed.

"Is it much farther?"

"Only another half hour or so." He glanced over at her. "You look exhausted, Jo. Why don't you put your head back, close your eyes and rest for a while?"

"I'm not tired, I'm just..." She stopped in midsentence. How stupid she was. David's suggestion had been meant as much for himself as for her. He might be taking her home but he didn't have to spend an hour and a half trying to make polite conversation. "You're right," she said, and shot him a quick smile, "I think I will."

Joanna lay her head back and shut her eyes. This was better anyway, not just for him but for her. Let him think she was tired. Otherwise, she might just blurt out the truth.

The closer they got to their destination, the more nervous she felt.

Nervous? She almost laughed.

Be honest, she told herself. You're terrified.

All her babbling about wanting to go home was just that. What good could come of returning to a house she wouldn't recognize with a man she didn't know?

Mars might be a better place than "home."

She looked at David from beneath the sweep of her lashes. Oh, that rigid jaw. Those tightly clamped lips. The hands, white-knuckled on the steering wheel.

She wasn't the only one with second thoughts. It was clear

that her husband regretted his spur-of-the-moment decision, too.

Why? Had their marriage really been so awful? It must have been. There was no other way to explain the way he treated her, the careful politeness, the distant, unemotional behavior.

The only real emotion he'd shown her had been the night in her hospital room, when he'd kissed her.

The memory made her tingle. That kiss…that passionate, angry kiss. It had left her shaken, torn between despising his touch and the almost uncontrollable desire to go into his arms and give herself up to the heat.

Joanna's breath hitched. What was the matter with her? She'd been so caught up in wanting to go home that she hadn't given a moment's thought to what it might really mean. She and David were husband and wife. Did he expect…would he expect her to…? He hadn't so much as touched her since that night in the hospital, not even to kiss her cheek. Surely, he didn't think…

She shivered.

"Jo? What is it?"

She sat up straight, looked at David, then fixed her eyes on the ribbon of road unwinding ahead.

"I…I think you're right. I am feeling a little cold."

"I'll turn on the heat." He reached for a knob on the dashboard. "You always said that the heating system in this old heap was better suited to polar bears than people."

"Did I?" She smiled and stroked her hand lightly over the seat. "Actually, I can't imagine I ever said an unkind word about this beautiful old car."

He looked over at her. "Beautiful?"

"Mmm. What kind is it, anyway? A Thunderbird? A Corvette?"

"It's a '60 Jaguar XK 150," he said quietly.

"Ah," she said, her smile broadening, "an antique. Have you had it long?"

"Not long." His tone was stilted. "Just a few years."

"It must take lots of work, keeping an old car like this."

"Yeah." His hands tightened on the steering wheel. "Yeah, it does."

Her fingers moved across the soft leather again. "I'll bet you don't trust anybody to work on it."

David shot her a sharp look. "What makes you say that?"

"I don't know. It just seems logical. Why? Am I wrong?"

"No." He stared out at the road, forcing himself to concentrate on the slick asphalt. "No, you hit it right on the head. I do whatever needs doing on this car myself."

"Untouched by human hands, huh?" she said with a quick smile.

A muscle knotted in his jaw. "Somebody else who worked on the car with me used to say that, a long time ago."

"A super-mechanic, I'll bet."

"Yeah," he said briskly, "something like that." There was a silence and then he shifted his weight in his seat. "Will you look at that rain? It's coming down in buckets."

Joanna sighed. For a minute or two, it had looked as if they were going to have a real conversation.

"Yes," she said, "it certainly is."

David nodded. "Looks like the weatherman was wrong, as usual."

Such banal chitchat, Joanna thought, but better by far than uncomfortable silence.

"Still," she said brightly, "that's good, isn't it? One of the nurses was saying that it had been a dry Spring."

David sprang on the conversational lifeline as eagerly as she had.

"Dry isn't the word for it. The tulips in the park barely bloomed. And you know those roses you planted three summers ago? The pink ones? They haven't even…"

"I planted roses? I thought you said we lived in New York."

"We do." His hands tightened on the wheel. "But we have another place in…" His words trailed off in midsentence. "Hell," he muttered, "I'm sorry, Jo. I keep putting my foot in it today. I shouldn't have mentioned the damned roses or the house."

"Why not?"

"What do you mean, why not?" He glared at her. "Because you can't possibly remember either one, that's why not."

"That doesn't mean you shouldn't talk about them. If we're going to avoid mention of anything I might not remember, what will there be left to talk about? Nothing but the weather," Joanna said, answering her own question, "and not even we can talk about the possibility of rain all the time."

"I suppose you're right."

"Of course I'm right! I don't expect you to censor everything you say. Besides, maybe it'll help if we—if you talk about the past."

"I just don't want to put any pressure on you, Joanna. You know what the doctors advised, that it was best to let your memory come back on its own."

"If it comes back at all." She flashed him a dazzling smile, one that couldn't quite mask the sudden tremor in her voice. "They also said there were no guarantees."

"You're going to be fine," he said with more conviction than he felt.

Joanna turned on him in sudden fury. "Don't placate me, David. Dropping platitudes all over the place isn't going to…" The rush of angry words stuttered to a halt. "Sorry," she whispered. "I didn't mean…"

A jagged streak of lightning lit the road ahead. The rain, which had been a steady gray curtain, suddenly roared against the old car. Fat drops, driven by the wind, flew through Joanna's window. She grabbed for the crank but it wouldn't turn. David made a face. He reached across her, grasped it and forced it to move.

"Got to fix that thing," he muttered. "Sorry."

Joanna nodded. She was sorry, he was sorry. They were

so polite, like cautious acquaintances. But they weren't acquaintances, they were husband and wife.

Dear heaven, there was something terribly wrong in this
relationship.

Her throat tightened. Whatever had possessed her to want
to go home with this man?

She turned her face to the rain-blurred window and
wished she had stayed at Bright Meadows. It hadn't been
home, but at least it had been safe.

David looked at his wife, then at the road.

Well, he thought, his hand tightening on the steering
wheel, wasn't that interesting?

His soft-spoken, demure wife had shown her temper
again.

A faint smile touched his lips.

Four years ago, that quick, fiery display wouldn't have
surprised him. Not that the Joanna he'd married had been
bad-tempered. She just hadn't been afraid to let her emotions
show. In his world, where people seemed to think that sort
of thing wasn't proper, his wife's willingness to show her
feelings had been refreshing and endearing.

Not that it had lasted. Not that it could. David's hands
clamped more tightly on the steering wheel. It had been a
pose. His beloved wife had worn a mask to win his heart
and once she'd decided it was safe to let it slip, she had.

As Morgana had pointed out, no one could keep up the
innocent act forever.

He just wished to hell he knew who this was, seated beside him. This Joanna wasn't the woman he'd married nor
the one he was divorcing. Everything about her was so familiar... And so unfamiliar. He'd known it ever since she'd
regained consciousness after the accident, but he was uncomfortably aware of it today, starting with the minute she'd
walked to the Jag to start the trip home.

He'd waited for her to make a face and ask where the
Bentley was but she hadn't. Well, why would she? he'd

reminded himself; she didn't remember how she'd felt about either car.

What he hadn't expected was the way she'd smiled when she'd settled in beside him, how she'd asked if the car really could go as fast as it looked. And then all those musings about how he probably never let anyone but him work on it.

That had struck too close to home. The Jag had been their project. They'd bought it together, tackled its restoration together, Joanna learning as fast as he could teach her until she was damned near as good at puttering under the hood as he was.

A bittersweet memory sprang into his head. They'd spent the week in Connecticut. He'd been called back to the city on business that he'd disposed of in record time and he'd gotten back to the house early, to find Joanna bent over the Jag's engine with her coverall-clad bottom in the air.

"Oh, David," she'd said, laughing as he'd grabbed her and whirled her around, "I was going to surprise you with this new—"

He'd never let her finish the sentence. He'd kissed her instead, and swung her up into his arms and carried her to their bedroom where he'd stripped away the bulky coverall to find her wearing nothing underneath but a tiny pair of white lace panties that he'd eased down her long, lovely legs...

He glanced over at those legs now. Her skirt had climbed up during the drive so that it was mid-thigh. She hadn't thought to adjust it. She hadn't thought to adjust her hair, either; the wind had tugged several strands loose from their moorings of pins and lacquer so that dark wisps curled sexily against her throat. David's gaze drifted lower. The quick burst of raindrops had dampened her silk blouse, the chill kiss of it tightening her nipples so they thrust against the fabric.

The Joanna he knew would have surely been aware of that. She would have fixed her hair, tugged down her skirt, crossed her arms over her breasts if she'd had to, done whatever it took to keep him from noticing that she was female, that she had sexual reactions if not sexual instincts.

David forced all his powers of concentration back to the rain-slicked road.

He had to stop thinking of Joanna as if she weren't Joanna. She had lost her memory but he had not lost his. He knew her. He knew the real woman.

And he had the increasingly uncomfortable feeling that he should have left her back at Bright Meadows, where she belonged.

The city glittered beneath the rain. It was beautiful, Joanna thought, and there was a vague familiarity to it the way there is to a place you've never visited but only seen in photographs.

David gave her a comforting smile.

"Just another couple of blocks," he said.

She nodded. Her hands lay in her lap, so tightly clasped that she could feel her nails digging into her flesh.

Would she recognize something? Would there be a moment when her memory would come rushing back?

In a movie, perhaps. But this was the real world, not one played out on the silver screen. The car made its way through clots of heavy traffic, turned onto Fifth Avenue, then down a side street. It was quiet here, the curb lined with plane trees in leaf, the town houses shouldering against each other in a way that spoke of money, power and elegant antiquity.

David pulled the car to the curb and shut off the engine. Joanna stared blankly at a building she had never seen before.

She'd asked him to tell her about their house when they'd first set out from Bright Meadows. Now, she could see that he'd described the place right down to the last detail. There was the gray stone facade and the windows with their black shutters; there were the black wrought-iron banisters and the stone steps leading to the front door.

Her stomach knotted in panic. "David," she said, swinging toward him...

But he'd already opened the car door and stepped out into the pouring rain.

"Stay put," he said, raising his voice over the deluge. "I'll go inside and get an umbrella and then I'll put the car away."

She flung her door open and got out. "No. No, wait..."

Her voice died away and she stood staring at the house, oblivious to the cold beat of the rain.

This is our home, she thought, mine and David's.

Her stomach twisted tighter. I want to go back to Bright Meadows, she thought desperately, oh, please...

"Dammit, Jo, what are you doing?"

David's voice broke through her frantic thoughts. He put his arm around her waist and began urging her forward.

"Come inside," he growled, "before you're soaked to the skin!"

She shook her head and pulled back against the tug of his arm. She didn't want to go into that house. She hated this place, *hated* it!

"For god's sake," David muttered, and he swung her into his arms. Caught off balance, she had no choice but to fling her arms around his neck.

Time seemed to stand still. The wet street, the rain...everything faded to insignificance. She was aware only of the feel of her husband's hard shoulders as she clutched them, the warmth of his powerful body against hers.

His eyes met hers; his arms tightened around her...

The door to the house swung open. "Sir," a voice said, "we had no idea..."

The moment of awareness shattered. "No," David said coolly, as he strode up the steps, "neither did I."

A tall, spare man with thinning hair stood in the doorway.

Joanna recognized him as the chauffeur who'd driven her to Bright Meadows. Now, seeing him at the entrance to the town house, her mouth fell open in surprise.

"That's the limousine driver," she whispered to David. "What's he doing here?"

"His name is Hollister, Joanna. He lives here."

"Lives here?" she repeated stupidly.

"Madam," Hollister said, inclining his head as David moved past him, "welcome home."

"Hollister," David said, "is our chauffeur."

"You mean…that huge car we took to Bright Meadows belongs to us?"

"It does. Hollister drives it." He shot the man a wry smile. "And when he's not driving the Bentley, he's our butler."

"Our butler?" Joanna said, even more stupidly, craning her neck for a last glimpse of Hollister's bony, expressionless face. "David." Her voice fell to a whisper. "David, please, put me—"

"How do you do, madam."

A stern-faced woman in a dark dress stepped out of the gloomy darkness of the oak-paneled foyer.

"And this," David said, "is Mrs. Timmons. Our housekeeper."

A housekeeper, too? Joanna forced a smile to her lips.

"Hello, Mrs. Timmons." She bent her head toward David and this time there was an urgency to her whispered words. "David, really, what will they think? If you'd just put me down—"

"And that," David said, as he started up a flight of long stairs, "is Ellen."

Joanna caught a flash of ruffled white apron, red hair and wide blue eyes.

"Madam," a girlish voice said shyly.

"Ellen," Joanna repeated numbly. She stared over David's shoulder as Ellen smiled and bobbed a curtsy. *A curtsy*? Did people really still do such things?

"A butler? A housekeeper? And a maid?" she whispered incredulously as they reached the second floor hall. "Do all those people really work for us?"

David smiled tightly. "You might say that."

"What do you mean, I might say…"

"Except for Mrs. Timmons, it's probably more accurate to say that the staff is yours." He shouldered open a door, stepped through it, and hit the light switch on the wall beside him with his elbow. "The staff," he said, lowering her to her feet, "and this bedroom."

Whatever questions Joanna had intended to ask flew out of her head as she stared in disbelief at her surroundings.

Last night she'd watched a program on television at Bright Meadows, something about Versailles or Fontainebleau; one of the glittering French palaces. Now, she wished she'd paid closer attention.

Whoever had designed this room must have taken their cue from a palace. The walls were covered with cream silk that matched the drapes at the windows and the coverings and hangings on the canopied bed. The floor was laid with richly patterned rugs. The furniture was white brushed with gold, except for a mirrored vanity table on the opposite wall. Its glass surface was covered with an assortment of stoppered bottles and jars, enough to stock a cosmetics shop.

The room was feminine and deeply sensual…and yet it wasn't. It was like a stage set; Joanna had the feeling that if she looked behind the walls and the furniture, she'd find out they were made of painted canvas.

She turned toward David in bewilderment. "This can't be my room."

He looked at her, his expression unreadable. "It is, I assure you. Now, get out of that wet dress while I go and get Ellen."

"No. I mean, I'd rather you didn't. I need a couple of minutes to…to…" She gave a hesitant laugh. "David, are you sure this room is…?"

He smiled sardonically. "It certainly isn't mine. I'm afraid vanities and frills aren't my style."

"You mean, we don't share a…"

She caught herself before the next word had tumbled out but it was too late. David's expression changed; she saw it before he turned away.

"No," he said. "We don't."

"Oh."

Oh? she thought, staring after him as he went into the adjoining bathroom. She'd just found out that she slept in a room only Marie Antoinette would have envied, that she and her husband didn't share a bedroom, and "Oh" was all she could manage?

Not that that part disappointed her. Sharing a room with a stranger wasn't what she wanted at all, it was only that the news had caught her by surprise…

"I've started the water in the tub."

She looked up. She could hear the water thundering in the bathroom as David came toward her. He'd pushed up the sleeves of his blue shirt; his forearms were muscled and tanned and dusted with dark hair.

"Joanna? I said—"

"I heard you." She cleared her throat. "Thank you."

"There's nothing to thank me for. Running a bath doesn't take any great effort."

"I meant…thank you for what you've done. For bringing me…home."

"Don't be silly," he said briskly. "You've every right to be here. Now, come on. Get out of those wet things and into a hot tub."

"David…" She reached out and put her hand lightly on his arm. "I know this isn't easy for either one of us. But I…I'm sure that my memory will come back soon."

His muscles tightened under her fingers. "Are you saying things seem familiar?"

"No," she admitted, "not yet. But they will. They have to," she said, with just a hint of desperation. "My memory will come back and then you and I can go back to living our normal lives.''

David's eyes, as deep and as green as a winter sea, met hers.

''Our normal lives,'' he said.

''Yes.'' She gave a forced little laugh. ''Whatever that may mean.''

A muscle knotted in his jaw. For just a moment, she was certain he was going to say something, something she didn't think she wanted to hear, but the seconds ticked away and then he nodded.

''Of course,'' he said politely. ''Now go on, take your bath. I'll tell Mrs. Timmons to make you a light supper and serve you here, on a tray.''

''Alone, you mean?''

''I think it's best, don't you? I have some work to do and this way you can just get out of the tub, put on a robe and relax.''

Joanna felt the sharp prick of tears behind her eyes, and felt immeasurably silly.

She was home, which was what she'd wanted, and her husband had shown nothing but kindness and consideration. He'd carried her up the stairs, drawn her bath and now he was offering her the chance to end the day quietly...

''Joanna?''

She looked up and smiled brightly. ''That's very thoughtful of you, David. Yes, please, if you don't mind I think I'd like to have my supper alone. I'm...I'm awfully tired. You understand.''

''Of course.'' He walked to the door and looked back at her, his hand on the knob. ''I'll see you in the morning, then.''

''In the morning,'' she said, ''sure.''

She held her bright smile until the door had shut after him. Then she walked slowly into the bathroom, sat down on the edge of the oversize circular tub and shut off the taps. The air was steamy, almost thick, and all at once the tears she'd fought against moments ago flooded her eyes and streamed down her face.

David was everything a woman could hope for.

But he wanted nothing to do with her. He didn't love her. He didn't even like her. She was not welcome in this house or in his life.

And she had absolutely no idea why.

CHAPTER FIVE

JOANNA had told David she'd see him the next morning, but he was gone by the time she came down the stairs at eight o'clock.

That was fine. The last thing she wanted to do was try and make small talk on her first day in this unfamiliar place that seemed more like a museum than a home.

She had breakfast under the cool, watchful eye of Mrs. Timmons, who seemed to offer silent disapproval of a meal made up of half a grapefruit and a cup of black coffee. Then she wandered from room to room, waiting for something to strike a familiar chord.

Nothing did.

At noon, as she was sitting in solitary splendor at a dining room table designed to seat twelve, David telephoned.

Hollister brought her the telephone.

How was she feeling? David asked politely. Did she need anything?

Joanna looked around her. A crown and a scepter, she thought, suppressing a rise of hysterical laughter.

"Don't worry about me," she said, very calmly, "I'm fine."

The conversation took no more than a minute. When it ended, Hollister gave a little bow and took the phone away. Mrs. Timmons marched in after him, bearing a huge lobster salad.

"You used to like this," she said in a crisp, no-nonsense voice, "or aren't I supposed to mention that kind of stuff?"

The frank, unsmiling face and blunt words were as out of place in this elegant setting as they were welcome. Joanna smiled.

"Mention whatever you wish," she said, "otherwise I'm liable to end up biting into cardboard, just to find out if it was ever to my taste."

The housekeeper almost smiled. "Fine," she said, and clomped out.

After lunch, Joanna went outside and sat in the pocket garden behind the house. It was a sad, forlorn little place with one scrawny maple doing its best to survive.

Just like me, she thought, and she shuddered and went back inside and up to her room. She napped, woke up and read a magazine, then wandered through the rooms some more.

Mrs. Timmons was in the kitchen, slicing vegetables at the sink.

"Anything I can do to help?" Joanna asked from the doorway.

The housekeeper looked at her as if she were suffering not just from amnesia but from insanity.

"No, thank you, madam," she said, and went back to her work.

At six, David phoned again, with apologies. He'd tried everything to get out of a sudden meeting but it was impossible. Would Joanna mind having dinner without him?

She bit her lip to keep from saying that she'd already had dinner without him last night; what would be the difficulty in doing it again?

"Of course not," she said briskly. "We'll have dessert and coffee together, when you get home."

But he didn't get home until almost ten, and by then she was in bed.

She heard his footsteps first on the stairs, then coming down the hall. They stopped just outside her closed door and her heart stopped, too.

Joanna held her breath, imagining her husband's hand on the knob, imagining the door slowly opening...

The footsteps moved on. Further down the hall, a door

opened, then softly shut and she fell back against the pillows in relief.

It *was* relief she felt, wasn't it?

Of course it was. What else could it be?

He was waiting for her in the dining room when she came down the next morning.

"Good morning," he said. "Sorry about last night."

"No problem," she said with a shrug of her shoulders. "I needed an early night anyway. I'm not operating on all burners yet."

David nodded. His hair was damp, as if he'd just finished showering, and suddenly she remembered what he'd said about running in the park early each morning.

"Were you out running?"

"Yes. I didn't wake you, did I? Going out so early, I mean."

"No, no, I slept like a log. I was only going to say..."

"What?"

What, indeed? They'd already talked about running together and he'd made it crystal clear that he hadn't wanted her company in the past. Why on earth would he want it now?

"I was only going to say that...that I'll have to get out for a walk, considering we're so near the park."

"Next week."

"What?"

"I said—"

"I heard what you said, David, I just didn't believe it. Or am I in the habit of asking your permission before I do something?"

His mouth twisted. "I only meant that you should wait until you're stronger."

"I am not ill," she said, her eyes flashing. "I've told you, I'm not—"

"An invalid. Yes, so you have. But going out alone, in a neighborhood that's strange to you, might be daunting."

She smiled through stiff lips. "New York still has street signs, doesn't it? Believe me, I'll find my way home without sprinkling bread crumbs behind me."

To her surprise, he laughed. "I'll bet you will." His smile faded. They stood looking at each other in an increasingly uncomfortable silence and then he cleared his throat. "Well, it's getting late. You'll forgive me if I hurry off, Jo, won't you?"

"Of course."

She smiled brightly as he picked up a leather briefcase from a table near the door. After a barely perceptible hesitation, he bent and dropped a light kiss on her forehead.

"Have a good day," he said. And he was gone.

A good day, Joanna thought. Tears stung her eyes.

"Mrs. Adams?"

Joanna blinked hard, took a steadying breath and turned around to see the housekeeper standing in the doorway to the dining room.

"Yes, Mrs. Timmons?"

"Your breakfast is ready. Half a grapefruit and black coffee, as usual."

"Oh. Thank you. I'll be... Mrs. Timmons?"

"Madam?"

"Was that my usual? My breakfast, I mean. Grapefruit and black coffee?"

The housekeeper's lips thinned in disapproval. "For as long as it mattered, it was."

"Do you think we might try something different?"

Mrs. Timmons's brows lifted a little. "We could, if you wish. What would you like?"

Joanna blushed. "I don't really know. I mean...I'm open to suggestion."

"Cinnamon toast," the housekeeper said, her eyes on Joanna's face, "orange juice, and hot chocolate."

"Hot chocolate!" Joanna laughed. "No, I don't think so."

"Coffee, then, but with sugar and cream. How does that sound, madam?"

"It sounds lovely." Joanna took a breath. "Do you have a minute to talk, Mrs. Timmons?"

The housekeeper's eyes narrowed. "If you wish."

Joanna ran the tip of her tongue over her lips. "Well, to begin with, I'd be pleased if you called me 'Joanna.'"

Mrs. Timmons's face paled. "I couldn't possibly do that, madam."

"Then call me 'Mrs. Adams.' Just don't…don't keep calling me 'madam.'" Joanna gave a little laugh. "I have enough trouble thinking of myself as 'Joanna,' let alone as anybody called 'madam.'"

The older woman's mouth opened, then shut again. After a moment, she nodded.

"I'll try and remember that, ma…Mrs. Adams."

"And I was wondering… Do you know who…uh, who furnished this house?"

"Why, you did, of course."

Joanna sighed. The answer was unpleasant, but not exactly a surprise.

"There's just one last thing…" She hesitated. "What did I usually do with my days?"

"Breakfast at eight, your health club at ten, and then, of course, your afternoons were quite full."

"Full? Do you mean…do I have some kind of part-time job?"

Joanna had the uneasy feeling that it was all Mrs. Timmons could do to keep from laughing.

"Certainly not, Mrs. Adams. You had your lunches, your charity commitments, your board meetings."

"Oh. I see."

"And then there were your three times a week hairdresser's appointments—"

"I had my hair done three times a week?" Joanna said, her voice rising in disbelief.

"You have a standing appointment on Friday at the nail salon, and, of course, there are your massages..."

"My massages," Joanna echoed faintly. She wanted to laugh. Or maybe she wanted to cry. It was hard to know which.

"You might wish to check your appointment book. Perhaps it's in the library. Or in your desk, in your bedroom."

"That's all right," Joanna said quickly, "I'll, ah, I'll forego all that for a while, until I'm feeling more like my old self..."

Her old self, who was beginning to sound more and more like one absolutely, monumentally pretentious bore.

The day was a duplicate of the one before.

She wandered through the house. She read. She sat in the garden. She had lunch, took a nap, and woke as restless as a tiger.

In midafternoon, she took a light jacket and headed for the door. Hollister, appearing from out of nowhere, reached it the same instant.

"If madam wishes to go anywhere," he said, "I am at her disposal."

"Thank you," Joanna said politely, "but I'm going for a walk."

"A walk, madam?"

"Yes," she said. "You know, left foot, right foot...a walk. In the park."

"Madam might wish to reconsider..."

Joanna yanked open the door. "Madam is out of here," she said, and slammed the door behind her.

The walk cleared her head.

She'd snapped at David this morning, and then at Hollister. There was no reason for it; everyone meant well, and she knew it.

It was she who was being difficult, not the staff or her husband.

It was just that it all seemed so strange…a wry smile curved over her lips as she made her way up the stairs to her room. This was the life she'd led, but was this the life she'd wanted?

It didn't seem possible.

Ellen was in the bathroom, pouring perfumed oil into the tub.

"There you are, ma'am. I'm just running your bath."

Joanna sighed and sat down on the edge of the bed.

"Ellen, do you think you could stop calling me 'ma'am'? I keep expecting to turn around and find the Queen of England hovering just over my shoulder."

Ellen giggled. "As you wish, madam."

"What I wish," Joanna said, "is that you'd call me Mrs. Adams."

"Oh, but, madam… You were very specific when you hired me, you said I was to address you as 'ma'am' or 'madam.'"

"Just forget whatever I said," Joanna said, more sharply than she'd intended. "I mean…things have changed. Besides, if you call me 'Mrs. Adams' it will help me get used to the sound of my own name."

"Yes, Mrs. Adams."

Joanna smiled. "Thank you. Now, what's this about running a bath?"

"Well, you bathe every day at this time, ma…Mrs. Adams. Then you dress for dinner."

"Dress?" Joanna looked down at herself. She was wearing a navy dress and matching kidskin pumps. Dreary, she thought, and frowned.

"Yes, Mrs. Adams."

"As in, long gown, white gloves and tiara?"

"Not quite so formal," Ellen said seriously. "A short dress, no gloves, and I suppose I could find a comb for your chignon, if you like."

"Do I do this every night? Dress for dinner, I mean?"

"Oh, yes, Mrs. Adams, you do."

Joanna's smile faded. A morning spent doing a lot of nothing, then an afternoon doing more of the same, followed by a soak in a perfumed bath while she considered what dress to wear for dinner.

What a useless existence.

Was this what it meant to be David Adams's wife? She thought of how he'd looked on Sunday, when he'd taken her away from Bright Meadows. The faded jeans, so worn and snug they'd outlined his body, the sweatshirt, straining over his broad shoulders. She thought of his admission that he never let anyone work on his car except him.

Why would a man like that marry a woman who made an art of doing nothing?

"My—my husband dresses for dinner, too?"

"Oh, yes. Mr. Adams showers and changes to a dark suit." Ellen sighed. "I think it's just so old-fashioned and romantic."

Old-fashioned. Romantic. Joanna's pulse quickened. Perhaps she was getting the wrong picture. Dressing for dinner didn't have to be stuffy, it could be everything Ellen had just called it.

"All right," she said, "I'll tell you what. I'll shower, and you pick a dress for me to wear tonight."

"Shower? But—"

"Trust me, Ellen. Unless I'm shivering cold or dying of the flu, I'm not a bath person."

The maid looked at her, her face puzzled. Two out of two, Joanna thought, remembering the way Mrs. Timmons had looked at her this morning. Neither her maid nor her housekeeper could fit the present Joanna Adams inside the skin of the old, and if you added Joanna Adams herself, the score went to a perfect three out of three.

It was a sobering, even frightening, thought.

*   *   *

At seven, dressed in black *peau de soie*, Joanna started down the stairs.

The dress wasn't much to her liking—it was blousey, almost shapeless, not short enough to be sexy or long enough to be fashionable, and it made her feel twice her age. But then, that description pretty much fit everything in her closet.

Why on earth had she bought all that clothing?

She'd as much as asked the question of Ellen, who'd shrugged.

"You shopped at all the best stores, Mrs. Adams."

"Did I?" Joanna had said softly, staring into the mirror.

Maybe she'd forgotten more than the details of her own life, she thought as she reached the bottom of the staircase; maybe she'd forgotten the tenets of high fashion.

She hung on to that thought as she paused in the doorway to the library. She could see David waiting for her before the fireplace, his back to her, one foot up on the edge of the stone hearth, his hands tucked into the pockets of his trousers.

What a handsome man he was, even from this angle. Those incredible shoulders. Those long legs and that tight bottom…

Her taste in furniture, clothes and hairstyles might be in doubt. But her taste in men seemed to have been impeccable.

David turned around.

"Joanna," he said.

Color flew into her cheeks.

"David." She swallowed dryly. "Hello."

His gaze swept over her. She waited for him to say something complimentary about her appearance but he didn't. She studied his face, trying to read his expression, but it was like trying to read the face of a statue.

"Well," she said brightly, "how was your day?"

"It was fine," he said evenly. "How was yours?"

Her heart sank. They were going to have another one of their standard, oh-so-polite conversations. How was your day? he'd asked and she was supposed to say it was fine, it was pleasant, it was…

"Dull."

David's eyebrows lifted. "Dull?"

"Well, yes. I didn't do anything."

His eyes narrowed. "You did something. You went for a walk."

Her head came up. "Ah, I see Hollister reported in, did he?"

"Hollister was only following orders."

"You mean, you told him to spy on me?"

David ran his hand through his hair. "It's been a long day, Jo. Let's not quarrel."

"Do we?" Joanna said quickly. "Quarrel, I mean?"

"No," he said, after a pause, "not really." It was true. Even their decision to divorce had been reached in a civilized way. No raised voices, no anger…no regrets. "Why do you ask?"

Because at least, if we quarreled, there was something more than this terrible nothingness between us…

She sighed. "No reason. I just wondered."

"Look, I'm only trying to make sure you don't overdo."

She sighed again. "I know."

"Before you know it, you'll be phoning up old friends, going to lunch, maybe even attending one or two of those meetings of yours."

"Yuck."

"Yuck?" David laughed. "Did you say 'yuck'?"

She blushed. "I meant to say that, uh, that doesn't sound very exciting, either."

Why had she let the conversation take this turn? David was watching her with a sudden intensity that made her feel like a mouse under the eye of a hungry cat. There was no way she could explain what she felt to him when she couldn't even explain it to herself.

"Don't pay any attention to me," she said with a little laugh. "I've probably been lying around feeling sorry for myself for too long." She turned away from him, searching desperately for a diversion. Her gaze fell on the built-in bar across the room. "What great-looking hors d'oeuvres," she said, hurrying toward them. "Cheese, and olives...what's this?"

"*Chèvre*," David said as she picked up a tiny cracker spread with a grainy white substance and popped it into her mouth.

"*Chèvre*?"

"Goat cheese."

Joanna stared at him. "Goat cheese?" Her nose wrinkled.

"Yeah. You love the stuff."

She shuddered, snatched up a cocktail napkin, and wiped her mouth.

"Not anymore."

He grinned. "It's even worse than it sounds. That's not just goat cheese, it's goat cheese rolled in ash."

"Ash?" she repeated in amazement. "As in, what's on the end of a cigarette?"

His grin widened. "I don't think so, but does it really matter?"

"You're right, it doesn't. Ash. And goat cheese." She laughed. "What will they think of next?"

"Chocolate-dipped tofu," he said solemnly. Her eyes widened and he held up his hand. "Scout's honor. It was part of the buffet at a business dinner last week. The Halloran merger. You remem... A deal I've been working on."

Her smile slipped, but only a little. "And how was the chocolate-dipped tofu?"

"I didn't touch the stuff. Morgana tried it and said it was great, but you know..." He frowned. "Sorry, Jo. I keep forgetting. Morgana is my P.A."

"Your...?"

"Personal Assistant."

Joanna nodded. "Oh. And she—she went to this dinner with you?"

"Of course." He hesitated. "She'd like to stop by and

see you. She's wanted to, ever since the accident, but I told her I wasn't sure if you were up to seeing visitors, even when they're old friends.''

Old friends? A woman named Morgana, who spent more time with her husband than she did? His assistant? His personal assistant?

"That was thoughtful of you, David. Please tell—Morgana—that I need just a little more time, would you?"

"Of course."

Joanna smiled at him, her lips curving up softly, and he realized that she'd inadvertently wiped away all that bright red lipstick she favored and he despised. Her mouth was full, pink and softly inviting, and he suddenly wondered what she'd do if leaned down and kissed it. He wouldn't touch her; he'd just kiss her, stroke the tip of his tongue across that sweet, lush flesh...

Hell!

"Well," he said briskly, "how about a drink?"

He didn't wait for an answer. Instead, he poured some bourbon for himself and sherry for Joanna. Her fingers closed around the delicate stem of the glass as he handed it to her.

"To your recovery," he said, raising his glass.

She echoed the sentiment, then took a sip of her drink. The pale gold liquid slipped down her throat and she grimaced.

"What's wrong?" David said. "Has the sherry gone bad?"

"It's probably just me. This is just a little bit dry for my taste, that's all."

He looked at her. "Is it?"

"But it's good," she said quickly. "Really."

"Come on, Jo. I can see that you don't like it."

She hesitated. "But...but I used to," she said in a suddenly small voice, "didn't I?"

"Tastes change," he said with studied casualness. "I'll pour you something else. What would you prefer?"

A picture popped instantly into her head. A bottle, dark amber in color, with a red and white label...

"Jo?"

She smiled uneasily. "I know this is going to sound ridiculous, but...I just thought of something called Pete's Wicked Ale."

David went very still. "Did you?"

"Isn't that crazy? Who'd name something... What's the matter?"

"You used to drink Pete's." His voice was low, almost a whisper. "A long time ago, before you decided that sherry was...that you preferred sherry to ale."

Joanna began to tremble. "Oh, God!"

"Easy." David took the glass from her hand. He led her to the sofa and helped her sit. "Put your head down and take a deep breath."

"I'm...I'm OK."

"You're not OK, you're as white as a sheet."

"I just...what's happening to me, David?" She lifted her face to his and stared at him through eyes that had gone from violet to black.

"You're remembering things, that's all."

"It's more than that." Her voice shook. "I feel as if I'm trapped inside a black tunnel and—and every now and then I look up and I see a flash of light, but it never lasts long enough for me to really see anything."

"Dammit, Joanna, put your head down!" David put his hand on her hair and forced her face toward her knees. "I knew this would happen if you went sailing off as if nothing had happened to you."

"I'm not sick!" She shoved at his hand and leaped to her feet. "Didn't you listen to anything I said? I'm—I'm lost, David, lost, and I can't...I can't..."

Her eyes rolled up into her head and she began to slump to the floor. David cursed, caught her in his arms, and strode from the dining room.

"Ellen," he bellowed. "Mrs. Timmons!"

The housekeeper and the maid came running. When Mrs. Timmons saw David hurrying up the stairs with Joanna in his arms, her hands flew to her mouth.

"Oh, my Lord, Mr. David, what happened?"

"Ellen, you get some ice. Mrs. Timmons, you call the doctor. Tell him my wife's fainted and I want him here now."

"Yes, sir. I'll do my best but it's after hours and—"

"Just get him, dammit!" David shouldered open the door to Joanna's room. Her eyes fluttered open as he lay her down gently on the bed.

"David?" she whispered. "What...what happened?"

"You're all right," he said gently. "You fainted, that's all."

"Fainted." She made a sound he supposed was a laugh. God, her face was as pale as the pillow sham. "I couldn't have fainted. It's—it's so Victorian."

"Sir?" David looked around. Ellen was standing in the doorway, her eyes wide, with a basin of ice and a towel.

"That's fine, Ellen. Just bring that to me—thank you. And shut the door after you when you leave."

Joanna stared up at him, her face still pale. "I can't believe I fainted."

"Well, you did. You overdid," he said grimly. "Too much, too soon, that's all. Can you turn your head a bit? That's the way."

"My head hurts," she said, and winced. "What are you doing?"

"What does it look like I'm doing? I'm getting you out of this dress."

She caught his hand but he shrugged her off and went on opening the tiny jet buttons that ran down the front of the black silk dress.

"David, don't. I'm OK. I can—"

"You can't," he said, even more grimly, "and you won't. Dammit, woman, how can a dress be tight enough at the throat to cut off your air and so loose everyplace else that it turns you into a sack of potatoes?''

"A sack of…" Joanna flushed. "You don't like this dress?"

"I don't like flour sacks. What man does? And what the hell does what I like or not like have to do with what you wear? Sit up a little. That's it. Now lift your arm…the other one. Good girl."

She stared at him as he tossed the dress aside. "But I thought…I assumed…" She thought of the closetful of ugly clothes, of the awful furniture in the room, of the servants David had so pointedly said were hers, and her mouth began to tremble.

"I don't understand," she whispered.

"Turn on your side."

She obeyed without thinking. His voice was toneless, his touch as impersonal as a physician's. She felt his hands at the nape of her neck, and then her hair came tumbling down over her shoulders.

"There," he said, "that's better. No wonder your head hurts. You've got enough pins stuck into your scalp to… to…"

His angry, rushed words ground to a halt. He had turned her toward him again and as he looked down at her, his heart seemed to constrict within his chest.

She was so beautiful. So much the woman he still remembered, the woman he'd never been able to get out of his mind. Stripped of the ugly dress, her hair flowing down over her creamy shoulders, her eyes wide and fixed on his, she was everything he remembered, everything he'd ever wanted, and the name he'd once called her whispered from his lips.

"Gypsy," he said huskily.

Who? Joanna thought, who? It wasn't her name, surely…and yet, as she looked up in David's eyes and saw the way he was looking at her, she felt as if she were falling back to another time and place.

Gypsy, she thought, oh, yes, she would be his Gypsy, if that was what he wanted, she would dance for him by firelight, she would whirl around him in an ever-tightening circle until she fell into his waiting arms. She would do whatever he asked of her, she would love him forever...

"Joanna," he whispered.

He bent toward her, then hesitated. Joanna didn't think, she simply reached up, clasped his face and brought him to her.

His mouth closed over hers.

His kiss was gentle, soft and sweet. But she could feel him trembling and she knew what was happening, that he was fighting to control what was raging through him, the need to plunder her mouth, to ravage her until she cried out with need. She knew, because it was raging through her, too.

"David," she sighed.

He groaned and his arms swept around her as he came down on the bed beside her. Her body was soft as silk and hot as the sun against his; his hand swept up and cupped her breast; she moaned and he felt her nipple spring to life beneath the silk of her slip and press against his palm...

"Mr. Adams?"

He raised his head and stared blindly at the closed door. Someone was knocking on it and calling his name.

"Mr. Adams? It's Ellen, sir. Dr. Corbett's arrived. Shall I send him up?"

David looked down at Joanna. Her face was flushed with color, her eyes were dark as the night. Her mouth was softly swollen and pink from his kisses....

But it meant nothing. Nothing. If he valued his own sanity, he had to keep remembering that.

His wife, his beautiful, lying wife, was unexcelled at this game. Her body still remembered how to play, even if her mind did not.

"David?"

Her voice was as soft as it always was. It was her heart that was hard.

"David," she said again, and he stood up, took her robe from where it lay at the foot of the bed, and tossed it to her.

"Cover yourself," he said coldly, and then he turned his back on his wife and on temptation.

CHAPTER SIX

JOANNA was stunned by the tone of cold command in her husband's voice.

"What?"

"You heard me," he growled. "Cover yourself—unless you don't object to Corbett knowing what you were up to a minute ago."

She felt the blood drain from her face. "What *I* was up to?"

"All right. What we were up to. Does that make you feel better?"

She grabbed the robe he'd tossed to her and shoved her arms through the sleeves. She was trembling, not with the aftermath of desire but with the fury of humiliation.

"Nothing could make me feel better," she said shakily, "except being able to start my life beginning the day before I met you."

"My sentiments exactly. The sooner you get your memory back, the better it will be for the both of us."

Joanna swung her legs to the floor and stood up, stumbling a little as she did. David reached out to help her but she swatted his hands away.

"Don't touch me. Don't you ever touch me again. Do you understand?"

David stared at his wife. Her eyes blazed black in her face. Suddenly, he was overcome with guilt. What had just happened was as much his fault as hers. Hell, who was he kidding? It was all his fault. She had no memory but he— he remembered everything. And she was right. She hadn't started this ugly scene, he had.

"Joanna," he said, "listen—"

"Get out of my room."

"Jo, please, I'm trying to apolo—"

She snatched a perfume bottle from the vanity and hurled it at him. He ducked and it whizzed by his head and shattered against the wall just as the door banged open.

Doctor Corbett paused in the doorway. He looked at the shards of glass that glittered against the carpet, then cleared his throat and raised a politely inquisitive face to David and Joanna.

"Excuse me," he said, "is there a problem here?"

"Yes!" Joanna glared at David. "I want this man out of my room!"

Corbett turned to David. "Mr. Adams," he said gently, "perhaps you'll give me a few moments alone with your..."

"Be my guest, Doctor. Take a few years, if you like," David snarled.

The door slammed shut after him. The doctor waited and then cleared his throat again.

"Well, Mrs. Adams," he said briskly, "why don't you tell me what's going on here?"

Joanna swung toward him. "I'll tell you what's going on," she said furiously. "I'll tell you what's...what's..." Her shoulders slumped. She felt the rage that had been driving her draining from her system. "Oh, hell," she muttered, "hell!" She sank down on the edge of her bed and wiped her sleeve across suddenly damp eyes. "I want my memory back," she said in a choked whisper. "Is that asking so much?"

"My dear Mrs. Adams—"

"Don't call me that!" Joanna's head snapped up, her eyes gleaming once again with anger. "It's bad enough I'm married to that—that cold-blooded Neanderthal! I certainly don't need to be reminded of it all the time."

Corbett sighed. Then he pulled a Kleenex from a box on the table beside Joanna's bed and handed it to her.

"Suppose you tell me what happened tonight," he said

quietly. "All I really know is that your housekeeper phoned my service and said you'd collapsed."

"I didn't collapse!" Joanna dabbed at her eyes, wiped her nose, then balled up the tissue and threw it into a wicker wastebasket. "David blew what happened out of all proportion. I just felt woozy for a minute, that's all."

"Woozy," Corbett repeated.

"Yes. I know it's not the sort of fancy medical term you use, but…" She stopped, bit her lip, and looked at him. "I'm sorry, Doctor. I don't know why I'm letting my anger out on you."

"That's all right."

"No, it isn't. It's myself I'm angry at."

"For what?"

"What do you mean, for what?" She threw her arms wide. "For everything! For having something as stupid as amnesia, that's for what!"

"There's nothing 'stupid' about amnesia," Corbett said gently. "And you didn't have a choice in acquiring it. You suffered a head injury, and it's going to take time to heal."

"It will heal though, won't it? You said—"

"There are no guarantees but, as I've told you, I've every reason to believe your memory will return." Corbett drew out the bench from the vanity table and sat down facing her. "Right now, I'm more concerned about what you call this 'wooziness' you felt tonight. Did it come on suddenly? Or was it precipitated by some event?"

She sighed. "It didn't happen out of the blue, if that's what you're asking. I…I remembered something. Not much, there was just a momentary flash…but it startled me."

"So, it was the shock of remembering that made you feel…what? Dizzy? Weak?"

She nodded. "Yes."

"And then?" Corbett prompted.

"And then, David told Mrs. Timmons to phone you and he brought me up here and…and…" Her voice trailed off.

"And you quarreled?"

She thought of how David had undressed her, of how he'd let down her hair. Of how he'd kissed her and how she'd responded with heated, almost unbearable passion…and of how he'd reacted then, with an anger that had bordered on disgust.

"Joanna?"

Color washed over her skin. "You could say that," she murmured, and looked down at her lap.

Corbett reached for his leather medical bag. "Very well. Let's just check a few things, shall we?"

"Check whatever you like. There's nothing wrong with me. Not physically, anyway."

She was right. The doctor's examination was thorough and when it was over, he pronounced her in excellent health.

"In excellent health," Joanna said with a bitter smile. "It's like that awful old joke, the one about the operation being a success but the patient dying."

"You're making fine progress. You've started to remember things."

"A picture of a bottle of beer flashing through my head isn't exactly the same as getting my memory back, Doctor."

"Joanna." Corbett took her hand in his. "You must have patience. I know this is difficult for you and for your husband, but—"

"Oh, please!" Joanna snatched back her hand. "Don't waste your sympathy on David!"

"Surely, you realize your condition is affecting him as well as you?"

"Look," she said, after a brief hesitation, "I know I must sound like a shrew. But you can't imagine what David's like."

"No," Corbett said mildly, "I can't. I only know what I've observed, that he came to the hospital every evening of your stay, that he agreed to bring you home when you seemed unhappy at Bright Meadows, that he's stood by you during a most difficult period."

Joanna stared at the doctor. Then she gave a deep, deep sigh.

"You're right, I suppose. And I have tried to keep in mind that this can't be easy for him."

"Joanna, the worst thing about loss of memory is the pressure it brings to bear on a relationship. That's why you both need to be patient as you restructure yours."

"Yes, but..." She hesitated. "But it's hard," she said softly, "when you don't know what things were like between you in the first place. I mean, what if...what if things had been shaky for a couple—a hypothetical couple—in the past? How could they possibly restructure a relationship successfully? One of them would know the truth and the other—the other would be working in the dark."

Corbett smiled. "There are those who would say the one working in the dark was fortunate."

"Fortunate?" Joanna's head came up. "That I don't know—that this hypothetical person doesn't know what sort of marriage she had?"

"Without a past, there can be no regrets. No anger, no recriminations... It's like starting over again with a clean slate."

Joanna laughed softly. "I didn't know they taught Optimism in med school."

"Philosophy was my love before I decided on medicine." Corbett chuckled. "Sometimes, it still comes in handy." He patted her hand, then stood up. "I'm going to give you something to help you sleep. And I'm going to leave you a prescription you must promise to follow."

"What kind of prescription? You said I was healthy."

"I want you to stop worrying about the past. *Carpe diem*, Joanna. Seize the day. The past is lost to *all* of us, not just to you. It's today and tomorrow that matter."

A slight smile curved across Joanna's lips. "More leftover class notes from Philosophy, Doctor?"

"Just an old-fashioned mother who loved quoting the classics." Corbett took a vial of tablets from his bag, shook two into her palm and poured her a glass of water from the thermos jug on the night table. "It's time you started living your life again."

"That sounds terrific, Doctor Corbett, but I don't know what 'my life' is."

"Then find out," he said briskly, snapping shut his bag. "Surely you had friends, interests, things you enjoyed doing…?"

"From what I can gather, I seem to have made an art of doing as little as possible," she said with a faintly bitter smile.

"Then try something new. Something you can share with David, perhaps. But don't go on moping and feeling sorry for yourself."

"Me?" Joanna handed him the glass. Her voice rose in indignation. "But I haven't…" Her gaze met Corbett's. She laughed and fell back against the pillows. "That's some combination," she said wryly, "philosophy and medicine."

Corbett grinned. "Just think of me as Ann Landers, M.D." He waved a hand in salute and shut the bedroom door.

The doctor's advice made sense.

She couldn't recall the past. Much as it upset Joanna to admit it, she didn't even have any guarantee that she ever would.

So whatever condition her marriage had been in didn't matter. It was what she made of it now that counted.

David didn't seem to like her very much. Well, she thought early the next morning as she pulled on a pair of cotton shorts and a tank top, maybe she hadn't been a very likeable person.

No. That couldn't be, she thought with a smile…

But it was possible, wasn't it?

Or maybe they'd hit a rough patch in their marriage. Maybe they'd begun to drift apart.

Not that it mattered. The doctor was right. *Carpe diem.*

The past was gone and only the present mattered, and when you came down to it, she didn't know all that much about the present, either, especially as it related to her husband.

Share something with David, Corbett had advised.

But what? What did her husband do with his spare time? What were his interests? Who were his friends?

Joanna glanced at her watch as she pulled her hair back into a ponytail and secured it with a coated rubber band. She had lots of questions and hardly any answers. Well, starting today, she was going to go after those answers.

Quietly, she opened the door to her bedroom and stepped out into the corridor.

David was in for a surprise.

"Surprise" wasn't the right word.

"Shocked" came closer to the truth, judging by the look on his face when he came trotting down the steps ten minutes later and saw her.

"Joanna?" He stared at her as if she might be an hallucination. "What are you doing up at this hour?"

She smiled at him over her shoulder. She'd been doing stretching exercises while she waited, using one of the marquetry benches that flanked the foyer door for support.

"Good morning," she said, as she finished her last stretch. "And it's not really so early, is it?"

He tore his astonished gaze from her and glanced at his watch.

"Are you kidding? It's just after six."

"Well, I was awake so I figured, instead of just lying in bed vegetating, I might as well get up and do something useful." She jerked her head in the direction of the kitchen. "I made a pot of coffee."

"Yes. Yes, I thought I smelled coffee."

"Would you like some?"

"No. Ah, no, thank you." He edged past her, as if she might vaporize if touched. "I prefer to wait until after my run but you go ahead and, ah, and have a cup."

"I already did." She followed after him, to the front door. "You don't mind, do you?"

"That you made coffee? No, of course not."

"That I've decided to run with you."

He swung toward her. "That you've…?" His gaze flew over her again, taking in her gray sweat shorts, her tank top, her ponytail, her running shoes. She'd decided to run with him? His brain couldn't seem to process the information. She hadn't run with him in months. In years. She hadn't done any of this in years, gotten up at this hour, put up the morning coffee, worn this tattered outfit that had once made his pulse beat quicken…hell, that *still* made his pulse beat quicken because she was the only woman he'd ever known who could fill out a shirt that way, or pair of shorts, the only one whose early morning, unmade-up face was a face that would have put Helen of Troy to shame…

Dammit, Adams, are you nuts?

"David? Do you mind?"

He frowned, shook his head. "No," he said coldly, "I suppose not."

She smiled. "Thanks. I was hoping you wouldn't mi—"

"It's a free country," he said as he swung the door open and started down toward the street. "And a big park. Just do your best to keep up, Joanna, because I don't feel much like tailoring my pace to suit yours."

Gracious. That was the word to describe her husband's acceptance of her presence, Joanna thought sarcastically as she panted after him half an hour later, gracious and charming and oh-so-welcoming.

But she was matching the pace he'd set, even if her legs were screaming and her breath was wheezing in lungs that felt as if they were on fire.

It had occurred to her, one or two times, that David was deliberately trying to exhaust her but why would he do that?

No. She was just out of shape, that was all.

But she'd be damned if she'd admit it.

* * *

Stupid. That was the word to describe his acceptance of his wife's presence, David thought grimly as he pounded through the park, stupid and pointless and all-around dumb.

Why hadn't he just told her he didn't want any part of her? That he was perfectly happy with the way things had been for the past few years, thank you very much, with him running alone and her doing her la-di-da exercises at her fancy health club.

She'd caught him off guard, that was why. Well, it wouldn't happen again. He couldn't imagine what insanity had gotten into her today, especially after what had happened between them last night. Corbett had come down from her bedroom looking smug and mysterious; he'd said she was in excellent health and that he'd advised her to get on with the business of living.

Was this Joanna's idea of how to do that?

David didn't think so. The real Joanna hadn't thought so, either, and if he was playing his cards right, this new one would soon come to the same conclusion.

He was running harder and faster than he'd run in years, running in a way that would exhaust anybody, especially a devotee of glitter Spandex, odor-free sweat and fancy treadmills.

By the time they got back to the house, she'd be finished with early morning runs and whatever foolishness had sent her along on this one.

Still, he had to admit, she was keeping up.

He frowned, put his head down, and ran harder.

But she wasn't finished with early morning runs, not by a long shot.

She was waiting for him the next morning, and the morning after that. By the third day, he adjusted his pace back to where it had been before Joanna had intruded.

He did it for her sake. Hell, it wasn't fair to tax her so, even if Corbett said she was fine.

He certainly didn't do it for his. And he certainly didn't enjoy having her tag along.

But when she wasn't bent over the bench in the foyer Friday morning, doing those stretching exercises that tilted her sexy little bottom into the air, David paused on the steps while he tried to figure out what the strange emotion stealing over him might be.

Disappointment?

No. Hell, no, why would he—

"Hi."

Joanna was standing in the door to the library, clutching a cup of coffee in her hands, smiling at him over the rim.

His heart did something absolutely stupid, as if it were on a string, yo-yoing in his chest.

"Hi," he said, and managed not to smile back.

"You're early."

"Am I? Well, that's OK, if you're not ready to—"

"I'm ready. Just let me put this cup in the sink and I'll be—"

"Jo?" He shoved his hand into his hair and scraped it back from his forehead.

"Yes?"

"I was going to say...I was going to say..."

He knew what he'd been going to say, that they might skip this morning's run, take their coffee out into the little garden, drink it together at the minuscule wrought-iron table under the tree and talk about nothing in particular and everything under the sun, just the way they used to, a million years ago.

"Yes, David?"

He looked at her. Was he crazy? He had to be. It was bad enough they'd started running together but they'd also started spending the evening together, too. Joanna waited for him to get home, no matter how late, before sitting down to dinner. He'd even begun to look forward to it, just sharing their mealtime, talking, telling her about the inconsequential bits and pieces of his day...

Why was he letting these things happen? Nothing, *nothing*, had changed. Joanna had lost her memory but sooner or later she'd get it back. She'd remember who she was and what she wanted. She'd turn into the real Joanna Adams again, the one that lay hidden beneath that mask of sexy innocence, and when she did...when she did, he had no intention of watching it happen again.

Feeling disappointment turn to despair once in a lifetime was more than enough.

He stood straighter and, with a cool smile, pulled the door open.

"I'd rather not wait, if it's all the same to you," he said politely. "I'd prefer running by myself today." The sudden hurt in her eyes knotted in his gut and his irritation with himself only made him twist the knot tighter. "Oh, by the way, Joanna...don't expect me for dinner tonight. There's a fund-raiser at the Gallery of Alternative Arts and I've agreed to attend."

Joanna stared at her husband. It had taken him no time at all to undo the progress of the past days. She wanted to weep; she wanted to slug him. Instead, she did the only thing she knew she ought to do, which was to smile brightly.

"How nice for you," she said.

"Yes, isn't it?" he answered, blithely ignoring the fact that tonight's event was just the kind of thing he hated, a bunch of fat cats standing around stroking each other's fur, telling themselves they were helping the world when all they were really doing was making asses of themselves. He hadn't even intended to go to the damned gala until desperation had forced his hand a couple of seconds ago. "Morgana reminded me of it yesterday."

"Morgana," Joanna repeated, even more brightly.

"My Personal—"

"—Assistant." She nodded. "Yes, I know."

"Anyhow, don't wait up. These things usually run late."

"Oh, of course. Well, have a good run. And a good day.
And a good..."

He was gone.

Joanna stood in the open doorway, watching her husband.
His stride was long and loose as he ran toward Fifth Avenue
without so much as a backward glance.

Her bottom lip trembled.

So much for sharing.

So much for getting back into life.

So much for letting herself think there might be a human
being lurking inside the man she was married to.

She slammed the door, made her way back to the kitchen,
rinsed out her cup and put it away.

"*Carpe diem*, my foot," she muttered.

Dr. Corbett's advice had been useless. Useless. She'd
wasted her time, wasted her hopes.

*That's right, Joanna. You might as well go back to sitting
around and feeling sorry for yourself.*

Her head jerked up.

"I'm not feeling sorry for myself!"

*Sure you are. You're thinking that he could have waited
while you rinsed your coffee cup, that he could have asked
you to go with him tonight.*

Unless, of course, he was taking the ever-present, ever-
helpful Morgana.

A muscle ticked in Joanna's cheek. She put her cup down,
trotted up the stairs to her room and to the Queen Anne
secretary that stood on one wall. There was a white-leather
appointment book in the top drawer; she'd flipped through
it a couple of times, shuddering at the stuff she saw scrawled
over the weekly calendar pages, nonsense about hairdresser's appointments and dress fittings and luncheons and
meetings that sounded senseless and silly...

There it was, under today's date, in her handwriting.

Eight p.m., Gal. of Alt. Arts, benefit for Tico the Chimp.

Her eyes widened. Tico the Chimp?

She closed the book, lay it aside, and stared into space.

Tico the Chimp. The elusive Morgana. And David, all under one roof.

Joanna shucked off her running clothes and headed for the shower.

CHAPTER SEVEN

AMNESIA, as Joanna was quickly learning, was a strangely elective ailment.

She didn't remember any of the details of her own life. But when she thought back to what Ellen had said—that she shopped in only the best stores—a list came quickly to mind.

And though she'd apparently bought only dark, conservative clothing in those fashionable shops, surely they also carried other things. They had to sell dresses that were bright in color and didn't have sleeves to the wrist and hems to mid-calf, that didn't make a woman look as if she were…what had David said? As if she were a sack of potatoes?

There was only one way to find out.

Joanna dressed quickly, without giving much thought to her selections. What was there to think about, when all her clothing had a grim sameness? Even her underwear was dowdy and utilitarian.

She paid even less attention to her hair. She hadn't yet grasped the knack of neatly knotting it low on her neck. Ellen had been fixing it, most mornings, but today was her maid's day off and even if it hadn't been, Joanna was too impatient to wait while her curls were brushed and sprayed into submission. So she simply caught her hair in one hand, gave it a twist, then pinned it into place.

Ugh, she thought, grimacing as she caught a glimpse of herself in the mirror, she looked even more funereal than usual.

Not that it would matter, after this jaunt…

My God, Joanna, are you sure you know what you're doing?

"No," she said, into the silence, "I don't."

She thought of her husband's biting comments about her dress, about the way she wore her hair. She thought of her doctor's admonition that she give up searching for the past and instead concentrate on the present and the future.

She thought of Morgana, and tonight's party.

And then she took one last deep breath and set out to face New York.

She let Hollister drive her to the first store on her list, then told him not to wait.

It was not an order that pleased him.

"But, madam…"

"Go on, Hollister. Go to the park or something. Take your girl out for a spin." Joanna laughed at the look on his face. "You do have a girl, don't you?"

"Madam, really—"

"Hollister, really," she said gently, "I much prefer to do my shopping on my own."

Once inside the store, the giddiness that had been bubbling inside her since she'd read the entry in her appointment book was all but swept away by a sense of near panic.

The store was so big… Why had she come? Nothing about it was familiar; she had no idea where to start or even what to start looking for.

"Madam? May I help you?"

Joanna turned toward the smartly dressed young saleswoman who'd materialized at her elbow.

"Yes," she said gratefully. "I'd like to buy a dress. Something—something special, to wear to a party tonight."

The girl's eyes moved quickly and professionally over her.

"Certainly, madam," she replied, "if you'll just come with me…?"

Within moments, Joanna found herself in a sea of dresses.

"Here we are, madam. Did you have a preference as to color?"

"Does it matter?" Joanna said with a little laugh. She turned in a slow circle. "The only color I see is black."

The salesgirl smiled coolly. "Black is always fashionable, as madam can attest."

Joanna looked down at herself. She was wearing the first thing that had come to hand in her closet, a long-sleeved, long-skirted, incredibly expensive and incredibly unattractive two-piece dress and yes, indeed, it was black.

"Always," she said, and smiled politely at the salesgirl, "but not always interesting. Haven't you got other colors? Something in yellow, perhaps, or pale blue?" Her gaze lit on a mannequin in the next department. "Something like that, for instance."

"That?" the clerk said, her voice losing its cultured purr and rising in dismay. "But that dress is…it's heliotrope!"

"I'd have called it violet," Joanna said. The girl trailed behind as she walked toward the mannequin. "But perhaps you're right. It's lighter than a true violet."

"I don't think this is quite what madam is looking for," the clerk said with a quick, artificial smile. "The neckline is rather low."

"Shockingly low."

"The skirt is very short."

Joanna nodded. "It seems to be."

"This dress is definitely not madam's style."

"How do you know that, Miss…" Joanna peered at the salesgirl's identification tag. "How do you know that, Miss Simpson?"

"Why, from looking at…I mean, it's my job to listen to what a customer tells me and then determine what will best meet her needs."

"Then do it, please," Joanna said with a pleasant smile. "I've told you I need a special dress for this evening, and that I particularly like this one. Please show me to the fitting room and bring me this dress in a—what would you think? A ten?"

The baffled clerk stared at her. "I don't know, not for

certain. It's difficult to assess madam's proper weight and shape in the dress she's wearing.''

Joanna smiled wistfully. ''So I've been told.''

Size ten was too big.

Eight was perfect. And so was the dress, Joanna thought, staring at herself in the three-way dressing room mirror.

The color was wonderful, almost the same shade as her eyes and a perfect foil for her creamy skin and dark hair.

The neckline certainly was low and the skirt certainly was short...not that Fifth Avenue wasn't crowded with stylish women wearing their necklines just as deeply cut and the hems just as high. Still...

''Madam looks...'' The salesclerk's stunned eyes met Joanna's in the mirror. ''She looks beautiful!''

Joanna turned, frowned, and peered at herself over her shoulder. She had a sudden vision of David, seeing her in something so outrageous.

''I don't know,'' she said slowly. ''Maybe you were right. This dress is—''

''Stunning,'' the girl said. ''With your hair done differently and the right shoes...''

The women's eyes met in the mirror. Joanna could feel her courage slipping.

What are you doing, Joanna? What would David think?

There was no way of knowing. But I know what I think, she thought suddenly. I think I look—I think I look...

She reached behind her and gave the zipper a determined tug.

''I'll take it,'' she said, before she lost her courage completely.

The rest was easy.

The right shoes turned out to be conveniently waiting one department over, a pair of silver sandals with slender high heels and narrow straps, and there was a tiny purse on a silver shoulder chain to match. The right underthings—an ivory silk teddy with lacy garters and a pair of gossamer-sheer stockings—were just a couple of blocks away, almost calling out Joanna's name from the window of a stylish boutique.

There was only one last step to take.

Joanna stood before the mirrored door of a beauty salon. Her appointment book had confirmed that she had standing appointments at this trendy place three times a week.

The door swung open and the scent of hair spray and expensive perfume came wafting out, born on a cloud of lushly romantic music.

Joanna squared her shoulders and marched inside.

The girl at the reception desk did a double take. "Oh, Mrs. Adams," she squealed, "how lovely to see you again. We'd heard you were in an accident!"

Joanna admitted that she had been, assured the receptionist that she was well on the road to recovery and said she was here to have her hair done.

"I know it's not my day but I was hoping you could fit me in."

The girl smiled. "Of course." She motioned to the glittering mirrors beyond them. "Arturo's just finishing up with a client so if you wouldn't mind waiting just a couple of secs…?"

Joanna followed the girl's pointing finger. Arturo confirmed he was her usual hairdresser by waving his hand and smiling. He was a gray-haired man in late middle age, as was his client whose hair was being pinned and sprayed into a style that was the duplicate of Joanna's.

"That's OK," she said quickly, "someone else can do my hair today."

"We wouldn't dream of letting that happen, Mrs. Adams. I promise, Arturo will only be—"

"How about him?"

The girl's eyes widened. The man Joanna had indicated was young, with shoulder-length hair and a tiny gold stud in one earlobe. He was cutting the hair of a woman in her mid-twenties—just about my age, Joanna thought with a surprised start—and shaping it into a style that was swingy, sexy and feminine.

"Oh, but, Mrs. Adams," the receptionist said nervously, "I don't think Mick's the right guy for—"

"I think he's perfect," Joanna said, ignoring the butterflies swarming in her stomach. She smiled, sat down in an empty chair and piled her gaily wrapped packages beside her. "And I'll be happy to wait until he's free. Oh, by the way…the sign outside says you do cosmetic makeovers, too. Is that right?"

The girl's throat worked. "Uh—uh, yes. Yes, we do. In fact, Mick is the one who—"

"Great." Joanna plucked a magazine from a lamp table, opened it and buried her face inside. After a moment, the receptionist took her cue and fled.

Joanna let out a shuddering breath and thought how perfect it would be if only the butterflies would do the same.

She taxied home, locked herself into her bedroom. Then, like a cygnet exchanging its dull feathers for the glorious plumage of a swan, she took off her old clothes and replaced them with the new.

The teddy first, and the sheer stockings followed by the violet dress, which floated down around her like the petals of a flower. She slipped on the silver shoes. Thanks to Mick, her hair was now loose on her shoulders, layered just lightly around her face. It needed only a fluff of the brush, and her new makeup—eyeliner, mascara and a touch of pale lip gloss—was easy enough to touch up, even with trembling hands.

Because her hands were trembling now, and her teeth were tapping together like castanets.

What in the hell had prompted her to do this?

She swung toward the mirrored wall against which the

vanity table stood and stared at herself. She had awakened in a hospital room weeks ago, a stranger to herself.

Now, she'd replaced that stranger with another, one David had never seen before.

The enormity of what she was doing almost buckled her knees. But there was no going back now.

Joanna gave her reflection a shaky smile.

"Carpe diem, kid," she whispered, and gave herself a thumbs-up.

She hadn't only seized the day, she was about to wring it dry.

David was sitting behind his oak desk in his spacious office in lower Manhattan, his chair turned to the window and his back to the door, staring sightlessly over the gray waters of the Hudson River while he mentally cursed his own stupidity.

What other word could you use to describe the way he'd trapped himself into the upcoming evening of unrelieved boredom?

He'd attended parties like tonight's in the past. Joanna belonged to virtually every committee around; she'd dragged him from one mind-numbing gala to another, all in the name of what she considered to be "Good Causes," where the same dull people stood in little clusters talking about the same dull things while they chomped on soggy hors d'oeuvres and sipped flat champagne.

Finally, he'd put his foot down and said he'd write checks to Save the Somalian Snail and the Androgynous Artists of America but he'd be damned if he'd go to one more inane benefit on their behalf.

In a way, that had been the beginning of the end. He'd taken a good, hard look at the four years of his marriage and admitted the truth, that the Joanna he'd married had metamorphosed into a woman he didn't understand, a woman who was interested in knowing the right people and buying the right labels, whose only goal was to be accepted in the upper echelons of New York society...

...Who had loved his money and his position but not him. Never him.

He had to admit, she'd done a fine job of pulling the wool over his eyes. She'd been so young, so seemingly innocent, and he'd been so crazy about her that he'd even worried, at the beginning, that he might overwhelm her with the intensity of his love.

He'd admitted as much to Morgana, who knew him better than anyone after working beside him for five years, and she'd generously offered him the benefit of her insight into the members of her own sex.

"I understand, David," she'd said. "Joanna's a child, only twenty-two to your thirty, and a free spirit, at that. You must be careful that you don't make her feel trapped."

His mouth twisted. He needn't have worried. While he'd been busy trying to keep his wife from feeling trapped, she'd been busy rearranging his life until the night they'd been at some stupid charity ball and he'd suddenly realized that *he* was the one who was trapped, in a loveless marriage to a woman with whom he had absolutely nothing in common and never would have.

Until the accident. Until a bump on the head had wiped away Joanna's memory and turned her into...

"Dammit," he said.

It was dangerous to think that way. The accident hadn't "turned" her into anything but a woman struggling to recover her memory. Once she did, life would return to normal and so would Joanna.

And then they'd be back where they'd been a couple of months ago, with their divorce only days away, and that was just fine. It was better than fine, it was freedom. It was—

"David?"

He swung his chair around. Morgana had inched open the door to his office, just enough so she could peer around the edge.

"I'm sorry to bother you, David. I knocked, but…"

"Morgana." He straightened in his chair, feeling strangely guilty for having been caught with his thoughts anywhere but on the papers strewn across his desk, and smiled at his assistant. "Come in."

"Are you sure?" she said, as she stepped inside the office. "If you're busy…"

"Don't be foolish. I'm never too busy to talk to you and anyway, I really wasn't working. I was thinking about—about this party I'm supposed to go to tonight. Did you phone and say I'd changed my mind about not attending?"

"I did. And Mrs. Capshaw herself told me to assure you it wasn't too late. She wanted you to know that the entire Planning Committee would be delighted to know you'd decided to come."

David smiled thinly. "How nice."

"She asked if Joanna would be with you." Morgana's perfect features settled into serious lines. "I told her it was far too soon for Joanna to be up and about. Which reminds me, David, I haven't asked in days…I do so want to stop by for a visit. Do you think she's up to seeing anyone yet?"

"That's kind of you, Morgana, but—"

"It isn't kind at all. I've always liked Joanna, you know that. And I know how difficult this must be for her and for you both." She hesitated, the tip of her pink tongue just moistening the fullness of her bottom lip. "She hasn't shown any signs of recovery yet, I suppose?"

The muscle in David's cheek knotted. "No."

"It will be good for her, knowing you've gone to a party she helped plan."

"She doesn't know she helped plan it."

"Oh? But I thought—I assumed that was why you decided to attend."

David frowned. Morgana was his assistant and his friend, and from the time of his marriage, she'd been Joanna's friend, too. But he wasn't about to tell her that he'd decided to go to tonight's gala only to make it clear to his wife that their lives went in separate directions…

…And what a stupid thing that had been to do, when he could make the same point just as easily and far more comfortably by going home and asking Mrs. Timmons to serve him his supper on a tray in his study.

"Actually," he said with a little smile, "now that I think about it, I'm not sure why I decided to attend. Eating soggy hors d'oeuvres and drinking flat champagne while I stare at the paintings of some artist who probably needs a bath more than he needs a paintbrush—"

"It's Tico the Chimp."

"What's Tico the Chimp?"

"The artist. You know, they profiled him in the *Times* a couple of weeks ago. The party's in his honor."

"That's just great." David began to laugh. "Soggy hors d'oeuvres, flat champagne…and for the guest of honor, a bunch of bananas."

"The art critic for the *Times* called him a great talent."

"Why doesn't that surprise me? Morgana, do me a favor. Phone Mrs. Capshaw, offer my regrets—"

"The mayor's going to be there, and Senator Williamson, and the Secretary-General of the UN. I know they're all friends of yours, but—"

"Acquaintances."

"Either way, it can't hurt to touch bases with all three of them with this new project in our laps." A sympathetic smile softened his assistant's patrician features. "Besides, it will be good for you to get out a bit. I know it's not my place to say so, but these last weeks surely must have been a strain."

David nodded. Morgana was the only person, aside from his attorney and Joanna's, who knew he and his wife had been about to divorce when the accident had occurred. Of course, she didn't know any of the details. Still, it helped that he didn't have to pretend with her.

"Yes," he said quietly, "it has been." He drew a deep breath, then let it out slowly. "For Joanna, too."

"Oh, certainly."

Morgana sat down on the edge of his desk, as she often did, and the skirt of her pale yellow suit hitched a couple of inches above her knees.

He almost smiled. When she became engrossed in something, her skirt would often hitch up, or she'd forget that her neckline might delicately gape open as she leaned forward to draw his attention to an item in her hand.

He'd have thought such things were deliberate if any other woman had done them but Morgana, though beautiful, was incapable of playing such games. She was the complete professional, a quality he'd come to appreciate more and more during the years she'd been working for him.

She'd started in his office as his secretary.

"But I don't intend to stay in that position," she'd told him bluntly when he'd hired her.

David had admired her drive. And the company had benefitted from it. Morgana was single-minded in her pursuit of success; she was nothing like the girls who'd preceded her, who'd batted their lashes a lot better than they took dictation or kept his files.

Not that she didn't have a heart. When he'd come to work one morning and announced he'd married the girl he'd met not ten days before, Morgana had probably been as stunned as his colleagues. But she hadn't shown it. If anything, she'd gone out of her way to befriend his young wife and ease her into his sophisticated world.

Little had he or Morgana known that Joanna had been more than ready to do that by herself.

Ever since the accident, Morgana had put her private life on hold, pitching in to take up the slack when he'd been out of the office the first couple of days, then staying late to help him play catch-up while Joanna was at Bright Meadows. He knew she was right, that there'd be networking opportunities at tonight's party...

…Opportunities she could take advantage of all on her own.

David felt a load lift from his shoulders. Why hadn't it occurred to him before? Morgana would get the chance to enjoy herself—she was far better than he at putting on a polite, social mask. And he'd be off the hook.

"You know," he said, "you could use some time off, too."

"That's kind of you to say, David, but—"

"Would you like to go to that party tonight?"

Her lovely face lit. "Why…I would, yes."

He smiled. "Well, then, why not go?"

"Oh." She gave an uncharacteristically breathless laugh. "How generous. Thank you, David. I'd enjoy that very much."

"Here," he said, opening his desk drawer and digging out his tickets for the event. "You take these and—"

"No, you'd better hang on to them." Morgana got to her feet. "I'll have to go home and change first, but I promise, I won't take very long. I can meet you at the gallery. Will that be OK?"

"Morgana," he said quickly, "you don't—"

"Oh, it's lovely of you to say that, David." She laughed again, that same soft, breathless sound. "But I can't possibly go to a party dressed like this. I promise, I'll be there by eight and not a moment later."

A dull pain began to throb behind David's eyes.

"Don't worry about it," he said wearily. "We'll take a taxi to your place. I'll wait while you change."

Morgana's smile flashed like a thousand-watt bulb.

"Oh, David, you're so kind! I just know we'll have a wonderful time."

"Yeah." He smiled, too, and the pain in his head intensified. "I just know it, too."

The hors d'oeuvres weren't soggy. They were stale.

The champagne wasn't flat. It was awful.

As for Tico the Chimp…the animal loped around the gallery, hand in hand with his owner, both of them decked out in tuxedos complete with top hats and bow ties. Every now and then, Tico rolled back his lips and let loose with a cackling shriek.

It was, David thought, the most honest comment anybody in the packed room made all night.

The whole thing was ludicrous, right down to the wild blobs of color that hung on the wall, each of them bearing the chimp's official handprint. Or was it footprint? David fought back the wild desire to ask. Everybody in the place was taking things so seriously, even Morgana.

Well, no. She couldn't be, she was too intelligent to swallow garbage like this but she was certainly putting on an amazing face, peering intently at the paintings, nodding over the notes in the program. Now, as he waited patiently, she'd lined up to shake Tico's hand. Or his paw. Or whatever in hell you called it.

It was hard to imagine Joanna as part of the committee that had planned this event even knowing, as he did, the penchant his wife had shown for fitting readily into the time-wasting habits of the idle rich. It was especially difficult because, for some crazy reason, he kept thinking back to the first one of these things they'd attended together.

They'd only been married a couple of months then and half the reason he'd decided to go to the party was because he could hardly wait to show off his gorgeous bride.

"Are we supposed to dress up?" she'd asked him and he'd kissed away the worried frown between her eyebrows and assured her that whatever she wore, she'd be the most beautiful woman in the room.

And she had been. She'd worn a hot pink dress, very demure and proper except that beneath it there'd been the hint of her lush, lovely body; her hair had streamed down over her shoulders like a midnight cloud. She'd clung to his arm, trying to look suitably impressed by—what had been on exhibit that night?

A display of cardboard boxes, that was it, some arranged on the walls, some grouped on the floor, all of them with price tags attached that made them Art instead of cardboard. They'd strolled from one end of the room to the other and then he'd bent his head to Joanna's and whispered that when they got back to Connecticut, he was going to go through the entire house, sign every box he found and then donate them all to the museum.

Joanna had looked up at him, her eyes wide and her lovely mouth trembling, and then she'd burst into laughter so hard that she'd had to bury her face against his chest.

An ache, sharper than the pain behind his eyes, crushed David's heart. Why was he thinking such dumb thoughts? That had been a million years ago. And it hadn't been real, it had all been illusion, just like Joanna herself.

If only he could forget the look of her, the sound of her voice...

"Hello, David."

The words were soft but their power stopped his breath. He turned slowly and there she was, as he remembered her. No artifice. No cool, matronly elegance. She wore little makeup, her hair was a glorious tide of midnight waves that tumbled down her back. Her dress was almost the color of her eyes; it clung to her breasts and narrow waist before flaring into a short, full skirt that stopped above her knees and made the most of her long legs.

Had he gone completely around the bend? Had he conjured up this image? For a minute he thought that maybe he had...but then she gave him a tremulous smile and he knew that she was real, this was Joanna, this was his beautiful, once-upon-a-time wife standing before him like a remembered vision come to life.

"I know I should have phoned and told you I was coming but..."

Say something, he told himself fiercely. But what?

"I hope you're not angry. It's just that I looked in my appointment book and saw that I was supposed to be here tonight and I thought, well, perhaps it's time I began to pick up the pieces of my life, and so—and so..."

Damn! Joanna bit down on her bottom lip. She'd spent the ride to the gallery promising herself she wouldn't lose her nerve the minute she came face-to-face with David, but after one shocked look from his green eyes, she was stammering.

Stop that, she told herself sternly, and despite the way her heart was hammering in her throat, she forced a smile to her lips.

"And so," she said, "here I am. You don't mind, do you?"

Mind? *Mind*? David stared at his wife. He wanted to grab her by the shoulders, spin her around and point her toward the door. He wanted to pull her into his arms and kiss her until night faded into dawn. He wanted to corner Corbett and every other arrogant, insufferable M.D. in New York who pretended to know what in hell was happening inside Joanna's head but who obviously didn't know a damned thing more than he did...

"No," he said, very calmly, "I don't mind, Joanna, but are you sure you're up to this?"

Up to having her husband look at her as if he were hoping she'd vanish in a puff of smoke? To seeing the stunned expressions on people's faces as she'd entered the room? To have people say, "Hello, it's wonderful you're up and around, Joanna" as she went by and not to have the foggiest notion who they were?

Joanna tried her best not to laugh. Or to cry. Or to do an impossible imitation of both at the same time.

"I'm absolutely up to it," she said with a hundred times more assurance than she felt. "In fact, I think a night out will do me—"

"Joanna? Joanna, is it really you?"

The voice came from a woman who'd stepped out from behind David. She was tall and slender, with pale blond hair cut in a feathered cap that emphasized the perfect structure of her face. Her eyes were pale blue, her lashes dark as soot; her mouth was full and pink. She wore a white silk suit, severely cut yet designed so that it was clear it depended for the beauty of its line not on cut or fabric but on the flawless body beneath.

Joanna smiled hesitantly. She looked at David for help but his face was like stone.

"I'm sorry," she said to the woman, "but I'm afraid I don't…"

"I'm Morgana."

Morgana. David's P.A. This—this Nordic goddess with the flawless face and the marvelous body was Morgana?

Joanna felt a flutter of panic deep in her stomach.

"Morgana," she said, and held out her hand, "how…how nice to see you again."

Morgana seemed to hesitate. Then she took the out-stretched hand, leaned forward and pressed her cheek lightly to Joanna's.

"What a lovely surprise." She drew back, looked at David and smiled, and it struck Joanna that the smile seemed strained. "You never said Joanna would be joining us, David."

"No." His eyes held Joanna's. "But then, it's a surprise to me, too."

Joanna flushed and disentangled her fingers from Morgana's. "I only decided to come at the last minute," she lied. "I was just telling David, I…I suppose I should have let him know…"

"Ah-ha! Here we are. Tico, I do believe that this is the lovely lady we have to thank for tonight's marvelous party!"

Joanna swung around and blinked in astonishment. A man and a chimpanzee, dressed in identical tuxedos and trailed by a crowd of onlookers, had appeared at her side.

"You are Mrs. Adams," the man said, "are you not?"

"Why…why yes, I—"

"Joanna," someone called, "yoo-hoo, over here!"

Joanna looked past the man in the tux. A woman with diamonds blazing at her ears and throat was waving at her.

"I'm sorry," Joanna said, "I'm afraid I don't—"

"Tico insisted you weren't Mrs. Adams," the man in the tux said. Joanna turned toward him again and he shot her a blazing smile. "But I said, yes, of course you were, and I was right." He sighed dramatically. "Tico can be so stubborn."

"Jo? Over here. It's so great to see you again. You remember me, don't you?"

Joanna's gaze flew from face to face. "No," she said, "actually, I'm afraid that I—"

"Anyway, Tico was determined to meet you."

"Are you talking about, ah, about the chimp?" Joanna said, looking at the man in the tux again.

"We don't call him that. Not to his face, anyway. It tends to upset him, but then, you know how *artistes* are, they have such delicate…"

"Oh, Joanna," a voice squealed, "I didn't know they'd let you out. How lovely!"

"No one 'let me out'," Joanna said, staring at the blur of faces. "I mean, I'm not sick. Or crazy. I'm just—"

"…egos."

She swung back to the man with the chimp. "Egos?"

"Egos," he said, and nodded. "Delicate ones. All artists are like that, don't you agree?" He stepped closer and breathed into Joanna's face. She pulled back from the scent of…bananas? "Tico, particularly. It truly upsets him to be referred to as a primate."

"As a primate," Joanna repeated stupidly. She looked down at the chimp and it looked back at her.

"Exactly. Oh, do forgive me for not introducing myself. My name is Chico."

"Chico," Joanna repeated. A nervous giggle rose in her throat. "He's Tico? And you're…?"

"Mrs. Adams." A youngish man with his hair sprayed firmly into place shoved forward and stabbed a microphone into her face. "Tom Jeffers, WBQ-TV news," he said with a self-important smile. "Would you care to tell our viewers how you're feeling?"

"Well..." Joanna blinked as the hot lights of a video camera suddenly glared into her eyes. "Well, I'm feeling—"

"Is it true you lost your memory and that you were in a coma for two weeks?"

"No. I mean, yes, but—"

A lush, bleached blonde in a miniskirt jammed a tape recorder under her nose.

"Mona Washbourne, from the *Sun*. Mrs. Adams, what about the rumors that you'd broken all the bones in your body?"

"That's not true. I didn't—"

"How about the plastic surgery they had to do on your face. Any comment?"

"Actually, I—"

"Mrs. Adams." Chico and his tuxedo were all but bristling. "Tico is not accustomed to being kept waiting. If you wish to meet him, you'll have to—"

"All right," David said brusquely, "that's enough."

His arm, hard and warm and comforting, swept around Joanna's waist. She sagged against him, her knees weak.

"My wife has no comment."

"Of course she does," the blonde snapped. "Women are perfectly capable of speaking for themselves. Isn't that right, Mrs. Adams?"

Joanna shook her head in bewilderment. "Please," she whispered, "I don't...I can't..."

A flashbulb went off. Joanna cried out, turned and buried her face in David's chest.

"That's it," he said grimly, and he swung her into his arms. She made a strangled sound and wound her arms around his neck. Another flashbulb went off in her face. "Bastards," David snarled, and without any apologies he shouldered his way through the mob.

Joanna didn't lift her head until she felt the sudden coolness of the night air on her skin. Carefully, she looked up
and peered behind her.

"Oh, God," she moaned.

The crowd had followed them with Chico and Tico, in
their matching tuxedos, leading the parade.

"Mrs. Adams!" Chico's high-pitched voice trembled with
indignation. "If you don't speak with Tico this instant, he's
going to be dreadfully upset!"

"Give him the banana you were saving for yourself,"
David muttered. "How did you get here, Joanna? Did Hollister bring you?"

She nodded. "He said he'd wait around the corner."

"At least you did something right," he snapped.

A moment later, they were safely inside the Bentley, with
the privacy partition up, racing through the darkened streets
toward home. Joanna was still in David's arms, held firmly
in his lap.

Her heart thumped. He was angry. He was furious! She
could feel it in the rigidity of his body, in the way he held
her, so hard and close that it was almost difficult to breathe.

"David?" She swallowed dryly. "David, I'm sorry."

In the shadowed darkness, she could just make out the
steely glimmer of his eyes as he looked down at her.

"Really," she said unhappily, "I'm terribly, terribly
sorry. I never dreamed...I mean, I never thought..."

"No," he growled, "hell, no. You never dreamed. You
never thought. Not for one damned minute, not about anybody but yourself."

"That isn't true! I didn't mean to make a scene. It never
occurred to me that—"

"What did you think would happen, once the sharks
smelled blood in the water?"

"I'm trying to tell you, I never imagined they'd—"

"What in bloody hell was the point in my working my
tail off to keep them away from you in the hospital?"

"David, if you'd just listen—"

"And what were you thinking, showing up looking like this?"

Joanna's cheeks flushed. "OK, I suppose I deserve that. I know you prefer me to dress more demurely. It's just that the other night...I thought you said...I realize now, I must have imagined it, but I thought you said you didn't like my hair in a chignon and the kind of dress I was wearing, and... and..."

"Dammit, Joanna, you should never have showed up tonight!"

A rush of angry tears rose in her eyes. She put her hands against David's chest and tried to push free.

"You've made that abundantly clear," she said, "and I promise you, I won't bother you and your little playmate again."

"Playmate? What playmate?"

"Morgana," she said stiffly, "that's what playmate. Damn you, David, if you don't let me go I'll...I'll..."

"What?" he said, and suddenly his voice was low and soft and almost unbearably sexy. "What will you do, Gypsy?"

She tried to tell him, but she couldn't think of an answer. It wouldn't have mattered if she had because his arms tightened around her, his mouth closed on hers, and suddenly he was kissing her as if the world might end at any second.

Joanna hesitated. Then, trembling with pleasure, she buried her fingers in her husband's thick, silky hair and kissed him back.

CHAPTER EIGHT

His mouth was hot, and so were his hands.

And she was burning, burning under his touch.

This is wrong, Joanna's brain shrieked, *it's wrong…*

How could it be wrong, when the searing flame of David's kiss felt so wonderful?

She whispered his name and he drew her even closer, until she was lying across his lap, her hair spilling over his arm, her hands clutching his shoulders desperately as his mouth sought and found the tenderness of hers.

"Open to me, Gypsy," he breathed and she did, parting her lips under the heat of his, moaning softly as he nipped her bottom lip, then stroked the sweet wound with the tip of his tongue.

He groaned and she felt his fingers at the nape of her neck, undoing her zipper, sliding it down until the bodice of her dress fell from her shoulders.

"No," she said, clutching at the silky fabric, "no, David, we can't…"

He cupped the back of her hand, his fingers tangling almost cruelly in her hair as he tilted her head back.

"The hell we can't."

"Hollister…"

"The partition's up. Hollister can't see or hear us." In the dark, his eyes gleamed with an almost predatory brilliance. He bent to her and kissed her until she was trembling in his arms. "This is our own little world, Gypsy. No one can see us. No one even knows we're here." He kissed her again. "And you are my wife."

His wife.

Joanna's breath caught. The simple words were as erotic as any a man had ever whispered to a woman.

And he was right. In the night, surrounded by the anonymity of the city, she felt as if they were alone in the universe.

She sighed with pleasure as he kissed her throat, and then the delicate flesh behind her ear.

"I never forgot the taste of you," he whispered thickly. His kisses were soft as rain, warm as sunlight against her skin. "Like honey. Like cream. Like..."

His lips closed over her silk-encased nipple and she cried out softly and her body arched toward him, a tautly strung bow of consummate sensation.

"Yes," he said, as she whispered his name and wound her arms tightly around his neck.

He groaned softly and shifted her, positioning her over him so that she was kneeling on the leather seat, her short, full skirt draping over his legs like the downturned petals of a flower.

His hand slid under the skirt, cupping her, feeling her wetness, teasing it until finally he hooked his fingers into the fragile crotch of her silk teddy and tore it aside.

Joanna gasped and jerked her head back.

"We're alone, Gypsy," David whispered against her mouth. "There's no one here but you and me. And I want you more than I've ever wanted a woman in my life."

He kissed her, hard, and she responded with an ardor that equaled his. It was what she wanted, too. No preliminaries. No sweet words. Just this, the blinding passion, the urgent need, the coupling that their flesh demanded.

That her heart desired.

Joanna's breath caught.

How could she have been so blind? She loved him. She had always loved him, this stranger who was her husband.

Her injury might have made her head forget him but her soul and her flesh remembered. He was a part of her, he always had been, and now her blood was throbbing his name with each beat of her heart.

"Gypsy?"

He was waiting, waiting for her to give him her answer. And she gave it, blindly, gladly, lifting her mouth to his for the sweet, possessive thrust of his tongue, clasping his face in her hands and dragging it down to hers.

He groaned softly, a primitive sound of triumph and need.

"Unzip me," he said, and she hurried to obey, her hands shaking with the force of her desire.

Her fingertips brushed over the straining fabric of his trousers. She felt the pulsing hardness of his erection.

"Joanna," he said urgently, and his hand moved, his fingers seeking, finding, caressing her secret, weeping flesh.

She was sobbing now, aching for him, empty without him; she had been empty for a long, long time.

"David," she whispered, and her fingers closed on the tab of his zipper...

The Bentley lurched. A horn blared, and the big car lurched again.

Joanna blinked. She pulled back in David's arms. "What was that?"

David cursed softly. "I don't know." His arms tightened around her. "And I don't care."

"No. No, wait..." She lay her palms against his chest. "David, stop."

"Come back here!" His voice was rough with desire; he cupped her face in one hand and kissed her. "I'm crazy with the need to be inside you, Gypsy. I want to feel your heat around me, to hear you cry out my name as you come."

Joanna felt as if she were awakening from a deep, drugged sleep. The Bentley had slowed to a crawl. She turned her head to the window, peered out the dark glass. They were moving through a construction zone; yellow caution lights blinked in the road.

She felt her face grow hot. No one could see in, she knew that. The tinted glass made it impossible. But that didn't keep her from suddenly feeling as if she and David were on display.

His hand stroked over her naked shoulders.

"David," she said, "please..."

His mouth burned at her breast.

"No. Stop it." She began to struggle. "David," she said sharply, "stop!"

He lifted his head. His eyes were dark, almost unfocused; his breathing was ragged. A *frisson* of fear tiptoed down her spine. All at once, her husband seemed more a stranger than ever.

"David." She shoved harder against his chest and shoulders. "Let me go, please."

"Don't be a fool! You know you want this—need this— as badly as I do. Come back here and—"

"No!" She tried to twist away from him but he wouldn't let her. "You don't know the first thing about what I want."

"I know exactly what you want. And you damned well almost got it."

Her hand cracked against his jaw. They stared at each other and then David let go of her and she scrambled off his lap. He turned away and lay his forehead against the cool window glass.

What in hell was the matter with him?

Here he was, a grown man, sitting in the back seat of a limousine with his wife straddling his lap, the bodice of her dress down at her waist and her skirt hiked up to her hips, and if she hadn't stopped him he'd have taken her here, on the cold leather seat, with no more finesse than a boy out on his first date.

And he was angry at Joanna?

God, what a pathetic excuse for a man he was.

She hadn't done a thing. Not one damned thing. She'd simply appeared from out of the blue, looking the way he'd never stopped remembering her, sounding the way she'd once sounded, and against all the rules of logic and reason he'd gone crazy, first with rage and then with lust and all because the terrible truth was that he'd never stopped loving the woman he'd thought he'd married.

For all he knew he might never, ever stop loving her.

What a joke.

He'd called Joanna a fool but if she was a fool, what did you call a man who was in love with a woman who'd never really existed?

Whoever this Joanna was, once her memory returned, she'd vanish as quickly as she had the first time. And then they'd be right back where they'd been before the accident, two people with nothing in common but his status and their impending divorce.

It would have made things easier if she understood. But what could he tell her? That the loss of her memory had made her a better person? That while she prayed for the return of her memory, he dreaded it?

David drew a shuddering breath. Making love to Joanna would have been like making love to a dream.

It was a good thing she'd stopped him. A damned good thing.

It had probably taken all her courage to show up at the party and he'd repaid that courage by being a selfish bastard.

"Joanna?" He reached out his hand and she slapped it away. "Jo, listen, I know how you feel—"

She turned toward him. He'd expected to see anguish in her eyes, that her mouth—that soft, sweet mouth—would be trembling, but he was wrong.

What he saw wasn't anguish but rage.

"You're truly remarkable," she said bitterly. "First you know what I want, now you know what I feel."

"Jo, I'm trying to apologize. I should never have…"

The limousine pulled to the curb. The engine shut off and the silence of the night settled around them. Joanna glared at him in the darkness.

"If you ever touch me again," she said, "so help me, David, I'll—I'll…"

Her voice broke. The door swung open. He caught a quick

glimpse of Hollister's startled face as Joanna shoved past him, ran up the steps and disappeared inside the house.

At five in the morning, David was still sitting in the darkened living room.

He'd been there for hours, ever since they'd come in. His jacket was off, his tie was gone and the top few buttons of his shirt were undone. His shoes lay beside his chair. There was an open decanter of cognac on the table beside him and a glass in his hand. He wasn't drunk though, God knew, he'd done his best.

Footsteps sounded softly on the stairs.

He rose to his feet and ran his hand through his hair. Then he walked quietly to the door and into the pool of pale yellow light cast by the lamp in the foyer.

"Joanna?" he said softly.

She paused, midway down the stairs. She was wearing a long yellow robe, her hair was caught back in a loose braid, and if she was surprised to see him, it didn't show on her face.

"Hello, David," she said tonelessly.

"Are you all right?"

"I'm fine."

She wasn't. Shadows lay like bruises below her eyes.

"I was just…" He raised his cognac snifter. "Would you like some?"

"No. No, thank you." She lifted both hands to her face and lightly touched her fingertips to her temples. "Actually, I came down for some aspirin. I couldn't seem to find any in my bathroom."

"I'll get you some."

"I'll get it myself, thank you."

Her voice was cool. Don't argue with me, it said, and he decided it might be best to take the hint.

He sighed, went back into the living room and sat down, nursing his cognac, anticipating her return, trying to figure out what to say, hell, trying to figure out what he could possibly do, to convince her he was sorry.

The seconds passed, and the minutes, and finally he put down his glass, stood up and walked back out to the hallway.

"Joanna?"

There was a light at the end of the hall. He followed it, to the kitchen. Joanna was standing in front of the open refrigerator, in profile to him. Her body was outlined in graceful brush strokes of light: the lush curve of her breast, the gentle fullness of her bottom, the long length of her legs.

His throat went dry. His hands fisted at his sides as he fought against the almost overwhelming urge to go to her, to take her in his arms and hold her close and say, Don't worry, love, everything's going to be fine.

He cleared his throat.

"Did you find the aspirin?"

She nodded and shut the refrigerator door.

"Yes, thank you. I was just making myself some cocoa."

"Cocoa?" he said, and frowned.

She went to the stove. There was a pot on one of the burners. She took a wooden spoon from a drawer and stirred its contents.

"Yes. Would you like some?"

He shut his eyes against a sudden memory, Joanna at the stove in Connecticut, laughing as she stirred a saucepan of hot milk.

Of course it's cocoa, David. What else would anybody drink when there's a foot of snow outside?

"David?"

He swallowed, looked at her, shook his head.

"Thanks, but I don't think it would go so well with cognac."

She smiled faintly. Then she shut off the stove, took a white porcelain mug from the cabinet and filled it with steaming cocoa.

"Well," she said, "good night."

"Wait." He stepped forward, into the center of the room. "Don't go, not just yet."

"I'm tired," she said in a flat voice. "And it's late. And I don't see any point in—"

"I'm sorry."

Her head came up and their eyes met. Joanna's throat constricted. He looked exhausted and unhappy, and she imagined herself going to him, taking him in her arms and offering him comfort. But there was no reason for her to comfort him, dammit, there was no reason at all!

It was he who'd hurt her, who'd been hurting her, from the minute she'd awakened in the hospital.

Tears stung in her eyes. She blinked hard and forced a smile to her lips.

"Apology accepted," she said. "We've both been under a lot of pressure. Now, if you'll excuse me—"

"Joanna."

His hands closed on her shoulders as she walked past him.

She stood absolutely still, her back to him.

She'd been awake all the night, staring at the ceiling and telling herself that what she felt for her husband—what she'd thought she'd felt—had been a lie, that in her confusion and the loneliness that came of her loss of memory, she'd fooled herself into thinking he meant something to her.

And she'd believed it.

Then, why was his touch making her tremble? Why was she fighting the urge to turn and go into his arms?

Stop being a fool, she told herself angrily, and she slipped out from beneath his hands and swung toward him.

"What do you want now, David? I've already accepted your apology." She took a ragged breath. "In a way, I guess some of what happened was my fault."

"No. You didn't—"

"But I did. I showed up uninvited, as you so clearly pointed out. And…and I suppose I should have worn something more in keeping with…with my status as your wife."

"Dammit, Jo—"

"As for what happened in the limousine…" Her cheeks colored but her gaze was unwavering. "I'm not a child, David. I'm as responsible for it as you. I shouldn't have let you—I shouldn't have…"

"Will you listen to me?"

"Why? We have nothing to discuss…unless you want to talk about a separation."

He recoiled, as if she'd hit him again. She couldn't blame him. What she'd said had shocked her, too. She hadn't expected to say anything about a separation, even though that was all she'd thought about for the last few hours.

"What in hell are you talking about?"

"It would be best," she said quietly. "You know we can't go on the way we are."

"You're talking nonsense!"

"Just give me a couple of days to—to find a place to live and—"

His hands clamped down on her shoulders.

"Are you crazy? Where in hell would you go?"

"I don't know." Her chin lifted. "I'll find a place. All I need is a little time."

"You're ill, don't you understand that?"

"I'm not ill. I just—"

"Yeah, I know. You just can't remember." David's eyes darkened. "Forget it, Joanna. It's out of the question."

"What do you mean, it's out of the question?" She wrenched free of his grasp. "I don't need your permission to leave. I'm not a child."

"You're behaving like one."

They glared at each other. Then Joanna slammed the mug of cocoa down on the table, turned on her heel and marched out of the room.

"Joanna?" David stalked after her. She was halfway up the stairs. "Where in hell do you think you're going?"

"Stop using that tone of voice with me." She spun toward him, her eyes flashing with anger. "I'm going to my room. Or do I need your approval first?"

"Just get this through your head," he snapped. "There won't be any separation."

"Give me one good reason why not!"

"Because I say so."

Joanna's mouth trembled. "That's great. If you can't win a fight, resort to typical male tyranny…" Her words tumbled to a halt and a puzzled look came over her face. "Typical male tyranny," she whispered. Her gaze flew to his. "David? Haven't I…haven't I said that before?"

He came slowly up the stairs until he was standing a step below her. "Yes," he said softly, "you have."

"I thought so." She hesitated. "For a minute, I almost remembered…I mean, I had one of those flashes… Did we…when I said that to you, had we been quarreling over the same thing? About—about me leaving you?"

A smile curved across his mouth. He reached out his hand and stroked his forefinger along the curve of her jaw.

"We hadn't been quarreling at all," he said in a quiet voice. "We'd been horsing around beside the pond—"

"In Connecticut?"

He nodded. "I'd been threatening to toss you in and you said I wouldn't dare—"

"And—and you made a feint at me and I laughed and stepped aside and you fell into the water."

He was almost afraid to breathe. "You remember that?"

Joanna's eyes clouded with tears. "Only that," she whispered, "nothing else. It's—it's as if I suddenly saw a couple of quick frames from a movie."

He cupped her cheek with his hand. "I came up sputtering and you were standing there laughing so hard you were crying. I went after you, and when I caught you and carried you down to the pond to give you the same treatment, you said I was a bully and that I was resorting to—"

"Typical male tyranny?"

"Uh-huh." His voice grew husky. "And I retaliated."

Joanna stared at him. There was something in the way he

was looking at her that sent a lick of flame through her blood.

"How?"

His smile was slow and sexy.

"I didn't dump you into the pond. I carried you to the meadow instead."

"A…a green meadow," Joanna said. "Filled with flowers."

"…and I undressed you, and I made love to you there, with the sweet scent of the flowers all around us and the sun hot on our skin, until you were sobbing in my arms." He cupped her face with his hands. "Do you remember that, Gypsy?"

She shook her head. "No," she whispered, "but I wish… I wish I did…"

Silence settled around them. Then David drew a labored breath.

"Go to your room," he said quietly.

Joanna swallowed hard. "That's where I was going, before you—"

"Get dressed, and pack whatever you'll need for the weekend."

Her brow furrowed. "What for?"

"On second thought, don't bother." He smiled tightly. "It seems to me you left the skin you shed in the bedroom closet in Connecticut."

"What on earth are you talking about?"

"We're going away for the weekend. Trust me," he said brusquely, when she opened her mouth to protest, "it's a very civilized thing to do, in our circle."

"I don't care if it's the height of fashion! I'm not going anywhere with you. I absolutely refuse."

"Even if going with me means you might begin to remember?"

She stared at him, her eyes wide. "Do you really think I will?"

Did he? he thought. And if she did…heaven help him, was that what he really wanted?

"David?"

"I don't know," he admitted.

"But you think I might…?"

"Get going." His tone was brisk and no-nonsense as he clasped her elbow and hurried her to her room. "I'll give you ten minutes and not a second more."

"David?"

He sighed, stopped in his tracks halfway down the hall, and turned toward her.

"What now?"

Joanna moistened her lips. "Why do you call me that?"

"Why do I call you what?" he said impatiently.

"Gypsy."

He stared at her and the moment seemed to last forever. Then, slowly, he walked back to where she stood, put his hand under her chin and gently lifted her face to his.

"Maybe I'll tell you while we're away."

He bent his head to her. She knew he was going to kiss her, knew that she should turn her face away…

His lips brushed softly over hers in the lightest, sweetest of caresses.

The gentleness of the kiss was the last thing she'd expected. Her lashes drooped to her cheeks. She sighed and swayed toward him. They stood that way for a long moment, linked by the kiss, and then David drew back. Joanna opened her eyes and saw a look on his face she had not seen before.

"David?" she said unsteadily.

He smiled, lifted his hand and stroked her hair.

"Go on," he said. "See if you can't find some old clothes and comfortable shoes buried in that closet of yours and then meet me downstairs in ten minutes."

Joanna laughed. It was silly, but she felt giddy and girlish and free.

''Make it fifteen,'' she said.

Impetuously, she leaned forward and gave him a quick kiss. Then she flew into her room and shut the door behind her.

CHAPTER NINE

THERE'D been a time David would have said he could have made the drive to Fenton Mills blindfolded.

He hadn't needed to check the exit signs to find the one that led off the highway, nor the turnoffs after that onto roads that grew narrower and rougher as they wound deeper into the countryside.

It surprised him a little to find all that was still true.

Even after all this time, the Jag seemed to know the way home.

Except that it wasn't exactly "home" and hadn't been for almost three years.

A young couple who farmed some land up the road from the house were happy to augment their income by being occasional caretakers. They kept an eye on things, plowed the long driveway when it snowed and mowed the grass when summer came, even though David never bothered coming up here anymore.

Sometimes, he'd wondered why he bothered hanging on to the property at all.

His accountant had asked him that just a few months before.

"You get no financial benefit from ownership," Carl had said, "and you just told me you never use the house. Why not get rid of it?"

David's reply had dealt with market conditions, real estate appreciation and half a dozen other things, all of which had made Carl throw up his hands in surrender.

"I should have known better than to offer financial advice to David Adams," he'd said, and both men had laughed and gone on to other topics.

Remembering that now made David grimace.

He'd done such a good snow job on Carl that he'd damned near convinced himself that he was holding on to the Connecticut property for the most logical of reasons.

But it wasn't true.

He'd hung on to the house for one painfully simple, incredibly stupid reason.

It reminded him of a life he'd once dreamed of living with a woman he'd thought he'd loved.

With Joanna.

He'd bought the place years ago, with his first chunk of real money. He had no idea why. This was not the fashionably gentrified part of Connecticut, though the area was handsome. As for the house…it was more than two hundred years old, and tired. Even the real estate agent had seemed shocked that someone would be interested in such a place.

But David, taking the long, leisurely way home from a skiing weekend, had spotted the For Sale sign and known instantly that this house was meant for him. And so he'd written a check, signed the necessary papers, and just that easily, the house had become his.

He'd driven up weekends, with a sleeping bag in the back of his car, and camped out in the dilapidated living room, sharing it from time to time with a couple of field mice, a bat and on one particularly eventful occasion, a long black snake that had turned out to be harmless.

Carpenters came, looked at the floors and the ceiling, stroked their chins and told him there was a lot of work to be done. Painters came, too, and glaziers, and men with specialties he'd never even heard of.

But the more time David spent in the old house, the more he began to wonder what it would be like to work on it himself. He found himself buying books on woodworking and poring over them nights in the study of the Manhattan town house he'd bought for its investment value and its location and never once thought of as home.

He started slowly, working first on the simpler jobs, asking for help when he needed it. Had he undertaken such a restoration in the city, people would have thought him crazy but here, in these quiet hills, no one paid much attention. New Englanders had a long tradition of thrift and hard work; that a man who could afford to let others do the job for him would prefer to do it himself wasn't strange at all.

He found an unexpected pleasure in working with his hands. There was a quiet satisfaction in beginning a job and seeing it through. He learned to plane wood and join floor boards, and the day he broke through a false wall and uncovered a brick fireplace large enough to roast an ox ranked right up there with the day years before when he'd opened the *Wall Street Journal* and realized he'd just made his first million on the stock exchange.

Local people, the ones who delivered the oak boards for the floors or the maple he'd needed to build the kitchen worktable, looked at the house as it evolved under his hands and whistled in admiration. The editor of the county newspaper got wind of what he was doing and politely phoned, asking to do what she called a "pictorial essay."

David just as politely turned her down. Dumped on a church doorstep as a baby, he'd grown up the product of an efficient, bloodless state system of foster child care.

This house, that he was restoring with his own hands, was his first real home. He didn't want to share it with anyone.

Until he met Joanna.

He brought her to the house for a weekend after their second date. The old plumbing chose just then to give out and he ended up lying on his back, his head buried under the kitchen sink. Joanna got down on the floor with him, handing him tools and holding things in place and getting every bit as dirty as he got.

"You don't have to do this stuff, Gypsy," David kept saying, and she laughed and said she was having the time of her life.

By the end of that weekend, he'd known he wanted Joanna not just in his bed but in his heart and in his life, forever. Days later, they were married.

At first, he was wild with happiness. The usual long hours he spent at his office became less important than being with his wife.

Morgana came as close to panic as he'd ever seen her.

"I don't know what to tell people when they phone, David," she said. "And there are conferences, and details that need your attention…"

He pondered the problem, then flew to the coast for three intensive days with the latest Silicone Valley *wunderkind*. By the time he returned home, the problem was solved.

After a squad of electricians spent a week rewiring the house, a battery of machines came to beeping, blinking life in the attic. Faxes, computers, modems, laser printers, even a high-tech setup that linked David to his New York office by video…

There was nothing he could not do from home that he had not once done in Manhattan, though he still flew down for meetings on Thursdays and Fridays, and always with his beautiful, beloved wife at his side. Sometimes the meetings ran late. Joanna never complained but David was grateful to Morgana, who kept her occupied the few times it happened.

And then, things began to change.

It started so slowly that he hardly noticed.

Joanna suggested they spend an extra day in the city. "I'd really love to see that new play," she said.

An invitation to the opera came in the mail. He started to toss it away but Joanna caught his hand, smiled, and said she'd never been to the opera in her life.

Before he knew it, they were spending five days a week in New York, then the entire week. Joanna met people, made friends, joined committees.

Connecticut, and the simple life they'd enjoyed there, got further and further away.

Morgana, who knew him as well as anyone except his wife, sensed his unhappiness and tried to help.

"You mustn't be so possessive," she told him gently. "A woman needs room to grow, especially one as young as Joanna."

So he backed off, gave her room. But it didn't help. The gap between them became a chasm. Joanna gave up pretending she liked the country at all. She begged off lazy weekend drives and quiet evenings by the fire. She hinted, then straight out told him she preferred the luxury of their Manhattan town house, and before David knew what was happening, the town house was crammed with ugly furniture and his life was governed by the entries in his wife's calendar.

The girl he'd fallen in love with had changed into a woman he didn't like.

Joanna traded denim and flannel for cashmere and silk. She scorned hamburgers grilled over an open fire in favor of *filet mignon* served on bone china in chic restaurants.

And she'd made it clear she preferred her morning coffee brought to her bedside by a properly garbed servant, not by a husband wearing a towel around his middle, especially if that husband was liable to want to sweeten the coffee with kisses instead of sugar.

David's hands tightened on the steering wheel of the Jaguar. That had been the most painful realization of all, that his passionate bride had turned into a woman who lay cold in his arms, suffering his kisses and caresses with all the stoicism of a Victorian martyr.

Had she worn a mask all along, just to win him? Or had his status and his money changed her into a different person?

After a while, he'd stopped touching her. Or wanting her. He'd made a mistake, and he'd fix it.

Divorce seemed the only solution...

Until last night, when his kisses had rekindled the fire

they'd once known and she'd burned like a flame in his arms.

Was that why he'd suddenly decided on coming here this weekend? Not in hopes of jarring her memory, as he'd claimed, but because...

No. Hell, no. He wasn't going to make love to Joanna, not this weekend or any other. He'd brought her to Connecticut because she'd had another of those all-too-swift flashes of memory, and they'd all been connected to this house.

The sooner she remembered, the better. The sooner he could give up his sham of a marriage and get on with his life—

"We'll be there soon, won't we?"

Joanna's voice was soft and hesitant. David looked at her. She was staring straight ahead. The sun was shining on her hair, making it gleam with iridescence.

"Just another few miles," he said. "Why? Do things seem familiar?"

She shook her head. "No. I just had the feeling that we were coming close... What a pretty road this is."

"Yes, it is."

"I like the stone walls we keep passing. Are they very old?"

"Most of them date back to Colonial times. Farmers built them with the stones they cleared from the land as they plowed."

"So many stones... It must have been hard land to cultivate."

"They still say that stone's the only crop that grows well in New England."

She smiled. "I can believe it."

I can't, David thought. We're talking like two characters in a travelog.

"What kind of house is it?"

So much for travelogs. That was the same question she'd

asked the first time he'd brought her here, and in that same soft, eager voice. He remembered how he'd smiled and reached for her hand.

"A house I hope you'll love as much as I do," he'd said.

This time, he knew enough not to smile or to touch her, and the only thing he hoped was that this weekend would end her amnesia and his charade.

"It's an old house," he said, and launched into the safety of the travelog script again. "The main section was built in the 1760's by a fairly prosperous farmer named Uriah Scott. His son, Joseph, added another wing when he inherited the house in the 1790's and each succeeding generation of Scotts added on and modernized the place."

"The house stayed in the Scott family, then?" Joanna sighed. "How nice. All those generations, sharing the same dreams...that must be wonderful."

David looked sharply at his wife. She had said that the first time, too, and just as wistfully. The remark had seemed poignant then, coming from a girl who'd been raised by a widowed father who'd cared more for his whiskey than he had for her; it had made him want to give her all the love she'd ever missed...

What a damned fool he'd been!

"Don't romanticize the story, Joanna," he said with a hollow smile. He glanced into his mirror, then made a turn onto the winding dirt road that led to the house. "Old houses are a pain in the ass. The floors sag, the heating systems never work right no matter what you do to them, there are spiders in the attic and mice in the cellar—"

"Is that it?"

He looked at the white clapboard house with the black shutters, standing on the gentle rise at the top of the hill. It was a small house, compared to the newer ones they'd passed along the way; it looked lonely and a bit weary against the pale Spring sky. The winter had been harsher than usual; the trim would need to be painted as soon as it got a bit warmer and he could see that the winter storms had worked a couple of the slate roof tiles loose.

A bitter taste rose in his mouth.

What had he ever thought he'd seen in this place to have made it magical?

"Yes," he said, "that's it. I'm sorry if you expected something more but—"

"Something more? Oh, David, what more could there be? It's beautiful!"

What in hell was this, a game of *déjà vu*? That was another thing she'd said the first time they'd come here. Later on, he'd realized that it had all been said to please him.

He prided himself on being a man you could only fool once. He swung toward her, a curt retort on his lips, but it died, unspoken, when he saw the enraptured expression on her face.

"Do you really like it?" he heard himself say.

Joanna nodded. "Oh, yes," she whispered, "I do. It's perfect."

And familiar.

She didn't say that, though she thought it. It was far too soon to know if this weekend would jog her memory and there was no point in getting David's hopes up, nor even her own. And she sensed that he was having second thoughts about having brought her here. She was having second thoughts, herself. If she didn't begin to remember after this weekend the disappointment would be almost too much to bear.

"Jo?"

She blinked and looked up. David had parked the car and gotten out. Now, he was standing in the open door, holding out his hand.

"Shall we go inside?"

She looked into his eyes. They were cool and guarded. She had the feeling that he was hoping she'd say no and ask

him to turn around and go back to the city. But she'd come
too far to lose her courage now.

"Yes," she said quickly, "yes, please, let's go inside."

David wasn't sure what he expected once Joanna stepped
inside the door.

Would she clap her hand to her forehead and say, "I
remember"? Or would she take one look at the small rooms
and the old-fashioned amenities and say that she didn't remember and now could they please go home?

She did neither.

Instead, just as she had all those years ago, she almost
danced through the rooms, exclaiming with delight over the
wide-planked floors and the windows with their original,
hand-blown glass; she sighed over the banister he'd once
spent a weekend sanding and varnishing to satin smoothness.

He'd made an early morning phone call to the couple who
were his caretakers and he could see that they'd stopped by.
The furniture was dusted, the windows opened. There was
a pot of coffee waiting to be brewed on the stove and a
basket of home-baked bread on the maple table he'd built.
A jar of homemade strawberry jam stood alongside and there
was a bowl of fresh eggs, butter and a small pitcher of thick
cream in the refrigerator.

Joanna said it was all wonderful, especially the fireplaces
and the hand pump on the back porch. But she added, with
a happy laugh, that she was glad to see there was a modern
gas range and real running water and a fully stocked freezer
because she wasn't that much of a stickler for the good old
days.

And suddenly David thought, but these *were* the good old
days. This woman bent over the pump, inelegantly and in-
congruously attired in a pale gray cashmere sweater, trendy
black nylon exercise pants and running shoes… "It's the
only comfortable stuff I could find," she'd explained with
a little laugh, when she'd reappeared that morning…this

woman, with her hair hanging down her back and her face free of makeup, was everything he'd ever wanted, everything he'd thought he'd found when he'd found Joanna.

Dammit, what was wrong with him?

He muttered a short, sharp epithet and Joanna swung toward him.

"What's the matter, David?"

"Nothing."

"But you just said—"

"I, ah, I saw a mouse, that's all."

"A mouse? Where?"

"It ran out from under the sink. Don't worry about it. There are probably some traps in the barn out back. I'll set some out later."

"You don't have to do that. I'm not—"

"I'll show you upstairs," he said brusquely. "You didn't get much sleep last night, Joanna, and this trip has probably been tiring. I think it might be a good idea for you to take a nap."

"Oh, but…" But I'm not tired, she'd almost said.

But being tired had nothing to do with it. He wanted her out of the way for a while; she could hear it in his voice. They'd only just arrived and already he was sorry he'd brought her.

Joanna nodded. "Good idea," she said with a false smile. "You lead the way."

There were three closed doors upstairs. One opened onto a bathroom, one onto a steep flight of steps that led to the attic. The third gave way on a spacious bedroom with exposed beams and a fireplace, dominated by a massive canopied bed…

One bedroom? Only one?

Joanna stopped just inside the doorway. "Oh," she said. "I never thought…"

David understood. "It's not a problem," he said quickly. "There's another bedroom downstairs. I'll be perfectly comfortable there. You go on, Jo. Take a nap. When you get up, we'll go for a drive. I'll show you a little bit of New England. Who knows? Maybe something you see will jog your memory.''

''Sure,'' she said brightly, ''that'll be fun.''

She shut the door after him. Then she walked to the window, curled onto the wide sill, and stared out at the rolling hills dressed in the tender green of late Spring and wondered why in heaven's name she couldn't just bring herself to ask him, straight out, why they didn't share a bed or even a room.

And if, in fact, they ever had.

Joanna did nap, after a while, and when she awoke, she was amazed to see that there were long shadows striping the room.

She got up, padded across the narrow hall to the bathroom, washed her hands and her face. In the process, she caught a glimpse of herself in the mirror.

Ugh, what a mess! Her hair needed combing, and a touch of lipstick wouldn't hurt. And this silly outfit... There was a wall-length closet in the bedroom, and David had said something cryptic about her not needing to bring anything with her. Maybe there was something in the closet that would look and feel better than this.

She made a soft exclamation of surprise when she looked into the closet. It was filled with clothing, all things she must have bought and all very different from what hung in her closet back in New York. There were jeans and corduroy pants, worn soft and fine with age and washing. Cotton shirts, and sweaters. Sneakers and walking shoes, hiking boots and a pair of rubber things that were as ungraceful as anything she'd ever seen but would surely keep your feet dry and warm in snow.

And there were David's clothes, too. Jeans, as worn as hers. Boots and shoes, sweaters and flannel shirts...

Joanna's throat constricted. They had shared this room, then.

This room. And this bed...

"Jo? Are you awake?"

She spun toward the door, and toward his voice just beyond it. "Yes," she called, and cleared her throat, "yes, David, I am. Just give me a minute and I'll be down."

"Take your time."

Her fingers flew as she pulled off her clothes. She put on jeans, a pale pink cotton shirt and a pair of gently beat-up leather hiking boots that felt like old friends as soon as she got them on. Then she tied a navy blue pullover sweater around her shoulders and brushed her hair back from her face. She found a tube of pale pink lipstick in a tray on the maple dresser, put some on her mouth, and went downstairs.

"Hi," she said brightly, as she came into the living room.

David turned around. "Hi, yourself." His smile tilted as he looked at her. "Well," he said, "I see you found your clothes."

"Uh-huh." She caught her lip between her teeth. "David? What did you mean about me shedding my skin in Connecticut?"

His face closed. "It was a stupid thing to have said."

"But what did you mean?"

"Only that I knew you had a closet filled with stuff to wear."

"Yes, but—"

"What do you feel like having for dinner?"

"Dinner? I don't know. I haven't even thought about—"

"There's a place half an hour or so away that's supposed to have excellent French cuisine."

She laughed. "French cuisine? Here?"

David smiled. "We're not exactly on the moon, Jo."

"Oh, I know. I just meant... I know you're going to think I'm crazy..."

"What?"

"No. Never mind. French is fine." She smiled and gave a delicate shudder. "Just so long as they don't serve—what was that stuff? Goat cheese?"

He laughed, leaned back against the wall, and tucked his hands into the rear pockets of his jeans.

"Goat cheese will be the least of your worries," he said. "Go on, tell me what you were going to say."

She took a deep breath and somehow, even before she spoke, he knew what was going to come out of her mouth.

"You'll laugh, I know, but when I looked in the freezer before... David, what I'd really love for dinner is a hamburger."

It was a mistake.

The whole damned thing was a mistake, starting with the minute they'd left Manhattan straight through to now, sitting here on the rug beside the fireplace in the living room with his wife, his beautiful wife, watching her attack an oversize burger with total pleasure while smoky music poured like soft rain from the radio.

What in hell was he doing? Why was he pretending to listen to what she was saying when he couldn't hear a word because he was too busy thinking how the light of the fire danced on her lovely face?

He forced himself to concentrate. She was telling him a story about one of the woman at Bright Meadows who'd been convinced she'd been born on the planet Pluto.

"...know I shouldn't laugh," she said, licking a drop of ketchup from her finger, "but, oh, David, if you could have heard how serious she was..."

He laughed, because he knew she expected it. But he wasn't laughing inside, where it counted, because he was too busy admitting that the best thing that could come out of this weekend was that Joanna would remember nothing.

Heaven help him, he was falling head over heels in love with her all over again.

"...asked me where I was born and when I said, well, I couldn't really say because...David? What's the matter?"

David rose to his feet.

"Listen, Joanna..."

Listen, Joanna, we're leaving. That was what he'd intended to say. We're gonna get out of here while the getting's good.

But that wasn't what he said at all.

"Jo," he said, and held out his hand, "will you dance with me?"

Her eyes met his. Color, soft as the pink of a June sunrise, swept into her cheeks. She smiled tremulously, put her hand in his and got gracefully to her feet.

He led her to the center of the room and put his arms around her. There was no pretense, no attempt to pretend that dancing was really what this was all about. Instead, he drew her close against his hard body, his hands linked at the base of her spine. She stiffened and he thought she was going to resist. But then she gave a soft, sweet sigh, looped her arms around his neck and let herself melt into the music and his embrace.

It was wonderful, holding her like this. Feeling the sweet softness of her breasts against his chest, the warmth of her thighs against his. His hand dropped from the small of her back and curved over her bottom. He lifted her against his growing hardness so that she could know what was happening to him.

Joanna made a little sound as she felt him pulse against her. The knowledge that he wanted her was like a song drumming in her blood. He'd wanted her last night, too, but not like this. What had happened in the car had been about lust but this...

This was about love.

She was sure of it, as sure as she could ever be about anything. She loved David, she knew that with all her heart. And he loved her. She could feel it in his every caress.

She drew back in his arms and looked deep into her husband's eyes.

"David?" she whispered.

"Gypsy," he said softly, "my Gypsy," and then his mouth was on hers and his hands were on her breasts and he was drawing her down to the rug in front of the fireplace and into a drowning whirlpool of passion.

CHAPTER TEN

THE wind sighing through the trees and the rain pattering gently against the roof woke David from sleep.

He lay unmoving, struggling to get his bearings in a darkness broken only by the flickering light of the fire on the hearth. Then he felt the sweet warmth of Joanna's body curled into his, smelled the fragrance of her hair spilled across his shoulder, and joy filled his heart.

His wife lay in the curve of his arm, snuggled tightly against him. Her head was nestled on his biceps, her hand lay open and relaxed on his chest. Her leg was a welcome weight thrown over his.

It was the way they'd always fallen asleep after they'd made love, the way it had been in those days so long gone by, days he'd never dreamed of recapturing.

But they had.

Was it a miracle? Or was it some cruel trick of fate? Would his wife stay as she was, even after she recovered her memory…or would she go back to being the cool, acquisitive stranger he'd been about to divorce?

There were so many questions, but there were no answers.

David eased onto his side, slid his other arm around Joanna and drew her close. The last, faint light of the dying fire played across her face, highlighting the elegant bones. She was so beautiful, and never more so than after they'd made love, and he knew that the questions didn't matter, not tonight.

All that mattered was this.

He buried his face in her hair, nuzzling it back from her shoulder, and pressed his mouth gently to the curving flesh. Still asleep, she sighed and snuggled closer.

The scent of her rose to his nostrils, a blend of flowers and sunshine and the exciting muskiness of sex. He kissed her again, his lips moving up her throat and to her mouth.

"Mmm," she said, and stirred lazily in his arms.

His hand cupped her breast.

"David," she sighed, and linked her hands behind his neck.

He smiled against her mouth. "Hello, sweetheart."

"Was I asleep?"

"We both were." He bent his head and kissed her with a slow, lazy thoroughness. "It's late."

"Mmm."

"The fire's almost out, and it's pitch black outside."

"Mmm."

"We should go to bed."

Joanna's laugh was soft and wicked. "What do we need a bed for? I thought we managed just fine."

His hand slid down her body and slipped between her thighs. She made a small sound of pleasure as he cupped her warm flesh.

"Better than fine," he murmured. "But now I want to make love to my wife on soft pillows and under a down comforter."

"That sounds wonderful." Joanna's smile tilted. "David? We...we shared a bedroom, didn't we? Before my accident, I mean."

She felt him stiffen in her arms and she cursed herself for ruining this perfect night. But instead of rolling away from her, as she'd half expected, he sighed and lay back with her still in his arms.

"Yes," he said, after a long silence. They had shared a bedroom, they'd shared everything...a long time ago. But he couldn't tell her that, not without telling her all the rest, about the divorce, about how different she was now...

"Yes," he said again, "we did."

Joanna rolled onto her stomach, propped her elbows on

the rug and her chin in her hands and looked down into her husband's face.

"Even back in the city?"

"Yes, even there." He reached up his hand and gently stroked her tangled curls back from her face. "We used to share my bedroom until…"

"Until what? Why did we…why did we decide on separate rooms? And when? Have we been sleeping separately for a long time?"

He sighed. Trust this new Joanna to come up with some damned good questions. And trust him not to have any good answers.

The truth was that they'd never "decided" on separate rooms; it had just happened. He'd started spending occasional nights in his study, stretching out on the leather sofa after working late. The excuse he'd offered himself, and Joanna, was that he hadn't wanted to wake her by coming to bed after she was asleep.

And Joanna had said there was no reason for him to spend the night on a sofa when they had a perfectly usable extra bedroom available. She'd been thinking of converting it into something more to her tastes, she'd added with a brittle smile. Would that be all right?

Of course, he'd told her, and not long after that he'd come home and found Joanna's clothes gone from the closet in the master suite and what had been the guest room remade into something that looked like a bad layout from a trendy magazine…

"David?"

He looked at his wife. She was still waiting for an answer and he decided to give her the only one he could. An honest one, as far as it went.

"I can't really tell you, Jo." Gently, he clasped her shoulders and rolled her onto her back. "It just happened. I'm not even sure exactly when."

"I asked you once if we'd been unhappy," Joanna said,

"and you gave me the same kind of answer. But we weren't happy, David, I know we weren't."

In the shadowy darkness, he could see the tears welling in her eyes. For one wild moment, he thought of telling her the truth. No, he'd say, hell, no, we weren't happy...

But they had been, once. And they could be again. The thought surged through him, pushing aside everything else.

"I mean," she said, her voice trembling, "if we were sleeping in separate beds, leading separate lives..."

David didn't hesitate. He crushed his mouth to hers, silencing her with a deeply passionate kiss.

"That's over," he said fiercely. "No more sleeping apart, Gypsy. And no more separate existences. You're going to be my wife again."

"Oh, yes, that's what I want. I..." She caught herself just in time. I love you, she'd almost said, I love you with all my heart.

But the idea of being the first to say the words frightened her. It was silly, she knew; there was nothing frightening about telling your husband you loved him—unless you couldn't recall him ever saying those three simple words to you.

"I want to be your wife," she whispered instead, and she smiled. "And I want to know why you call me Gypsy. You said you'd..." Joanna's breath caught. "David! What are you...?"

"I'm getting reacquainted with my wife," he murmured, his breath warm against her breasts and then against her belly. "Your skin is like silk, do you know that? Hot silk, especially here."

She cried out as he buried his face between her thighs and kissed her, again and again, until she was sobbing with the pleasure of it. And after she'd shattered against his mouth he rose over her and buried himself deep inside her, riding her with deep, powerful thrusts until she climbed that impossible mountain of sensation once again, then tumbled from its peak as he exploded within her.

There were tears on Joanna's cheeks when David at last withdrew from her. He tasted their salinity as he kissed her.

"Don't cry, sweetheart," he whispered.

"I'm not," she said, and cried even harder, "I'm just so happy."

He kissed her again as he gathered her into his arms.

"Joanna," he said, "I…"

He bit back the words just in time. Joanna, he'd almost said, I love you.

But how could he tell her that? It was too soon. He couldn't even let himself think it, not so long as he both knew and didn't know the woman he held in his arms.

"I'm glad," he said softly, and then he rose to his feet and carried her up the stairs to their bedroom, where he held her tightly in his arms all through the rest of the long night.

When he awoke again, it was morning.

The rain had stopped, the sun was shining, a warm breeze was blowing through the open window.

And the wonderful scent of fresh coffee drifted on the air.

David rose, dragged on a pair of jeans and a white T-shirt. He made a quick stop in the bathroom. The shower curtain was pulled back and there was a damp towel hanging over the rod.

Barefoot, thrusting his fingers into his hair to push it back from his forehead, he made his way down to the kitchen.

Joanna was turned away from him, standing in the open back door so that the morning sunlight fell around her like a golden halo. Her hair was still damp and fell over her shoulders in a wild tumble. She was barefoot and wearing a pair of incredibly baggy shorts that sagged to her knees and an old cotton shirt of his that still bore traces of the buttercup yellow paint they'd used to paint the pantry years before.

My wife, he thought, my beautiful wife.

His heart felt as if it were expanding within his chest. Back in his college days, during one of the all-night bull sessions that had been, in their way, as valuable as any class time, a guy who'd had one beer too many had said something about there being a moment in a man's life when everything that was important came together in a perfect blend.

David knew that this was that moment. No matter what the future held, there would never be an instant more right than this one, with Joanna standing before him, limned in golden sunlight, after a night spent in his arms.

"Good morning," he said, when he could trust his voice.

She spun toward him. He saw the swift race of changing emotions on her face, the joy at seeing him warring with the morning-after fluster of a woman new to a man's bed, and he smiled and held out his arms. She hesitated for a heartbeat, and then she flew into his embrace.

"Good morning," she whispered, tilting her face up to his. He accepted the invitation gladly and kissed her. She sighed and leaned back in his arms. "I didn't wake you, did I?"

He shook his head and put on a mock ferocious scowl. "No. And I want to talk to you about that."

Joanna's brows rose. "What do you mean?"

"I like it when you wake me." The scowl gave way to a sexy grin. "Very much, as a matter of fact. There I was, all ready to greet the day with a special pagan ritual—"

"A special pagan…?"

"Uh-huh. And I had all the ingredients, too. The sun, the bed, my ever-ready male anatomy…"

"David!" Joanna blushed. "That's awful."

His arms tightened around her. "You didn't think so last night."

"Well, no. I mean, *that's* not terrible. I mean…" She giggled, then dissolved in laughter. "Sorry. I never thought about your 'ever-ready male anatomy.' I just thought about being desperate for coffee."

"I'm desperate, too." He lifted her face to his. "For a kiss."

Joanna sighed. "I thought you'd never ask."

Their kiss was long and sweet. When it ended, David kept his arm looped around Joanna's shoulders while he poured himself a cup of coffee.

"What do you want to do today?"

She smiled up at him. "You pick it."

"If it's left to me to choose," he said, bending his head to hers and giving her another kiss, "we'll go back to bed and spend the day there."

She blushed again, in a way he'd all but forgotten women could.

"That doesn't sound so terrible to me," she whispered.

David put down his cup, took Joanna's and put it beside his.

"I don't want to tire you out, Jo," he said softly. "I know, I know, you haven't been ill. But you've been under a lot of stress."

Joanna put her arms around his neck. "Making love with you could never tire me out. But I have to admit, I'd love to see more of the countryside. It's so beautiful here."

"Beautiful," he agreed solemnly, and kissed her again. When the kiss ended, he knew he had to do something or he'd end up carrying her back to bed and keeping her there until neither of them had the strength to move. So he took a deep breath, unlinked her hands from around his neck, and took a step back. "OK," he said briskly, "here's the deal. I'll shower, then we'll go get some breakfast."

"I can make breakfast. We've got those lovely eggs in the fridge, and that fresh butter and cream…"

"Lovely eggs, huh?" David grinned. "OK. Just give me ten minutes to shower… Come to think of it, that was another thing I'd planned."

"What?"

"Well, first the pagan ritual to greet the day, then a shower together." A wicked gleam lit his green eyes. "What the heck. I had to do without the pagan bit but there's no reason to ditch both ideas."

"David?" Joanna danced away as he reached for her.

"David, no! I already took a shower. See? My hair is...
David? David!" Laughing, she pounded on his shoulders as
he caught her in his arms, tossed her over his shoulder, and
headed for the stairs. "You're crazy. You're impossible.
You're..."

But by then, they were already in the shower, clothes and
all, and she shrieked as he turned on the water and it cas-
caded over them. And somehow, in the process of stripping
off each other's soaked clothing, somehow, they ended up
worshiping the sun and each other, after all.

"Tell me again," Joanna said, wiping a ribbon of sweat
from her forehead with the back of her hand, "we really
used to do this?"

David nodded. They were standing in the midst of what
looked like an automotive graveyard.

"All the time," he said absently. "Hey, is that what I
think it is?"

"Is what what you think it is?" Joanna followed after
him as he wove his way through the rusting hulks of what
had once been cars.

"It is," he said triumphantly. He plucked something from
the nearest pile of rubble and held it out. "Ta-da!"

"Ta-da, what?" She poked a finger at the thing. It looked
like a metal box with pipes attached. "What is that?"

"A heat exchanger. If you knew how long I've been looking for one..."

Joanna laughed. "Yeah, well, to each his own, I guess.
This place is amazing. To think anybody would save all this
junk..."

"It's not junk," David said firmly, "it's a collection of
what may be the best used sports car parts in the northeast."

"Uh-huh."

"And this heat exchanger, woman, is the catch of the
day."

"Will it fit the Jag?"

"Of course."

"Do you need it?"

David shot her a pitying look. "I don't. But you thin-blooded types do. Come on, give me your hand and we'll go pay the man for..." He turned toward her. "That's just what you used to ask me," he said softly.

"What?"

"Do you need it?" He lay his hand along the curve of her cheek. "We bought the Jaguar together. And we worked on it together. And we had a great time, but you used to tease me, you'd say that you didn't know buying the car meant we'd have to poke through—"

"—through every junkyard in the lower forty-eight," Joanna said, "with long-term plans for Hawaii and Alaska." Her eyes flew to his. "That's what I used to say, wasn't it?"

David nodded. "Yes."

"I can hear myself saying it." Her throat worked dryly. "David? What if...what if my memory comes back and—and spoils things?"

Her fear mirrored his, but he'd be damned if he'd admit it.

"Why does it have to?" he said, almost angrily.

"I don't...I don't know. I just thought—"

"Then don't think," he said, and kissed her.

They stopped for lunch at a tiny diner tucked away on a narrow dirt road.

"No menus," David said, waving away the typed pages the waitress offered. "We'll have the chili. And two bottles of—"

"—Pete's Wicked Ale," Joanna said, and smiled. She waited until the woman had gone to the kitchen before she leaned toward David.

"Do I like chili?" she whispered.

He grinned. "Does the woman like chili? I used to say you must have been born south of the border to love chili as much as you did."

"Is that why you call me Gypsy? Because you teased me about being born in Mexico?"

His grin faded. "Gypsies don't come from Mexico. You've got your continents mixed."

"I know. But every time I try to get you to tell me why you call me that name, you change the subject." She reached across the scarred tabletop and took hold of his hand. "So I figured I'd back into the topic."

"Cagey broad," David said, with a little laugh. He sighed and linked his fingers through hers. "There's no mystery, Jo. It just…" It hurts me to remember, he wanted to say, but he didn't. "It just happened, that's all."

"How?"

"Because that's how I thought of you." He looked at her and smiled. "As my wild, wonderful Gypsy."

"Was I wild?"

"Not in the usual sense. You just had a love for life that…"

"Ale," the waitress said, putting two frosted bottles in front of them. When she'd left, David leaned forward.

"You were nothing like the women I knew," he said softly. "You didn't given a damn for convention or for the rules."

"Me?" Joanna said, her voice rising in a disbelieving squeak as she thought of her conventionally furnished town house, her chauffeured car, her clothing, her life as it was mirrored in her appointment book.

"The first time I saw you, you were wearing hiking boots, wool socks, a long wool skirt and a lace blouse with big, puffy sleeves that narrowed at your wrists."

"Leg-o'-mutton," she said, frowning. "Where was I? At a costume party?"

He laughed. "You were sitting at the reception desk at Adams Investments."

Joanna's eyes rounded. "I was what?"

"Our regular receptionist had called in sick. She said she

had the flu and she'd be out for the week. So Morgana phoned a temp agency and they sent you over.''

"Morgana," Joanna said, frowning.

"Yeah." David chuckled. "She didn't want to hire you, she said you didn't fit our image."

He paused as the waitress served their chili.

"And I agreed with her," he continued, after they were alone again. "But we were desperate. There were six people in the waiting room, the telephones were ringing off the walls, and who else could we have come up with on such short notice?"

Joanna smiled. "It's so lovely to be hired because you're wanted," she said sweetly. "Thank you, David." She spooned some chili into her mouth and rolled her eyes in appreciation.

"Good?"

"Wonderful. So, go on. I looked like a refugee from a thrift shop but you hired me anyway, and—"

"And I offered to drive you home that night, because we worked late."

"I'll bet that didn't thrill Morgana."

He frowned. "You don't like her very much, do you?"

"Don't be silly," she said quickly. "How could I not like her when I hardly know her?"

David reached across the table and took Joanna's hand. "She was a good friend to you, Jo. After you and I married, you felt a little, well, lost, I guess. And Morgana did everything she could to help you settle in."

"Settle in?"

"Yeah." He cleared his throat. "It was all new to you. Living in Manhattan, entertaining…"

"You mean, I was the poor little match girl who married the handsome prince and went to live in his luxurious castle," she said softly.

"No. Hell, no." His fingers tightened on hers. "You weren't accustomed to…" *To money. To status. But, by God, she'd grown accustomed quickly enough…*

"I understand." Joanna sighed. "And I'm sure Morgana was terrific. I don't know why…" She sighed again and gave him a little smile. "Actually, I do know. It's because she's so gorgeous and she gets to spend so much time with you. For a while there, I even thought—I imagined…"

"Morgana is my right-hand man," David said, dragging his thoughts from where he wished they hadn't gone. "She's efficient, and very bright, and I trust her implicitly. But that's all she is and all she ever has been."

"I'm glad to hear it," Joanna said, and smiled. "Go on. Tell me what happened when you drove me home."

He felt some of the sudden tension ease from his muscles. He grinned, let go of her hand and picked up his spoon.

"What do you think happened?"

"What?"

"Nothing."

"Nothing?"

"Cross my heart. You were the soul of propriety, and so was I."

"Good." She laughed. "For a minute there, you had me thinking that—"

"I wanted you so badly that I ached."

Color swept into her face. "Right away?"

"Oh, yeah." He spooned up some chili. "The minute I saw you. But I did the right thing," he said, deadpan. "I waited until our second date."

"Our second…" Joanna's color deepened. "Tell me you're joking!"

"We made love," he said, smiling into her eyes, "and it was incredible."

"Incredible," she whispered, as fascinated as she was shocked.

"Uh-huh. And a few days after that, we got married."

Joanna's spoon clattered against the tabletop.

"Got married? So fast? After knowing each other, what, two weeks?"

"Ten days," he said, making light of it, wishing he could

tell her how he'd proposed with his heart in his mouth for fear she'd turn him down and walk out of his life…and how, not even a year later, he'd wished she had.

Ten days, Joanna thought. Well, why not? It couldn't have taken her more than ten minutes to have fallen in love with David.

But what about him? She'd been the soul of propriety, he'd said. What had happened? Had he wanted her to sleep with him—the ever-ready male anatomy at work—and when she'd refused, had he made an impulsive offer of marriage and ended up regretting it?

Was that what had gone wrong between them? Had he simply looked at her across the breakfast table one morning and asked himself what in hell she was doing there?

When the sexual excitement of this weekend was over, would he look at her and think that same thought again?

"Jo?" David reached for her hand. "What is it? You're so pale."

Joanna forced a sickly smile to her lips. "I think…I think you were right when you said I shouldn't overdo." Carefully, she pushed her bowl of chili away. "Would you mind very much if we went back to the house now?"

He was on his feet before she'd finished speaking. "Let's go," he said, tossing a handful of bills on the table. She stood up, he put his arm around her and the next thing she knew, he was carrying her from the diner.

"David, put me down. This is silly. You don't have to pick me up every time I—"

He kissed her, silencing the quick flow of words in a way that made her heartbeat stutter.

"I love holding you," he whispered fiercely. "I'd hold you in my arms forever, if I could."

He tucked her gently into the car, buckled her seat belt, then got behind the wheel and drove slowly home. And all the time, she wondered if he'd meant what he'd said, if it would last or if everything that had happened between them would end when the weekend did.

He insisted on lifting her from the car and carrying her into the house.

"I'm going to take you upstairs and put you to bed," he said. "And when you're feeling better, I'll make us some supper."

"Don't be silly. I feel better already. I'll cook."

"What's the matter? Afraid of trying my extra-special canned chicken soup?"

Joanna laughed. "At least let me lie down in the living room so I don't feel like a complete invalid."

"Deal." He lowered her gently to the couch and smiled at her. "And since you're feeling better, I'll let you have a vote."

"A vote on what?"

David grinned. "Raise your hand if you want us to stay right where we are for the rest of the week."

Her eyes widened. "Do you mean it?"

"Scout's honor."

"Oh, that would be wonderful. But your office…"

"They'll manage." He leaned down, brushed his mouth lightly over hers. "Lie right there and don't you dare move an inch. I'll put up the kettle for some tea and phone Morgana." He smiled. "She'll probably be delighted at the chance to run things without me for a while."

Joanna smiled and lay her head back as David made his way to the kitchen.

Had she ever been so happy in her life?

Even the fears she'd had just a little while ago didn't seem quite so awful now. There was more to her relationship with David than sex. There had to be. That he wanted to stay here with her, away from the rest of the world, was wonderful.

Regaining her memory no longer seemed as quite as important as it had. What mattered now was getting her husband to admit that he loved her.

"Jo?"

She looked up. David was coming slowly toward her, his smile gone.

"David, what's wrong?"

"Nothing, really." He squatted down beside her and took her hand in his. "I mean, it's not like it's the end of the world or anything…"

"But?"

He sighed. "But Morgana said she'd been just about to phone me. I've been working on this project for the Secretary of Commerce… Hell," he said with an impatient gesture, "the point is, the White House has become interested."

Joanna gave a little laugh. "The White House? Are you serious?"

David nodded. "The Secretary wants a meeting. Gypsy, there's no way I can put him off."

"Of course not."

"If it was anything else…"

"David, you don't have to explain. I understand."

"Look, we'll go back to New York tomorrow, I'll meet with the Secretary and his advisors and next weekend, we'll drive up again and stay for the week. OK?"

Joanna nodded. "Sure."

She hoped she sounded as if she meant it but as she went into David's arms and lifted her face for his kiss, there was a hollow feeling in the pit of her belly, as if she knew in her heart that they would not be returning to this house again.

CHAPTER ELEVEN

THE servants in the Adams town house were in the habit of taking their mid-morning coffee together.

It was Mrs. Timmons's idea and though it made for a pleasant start to the day, it was a ritual that had less to do with congeniality than with efficiency. The housekeeper had found she could best organize the day with Ellen and Hollister seated opposite her at the kitchen table.

But she could see instantly that that wasn't going to work this morning.

Nothing was going according to schedule. And she had the feeling that nothing would.

The Adamses had returned from their weekend outing late last night. Mrs. Timmons had been watching the late news on the TV when she'd heard them come in and she'd risen from the rocking chair in her bedroom cum sitting room off the kitchen, hastily checked her appearance in the mirror, and gone out to see if she were needed.

What she'd seen had made her fall back into the shadows in amazement.

There was Mr. David, carrying his wife up the stairs. He'd done that the day he'd brought her home from the rehabilitation center, but this…oh, this was very different.

Mrs. Adams's arms were tightly clasped around her husband's neck. They were whispering to each other, and laughing softly, and halfway up the stairs Mr. David had stopped and kissed his wife in a way that had made Mrs. Timmons turn her face away. When she'd dared look again, the Adamses were gone and the door to Mr. David's bedroom was quietly clicking shut.

Now, at almost ten in the morning, the door to that room

had yet to open. Neither of the Adamses had come down for breakfast and Mr. David had even foregone his daily run.

"Never happened before," Hollister said, dipping half a donut into his coffee.

"Of course it has," Mrs. Timmons said briskly, "it's just that you weren't here at the beginning."

"The beginning of what?"

"I'll bet she means when they were first married," Ellen said with a giggle, "when they were still newlyweds. Isn't that right, Mrs. Timmons?"

Ellen blanched when the housekeeper fixed her with a cold eye. "Isn't this your day for organizing the clothing for the dry cleaner?"

Hollister came to Ellen's defense.

"She was only picking up on what you'd just said," he began, then fell silent under that same stern gaze.

"And you," Mrs. Timmons said, "are supposed to be polishing the silver."

Hollister and Ellen looked at each other, shrugged their shoulders and pushed back their chairs.

"We can take a hint," Hollister said with quiet dignity.

Mrs. Timmons began clearing the dishes. "Good," she said grumpily. But after the door had swung shut and she was alone in the kitchen, she stood still.

She had worked for David Adams for many years and she'd come to respect him. She supposed, if pressed, she might even admit she'd developed a certain liking for him.

"Damnation," she muttered.

The truth was that she'd come to think of him as if he were a kind of son. Not that she'd ever let him or anyone else know it. That would not have been proper.

But if Joanna Adams, who had broken his heart once, had somehow got it into her head to break it twice…

The coffee cups clattered against each other as Mrs. Timmons all but jammed them into the sink.

No. It was just too impossible to contemplate.

Not even fate could be that cruel.

* * *

Upstairs, in the master bedroom suite, David stood gazing down at Joanna, who lay fast asleep in his bed.

The weekend, and the night they'd just spent together, had been wonderful.

His gaze moved slowly over his wife. She was lying on her belly, her head turned to the side so that he could see her dark lashes fanned down over her cheek. The blanket was at her hips, exposing the long, graceful curve of her back. Her hair, black as night against the white linens, streamed over her shoulders.

He loved her, he thought. Lord, he loved her with all his heart.

If only he dared tell her so.

Joanna sighed. She stretched lazily, rolled onto her back and opened her eyes. Her face lit when she saw her husband, standing beside the bed.

"David," she whispered, and without any false modesty or hesitation, she raised her arms to him.

He came down to her at once, his freshly pressed suit, crisp white cotton shirt and perfectly knotted silk tie be damned, and folded her tightly into his embrace.

"Good morning," he said softly, and when she smiled, he kissed her.

It was a slow, gentle kiss but almost instantly he felt his body begin to react to the warmth and sweetness of hers.

"Mmm," he whispered against her mouth, and he moved his hand to the silken weight of her breast. His fingers stroked across her flesh and then he bent his head and drew her nipple into his mouth.

Her response was swift and exciting. She made a soft little sound that was enough to drive him crazy all by itself but when she arched toward him, murmuring his name, her hand cupping the back of his head to bring his mouth even harder against her, it was almost his undoing.

With a groan, he lifted his head, kissed her lips, and drew back.

"I can't, darling," he said softly. "My meeting is in less than an hour."

Joanna smiled and smoothed his hair back from his forehead.

"I understand."

"I should have told Morgana to say I couldn't make it."

"No, you shouldn't. It's OK, David. Really. I do understand."

David took her hand and brought it to his lips. "I'll be back as soon as I can."

She sat up, put her arms around his neck, and kissed him.

"I'll be waiting," she whispered.

He stroked his hand down her cheek. Then he stood, straightened his clothes and headed for the door while he could still force himself to leave.

This Joanna, this woman he'd fallen in love with all over again, couldn't be a temporary aberration. She had to be real, and lasting.

He could not suffer her loss again.

Not even fate could be that cruel.

Morgana picked up the papers on David's desk and squared them against the blotter though she'd done the same thing only moments before. She looked at the onyx desk clock.

David was late. Twenty minutes late. That wasn't good.

He was never late. Not for the past couple of years, at any rate; not since he'd stopped being cutesy-cozy with his adoring little minx of a wife.

Morgana's sculpted lips pressed together with distaste. David's marriage had almost marked the end of all her plans. Until then, it had only been a matter of time before he'd have realized what she, herself, had known from the first day she'd come to work for him.

She and David were meant for each other.

One look, and she'd fallen deeply in love. David...well, he was a man. It took men longer to realize such things. For a long while, it had been enough that he'd found her the best P.A. he'd ever had. Morgana had taken each compliment on her efficiency, her dedication, and clutched them to her heart.

Soon, she had told herself, soon he'd know.

Instead, he'd been captivated—seduced—by a common piece of baggage from out of nowhere.

Morgana shot a look of pure venom at the photo of Joanna that stood on the corner of David's desk.

"Just look at her," she muttered under her breath.

The hair, blowing in the wind; the oversized denim shirt tucked into torn jeans. And that smile, that oh-so-innocent smile.

Morgana smiled, too, but her smile was as frigid as a January night.

At first, it had seemed an insurmountable problem. It had been bad enough that David had gotten married. But when he'd begun spending less and less time at the office, Morgana had suffered in silence, watching as her plans for a future with him began to fall apart.

Until one day, she'd seen her chance.

David had made a comment, a light one, really, something about not wanting to overwhelm his bride with the pressures of her new life. But Morgana had sensed real concern behind his words.

All smiles, she'd offered to befriend Joanna.

The girl had been so young. Stupid, really. She'd swallowed everything Morgana fed her, hook, line and sinker.

"I'm so happy for you," Morgana had purred. "It must be so wonderful, up there in Connecticut. Why, David's missed several important meetings because he didn't want to leave. He didn't tell you? No? Oh, dear, I suppose I shouldn't have said anything."

"No," Joanna had replied, "no, I'm glad you did. I surely don't want to interfere in David's life."

After that, it had been easy. A few woman-to-woman chats about things like David's status. His position. His importance on the national and international scenes. His need to entertain, to network with his peers.

"But why hasn't he told me these things?" Joanna had said pleadingly, each time Morgana worked around to the topic, and Morgana sighed and said, well, because he loved her and he was afraid of making too many demands on her too soon.

"Perhaps if you were the one to suggest that you'd like to make some changes," Morgana had said in her most kindly way. "I mean, if David thought you wanted to move back to the city, mingle with his old crowd, if he saw you beginning to adapt yourself to his sort of life…that would please him so, Joanna, and he wouldn't have to feel guilty about asking *you* to change for *him*, do you see?"

Morgana's heels tapped briskly across the Italian tile floor of David's office as she headed out the door to her own desk. It had been as simple as striking a match to start a fire. Joanna made changes, David reacted with disappointment, Joanna—the stupid girl—reacted by making even more changes, and the fire grew larger.

It had been difficult, watching David's growing distress, but it was for the best. His marriage was an error; it was up to Morgana to make him see that.

Finally, he had.

He'd come in one day, called Morgana into his office. Grim-faced, he'd told her that he and Joanna would be getting a divorce.

Morgana had made all the right sounds of distress and concern, even though she'd wanted to throw her arms around him and shout for joy. But she'd told herself she had only to bide her time, that once the divorce was over, she could carefully offer consolation.

Her jaw clenched as she sat down at her desk.

And then Joanna had her accident. If only that taxi hadn't just hit her a glancing blow, if only it had done a proper job…

Morgana took a trembling breath. She put her hands to her hair and smoothed the pale strands.

This had been a long, and terrible, weekend. When she'd gotten the call from David, telling her he was in Connecticut, she'd known immediately that the little slut had seduced him again. It was there in his voice, that soft hint of a male who had been pleasured.

And in that instant, Morgana had known she could no longer wait to see if Joanna's memory would come back, that she'd have to take action if she wanted the fire that she'd started to consume that interfering little bitch.

She would not lose David again. She'd worked too hard to let that happen.

"Good morning."

She looked up. David was coming through the smoked-glass doors toward her. A smile curved across her mouth. How handsome he was. How much she adored him.

"Good morning," she said in her usual, businesslike manner. "There have been some calls for you. I put the memos on your desk." She rose and hurried after him as he went into his office. "A couple of faxes came in from Japan during the night, nothing terribly urgent. Let's see, what else? John Fairbanks phoned to see if you could make lunch today. I said you'd call him when you came in. Oh, and the Mayor's office wanted you to—"

"What time are they coming in?"

Morgana looked blank. "Who?"

"The Secretary and his people." He yanked out his chair, sat down, and began to leaf through the stack of memos and faxes. "Didn't you say something about noon?"

Morgana frowned. What was the matter with her? Yesterday, all she'd thought of was that she had to get David back into his real life and away from his wife.

Now, suddenly remembering how she'd accomplished that, she scrambled for words.

"Oh," she said, "oh, that..."

David looked up at her. His hair was neatly combed, he

was clean-shaven, his shirt and tie and suit were impeccable...but she could see beyond all that, she could see the satiation in his face, she could almost smell the damnable stink of that woman.

"Yes," he said impatiently, his voice politely echoing hers, "that. When are these guys supposed to put in an appearance? I don't much feel like cooling my heels today, Morgana."

"They called a few minutes ago," Morgana said quickly, "and changed the time to one o'clock."

That would do it. By one, she'd have David up to his eyeballs in work. Thoughts of his little wife would be relegated to the back burner, where they belonged. And by six or seven, when Morgana suggested she phone out for supper...

"Hell," David muttered, looking at the onyx clock. He ran his hand through his hair. "All right, then, let's not sit around and watch dust settle. Get your notebook and we'll deal with these faxes."

Morgana smiled happily. "Yes, David."

By noon, David had his jacket off and was deep in work.

Morgana sent out for sandwiches. He nodded his thanks and ate what she'd ordered without comment.

At ten of one, she excused herself, and went out to her desk, dialed the phone company and said she thought her telephone might be out of order and would they please ring her right back?

When her phone rang, she picked it up, said thank you, then hung up. She waited a couple of minutes before going into David's office.

He looked up from his desk. He was scowling. A good sign. It surely meant that he was engrossed in his work.

"David, that was a call from Washington. The Secretary sends regrets but he can't make it today."

"Damn!" David tossed down his pen. "You'd think they'd have called sooner."

"Well," Morgana said apologetically, "you know how these people are."

"To think I rushed all the way back to the city for this…"

"But it's a good thing you did," Morgana said quickly. "Just look at all the work you've done."

"Yeah." He pushed back from his desk. "Terrific."

Something in his voice made her scalp prickle. "You know, you never did answer that letter that came in last week from—"

"I suppose, as long as I'm here, I might as well put the rest of the day to good use."

Morgana smiled. "Exactly. That letter…"

David wasn't listening. He'd pulled his telephone toward him and he was dialing a number.

"This is David Adams," he said. "I'd like to speak with Doctor Corbett."

"David," Morgana said urgently, "there's work to do."

David held up his hand. "Corbett? I'm fine, thank you. Look, I've been thinking… Do you have some time free this afternoon, Doctor? I really need to talk to you."

"David," Morgana hissed, "listen—"

"Half an hour from now, in your office? Yes, that's fine. Thanks. I'll be there."

David hung up the phone and got to his feet. He grabbed his suit jacket from the back of his chair and put it on as he walked to the door.

"Where are you going?" Morgana demanded. "Really, David…"

"Joanna's just the way she used to be," he said, and smiled at her. "She's…hell, she's wonderful! Do you remember what she was like, Morgana?"

Morgana's mouth whitened. "Yes," she said, "I do."

"What occurred to me was…I know it sounds crazy, but maybe that blow to the head changed her personality."

"Honestly, you can't believe that."

"Why not? Something's happened to change her." He

smiled again, even more broadly. "I've got to talk to Corbett about it. Maybe he can shed some light on things."

"David, no! I mean, that's crazy…"

He laughed. "No crazier than me falling in love with my wife all over again. I'll see you tomorrow." He grinned. "Or maybe I won't. Maybe I'll whisk Joanna off to Paris. Hell, who knows what will happen? I'm beginning to think that anything is possible."

Morgana stared at the door for long minutes after he was gone. Then, her mouth set in a thin, hard line, she collected her jacket and her purse and left the office on the run.

Joanna sat on the delicate, silk-covered sofa in her own living room and wondered if it was possible to feel more out of place than she felt at this moment.

Morgana, an unexpected visitor, sat in an equally delicate chair across from her. In her ice blue, raw silk suit, with her blonde hair perfectly arranged and her hands folded in her lap, she looked completely at home.

Joanna, caught in the midst of trying to bundle most of the contents of her clothing closet for the Goodwill box, knew she looked just the opposite. She glanced down at her jeans, dusty from her efforts, and her sneakers, still bearing grass and mud stains from the weekend in the country. Her hair was a mess, with some of the strands hanging in her eyes. Her hands were grungy and she saw now that she'd broken a nail…

Quickly, she laced her fingers together but it was too late. Morgana was looking at the broken nail as if it were something unpleasant she'd found on her dinner plate.

"You really need to see Rita," she said.

Joanna cleared her throat. "Rita?"

"Yes. The girl who does your nails. You have a standing appointment, hasn't anyone told you?"

"No. I mean, yes, I know I do but I haven't…I mean, the thought of going to a nail salon seems so weird."

Joanna took a breath. This was ridiculous. This was her

house. Morgana was her guest. An uninvited one, at that. There was no reason to feel so…so disoriented.

"Morgana," she said, and smiled politely, "would you care for some tea?"

"Thank you, no."

"Coffee, then? It's Mrs. Timmons's afternoon off, and Ellen's out running errands, but I'm perfectly capable of—"

"No."

"A cool drink, then?"

"Joanna." Morgana rose in one graceful movement and dropped to her knees before Joanna. "My dear," she said, and clasped Joanna's hands in hers.

"Morgana," Joanna said with a nervous laugh, "what is this? Please, get up."

"Joanna, my dear Joanna." Morgana's sympathetic blue eyes met Joanna's wary violet ones. "I've felt so badly for you, ever since that dreadful accident."

"I don't want to talk about the ac—"

"And for David, too."

"Morgana, really, get up. You're making me uncomfort—"

"He told me today why you went away for the weekend. That you'd both hoped the time in the country might help you recover your memory."

It was a shot in the dark, but an accurate one. Joanna flushed. "He told you that?"

"Oh, yes. David and I are very close, Joanna. Surely you remember…well, no, I suppose you don't."

"I know that he thinks very highly of you," Joanna said cautiously.

"Of course he does." Morgana squeezed her hand. "But it's you I'm thinking of now, my dear."

"I don't…I don't follow you."

Morgana sighed and got to her feet. "You were intimate with David this weekend, Joanna."

Joanna blanched. "How did you…"

"He told me."

"David told you...?" Joanna shot to her feet. "Why? Why would he tell you something so...so personal about us?"

"We're very close, I've told you that. And perhaps he was feeling guilty."

"Guilty?" A chill moved over Joanna's skin. "Guilty about what?"

"Are you sure you're up to this? Perhaps I've made a mistake, coming here. I wrestled with my conscience all day but—"

"I feel strong as an ox. Why should my husband have told you that he and I...that we were together this weekend? And why should he have felt guilty about it?"

Morgana's teeth, very tiny and very white, closed on her bottom lip. "Because he's done a cruel thing to you, and he knows it." She took a deep breath. "I can't stand by and see him do it. You see, Joanna, David intends to divorce you."

Joanna felt the blood drain from her face. "What?"

"He should have told you the truth weeks ago. I tried to convince him. So did his attorney, but—"

"His attorney?"

"Yes." Morgana clasped Joanna's hands. "You must be strong, dear, when I tell you this."

"Just tell me," Joanna said frantically, "and get it over with!"

"The day of your accident," Morgana said slowly, "you were on your way to the airport. You were flying to the Caribbean, to get a divorce."

Joanna pulled her hands from Morgana's. "No! I don't believe you. I asked David about our marriage, he never said—"

"He listened to the doctors, who said it was vital you have no shocks to your system."

"I don't believe you. It isn't true..."

Joanna's desperate words halted. She looked at Morgana

and then she gave a sharp cry of despair, and spun toward the window and the sad little garden beyond.

It *was* true. Every word. What Morgana had just told her made a terrible kind of sense.

David's unwillingness to bring her home from the hospital. His coldness. His silence. His removal.

Their separate rooms...

But their rooms hadn't been separate this weekend.

"I suppose," Morgana said kindly, as if she'd read Joanna's thoughts, "that it's difficult to accept, especially after the intimacy of the past weekend." She sighed. "But if you could only remember the past, you'd know that... well, that sex was all you and David ever had together. It's what led up to your marriage in the first place."

Joanna looked at her. "What do you mean?"

"Surely you know that David is a man with strong appetites. There have been so many women... They're in his life for a while and then, poof, they're gone. And then he met you. You were so young..." Morgana struggled to keep the anger and hatred from her voice. "He's a moral man, in his own way. I suppose, afterward, he felt an obligation." Morgana smiled pityingly. "Unfortunately, it wasn't love. Not for David."

Joanna's legs felt as if they were going to give out. She made her way to the couch and sat down.

"He said things this weekend," she whispered while the tears streamed down her face, "we planned things..."

"Yes, I'm sure. He was full of regrets for what had happened in Connecticut. I was blunt, I said, 'David, it's your own fault, you shouldn't have listened to the doctors, you should have told Joanna the truth, that your marriage had been an impetuous mistake and you were in the process of ending it...'"

And, with dizzying swiftness, Joanna's memory returned.

"Oh, God," she whispered, "I remember!"

Pictures kaleidoscoped through her head. She saw herself

coming to New York from the Midwest, looking for a new life and finding, instead, the only man she would ever love.

David.

He was almost ten years older and he moved in such exalted circles... It was hard to imagine him taking notice of someone like her.

But he had, and on their very first date, Joanna had fallen head over heels in love.

She remembered the passion that had flamed between them, how she, the girl her friends had teasingly called the eternal virgin, had gone eagerly to his bed soon after they'd met.

Oh, the joy of his proposal. The excitement of flying to Mexico to get married, the honeymoon in Puerto Vallarta, the weeks of happiness and ecstasy...

And then the slow, awful realization that she wasn't what David had wanted at all.

He'd never said so. He was too decent. But it was a dream that could not last and the signs of its ending had been easy to read.

David had given up his everything. His friends. His charities. He stopped going to the office, saying he preferred living in Connecticut but Joanna knew that everything he'd done was based on his conviction that she wouldn't fit into the sophisticated life he led in the city.

When Morgana offered her help, Joanna leaped at the chance to salvage her marriage.

What she needed, Morgana told her, was a life of her own, a life that would make David see her as more than just a woman he was responsible for but as someone as proficient in her sphere as he was in his.

"A man of his energies needs challenge to perform at his best, my dear," Morgana said. "By devoting so much time to you, he cheats himself. You must develop interests of your own. Show him you're equal to the position he holds in the world. Perhaps if you joined some clubs, or sat on some charity committees, you'd learn how to organize this house, how to look…''

Morgana clamped her lips together but it was too late.

"You mean," Joanna asked in a choked voice, "he's embarrassed by the way I look?"

"No, not at all," Morgana quickly replied.

Too quickly. Joanna understood that "embarrassed" was exactly what she'd meant.

But nothing she'd tried had been enough to halt the collapse of the marriage. David had grown more distant. The bed that had once been a place of intimacy and joy became the cold setting in which they ended each day by lying far apart until finally, Joanna had salvaged what little remained of her pride by moving into a separate room. Eventually, David had suggested divorce. Joanna had agreed. It had all been very civilized, though the day she'd set out for the airport and the legal dissolution of her marriage she'd been so blinded by tears that she hadn't seen the oncoming taxi until it was too late…

The memories were almost too painful to bear. Joanna buried her face in her hands while Morgana stood over her.

"Poor Joanna," she crooned. "I'm so sorry."

Joanna lifted her tear-stained face. "I can't…I can't face him," she whispered, "not after…"

It was difficult for Morgana to hide a smile of triumph.

"I understand," she said soothingly.

"I don't want to be here when David gets back. I don't want to see him ever again." Joanna grasped Morgana's hands. "Please, you must help me."

"Help you?"

"I have nowhere to go. I don't really know anyone in this city…except you."

Morgana frowned. Time was of the essence. She had to get Joanna out of here before someone showed up. Luck had been with her, so far. The maid and the housekeeper were out; the chauffeur was among the missing, too.

But David…David could come home at any minute.

She made a quick decision. "You can sleep on the pull-out sofa in my living room until we work out the details."

"Oh, no, I couldn't impose."

"Nonsense. Go on, now. And I suppose you'd best leave a note."

"A note?"

"Yes. Something clear and concise, so David understands why you've gone." *So he knows you've left him deliberately, so that he doesn't scour the streets, trying to find you...*

"But what shall I say?"

"Just the truth, Joanna, that you've recovered your memory and you wish to proceed with the divorce."

Joanna nodded. Still, she hesitated.

"Morgana? I'm almost ashamed to admit it but when I first heard David talk about you, I was...I was jealous."

"Of me?" Morgana's smile felt stiff. "What nonsense, Joanna. David's never even noticed that I'm a woman."

But he would notice it, at long last, she thought as Joanna left the room.

Finally, *finally*, she was about to take her rightful place in David Adams's life.

CHAPTER TWELVE

"DAVID," Morgana said, "you must calm down."

"How the hell can I calm down?" David, who had been pacing the floor of his office for the past ten minutes, swung toward Morgana. "It's a week since Joanna disappeared. A week, dammit! And all these damned private investigators are no closer to finding her than they were when I first hired them!"

"Getting yourself all upset won't help."

"I am not getting myself all upset," he snarled, "hell, I'm already upset!" He strode to the triple window and looked out. "Look at the size of that city! Jo could be out there anywhere, alone and hurt and in God only knows what sort of trouble."

"She's not in trouble, and she didn't disappear. She simply left you, David. I mean," she added quickly, when he swung toward her, "that's what you told me. You said she wrote a note."

"Yeah, but what does that prove? She'd been ill. She'd been in an accident. She'd hurt her head..." His face, already pale beneath its usual tan, seemed to get even whiter. He kicked the chair out from behind his desk, sighed and sank down into it. "If only I knew she was OK."

"She is."

"You don't know that."

But I do, Morgana thought smugly, *I surely do*. Joanna Adams was as well as could be expected for a woman who moped around Morgana's apartment all day, looking as if she'd lost her best friend.

It was definitely time to get her out from underfoot. Joanna thought so, too; Morgana had come home two days ago and found her unwelcome boarder with her suitcase packed. She was moving into a hotel, Joanna had said, and though Morgana's first instinct had been to applaud, common sense had prevailed.

If Joanna were on her own, there was no telling what might happen. Suppose she changed her mind and decided to confront David? Or suppose she and David simply bumped into each other? Manhattan was a big island, jammed with millions of people and the odds on that happening were small but still...

Morgana's brain had recoiled from the possibilities. She had to keep Joanna on ice just a little longer. So she'd thought fast and come up with a story about David cutting off Joanna's credit cards and bank accounts.

"The bottom line," she'd said with a gentle smile, "is that you'll just have to stay here a little while longer, dear."

What could Joanna have done but agree?

The only problem was that things weren't going quite as Morgana had expected. She'd assumed David would be distraught, yes, but not...what was the word to describe his behaviour the last several days? Disturbed? Upset?

Frantic, was more like it. He'd gone half crazy when he learned his wife had left him, calling the police, hiring private detectives...

And brushing off all Morgana's attempts to offer comfort.

She looked at him now, sitting behind his desk with his head buried in his hands. It was ridiculous, that he should mourn the loss of a girl as common as Joanna.

"Ridiculous," she muttered.

David's head came up. "What's ridiculous?"

Morgana flushed. "That—that the police haven't found her yet."

David sighed wearily and scrubbed his hands over his face. He hadn't slept more than an hour at a time since he'd come home to find Joanna gone and exhaustion was catching up with him.

"Jo left a note...it means she's not technically a missing

person. If it wasn't for her having amnesia, they wouldn't bother looking at all.''

''She doesn't have amnesia, not anymore. She remembered everything.''

David's eyes narrowed. ''How do you know that, Morgana?''

''Well...'' She swallowed dryly as she searched for the right words. ''Well, you said that was in the note. That she'd gotten her memory back.''

''Yeah, but what does that mean? What does she remember?'' He put his hands flat on his desk and wearily shoved back his chair. ''Corbett says memory sometimes returns in bits and pieces. For all I know, she doesn't remember the things that matter.''

A look came over his face that made Morgana's stomach curdle.

''Honestly, David,'' she snapped, ''one would think *you'd* remember the things that matter, too.''

The look he gave her all but stopped her breath.

''Maybe you'd like to explain that,'' he said with sudden coldness.

Morgana hesitated. Well, why not? It might be time for a little straight talking, if she could do it with care.

''I mean,'' she said, ''that you seem to have forgotten that your marriage to Joanna was always doomed.''

''Doomed?'' David rose to his feet. ''What in hell gives you that idea?''

''David, don't let your irritation out on me!''

''I just want a simple answer to a simple question, Morgana. Why would you think my marriage had been doomed?''

Morgana's lips pursued. ''Honestly, you act as if I weren't privy to the divorce proceedings. And to the years that led up to them. I know, better than anyone, how badly things had gone for you and Joanna.''

David's mouth thinned. ''You weren't privy to how much

I loved her," he said coldly. "As for the divorce proceedings…that was behind us."

"After she'd lost her memory, of course, but—"

"Memory be damned!" He slammed his fist on the desk. Morgana jumped, and papers went flying in all directions. "I love her, do you understand? Even if she'd recovered her memory, there was no reason to think we couldn't have worked things out. Corbett made me see that. I'd loved the woman Joanna had once been, I loved the woman she'd become… Hell, there had to have been a reason she'd changed during our marriage. And I came home that day, knowing it was time to tell her the truth and to tell her that, together, we could find the answers…"

He turned away sharply and his voice broke. Morgana hesitated. Then she went slowly to where he stood and put her hand on his back.

"David," she said softly, "you've got to accept what's happened."

"I don't know what's happened, don't you understand?"

"Joanna remembered. And when she did, she knew she wanted just what she'd wanted before the accident, to be free of you—"

She cried out as he swung around and grabbed hold of her wrist.

"How do you know that?"

Morgana stared at him. "Because…because that's the way it was," she stammered. "You told me—"

"Never."

"You did! You said she wanted a divorce."

"I said we'd agreed on a divorce." David's eyes were cold as the onyx clock on his desk as they searched Morgana's face. "I never said Jo wanted to be free of me."

"Well, I suppose I just assumed…" Morgana looked at his hand, coiled around hers. "David, you're hurting me."

"Hell," he muttered. He let go of her wrist and drew a ragged breath. "I'm sorry. I don't know what I was thinking."

"It's all right. I understand."

"If only I'd gotten home earlier."

"You mustn't blame yourself."

"If only the maid or the housekeeper had been there."

"David, please. Try and relax."

"Even Hollister was gone. He had to pick that damned afternoon to get the oil changed in that miserable car."

"Oh, David, my heart breaks for you. If there were only something I could… What are you doing?"

David shrugged on his jacket. "I'm going home. It's better than pacing a hole in the floor."

"Oh, don't! Let me make us some tea."

"I need an hour's sleep more than I need tea. You might as well take the rest of the day off, too."

"But it's only midafternoon. We can't just abandon the office!"

He smiled. "Trust me, Morgana. We can."

"But…"

It was useless to protest. He was gone.

Morgana walked around David's desk and sat down in his chair. Her mouth twisted.

Damn Joanna! She might have been gone but she wasn't forgotten. And she was an ever-present threat, so long as she remained in New York. She didn't belong here. She never had. She wasn't sophisticated enough, or clever enough, or beautiful enough. Not for the city and not for David.

Joanna belonged back in whatever hick town she'd come from.

Morgana's grimace became a smile. She shoved back the chair and marched to the door.

And the sooner, the better.

Morgana's apartment held the deep silence of midafternoon.

"Joanna?" She slammed the door and tossed her purse and briefcase on a chair. "Joanna, where are you? We have to talk."

Not that she'd give the little slut the chance to talk. She'd simply hand the girl a check, tell her to buy herself a one-way bus ticket, and that would be that.

Life would return to normal. To better than normal, because now David would need solace.

And Morgana would be there to offer it.

What was that?

Her heart began to hammer as soon as she saw the note propped against the toaster in the kitchen. The quiet and that folded piece of white paper filled her with foreboding.

She opened the note, smoothed it carefully with her fingers.

Dear Morgana,
You've been so kind but I can't go on imposing. This morning, I remembered a small cache of money I'd tucked away. I'm going home to get it and then...

"No," Morgana whispered. She crumpled the note in her hand. "No," she said, her voice rising to a wail, and she raced from the apartment.

It didn't take Joanna very long to find what she was looking for.

The couple of hundred dollars she'd squirreled away more than a year ago was in her night table, right where she'd left it. She'd put the money aside last year, to buy David a special birthday gift...

As if that would have changed anything.

Her eyes misted and she rubbed them hard with the heel of her hand. It was stupid, thinking about that. Those days were over and gone. Now, what she had to do was concentrate on the future.

And on slipping out of the house as quietly as she'd slipped in.

It was foolish, she knew, but she didn't want to see anybody. Her timing was right. At this hour on a Friday, Mrs. Timmons would be out marketing. Ellen and Hollister would be in the kitchen, eyes glued to their favorite soap operas.

Joanna made her way quietly down the stairs. The house lay in midafternoon shadow, adding to its natural gloom. She shuddered and thought that she would not miss these over-furnished, cold rooms.

The only thing she'd miss was David, and that was just plain stupid. Songs by the truckload had been written about the pain of unrequited love but in the real world, how could you go on loving someone who didn't love you?

Before the accident, she'd come to terms with that fact. She'd accepted the truth of their impending divorce, and she would again. Her weepiness this past week, her anguish at the thought of losing her husband…it was just a setback, and perfectly understandable in light of all that had happened to her, first the amnesia and then the shock of her recovery, and in between that long, wonderful weekend…

No. It hadn't been that at all. The weekend had been a lie. And she could never forgive David for that, for what he'd stirred in her heart while she'd lain in the warmth of his arms…

The front door swung open just as she reached it. Startled, Joanna jumped back, expecting to see Mrs. Timmons's dour face.

But it wasn't the housekeeper who stood framed in the doorway, it was David.

They stared at each other, the both of them speechless. Joanna recovered first.

"Hello, David," she said. He didn't answer but he didn't have to. The look on his face was far more eloquent than words. He was glaring at her, his amazement giving way to repressed rage. "I—I suppose you're surprised to see me."

Surprised? He was stunned. He was a man who'd never been at a loss for words in his life but at this moment, he was damned near speechless and torn by half a dozen con-flicting emotions, all of them warring to get out.

Anger, born of a week's worth of pain and fueled by the way Joanna was looking at him, as if he was the last man on earth she'd ever wanted to see, won out.

"Where in hell have you been?"

Joanna winced. "You don't have to yell, David, I'm not deaf."

"Thank you for the information." A muscle jumped in his cheek. "Now answer the question. Where have you been?"

"I didn't come here to quarrel," she said carefully.

"No?"

"No."

David slammed the door behind him. He took a step toward her and she held her ground through sheer determination.

"Why did you come here, then? To see if I'd torn the wallpaper as I climbed the walls while I tried to figure out if you were dead or alive or maybe just sitting in an alley someplace, singing *Hey Nonny Nonny* while you wove flowers into your hair?"

Color swept into her cheeks. "I am perfectly sane. I've told you that before."

"Yeah?"

"Yeah," she said, and this time when he moved toward her she couldn't keep from taking a quick step back because if she hadn't, they'd have been nose to nose. Or nose to chest, considering the size of him...

"Well, lady, you sure could have fooled me."

Joanna's chin lifted. "I didn't come here to be insulted."

"Fascinating." He unbuttoned his jacket and slapped his hands on his hips. "You didn't come here to quarrel. You didn't come to be insulted. Near as I can figure, that only leaves us with a couple of thousand other possibilities. Are we going to go through them one by one or are you going to tell me how come you decided to honor me with your presence?"

It took a few seconds to get enough moisture into her mouth so she could swallow.

"I came to get something."

"Something?"

"Yes."

David folded his arms over his chest. "I never much cared for Twenty Questions to start with, Joanna, and I find I'm liking it less and less as this conversation goes on."

"It isn't a conversation, it's an inquisition!"

His smile was quick and chill. "No, it's not. Not yet, anyway, but if I don't start getting some straight answers it's sure as hell going to become one."

Joanna folded her arms over her chest, too.

"I came to get some money I'd put…"

She bit her lip. Hollister and Ellen had materialized in the hallway and were staring at them both with wide eyes. David frowned and swung around, following her gaze.

"Well?" he barked. "What do you want?"

"Nothing, sir," Hollister said quickly. "We simply heard the door slam, and then voices…" He looked at Ellen. "Well, uh, we'll just go be getting back to the kitchen."

"You do that," David said coldly. "Better still, go for a walk. Or a drive. Just leave us alone."

Hollister nodded, grabbed Ellen's arm and hustled her away. Joanna, trying to take advantage of the interruption, headed for the door. David reached out and clamped his hand around her wrist.

"Let go," she demanded.

"The hell I will. You were about to explain why you came here."

"I told you, I'd put away some money. I came to get it." Her chin lifted. "I admit, it was yours to begin with but I—"

David cursed, with an eloquence that made her blush.

"Your money? My money? What kind of garbage is that? Money is money, that's all. It always belonged to the both of us."

"I only meant that I'd saved this on my own."

"And what, pray tell, do you need this little 'nest egg' for?"

Joanna licked her lips. "To leave town,"

"Leave town," David repeated. His voice was flat but the muscle was jumping in his cheek again. "As in, cut and run without having the decency to face me and tell me you were leaving me?"

"I *did* tell you," Joanna said, wrenching out of his grasp. "I left you a note."

"Oh, yeah, you certainly did. 'Dear David, My memory came back and I want the divorce.' Yours Very Truly…"

"I didn't say that," she snapped, her cheeks flaming.

"No," he said coldly, "not the 'Yours Very Truly' part but you might as well have."

"David, this is senseless. I told you, I didn't come to argue."

"Right. You came for money you'd squirreled away, I suppose for just such an occasion, so you could do a disappearing act if the going got tough."

She moved so fast that her fist, slamming into his shoulder, was a blur.

"Hey…"

"You…you rat!" Her eyes, black with fury, locked on his. "I saved that money so I could buy you a carburetor for your last birthday!"

David's face went blank. "A what?"

"A carburetor. That—that thing you kept drooling over in that stupid car parts catalog, the Foley or the Holy…"

"Holley," he said in a choked whisper. "A Holley carb."

"Whatever. You had this dumb thing about just ordering it from the catalog, all this crazy male macho about it being better to stumble across it yourself in some stupid, dirty junkyard…"

"It isn't male macho, it's simple logic," David said with dignity, "and what were you doing, buying me a Holley carb in the first place? It sure as hell didn't go with your image.''

''No,'' Joanna said, and all at once he could see the anger drain from her face. ''It didn't. But then, just before your last birthday I was still fool enough to think—to hope—that maybe buying you a gift would remind you of how things had once been for us…''

She stared at him, her mouth trembling, despising herself for what she'd almost blurted out, that she loved him, that she would always love him…

A choked sob burst from her throat. Eyes blinded with tears, she turned away. ''Goodbye, David. I'll let you know where to send my things. On second thought, you can give them away. Maybe the Goodwill people want—''

She cried out as he hoisted her unceremoniously into his arms and stalked into his study.

''David, are you crazy? Put me…''

He dumped her on her feet, slammed the door shut behind them, and glared at her.

''You're not going anywhere until we've had this out,'' he said grimly.

''We have nothing to talk about.''

''No?''

''No.''

''What was all that, about you caring how things once were between us?''

Joanna's shoulders slumped. ''I was just babbling. Besides, it doesn't matter anymore.''

''The hell it doesn't!'' He caught her face in his hand and forced her eyes to meet his. ''Does it really matter to you, how things used to be?''

She stared at him, warning herself not to let go, to hang on to what little remained of her self-respect…but it was too late. The words were there, bursting from her heart and her lips.

''Damn you, David,'' she cried, ''I'll always care!'' Color stained her cheeks, giving her a wild, proud look. ''Do you feel better, now? Wasn't it enough that I couldn't live up to your standards?''

''What the hell are you talking about? What standards?''

''Your wealth. Your status. Your friends. You married me without really thinking about whether or not I'd fit into your life, and then you woke up one morning and realized that I didn't.''

''You mean, I woke up one morning and discovered that my beautiful Gypsy had changed into a…a…'' David let go of her, flung up his arms and paced across the room. ''I don't know how to describe what you'd become! A woman who cared more about other people than about me, who was determined to turn this damned house into a mausoleum, who didn't want me to touch her—''

His words faded way. He looked at her, and suddenly Joanna could see the anguish in his eyes.

''Why, Jo? Why did you turn to ice whenever I tried to make love to you? More than anything else, that damn near killed me.''

''Because…because…'' Joanna took a deep breath. It was a moment for truth, and she would see it through. ''Because I was ashamed of…of how I was, whenever we…we made love.''

David stared at her in disbelief. ''Ashamed? My God, why?''

Joanna's head drooped. Her voice came out a whisper. ''She never said anything, not about that. I'd never mentioned—I would never talk about something so intimate.'' She laced her hands together to stop their trembling. ''But…but she'd hinted. About certain things that I might do or say that would seem coarse…''

David crossed the room with quick strides. ''Who?'' he said through his teeth. ''Who hinted?''

''I did try, David. To do what she said. To be the right wife for you.''

''Who told you these things, Joanna?'' But with gut-wrenching swiftness, he knew, and he could feel the blood heating in his veins. "Who told you that you weren't what I wanted in a wife?"

"Morgana," Joanna whispered. "She tried so hard to help me make myself over, but it was useless."

David's arms swept around her. "Listen to me," he said. "And look at me, so you'll know that what I'm about to tell you is the truth." He waited until she raised her head and then he took a deep breath. "I never wanted you to change, Gypsy. I loved you, just as you were."

"But Morgana said…"

"She lied."

"Why? Why would she have lied, David? She was so kind to me. Even this week, when I had nowhere to go, she took me into her apartment…"

David's eyes darkened with rage. "You spent this week with Morgana? I was tearing this miserable city upside down to find you and she had you tucked away all the time?"

His voice was cold as stone, and just as hard. It sent a shudder down Joanna's spine.

"Yes. After she told me about the divorce, after I remembered everything…" Joanna caught her breath. "Did you say you'd tried to find me?"

David drew her closer. "I went crazy this past week," he said gruffly. "Don't you know how much I love you?"

Joanna sighed. She lifted her arms and looped them around his neck.

"No," she said, with a little smile. "You're just going to have to tell me."

"For the rest of our lives," David said, and just then the door burst open.

"Mr. David?" Mrs. Timmons said, "are you…?" Her eyes widened. "Mrs. Adams. I didn't know you'd come back, ma'am. I'm terribly sorry to disturb you, but—"

Morgana pushed the housekeeper aside and came sweeping into the room.

"David," she said importantly, "I've seen Joanna, and I think you should know…" Her face turned white with shock but she recovered quickly. "She's here already, I see. David, I don't know what she's told you but I assure you, it's all lies!"

David put his arm around Joanna's shoulders. The green chips of sea ice that were his eyes told the whole story.

"If you were a man," he said softly, "I'd beat the crap out of you and smile while I did it."

"Please, David, I can explain—"

"Get out!"

"This snip of a girl isn't for you. She's…she's…"

David let go of Joanna and took a step forward. "You lying bitch! If I ever see your face again, I won't be responsible for my actions. Now, get out of this house and out of our lives or so help me, I'll throw you out!"

Morgana drew herself stiffly erect. "You'll regret losing me some day, but it will be too late then. I'm giving you one last chance to come to your senses—"

She cried out as Mrs. Timmons grasped the back of her collar and hustled her out of the room. The door slammed shut. There was a cry of outrage, then the sound of the front door opening and closing, and then there was silence.

"David?" Joanna looked up at her husband. "Do you think she's all right?"

David drew his wife into his arms. "I don't really care," he said. His mouth twitched. "Yes, I'm sure she's fine. But after this I'll think twice about ever crossing Mrs. Timmons."

Joanna laughed softly and linked her hands behind his neck.

"Have I told you lately that I love you, Mr. Adams?"

David smiled. "Welcome home, Mrs. Adams," he said softly and then, for long, long moments, there was no need for either of them to say anything at all.

EPILOGUE

Five years later

"KATE? Benjamin? Where are you?"

Joanna sighed as the sound of childish giggles spilled from the old-fashioned country kitchen behind her.

"Your daddy's car is going to be coming up that road any minute and if you want to be ready to go outside and greet him, you'd better show yourselves and let me get your boots on." She waited. "OK," she said, "I'm going to count to three and then whoever's not standing right in front of me is going to have to wait in the house. One. Two. Th—"

"Here I am, Mommy."

A little girl with dark hair and eyes the color of violets raced like a whirlwind into the living room.

"That's my girl," Joanna said. She hugged her daughter close and gave her a big kiss. "Now, where's that brother of yours?"

"Here, Mommy," her son sang out, and hurled his chubby, three-year-old self into her outstretched arms. "Daddy's gonna be here soon."

"That's right, darling. Sit down and let me get these boots on."

Benjamin collapsed on the carpet next to his twin sister.

"He's gonna bring me a truck," he said importantly, "with big wheels and a horn that goes beep."

Joanna laughed. Her son was the image of his father, with his dark hair and his green eyes. He had his father's passion, too, for anything on wheels.

186

"There we go," she said. "Almost ready. Just let's button you guys up..."

"Ugh," Kate said.

"Ugh," Benjamin echoed.

"Yes, I know, but it's cold out and there's lots and lots of snow..."

A horn sounded outside the snug Connecticut farmhouse. The children screeched happily and flew out the front door, trundling down the steps clumsily in their boots and snow-suits just as a black Land Rover pulled up. The door opened and David stepped out.

"Hey," he said, grinning as he squatted down and opened his arms. The children raced into them and he kissed them both, then scooped them up, one in each arm. "Did you miss me?"

Kate laughed. "Silly Daddy. You were only gone one day." Then she leaned forward and planted a wet kiss on his cheek. "I missed you every minute," she whispered.

"Me, too," Benjamin said, and delivered an equally sloppy kiss on the other side of his father's face. Then he craned his neck and peered over David's shoulder. "Did you bring my truck, Daddy?"

"Let's see," David said thoughtfully, as he set his children on the ground. "Did I bring Benjamin a truck? Well...I think maybe I did." He pulled a gaily wrapped package from the Land Rover and handed it to his son, who promptly sat down in the snow and began ripping it open. "There might even be something in here for Kate...yup, by golly, there is." Wide-eyed, his daughter accepted a box almost as big as she was. She plopped herself down beside her brother and set to work. "And there might even be one more thing in here someplace..."

For the first time, David looked up at the porch where Joanna stood framed in the doorway. After nine years of marriage and two babies, she was more beautiful than ever and his heart did what it always did at the sight of her, rose straight up inside his chest until he felt as if he could float.

"Hello, wife," he said softly.

Joanna smiled. "Hello, husband."

He mounted the steps slowly, his eyes never leaving hers, and when he reached the porch she went into his arms and kissed him.

"A year," she whispered, her lips warm against his cold cheek. "That's how long it seems since you left yesterday morning. A year or maybe a month or—"

David kissed her again. "I know. The next time I have to go into the city, you and the kids are coming with me."

"That sounds like a wonderful idea. How's the apartment?"

"Fine. Mrs. Timmons sends her best." David drew back, then held out the package. "I brought you something."

Joanna looked at the box and smiled. "Do I get to guess what it is?"

"Sure. Three guesses, then you pay a penalty."

She pursed her lips. The box was blue. It was small and square. It came from Tiffany's...

"A bread board?" she asked innocently.

David's lips twitched. "Try again."

"Um...a vacuum cleaner?"

"Last shot, coming up."

"Let's see...a new washing machine?"

He sighed. "Not again."

"Well, that's what happens when you have twins. The washing machine just works itself to death."

"Yeah." He smiled. "And you've used up all three guesses, Mrs. Adams. So I guess you'll just have to pay the penalty."

Joanna laughed softly. "Oh, my."

His grin turned wickedly sexy. "Oh, my, indeed."

"At least let me see what's in that box..."

"Uh-uh," he said, taking it out of her reach. "Not until you pay up."

Joanna batted her snow-tipped lashes at him. "Why, Mr. Adams, sir, whatever do you have in mind?"

David put his lips to his wife's ear and whispered exactly what he had in mind. She turned pink, laughed softly, and buried her face in his neck.

"That sounds wonderful. When?"

"Tonight, right after the kids are in bed. I'll build a fire, we'll open some champagne…"

Joanna's smile faded. She leaned back in her husband's arms and looked into his eyes. "I love you," she said softly.

David brushed his lips over hers. "My Gypsy," he whispered.

Then, together with their son and daughter, Joanna and David Adams went inside their home and closed the door.

Lee Wilkinson lives with her husband in a three-hundred-year-old stone cottage in a Derbyshire village, which most winters gets cut off by snow. They both enjoy travelling and recently, joining forces with their daughter and son-in-law, spent a year going round the world 'on a shoe-string' while their son looked after Kelly, their much loved German shepherd dog. Her hobbies are reading and gardening and holding impromptu barbecues for her long-suffering family and friends.

A HUSBAND'S REVENGE
by
LEE WILKINSON

CHAPTER ONE

SHE opened her eyes to a strange, underwater world of light and shade. After a moment her blurred vision cleared and she found herself looking at a bare, impersonal room, little more than a cubicle.

The walls and ceiling were painted sickly green; the floor covering was grey rubberised tiles. A metal locker and a wheeled trolley stood next to a white porcelain sink, where a tap dripped with monotonous regularity.

There were no curtains at the window, and bright sunshine slanted in. It was the only cheerful thing in the room. A panacea. Something to be filtered in between the fear and the smell of disinfectant.

She was wearing a much washed blue cotton gown that fastened down the back with tapes and lying on a hard, narrow bed. A hospital bed. It made no sense. Too tired to try and think, she closed her eyes once more.

The next time she awoke the sunshine had gone and dusk had taken its place. Shadows gathered in the room like a menacing crowd. Her throat was dry, her mouth parched. The tap was still dripping, and there was a red plastic beaker on the sink.

Pushing herself up on one elbow, she swung her bare feet to the floor. But when she straightened and attempted to take a step her head swam, and she was forced to hang onto the metal bar at the top of the bed.

At the same instant the door opened to admit a young and pretty dark-haired nurse, who hurried over and, after helping her patient back into the high bed, scolded, 'You shouldn't be trying to get out on your own.'

'I'm thirsty.' The words were just a croak.

'Well, stay where you are and I'll get you some nice cool orange juice.' She plumped up the thin pillows and switched on a harsh overhead light. 'The doctor will be pleased you're awake at last.'

Awake… Yes, she was awake. Yet it was as if her brain was still asleep. She was conscious of physical things—her head ached dully and her throat felt as if it was full of hot shards of glass—but she was dazed and disorientated, her mind a curious blank.

The nurse returned and handed her the promised glass of orange juice. While she drank eagerly there was a flurry of footsteps, and a short sandy-haired man hurried in. He wore a white coat, steel-rimmed glasses and an air of harassed self-importance.

Pulling a pencil-torch from his pocket, he shone it into her eyes before taking her pulse. Then, sitting down on the bed, he informed her, 'My name's Hauser. I'm the doctor in charge.'

His complexion was pasty, and he appeared so effete that he would have made a better patient, she decided wryly, and asked, 'In charge of what?'

Judging from his look of disapproval, he thought she was being facetious.

'I mean, what is this place?' Her voice was husky.

'The accident and emergency wing of the charity hospital.'

'Have I had an accident?'

'You were brought in earlier today by a cabby. He says you stepped off the sidewalk in front of him. His fender caught you and you fell and hit your head. As far as we can tell, you have no injuries other than minor bruising and slight concussion. Unfortunately you weren't carrying any means of identification, so we were unable to notify your next of kin.'

He made it sound as if she'd planned the whole thing just to annoy and inconvenience both him and the nursing staff.

'This is a very busy hospital, and it gets busier late at night. Especially at the weekend.' Having made that point, he headed for the door, saying over his shoulder, 'If you'll give the nurse details of who you are and where you live, we'll contact your family so someone can come and collect you.'

'But I don't know where I live...'

The forlorn statement brought him back.

'You've had a shock. Try and think. Are you a tourist?'

'A tourist? I don't know.'

'Do you remember your name?'

'No... I don't remember *anything*... Oh, dear God!'

'Don't worry.' He became a little more human. 'Temporary amnesia isn't uncommon after your kind of accident. It just means you'll have to stay.' His frown made it clear that this wasn't a popular option. 'Until either you regain your memory or someone misses you and checks the hospitals.'

Temporary amnesia. As the door closed behind him and the nurse began to make notes on her chart she did her best to cling to that thought, but a rising panic fought its way to the surface. 'I don't know if there's anyone to *make* enquiries... I don't know if I've *got* any family...'

A terrible sense of desolation swept over her. She covered her face with her hands. Her skin felt too tight for her bones, her cheeks and jaw all angles and sharp lines. 'I don't even know what I *look* like.'

Opening the locker, the nurse brought out a grubby, finger-marked mirror and handed it to her. 'Well, at least that should cheer you up.'

A pale, heart-shaped face surrounded by a cloud of dark silky hair stared back at her. There was an ugly purple bruise spreading over her right temple. Almond-shaped eyes, a short, straight nose, high, slanting cheek-bones and a disproportionately wide mouth, the lips of which looked bloodless, did little to cheer her.

The blue eyes, so deep they looked violet, and the fine, clear skin, seemed to be her best features. Well, my girl, you're no beauty, she told herself silently as she handed back the mirror.

Looking down at her hands, she saw they were slim and shapely, the oval nails free of polish, the fingers bare of rings.

She felt a peculiar relief.

When the nurse had rinsed the glass and refilled it with tap water, she said, 'It looks as if you'll be here for the night at least, so would you like a little supper?'

'No, thank you. I'm not hungry.'

'Then get some sleep. Perhaps by morning your memory will have come back.' Switching off the light, the nurse departed.

Oh, if only! It was *terrifying*, this feeling of being lost, isolated in a black void. She lay for what seemed hours, trying fruitlessly to shed some light on who she was and where she'd come from, before finally falling asleep.

Some time later she woke with a start, hugging her pillow in a death grip.

Someone was just closing the door. Failing to latch, it swung open a few inches, letting a crack of light spill into the room from the corridor.

'I've no intention of waiting until morning.' Just outside the door a masculine voice spoke clearly, decisively.

Sounding flustered, the nurse said, 'We don't normally release patients this late.'

'I'm sure you could make an exception.'

'Well, you'd have to speak to Dr Hauser.'

'Very well.'

They began to move away.

'I couldn't let her go without his permission, and I'm not sure if... Oh, here he is...'

Though she could still hear the murmur of conversation, the actual words were no longer clear. After a minute or two the voices came closer, apparently returning.

Dr Hauser was saying, 'We certainly need the bed, but I'm afraid I can't allow—'

That authoritative voice cut in crisply. 'I want her out of this place. Now!'

Stiffly, the doctor said, 'I have my patient's welfare to consider, and I really don't think—'

'Look—' this time the tone was more moderate, the impatience curbed '—I'm aware you do some very good work here. I'm also well aware that this kind of charity hospital is always drastically underfunded...'

There was a pause and a rustle. 'Here's a cheque made out to the hospital. It's blank at the moment. If you'll make the necessary arrangements for her immediate release, I'll be happy to make a substantial contribution towards the hospital's running costs.'

Sounding mollified, the doctor said, 'Will you step into my office for a moment?' and three pairs of footsteps moved away.

Sitting up against her pillows, torn between hope and anxiety, she waited. Was this someone come for her? If it was, and please God it was, surely a familiar face would bring her memory back?

It seemed an age before one set of footsteps returned and the door swung wider. 'Ah, you're awake. Good.' The doctor switched on the shaded night-light. 'Have you remembered anything?'

Her throat moved as she swallowed. 'No.'

He came to sit on the edge of the bed. 'Well, you'll be pleased to know you've been identified as Clare Saunders…'

The name meant nothing to her.

'And you're English. That accounts for the accent.'

Of course she was English. Yet both the nurse and doctor had *American* accents. That fact hadn't really registered until now, almost as if subconsciously she'd *expected* to hear American accents… 'But I've never been to the States.' She spoke the thought aloud.

'You mean until you came to live here?'

'I live in England.' Of that she was sure.

'At the moment you're living here in New York.'

'*New York!* No, I can't *possibly* be living in New York.' For some reason the idea scared her witless. 'You must have got the wrong person.'

He shook his head. 'You're Mrs Clare Saunders. Your husband has given us definite proof of your identity.'

'My *husband*! But I haven't got a husband!' That was something else she was sure of. 'I'm not married!'

Reacting to the note of rising hysteria in her voice, Dr Hauser said sharply, 'Now, try to stay calm. Amnesia can be extremely upsetting, but it should only be a matter of time before your memory returns in full.'

'What if it doesn't?'

'In the vast majority of cases it *does*,' he said a shade irritably. 'Believe me, Mrs Saunders, you have nothing

to fear. We are quite satisfied—both with your husband's
identity and with yours. We're prepared to let you leave
at once, and as soon as Mr Saunders has signed the papers that release you into his care, he'll be here.'

What would have been good news a short time ago
was all at once terrifying. If only she didn't have to go
tonight. By tomorrow her memory might have returned.

She caught at the doctor's arm. 'Oh, please, can't I
stay until morning?' But even as she begged she sensed
there was no help to be had from that quarter.

'Do you know where this hospital is situated?'

'No.' It was just a whisper.

'This downtown area is rough,' he told her. 'Late at
night we get a lot of drunks and people injured in brawls.
You obviously don't belong in a place like this, and I
can't blame your husband for wanting to take you home
without delay.'

He patted her hand. 'Don't forget, all your doubts will
be set at rest if you recognise him.'

And if she *didn't*?

But the doctor was satisfied, and that was all there was
to it. If he hadn't been, despite the contribution to the
hospital's funds—she closed her mind to the word
'bribe'—he wouldn't have released her.

Or would he?

The door swung open and a tall, dark-haired, broad-
shouldered man strode in. He was very well dressed, but
it was his easy air of power and authority, his natural
arrogance, that proclaimed him top of the heap.

As if by right he took the doctor's place on the edge
of the bed. He appeared to be in his early thirties, his
face was lean and tough, and his handsome black-
pupilled eyes were a light, clear green beneath curved
brows.

He was a complete stranger.

As though mesmerised, she found herself staring at his mouth. The upper lip was thin, the lower fuller, and with a slight dip in the centre that echoed the cleft in his chin. It was an austere, yet sensual mouth—a mouth that was at once beautiful and ruthless.

Suddenly she shivered.

Those brilliant eyes searched her face, apparently looking for some sign of recognition. When he found none, his own face hardened, as though with anger, but his voice was soft as he said, 'Clare, darling…I've been nearly frantic.'

Then, as without conscious volition she shrank away, he said, 'It's Jos… Surely you remember me? I'm your husband.'

If he was, why did she feel this instinctive fear of him? And why did she get the impression that he was cloaking his displeasure, playing the part of a loving husband to satisfy Dr Hauser?

He took her hand.

In a reflex action she snatched it away, cradling it against her chest as though he'd hurt it.

'You're not my husband! I know you're not.' Turning to the doctor, she cried desperately, 'I've never *seen* him before!' She held out her left hand. 'Look, I'm not even wearing a ring.'

The man who called himself Jos felt in his pocket and produced a wide band of chased gold and a huge diamond solitaire. 'You took your rings off when you showered this morning and forgot to put them back.'

No, she didn't believe him. Somehow she knew she wasn't the kind of woman who would lightly remove her wedding ring.

As she began to shake her head he caught her hand,

and, holding it with delicate cruelty when she would have pulled it free, slipped both rings onto her slender finger. 'See? A perfect fit.'

He gave her a cool, implacable stare, which sent a quiver of apprehension through her, before lifting her hand to his lips and kissing the palm. 'And if you want further proof that we're married...' Removing a marriage certificate and a couple of snapshots from his wallet, he held them out to her.

A marriage certificate might be anyone's, so she didn't even bother to look at it, but photographs couldn't lie. Afraid of what she might see, she forced herself to take the Polaroid pictures and look at them.

The first one had been taken in what appeared to be a cottage garden. She was smiling up at a tall, dark-haired attractive man. His arm was around her waist and she looked radiantly happy.

'That was the day we got engaged...and that was our wedding day.'

The second picture showed a couple just emerging from the stone porch of a village church. Dressed in an ivory satin bridal gown and holding a spray of pale pink rosebuds, she was on the arm of the same man, who now wore a well-cut grey suit with a white carnation in his buttonhole.

A man who was undoubtedly Jos.

'Do you still believe we're not married?'

She couldn't deny the evidence of her own eyes, but she knew that no matter what the picture suggested she didn't *want* to be married to this man.

'Well, Clare?'

'No.' It was just a whisper.

Standing in the background, Dr Hauser nodded his approval just as his bleeper summoned him. 'I must go. Try not to worry, Mrs Saunders. I'm sure your loss of memory will prove to be only temporary.'

The door had hardly closed behind him when there was a bump and it swung open again to admit the nurse, pushing a shabby wheelchair. 'Well, isn't this good news?' she asked her patient cheerfully. 'As soon as you're dressed, you can go home.'

Taking a small pile of clothing from the locker, she pulled back the bed-sheet and the single greyish cellular blanket. 'Shall I give you a hand with the gown? Or would you prefer your husband to help you?'

Jos eyed the hospital gown with distaste, and raised an enquiring brow.

Agitated, because she was naked beneath the faded cotton and he knew it, Clare folded her arms across her chest and hugged herself defensively. 'No, I...I don't need any help.'

He rose to his feet in one lithe movement and said smoothly, 'Then I'll wait outside.'

'You didn't remember him?' the nurse queried, unfastening the tapes.

Clare shook her head mutely.

'So I guess you're entitled to be shy. Though I'd have thought a man like that would have been impossible to forget. He's really *something*...'

Seeing nothing else for it, Clare swung her legs off the bed and stood up. Moving slowly, carefully, wincing as she touched her bruised ribs, she began to get dressed in clothes she didn't even recognise as hers.

The undies were pretty and delicate, the silky suit and sandals well-chosen and smart, but all of them appeared to be relatively cheap. Which didn't seem to tie in with *his* expensive clothes.

Her tongue loosened, the nurse was chattering on. 'I

must say I envy you. It's so thrilling and exciting. Like meeting for the first time and falling in love all over again…'

Clare wished she could see things in such a romantic light. Caught between an unknown future with a man who was a stranger to her and a blank past, all she could feel was alarm and dread.

All too soon she was dressed. With no further excuse for dawdling she took a few steps and, feeling weak, found herself glad to sink into the wheelchair the nurse was holding for her.

Standing at ease, showing no sign of impatience now, Jos was waiting in the bare corridor. He was very tall, six feet three or four, with wide shoulders and narrow hips.

He looked hard and handsome. And somehow dangerous.

Though he was so big, when he came towards them she saw he moved with the grace and agility of a man perfectly in control of his body.

'Shall I come down with you?' the nurse asked.

Anxious to put off the time when she'd be left alone with him, Clare was about to accept the offer when he said pleasantly, 'Thank you, but there's really no need. I'm sure I can handle a wheelchair.'

The smile accompanying his words held such devastating charm that the nurse almost swooned. She was still standing staring after them when they reached the lift.

It came promptly at his summons.

It probably didn't dare do anything else, Clare found herself thinking as the doors slid open. Then she was trapped with him in a small steel box. It was a relief when it stopped a few floors down and a hospital porter got in pushing a trolley.

As the doctor had predicted, things were hotting up. The main concourse was busy and bustling, with people and staff milling about.

At the reception desk a hard-pressed woman was trying to cope with a growing queue. A large calendar with a picture of Cape Cod on it proclaimed the month was June.

When they reached an area close to the entrance, where a straggling row of shabby wheelchairs jostled each other, Jos asked, 'Can you manage to walk from here?' His deep, incisive voice startled her. 'Or shall I carry you?'

The idea of being held against that broad chest startled her even more. Sharply, she said, 'Of course I can walk.' They were foolhardy words that she was soon to regret.

Struggling out of the chair, ignoring the hand he held out, she added, 'I've only lost my memory, not the use of my legs,' and saw his lips tighten ominously.

Once on her feet, Clare swayed a little, and he put a steady arm around her waist. As soon as she regained her balance she pulled away, leaving a good foot of space between them.

His face cold and aloof, he walked by her side, making no further attempt to touch her.

Somehow she managed to keep her chin high and her spine ramrod-straight, but, legs trembling, head curiously light and hot, just to put one foot in front of the other took a tremendous effort of will.

His car was quite close, parked in a 'Doctors Only' area. A sleek silvery grey, it had that unmistakable air of luxury possessed only by the most expensive of vehicles.

By the time he'd unlocked and opened the passenger door she was enveloped in a cold sweat and her head had started to whirl. Eyes closed, she leaned against the car.

Muttering, 'Stubborn little fool!' he caught her beneath the arms and lowered her into the seat. A moment later he slid in beside her and leaned over to fasten her safety belt.

'Have you had anything to eat?' he demanded.

As soon as she was sitting down the faintness began to pass and the world stopped spinning. Lifting her head, she answered, 'I wasn't hungry.'

'No wonder you look like a ghost!'

Knowing it was as much emotional exhaustion as physical, she said helplessly, 'It's not just that. It's *everything*.'

He started the car and drove to the entrance, giving way to a small ambulance with blue flashing lights before turning uptown.

The dashboard clock told her it was two-thirty in the morning, and, apart from the ubiquitous yellow cabs and a few late revellers, the streets of New York were relatively quiet though as bright as day.

Above the streetlamps and the lighted shop windows, by contrast it looked black—black towers of glass and concrete rising into a black sky.

It was totally strange. Alien.

As though sensing her shiver, he remarked more moderately, 'Waking up with amnesia must be distressing.'

'It is,' she said simply. 'Not to know *who* you are, *where* you are, where you're *going*—and I mean *know* rather than just being *told*—is truly terrifying.'

'I can imagine.' He sounded almost sympathetic.

'At first you just seemed to be…angry…' She struggled to put her earlier impression into words. 'As if you blamed me in some way…'

'It's been rather a fraught day… And I wasn't convinced your loss of memory was genuine.'

'You thought I was making it up! Why on earth should I do a thing like that?'

'Why does a woman do anything?' he asked bitterly.

It appeared that he didn't think much of women in general and her in particular.

'But I would have had to have some *reason*, surely?'

After a slight hesitation, he said evasively, 'It's irrelevant as you *have* lost your memory.'

'What makes you believe it now when you didn't earlier?'

They stopped at a red light and he turned his head to study her. 'Because you have a kind of poignant, lost look that would be almost impossible to fake.'

'I still don't understand why you think I'd *want* to fake it.'

He gave her a cool glance. 'Perhaps to get a little of your own back.' Then, as if conceding that some further explanation was needed, he went on, 'We'd quarrelled. I had to go out. When I came back I found you'd gone off in a huff.'

Instinctively she glanced down at her left hand.

'Yes—' his eyes followed hers '—that was why you weren't wearing your rings.'

It must have been some quarrel to make her take her wedding ring off. She racked her brains, trying to remember.

Nothing.

Giving up the attempt, she asked, 'What did we quarrel about?'

For an instant he looked discomposed, then, as the lights turned to green and the car moved smoothly forward, he replied, 'As with most quarrels, it began over something comparatively unimportant. But somehow it escalated.'

She was about to point out that he hadn't really answered her question when he forestalled her.

'I can't see much sense in raking over the ashes. As soon as your memory returns you'll be able to judge for yourself how trivial it was. Now I suggest that you try and relax. Let things come back in their own good time rather than keep asking questions.'

Questions he didn't want to answer?

Yet if not, why not? Unless he didn't *want* her to regain her memory?

Helplessly, she said, 'But there's so much I don't know. I don't even know where I…we…live.'

'Upper East Side.'

That figured. It went with his obvious wealth, his air of good breeding, his educated accent. She frowned. *His accent*… Basically an English accent?

'You're not American?'

'I was born in England.'

'How long have you been in the States?'

'Since I was twenty-one.'

'How old are you now?'

'Thirty.'

'Do your family still live in England?'

Glancing at his handsome profile, she saw his jaw tighten before, his voice repressive, he replied, 'I haven't any family.'

Plainly he was in no mood to be questioned. But, needing to know more about this stranger she was married to, about their life together, she persisted, 'Where did we meet…?'

He swung the wheel and they turned into a paved forecourt and drew to a halt in front of a huge apartment block.

'Was it in England?'

Curtly, he said, 'I thought I'd made it clear that I wanted you to rest rather than keep asking questions.'

Resenting the way he was treating her, she protested, 'But I—'

He put a finger to her lips. 'This is the Ventnor Building and we're home. Any further questions will keep until tomorrow.'

The light pressure of that lean finger against her mouth stopped her breath and made her lower lip start to tremble.

Watching her with hooded eyes, he moved it slowly, tracing the lovely, passionate outline of her mouth, and she was submerged by a wave of sensation so strong that it scared her half to death.

She saw his white teeth gleam in a smile, and suddenly felt terribly vulnerable. He knew only too well what effect his touch had on her.

As he got out and came round to open her door a blue-uniformed night-security guard appeared from nowhere.

'Mr Saunders, Mrs Saunders...' He gave them a laconic salute. 'Want me to park her for you?'

'Please, Bill.' Jos tossed him the keys and stooped to help Clare from the car. With a strong arm around her waist he led her past the main doors to a side entrance and slid a card into the lock.

The chandelier-lit marble foyer, ringed by glittering stores and boutiques, was vast and empty. Their footsteps echoed eerily in the silence as, watched by the glassy eyes of the elegantly dressed mannequins in the shop windows, they crossed to a bank of elevators.

He produced a key, and a moment later the doors of his private elevator slid to behind them.

'You live in the penthouse.' Her own certainty surprised her.

Brilliant eyes narrowed to slits, he turned to watch her like a hawk, his hard face all planes and angles. 'What makes you so sure?'

As they shot smoothly upwards she pressed her fingers to her temples and struggled to pin down the elusive recollection. It was like trying to trace one particular shadow in a room full of shadows.

She shook her head. 'I don't know.'

They slid to a halt, and with a hand beneath her elbow he led her across a luxuriously carpeted hall and into an elegant living room. The room must be on a corner of the building, she realised, because two walls at right angles seemed to be made entirely of lightly smoked glass panels which opened onto a terrace and roof garden.

She could see the shapes of trees and bushes and hear the splash of a fountain. It seemed strange when they were so far above the city.

With some trepidation, she said, 'I think I'm scared of heights.'

'Then perhaps you shouldn't have chosen to marry a man who lives in a penthouse.'

With a sudden sensation of *déjà vu*, she felt sure he'd said those mocking words to her once before, used the same coolly cutting tone.

Though unable to recall the precise terms of their relationship, she was certain it wasn't of the pleasant, friendly 'rub along together' sort, but rather the tempestuous 'strike sparks off each other' kind.

The kind where someone could get hurt.

No, not someone. *Her*. Every instinct warned her that Jos was dangerous, that he wanted to hurt her, would *enjoy* hurting her.

'Why do you want to hurt me?' The question was out before she could prevent it.

'Why should I want to hurt you?'

Glancing quickly at him, she saw his dark face was cool and shuttered. It would only reveal what he wanted it to reveal. He would only tell her what he wanted her to know.

'What makes you imagine I want to hurt you?' he persisted.

She made a helpless gesture with her hands. 'I don't know. I just get the feeling you don't like me very much.'

He moved towards her.

Instinctively she backed away.

Reaching out, he caught her wrist and pulled her against him. One arm held her while his free hand came up to encircle her throat lightly.

Something about his stillness, the tension in his muscles, warned her that he was waiting for her to struggle.

When she stood as if frozen, he bent his dark head and let his lips wander over her cheek and jaw. She caught her breath, aware of the faint scent of his skin, the slight roughness of stubble.

His lips brushed her ear, making her shiver, as he said, 'Liking is such a bloodless, insipid emotion. It has nothing to do with what I feel for you.'

Recognising something fundamental in his words, knowing she was close to an important truth, she felt her heart begin to race with suffocating speed. 'What *do* you feel for me?'

The sudden flare of anger in his eyes made her blood run cold. Before she could do or say anything he covered her mouth with his own.

While he deepened the kiss, ravaging her mouth with a savage, punitive expertise, she lay against him, lost and dazed, knowing only that if he released his grip she would fall.

When he finally lifted his head she was trembling in every limb, her breath coming in harsh gasps.

He looked down at her, studying the violet eyes that looked too big for her heart-shaped face, the swollen lips, the fine dew of perspiration on her forehead, and said tightly, 'You should know better than to try to provoke me.'

'I wasn't trying to provoke you,' she denied in a husky whisper.

With a muttered oath he let her go so suddenly that she staggered a little, and the beautiful room whirled sickeningly around her head.

A moment later he had swept her up in his arms and was carrying her into what was obviously the master bedroom.

'What are you doing?' she croaked.

'Taking you to bed.'

'No!' Every trace of colour drained from her face, leaving it ashen.

Setting her on her feet, he said coldly, 'Credit me with *some* sensitivity. I can see you've had about as much stress as you can handle, so for tonight at least I'll sleep in the guest room.'

She gave the kind of shuddering sigh a child might give.

The impatience dying out of his face, he opened one of the drawers and tossed her an ivory satin nightgown with shoestring straps and a matching negligee. 'Do you need any help?'

'No!' she snapped, then added more moderately, 'No, thank you.'

'You'll find your toilet things in the bathroom. I'll give you ten minutes.'

In the big, luxurious bathroom, hurrying as much as

her debilitating weakness would allow, she pulled off her clothes and dropped them into the dirty linen basket, showered, cleaned her teeth and dragged a brush through her damp hair.

She was safely in bed, leaning against the pillows, the lightweight duvet pulled chest-high, when he returned.

Sitting on the edge of the king-sized divan, he handed her a beaker of hot chocolate. 'Drink that before I tuck you in.'

The smell made her wrinkle her nose. 'I don't like hot chocolate.'

'Drink it all the same. It'll help you sleep soundly.'

Sipping obediently, she avoided his eyes.

As soon as the beaker was empty he put it on the bedside cabinet and then, rising to his feet, reached to flatten her pillows.

As she slid down his hand brushed her breast and she flinched away.

His chiselled mouth tightened. 'There's no need to look quite so alarmed. I am your husband, you know.'

But that was just it, she thought as the door closed behind him, she *didn't* know. As far as she was concerned he was a stranger.

But a stranger who had a devastating effect on her.

Earlier, when he'd kissed her, desire, terrifying in its intensity, had overwhelmed her. And, though his intention had clearly been to punish her, she'd sensed a fierce reciprocal hunger in him, which even such a cold, self-controlled man as he couldn't totally hide.

Their relationship, whatever other dark threads were woven into it, was undoubtedly a passionate one.

Suddenly she was even more afraid of what the future held than she had been when she'd left the hospital.

CHAPTER TWO

CLARE'S brain stirred into life slowly, unwillingly. Lying stretched on her back, eyes closed, she was aware of softness and warmth, of a physical comfort that went hand in hand with a kind of bleak mental anguish.

Bodily she was at ease, but her mind was a teeming mass of disturbing, shadowy thoughts. When she tried to hold onto them, to coax them into the light, they vanished like wraiths, leaving only a set of hard, handsome features indelibly printed there.

Jos. Her husband.

Her heart began to beat at a fast, suffocating speed. She recalled him coming to the hospital. Bringing her home. Kissing her. Innocuous enough memories except for the powerful black undercurrents which, like some deadly whirlpool, threatened to drag her down and drown her.

Undercurrents which, if she could only remember, would almost certainly explain why she had taken off her rings and walked out in the first place.

But had she just stormed off in a temper, as he'd tried to imply? Or had she meant to go for good?

If she *had* meant to leave him, surely she would have taken a case? Certainly she would have had a handbag. Some money…

Eyelids still closed, to help her concentration, she tried to think, but her memory would go back no further than awakening in the hospital.

Sighing, she opened her eyes to semi-gloom. Abruptly

the sigh turned into a gasp. The sight of Jos lounging in a chair by the bed, his eyes fixed on her face, made her jerk upright.

His mere presence brought a surge of dismay and excitement that took her breath and made her heart start to race again.

As though he'd run restless fingers through it, his hair, peat-dark, not quite black, was slightly rumpled, his jaw was smooth, clean-shaven, his lean face, with its fascinating planes and angles, heart-stoppingly attractive.

He was casually dressed in light trousers and a dark green cotton-knit shirt open at the neck, exposing his tanned throat, and with the sleeves pushed up his muscular hair-sprinkled forearms.

Pulling the duvet high, though her nightgown was perfectly modest, she demanded hoarsely, 'How long have you been there?'

His clearly delineated mouth curved slightly. 'Most of the afternoon.'

The idea of him sitting watching her sleep was disturbing, to say the least. Slowly, with an effort, she smoothed her face into a careful, unrevealing mask, before asking, 'Why didn't you wake me?'

Rising to his feet, he crossed to the wide window and drew aside the curtains, flooding the attractive blue and white room with light, before answering, 'I wanted you to wake up naturally. I thought perhaps...?' He allowed the question to tail off.

'It's no use...' She heard the desolation of her own despair. 'I can't remember anything prior to waking up in the hospital.'

Suddenly he was by her side again, looming too close. Tilting her chin, he examined her face, taking in the translucent skin stretched tightly over the wonderful bone structure, the paleness of her lips, the lost look in the long-lashed violet eyes.

His touch closed her throat and made her mouth go dry. Unconsciously, she ran the tip of her tongue over parched lips.

Something flaring in his green eyes, he followed the small, betraying movement. She froze, terrified he was going to kiss her, *wanting* him to kiss her…

He, who seemed never to miss a thing, obviously noted her reaction and smiled a little. Releasing her chin, he touched a bell by the bedhead before sitting down again. 'When you say ''anything''…?'

It took her a moment or two to recover. Then, forehead creased in thought, she said slowly, 'I remember the ordinary everyday things of life. How to read and write, add up and subtract…that kind of thing. It's *personal* memories that have gone…'

Were those memories so dark, so disturbing, that her subconscious *wanted* them blanked out? Had she *needed* to lose herself and the past in order to survive some emotional trauma?

Or was this feeling of being threatened by past and future alike merely symptomatic of her amnesia? When her memory returned would she find she was a perfectly ordinary woman with a perfectly ordinary marriage?

But suppose it *never* returned?

Fighting down a rush of blind panic at the thought, she went on, 'I don't know anything about myself. If I've got a middle name or what my maiden name was… I don't even know how old I am.'

'Your middle name is Linden, your maiden name was Berkeley and you're twenty-four. You'll be twenty-five on September the third. A Virgo,' he added, with a derisive twist to his lips.

Before Clare could react to what seemed to be a sneer, there was a tap at the door, and it opened to admit a dark-suited dignified man, carrying a tray. Pulling the metal supports into position, he placed it carefully across her knees.

Bending his balding head deferentially, he said, 'I'm delighted that madam is safely home.'

'Thank you, er…' She hesitated.

'This is Roberts,' Jos informed her. Then, to the man-servant, he said, 'I'm afraid Mrs Saunders still hasn't recovered her memory.'

Roberts looked suitably grave. 'Very upsetting for both of you, sir.'

After deftly removing the lid from a dish of poached salmon, he opened and shook out a white damask napkin. 'Mr Saunders thought a light meal… If, however, madam would prefer chicken, or an omelette…?'

'Oh, no… Thank you.' Then, sensing a genuine wish to please, she remarked with a smile, 'I'm sure this will be delicious.'

Roberts departed noiselessly.

'A butler instead of a housekeeper?' Sipping her tea, Clare spoke her thoughts aloud. 'I get the feeling you don't care much for women?'

'In one area at least I find a woman is indispensable.' His mocking glance left her in no doubt as to which area he referred to. 'I also employ a couple of female cleaners. But I happen to prefer a male servant to run the house-hold.'

Head bent, hoping to hide her blush, she asked, 'Has Roberts been with you long?'

'He came with the penthouse.' Then, with no change of tone, he added, 'Your salmon will get cold.'

Uncomfortably, she asked, 'Aren't you eating?'

'I had a late lunch a couple of hours ago, when it appeared that you were still in shock and were going to sleep the clock round.'

She glanced at her bare left wrist before asking, 'What time is it now?'

'Nearly four-thirty.' Lifting her hand, making the huge diamond solitaire flash in the light, he asked, 'Do you remember what happened to your watch?'

'Do I usually wear one?'

'Yes. So far as I know, always.' Letting go of her hand, he urged, 'Do eat something or you'll upset Roberts.'

Feeling suddenly ravenous, Clare began to tuck in with a will. Glancing up to find Jos's eyes were watching her every move, she hesitated.

'Don't let me put you off,' he said abruptly. 'You must be starving. It's over twenty-four hours since you were knocked down.'

Glancing once again at her empty wrist, she suggested, 'Perhaps I left my watch behind when I…with my rings…'

He shook his head emphatically. 'You wouldn't have left it behind.' Dark face thoughtful, he went on, 'When you arrived at the hospital you had no handbag with you. Didn't you think that was strange? Don't most women carry a bag?'

Putting down her knife and fork, she agreed, 'Yes, I suppose so.'

'It's my belief that when you were knocked down, by the time the cabby had pulled himself together and got out, your bag and watch had been stolen. It's a pretty rough area… Have you any idea what you were doing there?'

'No.' Then, harking back, she asked curiously, 'What

makes you so sure I wouldn't have left my watch behind?'

He rose to his feet and, lifting the tray from her knees, set it aside before answering, 'Because it was a twenty-first birthday gift from your parents.'

'My parents?' Her heart suddenly lifted with hope. 'Where do they—?'

'They're dead,' he said harshly, resuming his seat. 'They died in a plane crash in Panama a few months ago.'

'Oh…' She felt a curious hollowness, an emptiness that grief should have filled. 'Did you know them?'

After an almost imperceptible hesitation, he said, 'I knew of them.'

'Can you tell me anything about them?' she asked eagerly. 'Anything that might help me to remember? Our family background…where they lived?'

This time he hesitated so long that she found herself wondering anew if he would prefer her *not* to remember.

Then, as though making up his mind, he said, 'Yes, I can tell you about your family background.' His face hard, his green eyes curiously angry, he went on, 'Your father was Sir Roger Berkeley, your mother, Lady Isobel Berkeley. He was a diplomat and she was a well-known hostess, prominent in fashionable society.'

Clare could sense an underlying tension in his manner, a marked bitterness.

'You were born and brought up in a house called Stratton Place, a mile or so from Meredith.'

'Meredith?'

'A pretty little village not too far from London. A lot of rich people live there—bankers, stockbrokers, politicians… You went to an expensive boarding-school until you were eighteen, then a Swiss finishing-school.'

He sounded as if he resented their wealth and position,

and she wondered briefly if he'd come from a poorer environment. But that didn't tally with his voice and his educated accent.

'You were an only child—and a mistake, I fancy.'

Chilled both by the concept and Jos's deliberate cruelty, she asked, 'How could you know a thing like that?'

He shrugged broad shoulders. 'I'm judging by the type of woman your mother was, and the fact that you were pushed off to boarding-school at a very early age...'

Clare felt impelled to defend the mother she couldn't remember. 'But are you in a position to judge? If you didn't really know her...'

'I know all I need to know. When your father was posted to the States she joined him in New York. The society gossip columns had a field-day. Men swarmed round her like flies, and she soon got quite a reputation as a goer...' There was contempt in the deep voice. Softly, he added, 'You're very like her.'

Every trace of colour draining from her face, she sat quite still. Surely she couldn't be the kind of woman he was describing?

Watching her expressive face mirror her consternation, he allowed a scornful little smile to play around his lips.

In response to that smile, she lifted her chin. No, she refused to believe it. Some fundamental self-knowledge told her he must be wrong.

'I can't answer for my mother,' she said calmly, 'but I'm sure *I'm* not like that.'

'You're the image of her in looks...'

'That doesn't necessarily make me *like* her.'

As though she hadn't spoken, he went on, 'You both have the kind of beauty that can drive any man wild.'

Clare shook her head. 'When I woke in the hospital I

had no idea what I looked like. The nurse gave me a mirror. I'm not even pretty.'

'You're far more than pretty. You're fascinating. Wholly bewitching.'

But the way he spoke the words made them a damning indictment rather than a compliment.

A shiver ran through her. 'I didn't bewitch you,' she said with certainty.

His voice brittle as ice crystals, he contradicted her. 'Oh, but my darling, you did.'

She didn't believe it for one moment. Almost in despair, she asked, 'Why did you marry me?'

'Why do you think?'

'I don't know. If I'm like my mother—' She broke off in confusion.

'You mean it wouldn't have been necessary?' He smiled like a tiger. 'If I'd only wanted a casual affair, it wouldn't have been.'

He spoke with such certainty that her blood turned to ice in her veins.

'But I wanted a great deal more than that…'

Without knowing why, she shivered. 'So what *did* you want?' Perhaps she needed to hear him put it into words, like some *coup de grâce*.

His mouth smiled, but his eyes were cold as green glass. 'I wanted to own you body and soul.'

She shivered again. Then slowly, almost as if in accusation, she said, 'You didn't love me.'

With no reason to dissemble, he told her matter-of-factly, 'I never pretended to. On the contrary, I went to great lengths not to mention the word ''love'', so there would be no possibility that you could have any illusions, be under any misapprehension…'

Filled with a lost, bleak emptiness that was far worse

than anything she had yet experienced, she accepted the fact that he had never loved her and she must have been aware of that.

Then why had she married him?

Recalling the overwhelming effect his kisses had had on her, one reason immediately sprang to mind. Yet surely common sense would have prevented her marrying a man simply because he attracted her physically?

Unless that attraction had developed into an infatuation and, more like her mother than she wanted to believe, she'd been unable to help herself...

'And neither was I...' Jos was going on, his voice like polished steel. 'I knew perfectly well why you agreed to marry me.'

Shrinking inwardly at the realisation that her sexual enslavement must have been obvious, she waited for him to crow.

Incredibly, he said, 'I was wealthy, and you wanted a rich husband.'

At that moment all she could feel was relief. The fact that he didn't realise how obsessed she must have been went some way towards salving her pride.

'Someone who could give you the right kind of life-style.'

'It's my impression that I already had that.' Somehow she kept her voice steady.

'Ah, but you didn't. When you left your smart finishing-school, for some reason—you never told me exactly what—you struck out on your own. You rented a small cottage in the village and took a job in a real estate office while you waited for the opportunity to catch a suitable husband.'

'Did I tell you that?' she asked sharply.

'You didn't need to.'

'And I suppose by "suitable" you mean…?'

'Stinking rich.' He spoke bitterly. 'Because of the kind of life your parents led—jet-setting, champagne parties, lots of entertaining—they always lived above their income, and I suppose you must have realised there'd be nothing left when they died. Therefore, you needed to hook a man with money.'

The picture he was painting of her was a far from pleasant one. Pushing back a tendril of dark silky hair, she objected, 'If I was an ordinary working girl, what chance would I have had of ever meeting any rich men?'

'Hardly *ordinary*. You still had that air of good breeding, that finishing-school gloss, and Ashleigh Kent, the firm you worked for, was an up-market one, dealing mainly with wealthy clients wanting country estates and the like. In fact that was where I met you—when I was over in England on a business trip.'

'And you blame me for hooking you?' That explained at least *some* of the hostility she sensed in him.

To her amazement, he shook his head. 'No, I don't blame you for that. It would be different if you'd used your wiles to try and captivate me, but you didn't, did you?'

'I don't know,' she admitted huskily. 'I don't know what I did, how I acted…'

'Like a perfect lady.' His lips twisted into a smile that wasn't a smile. 'You intrigued me from the first moment I laid eyes on you. Though you were obviously attracted to me, you looked at me with such composure, such cool reserve.'

Whereas a lot of women, she guessed, would drool over a man with his kind of looks and that amount of blatant sex appeal.

Slowly, she said, 'You seem pretty sure I was looking

for a rich husband…so if I didn't, as you put it, use my "wiles" to try to catch you…' She hesitated. 'Why *didn't* I?'

'When I first asked you to have dinner with me, you refused without giving a reason. I found out later that you already had Graham Ashleigh—who was worth quite a bit—in your sights.

'Though I didn't think the…shall we say attachment… on your side, at least, was too serious, and I had a great deal more to offer financially, it still took me over a week to persuade you to go out with me.'

He sounded annoyed.

Her smile ironic, she suggested, 'Perhaps I was just playing hard to get.'

Privately she thought it far more probable that she'd been chicken—scared stiff by all that overpowering masculinity.

He shook his head. 'Somehow I feel that playing hard to get isn't your style… It certainly wasn't your mother's.'

She flinched at his deliberate unkindness.

'But that's enough delving into the past for the moment,' Jos said decidedly. With a short, sharp sigh, he rose to his feet and stretched long limbs. 'Now I suggest a breath of air. If you have no objection to New Yorkers *en masse*, Saturday afternoon is a good time to take a stroll in the park. Feel up to it?'

His tone was neutral, neither friendly nor unfriendly, and, only too happy to leave the confines of the bedroom, she agreed eagerly. 'Yes, I'd like that.' Then, unwilling to get out of bed while he was there, she added, 'If you'll give me a few minutes…?'

His smile sardonic, he said, 'I'll use the dressing room to change.'

.As soon as the door closed behind him, Clare got out
of bed and made for the sumptuous bathroom. Whether
it was due to the food or to the prolonged sleep, she was
pleased to find that the worst of the weakness had gone
and she felt much better.

After cleaning her teeth and taking a quick shower,
she donned a terrycloth robe while she looked for some
fresh undies and something to wear.

A look at the clothes hanging in the walk-in wardrobe
suggested that her tastes were quiet and classical rather
than flamboyant. For which she was truly thankful.

Trying to rid herself of the feeling that she was rifling
another woman's things, she took out a grey and white
patterned dress, a white jacket and a pair of high-heeled
sandals. Rather to her surprise, everything fitted her perfectly.

When she was dressed she brushed the tangles from
her shoulder-length hair. Seeming to be naturally curly,
it settled in a soft, dark cloud around her face.

Wrinkling her nose in the mirror at the bruise on her
temple, she looked for some tinted foundation to mask
it. There was a range of light cosmetics in a pretty, daisy-
strewn bag—cream, cleansing lotion and lip-gloss. No
sign of any foundation or mascara. Perhaps with dark
brows and lashes and a clear skin she didn't use any?

In a side pocket of the bag she came across a narrow
flat packet, and froze. Each pill was packed separately
and marked with a day of the week.

But that didn't necessarily mean she was like her
mother, she told herself firmly. After all, she was a married woman—even if she didn't feel like one...

Hiding her nervousness, her uncertainty, beneath a veneer of calm, she squared her shoulders and went to find
Jos.

Everything was quiet and in perfect order. Too perfect. It struck her that the penthouse, with its impersonal opulence, was more like a luxury film-set than a home.

Without her knowing why, the thought made her sad.

In the living room, the long glass panels had been slid aside and he was standing on the terrace looking out across the green leafiness of Central Park. He'd changed into a lightweight suit, the jacket of which was slung over one shoulder and held by a crooked finger.

Clare could have sworn she had made no sound on the thick pale carpet, but, as though some sixth sense was at work, he turned to face her.

Though she didn't *know* him, he was no longer a stranger. Outwardly, at least, he was achingly familiar, and she could have picked him out unerringly from a thousand other tall, dark men.

His hair, brushed straight back from a high forehead, formed a widow's peak, his skin was tanned and his eyes were a clear, brilliant green between thick lashes. He looked tough and intelligent and heart-stoppingly handsome, with the kind of animal magnetism that would have made even an ugly man completely irresistible.

At her approach he held out his hand.

As if under a spell, she put hers into it.

He used the hand he was holding to draw her close, and, smiling into her eyes, bent his head.

Her nostrils were filled with the faint, masculine scent of his aftershave, and, feeling his warm breath on her cheek, she trembled inside while, eyes closed, lips parted, she waited transfixed for his kiss.

But the kiss never came.

When she lifted heavy lids he had drawn back. He was still smiling, but his smile was mocking, derisive.

She didn't need that smile to tell her he was amused

by her reaction. Feeling as though she had been slapped in the face, she snatched her hand free and turned away.

Why was he playing with her like this? To remind her that he could? To put her at a disadvantage? For his own entertainment? Or a combination of all three?

Chilled and alarmed, she began dimly to realise something of the power he had over her.

But until her memory returned, and she knew exactly how things stood between them, all she could do was stay calm and resist his potent attraction.

He put on his jacket and, a hand at her waist, accompanied her across the hall and into the lift. Though she was tall and wearing high heels, standing by her side he still seemed to tower over her.

Glancing down at her set profile, he remarked blandly, 'You're looking rather…militant. Something to do with a need for self-preservation?'

She studied his face with calm deliberation, then said, just as blandly, 'And you're looking rather conceited. Something to do with a mistaken belief in your own powers of attraction?'

To her surprise he laughed, and said appreciatively, 'You're starting to sound less like some forlorn waif and more like yourself.'

A moment later the lift slid to a halt and they emerged into the glittering foyer, now thronging with people.

His hand beneath her elbow, he escorted her through the main doors and out onto Fifth Avenue. That famous street was teeming with life and vitality, and had, Clare thought, an air of being *en fête*.

The early evening was hot and sunny, and the park was full of people. Bright summer dresses and colourful umbrellas blossomed everywhere; candy wrappers and soft drink cans littered the paths, radios blared, babies bawled, children played and perspiring joggers jogged.

It was a scene full of noise and gaiety, and Clare loved it.

Jos tucked her hand through his arm and, as he matched his pace to her slower one, they strolled in silence.

After a while, her thoughts busy, she remarked, 'You mentioned we met when you came over to England on a business trip. How did we get to know each other?'

Face guarded, green eyes suddenly wary, Jos answered, 'I'd approached Ashleigh Kent with the intention of buying a house...'

She frowned. Why would he want a house in rural England when he lived in New York?

'You were the representative they sent to show me around.'

A chill feathering over her skin, Clare stopped walking and stood stock-still. As a dim crystal ball, her mind produced a faint, intangible impression of a bare hall, open to the rafters, with dark galleries running round three sides, and a man standing looking up to a pair of high, narrow windows which threw lozenges of light onto the dusty stone flags three floors below.

Head bent, slim fingers pressed to her temples, she tried to seize the elusive memory that hovered almost within her grasp.

Just when she thought she had it, it vanished like a spectre. Suddenly convinced it held some terrible significance, she gave a low moan and began to tremble violently.

Jos took her shoulders. 'Clare, what is it? What have you remembered?'

'Nothing. I...I thought I had, but then it was gone.'

CHAPTER THREE

SHE was shaking so much that she could scarcely stand. Steering her to the nearest vacant bench, he pushed her onto it and stood over her. After a while the trembling stopped. Gathering herself, she looked up at him and said steadily, 'I'm all right now. We can go on.'

'I think not. You've done enough walking for today. Wait here a moment.'

He went a hundred yards or so to an intersection, where the path they were on was crossed by a wider one. Raising his hand, he snapped his fingers.

As he came back to offer his arm she heard the clatter of a horse's hooves, and by the time they'd reached the intersection a polished black carriage with a top-hatted driver was waiting. It had a festive, holiday air—the well-groomed horse wore yellow rosettes and the driver's whip was adorned with a matching bow of ribbon.

Jos helped her step up and then sat beside her. The driver clicked his tongue at the horse and they were off, bowling merrily through the park.

Clare looked at her companion with awe. 'And I didn't catch a glimpse of either the mouse or the pumpkin.'

He laughed, white teeth gleaming, charm momentarily banishing the hardness. 'There are plenty of these carriages about. The only magic is in knowing where to find an empty one.'

The word 'empty' reminded her of the memory she had so nearly grasped. 'The house I took you to see, was it—?'

'No more questions for the moment,' he broke in firmly. 'Just relax and enjoy the drive. Don't make any attempt to remember. Later on we'll try a spot of therapy, but I was planning to have a meal out first, if you feel up to it?'

So that was why he'd changed into a suit and tie.

'Oh, yes, that would be nice,' she agreed.

The sun shone and, despite the traffic fumes, the balmy evening air fanning her face felt fresh and clean. As they clip-clopped along Jos pointed out all the things of interest, and after a while Clare found herself enjoying the leisurely drive.

It was well past seven when they crossed the Grand Army Plaza and their carriage stopped alongside some others. Beyond rose the pale marble and glazed brick, the richly ornamented mansard of the Plaza Hotel.

'I thought we'd have dinner here tonight,' Jos told her as he helped her down and paid the driver. 'Tomorrow evening, if you like, we can go further afield.'

When he'd given her a glimpse of the celebrated hotel, with its fine shops, lounges and places to eat, he asked, 'Which of the restaurants do you prefer, Clare?'

'I really don't mind. I'll leave it to you.'

'In that case...' With a firm hand beneath her elbow, he steered her towards the nearest, where he appeared to be well known—the maitre d' calling him by name and ushering them to a secluded table for two.

The very air breathed luxury—the rich aroma of smoked salmon and caviare mingling with expensive perfumes and the sweet smell of success. Above the discreet murmur of conversation and an occasional laugh, ice buckets rattled and champagne corks popped.

As they sipped an aperitif and studied the menu Jos

made light conversation, giving Clare an opportunity to respond in kind.

She asked him what it was really like to live in Manhattan, and discovered that he was a born raconteur with a pithy way of expressing himself and a dry sense of humour.

'A taxi had just dropped me at Madison and Sixty-third one evening,' he told her, 'when footsteps hurried up behind me and a tough-looking character grabbed hold of my arm. He was picking himself up from the sidewalk for the second time before he managed to explain that I'd lost my wallet and he was trying to return it. To add to my chagrin, when we had a drink together I discovered he was a fellow colleague in the banking business.'

'Is New York a very violent city?' she asked, when she'd stopped laughing.

'There's not as much violence as the media might lead you to believe. Though, as with most big cities, it has its share.'

The food and wine proved to be excellent, and the service first class, but it was the atmosphere that Clare found herself enjoying most, and she said so.

He nodded agreement. 'That's why I come here.'

'Do we tend to like the same things?'

With a strange note in his voice, he said, 'Oh, yes. Though we *can* disagree and have stimulating arguments, it's been clear from the start that our tastes and minds mesh...'

For a moment she felt warmed, though common sense told her that as they didn't love each other there had to have been something, apart from sex, to draw them together.

'For one thing we both enjoy the good life and being rich.'

There was a bitter cynicism in his tone that chilled the warmth, and she recalled his certainty that she'd married him for what he could give her.

'Who wouldn't enjoy being rich?' she asked wryly. 'Though I doubt very much if money can buy real happiness.'

His brilliant gaze on her face, he enquired silkily, 'Still, it must have its compensations? You were prepared to sell yourself...'

'I've only your word that I did.'

'Don't doubt it.'

'But, J—' She broke off, biting her lip, somehow unable to call him by his name.

He reached across the table and took her hand, his thumb pressing menacingly against the soft palm.

'Did I forget to tell you what I'm called?'

'Wh-what?' she stammered.

The green eyes pinned her. 'Do you know what my name is?'

'Of course I know what your name is.'

'You seem unwilling to use it.'

She found herself scoffing, 'Why on earth should I be?'

'Then let me hear you say it.'

Reluctantly, and scarcely above a whisper, she said, 'Jos.'

'Again.'

When she hesitated, he lifted her hand to his lips, biting the fleshy mound at the base of her thumb.

'Jos, please...'

His smile was sardonic. 'That sounded more as if you meant it.'

That little show of dominance effectively spoiled the calm of the evening, and though he went on to prove himself an entertaining companion she was unable to relax.

They were sipping their coffee when, despite her long sleep, she found herself drooping, having to make an effort to sit up straight.

He noticed at once. 'Getting tired?'

'A little,' she admitted.

He signalled for the bill.

Outside, the summer evening was clear and warm, making the prospect of a short walk back to the Ventnor Building a not unpleasant one. As they began to stroll Jos took her hand.

She shivered, and it had absolutely nothing to do with the little night breeze that had sprung up.

The scent of flowering shrubs drifted across from Central Park, perfuming the air, and far above Fifth Avenue and the lights of the city stars shone in a deep blue sky.

But Clare scarcely noticed the beauty of the night. Tense and *aware*, with her hand imprisoned in his, their arms occasionally brushing, all her attention was focused on Jos.

When they got back to the penthouse though the lights were on there wasn't a sound, and the place appeared to be empty.

Confirming that, Jos remarked casually, 'It's Roberts' night off.'

The realisation that they were quite alone made her feel distinctly apprehensive.

He slid aside the glass panels and led her onto the lamplit terrace to look over the glittering panorama that was Manhattan by night.

As they approached the balustrade she held back.

Feeling her instinctive reluctance, he stopped. 'Have you always been scared of heights?'

'I'm not sure…I don't think so.' She wrinkled her smooth forehead. 'Maybe something happened that frightened me…' As she spoke her skin chilled and a shudder ran through her.

'What is it?' he demanded sharply. 'What do you know?'

'It's nothing… Just someone walking over my grave.' She tried to speak lightly. 'And all I know is, I feel safer back here.'

She was wearing her jacket draped around her shoulders, and as Jos slipped it off he brushed aside the dark silky cloud of hair and kissed her nape.

Feeling that frisson of fear and excitement she experienced every time he touched her, she caught her breath in an audible gasp.

Indicating a luxuriously cushioned swing-seat beyond the splashing fountain, he suggested blandly, 'Why don't you sit down and relax while I get us a nightcap?'

More than uneasy, with all her doubts and worries, her fear of both the future and the past suddenly crowding in on her, she shook her head. 'I think I'll go straight to bed.'

When he said nothing, she added awkwardly, 'Good-night…Jos.'

She was turning away when his hand shot out and grasped her wrist, bringing her to a halt, not hurting—not if she stood quietly—but keeping her where he wanted her. 'We haven't tried that therapy I mentioned.'

'Therapy?' she echoed unsteadily. 'What kind of therapy?'

'The kind that might help you to remember just what it's like between us.'

Recalling his apparent reluctance to answer some of her questions, and her own sneaking suspicion that perhaps he didn't *want* her to regain her memory, she was surprised.

Seeing that surprise, he smiled mirthlessly. 'Did you think I'd prefer you *not* to remember?'

'I wondered,' she admitted.

Green eyes gleaming beneath dark, well-marked brows, he shook his head. 'If you didn't get your memory back it would spoil my plans...'

That veiled statement seemed almost to hold a hint of menace, and she was about to ask him what he meant when he went on, 'However, as your remembering might prove to be a two-edged sword, until you're more able to cope I think we should take it easy and not try to hurry things. Except in one area...'

He used the wrist he was holding to draw her closer, so his other hand could raise her chin. His face was only inches away—a lean, attractive face, with beautiful hollows beneath the cheekbones and a mouth that gave her goosebumps.

She felt his breath on her cheek and shivered, her lips suddenly yearning for his. As though he knew, he bent his dark head to touch his mouth to hers.

Last time his kiss had been hard and punishing. This time it was light as thistledown, coaxing and tantalising until her lips parted for him. Then he deepened the kiss, cradling her face between his hands while his mouth made an uncompromising demand that sent her head spinning.

Somehow she knew that she was normally cool and in control, but this man had the power to heat her blood and arouse a fierce, almost overwhelming desire.

He kissed her skilfully, knowledgeably, with a kind of

leashed passion that made every nerve-ending zing into life. While he kissed her one hand slid to her nape and the other deftly dealt with the buttons of her dress and the front clip of her dainty bra.

Then his fingers were moving in a tactile exploration, discovering and lingering on the hammering pulse at the base of her throat, stroking across her smooth collarbone, cupping the warm, satiny curve of her breast.

She shuddered as his thumb found and teased the sensitive nipple, sending the most exquisite sensations running through her, making her muscles clench and a core of molten heat form in the pit of her stomach.

He knew exactly what he was doing to her, how to use his mouth and hands to heighten her pleasure and drive her slowly mad, and she was almost lost in a sensual maze of need and hunger when somewhere at the back of her mind a warning bell clanged and she stiffened. If she didn't stop him now, in a very short while she would be unable to.

A part of her protested. Did she *want* to stop him? He *was* her husband...

But a husband she didn't really know.

Using will-power as a whip, she mentally distanced herself. She might have lost her memory but she still had instincts, and every one of those instincts warned her that something was terribly wrong somewhere. If she slept with him now she would be committing herself before she knew what that something was.

Aware of her withdrawal, he stilled his hand and lifted his head to study her flushed face from beneath half-closed lids.

Despite its delicate bone structure, its poignancy, it held no sign of weakness. Indeed, her chin proclaimed a quiet strength, even a hint of stubbornness, and, though passionate, her mouth was set in lines of self-discipline.

Opening heavy lids, Clare saw that the green eyes fixed on her held no warmth or tenderness—no passion, even—only a kind of determination to probe beneath the surface and assess her defences, as if she was an enemy whose strengths and weaknesses he needed to know and calculate.

She hated that cold, impersonal inspection. It told her that whereas his lovemaking had reduced her to a quivering mass of wants and desires, he had been virtually unmoved, his own feelings held in check while with cool expertise he'd aroused hers.

But though he obviously cared little for her, he was her husband and a red-blooded male, and if she'd proved willing he would certainly have taken her to bed.

No doubt he still would.

The thought galvanised her into action. Drawing back abruptly, she caught at the edges of her gaping dress and dragged them together. Then, striving to sound calm, self-possessed, she said, 'I'm afraid your "therapy" hasn't produced any results.'

Seeing the rapid rise and fall of her breasts, and hearing the harshness of her quickened breathing, he observed with ironic amusement, 'Oh, I wouldn't say that. If we were to carry it a little further...'

'No!' Her alarm was evident.

Lifting his shoulders in a slight shrug, he accepted her decision. 'Very well. We'll just have to see what tomorrow brings.'

He wasn't making any attempt to push it—indeed, he was behaving in a thoroughly civilised way—but a hint of something primitive and dangerous hidden beneath his suave manner made her more than wary.

As if to add weight to that impression, he added, 'But bear in mind that you *are* my wife, and I don't intend to go on sleeping in the guest room.'

When he took a step towards her she caught her breath. But, holding her eyes, a cool challenge in his that dared her to protest, he reclipped her bra and fastened the buttons on her dress.

It was *she* who had called a halt, but *he* was very much in command of the situation—as he would be of any situation, she thought bleakly. And, though he was allowing her a free choice at the moment, he'd made it abundantly clear that this state of affairs would only last as long as he permitted it to.

Had his sexual arrogance, his masterfulness, become anathema to her? Was that one of the reasons she had attempted to leave him?

No, surely not. She must have realised what kind of man she was marrying, must have preferred a strong, virile partner to a wimp.

As most women would.

Turning away to stare across the dark trees to the art deco towers of Central Park West, she sighed. He was so blatantly, excitingly *male* that there would have been plenty of willing, not to say eager females flocking round. Small wonder he knew so well how to pleasure a woman…

Contemplating her profile, he offered, 'A penny for them…'

Without stopping to think, she admitted, 'You seem to have a great deal of experience…I was wondering how many women you've loved.'

His dark face sardonic, he said, 'If you're talking about *loved* then the answer's none. Nor have any loved me. I gave up wanting or expecting love a long time ago. But if you mean how many have I gone to bed with, I'm afraid I don't make notches on the bedpost. However, I'm more than willing to refresh your memory on how experienced I am...'

His words caused a convulsive clutch of desire deep in her stomach.

Shaking her head, praying he would take no for an answer, she wondered how long she could hold out against him, and tried to recall if this fierce attraction had been there from the start.

Some instinctive knowledge told her it had sprung into life at their first meeting.

But she had no idea how long ago that was.

Taking a deep breath, she asked jerkily, 'You said we met when you were in England looking for a house... when was that?'

Face guarded, green eyes suddenly wary, Jos answered evasively, 'A few months ago.'

So they couldn't have been married for very long.

It seemed strange to think that with a new husband such as he she couldn't remember what it was like to sleep with him.

But she could imagine the things his lean, skilful hands would do to her, could imagine his weight and the driving force of his body...

Her cheeks growing hot at her own erotic thoughts, she looked hurriedly away from those hard, too percep-tive eyes.

'Something bothering you?' he asked blandly.

Schooling her face into a careful blankness, she turned and said, 'I was just wondering how long we've been married.'

Though his lazy, slightly mocking expression didn't alter, she got the distinct impression that it was a question he'd been waiting for. A question he didn't particularly want to answer.

After the briefest pause, he said casually, 'Only a short time.'

'How short?'

He was watching her, eyes gleaming between half-closed lids. 'We were married two days ago.'

'Two days ago?' she repeated, startled. 'Then we're…'

'On our honeymoon,' he finished for her. 'So you can understand why I don't find the guest room to my taste.'

Heat running through her, she queried, 'Where were we married? Not here in New York?'

'No, in England. Meredith, to be precise.'

That explained the snapshots.

But if they'd only been married on Thursday, unless they had been lovers previously, they'd spent just one night together. If that…

Unable to ask directly, she said, 'Did we spend our… our wedding night travelling?'

His mocking expression told her he knew what she was getting at, but he answered her question with great exactness. 'No, we spent it here. After a morning wedding and a noon reception we drove to Gatwick and caught an early evening flight to JFK. Because of the time difference we were here at the penthouse by ten o'clock, our time.'

So the marriage had almost certainly been consummated, and she didn't for a moment doubt that he had been a fantastic lover, able to wring the most rapturous responses from her… Yet the very next morning she'd taken off her rings and bolted. Why? *Why?*

'Jos, won't you tell me what happened?'

He raised a dark brow. 'If you want a blow by blow

account of our wedding night, it would be easier and much more fun to take up my offer and let me *show* you.'

Hot-cheeked, flustered by his open mockery, she nevertheless stuck to her guns. 'I mean what happened next morning? What did we quarrel about?'

Harshly, he told her, 'I've already said I can't see much point in discussing it, and that still stands. It was merely a dispute that got out of hand.'

She was almost certain that he was lying.

Surely, in the circumstances, no mere falling out would have made her act that way? Their disagreement must have been over something pretty traumatic.

Something he had no intention of talking about.

She recalled his earlier words, 'your remembering might be a two-edged sword', and guessed that his feelings about it were ambivalent.

Though he'd said it would spoil his plans if she *didn't* remember, she had the strangest notion that he was scared of what it might do to her if she *did*.

So where did that leave them?

As though reading all her doubts and uncertainties, he went on more mildly, 'Look, after a few days in New York we were intending to go upstate. You'd expressed a desire to see Niagara Falls, and we have a suite booked at the Lakeside International on Lake Ontario. If we carry on with our honeymoon as planned—'

'No, I…I *can't*…' she cried in panic.

Controlling his obvious annoyance and frustration admirably, he suggested, 'Suppose we go on *your* terms.'

'You mean…?'

'I mean I'll sleep in the dressing room until you want me in your bed.'

'You won't try to pressure me?'

Grimacing at her caution, he said trenchantly, 'I promise I won't *force* you.'

It wasn't quite the same thing, but after a moment's hesitation she took a deep breath and agreed, 'All right.'

'Then tomorrow morning we'll head for Buffalo.' He took her face between his palms. 'And I suggest that for the next couple of weeks you make a real effort to relax. Don't keep worrying about the past. Give your memory a chance to come back of its own accord. OK?'

'OK.'

'Good girl.' He smiled and dropped a light kiss on her lips.

Almost more scared of his charm than his anger, she pulled away and fled.

They flew into Buffalo International Airport to find the rental car Jos had ordered waiting for them.

As they began their relatively short drive up to Lake Ontario the weather was clear and bright. Leaving the urban sprawl behind them, they drove with the car windows down, the sun warm on their arms and the breeze ruffling their hair.

Clare discovered that round the great lake was apple country, with mile upon mile of orchards.

'I'm afraid we're too late for the blossom,' Jos remarked, 'and too early for the fruit. But if you come in autumn I'll bet you'll never smell or taste anything more delicious than an Ida Red straight from the tree...'

As its name suggested, the Lakeside International, a quiet, exclusive hotel, was right on the shores of the lake. It was set in well-kept grounds which led down to a private stretch of sand bright with sun-loungers and huge beach umbrellas.

They were greeted by the manager himself, a grey-haired dapper man with a carnation in his buttonhole, and while Jos signed the register a uniformed bellhop hurried to bring their luggage from the car.

Their corner suite was on the ground floor, the green and gold decor throughout giving it an air of cool graciousness.

It had a sumptuous bedroom, with a king-sized canopied bed, an enormous *en suite* bathroom complete with a jacuzzi, and an elegant sitting room furnished with handsome period pieces.

From both the main rooms long French windows opened onto a paved terrace with a lovely view over the garden to the lake. There were several bowls of flowers scattered about, a basket of fresh fruit and a bottle of champagne waiting in an ice bucket.

The only thing it lacked was a dressing room.

Clare's eyes flew to her husband's face and she waited for him to ask to be moved, but, having thanked the bellhop and tipped him generously, he let him go.

As the door closed behind the youth she burst out, 'If you think for one moment...'

The cold blaze in his eyes made the words tail off. His voice brittle, he said, 'I'm sorry there's no dressing room, but, having booked the honeymoon suite in good faith, I don't intend to look a fool by asking to change now.'

Her heart in her mouth, she said, 'But you agreed not to pressure me.'

For a moment he looked furious, then the anger and irritation were swiftly masked. Coming up behind her, he folded his arms around her waist and leaned forward to rub his cheek against hers.

Softly, he asked, 'And you'd regard having to share the same bed as my pressuring you?'

Her heart began to race and fire ran through her, making her face grow hot and melting her very bones. Somehow she found her voice and said, 'Yes, I would. And you *promised*…'

'I only promised not to *force* you. And we both know force wouldn't be necessary…'

Frightened by the truth of his words, she played the only card she'd got. 'I should have had more sense than to trust you to keep to our bargain…'

For an instant his grip tightened, then with a sigh he let her go. 'Very well. As I gave my word, I'll sleep on the couch.'

The brocade-covered couch looked short and narrow and none too comfortable.

'I think I'd better take the couch,' she offered quietly.

'Over my dead body!'

Oh, well, it was up to him.

Keeping his darker side well hidden, and being careful not to upset or disturb her, except in what she guessed was a deliberately calculated *physical* way, with a kind of lazy, good-natured charm that was almost irresistible, Jos set himself out to disarm her and make the holiday a period of calm.

True to his word, he made no attempt to pressure her. Each night, having given up on the couch, he threw a pillow down and, without complaint, slept on the living room floor. But for the rest he insisted on a casual intimacy that continually threatened her composure.

For such a cool and in some ways austere man, he was very physical. He seemed to enjoy touching her.

When they walked he either held her hand or tucked her arm through his. If they were sunbathing, he liked to put sun-screen on her back. And when they lay side by side on the beach he often played with a strand of her hair or stroked the smooth, golden skin of her shoulder with a lean finger.

Keeping up the honeymoon image, he'd arranged for meals to be served in their suite, and, after spending the sunny days exploring the countryside, they ate romantic candlelit suppers on the terrace.

But the thing that disturbed her most was his goodnight kiss. Though he kept it light and easy, the touch of his lips invariably sparked all kinds of wild longings within her, and beneath the veneer of calm unconcern she managed to keep in place she felt breathless and aroused, and was forced to battle against a growing hunger.

Only some sixth sense, some prevailing instinct of danger, prevented her from giving in to the heated excitement that made the blood run through her veins like molten lava.

She felt as though she was walking a tightrope across the crater of a seething volcano. If she once lost her balance she would be lost indeed.

By tacit consent neither mentioned the past or her loss of memory, and though at times the hovering darkness would march forward and press in on her, for the most part Clare managed to exist in a kind of limbo that was far from unpleasant.

The weather remained glorious and, apart from an occasional idle hour or two spent sunbathing on the beach, they used every minute to explore the area.

They visited Oswego, at the lake's edge, Watkins Glen, with its car-racing and its vineyards second only to California's, the Finger Lakes, glacial gouges thought to resemble elongated fingers, and Old Fort Niagara, where uniformed volunteers gave a taste of life as it had been in the early seventeen-hundreds.

Jos proved himself to be a good-tempered, stimulating

companion, with an effortless ability to make every excursion enjoyable.

The only time the serenity of the holiday was ruffled, was the day they visited the charming little town of Rochester.

They were passing a high class jeweller's and, having noticed Clare glance at her bare wrist on more than one occasion, Jos paused to look in the window.

When she would have kept walking he held her back, a hand on her elbow. 'It's high time I bought you a wedding present.'

Unwilling to have him buy her anything, she protested, 'I don't need a wedding present.'

'But I want to buy you one.'

Throwing down the gauntlet, he propelled her into the shop and asked to look at some watches.

Having appraised Jos's casual, but clearly expensive clothes, the salesman produced several gold and jewel-encrusted bracelet watches.

Picking up the gauntlet, with barely a glance at them, Clare shook her head.

The next time the selection was slightly less ostentatious but just as pricey.

A cold knot of apprehension forming in the pit of her stomach, she objected, 'Really, I don't need a watch.'

Jos kept his patience admirably. 'Of course you need a watch, and I want to buy you one.'

'I'd rather you didn't,' she said in a tight little voice.

'Darling, I insist...' An icy fury hidden beneath the smiling endearment, he picked up the most expensive watch there and, holding her wrist in a grip that threatened to bruise the delicate bones, fastened it on. 'There, that looks nice.'

As soon as he let her go, she took it off and put it

back on the counter. Bolstered by anger, her stubbornness met and matched his. 'Thank you, darling—' she returned his smile while violet eyes met green in a silent clash of wills '—but I don't much care for that one.'

'Then perhaps you'd like to choose?' His voice was smooth as silk, but his eyes warned of the consequences of further rebellion.

Knowing she was committed now—she couldn't make him look a fool by just walking out—she turned to the salesman and said steadily, 'I'd prefer something much simpler.'

Glancing over an array in a glass showcase, she pointed to a neat, relatively inexpensive little watch on a black leather strap. 'Something like that.'

Disappointed, but too good a salesman to show it, the jeweller opened the case and took out the one she'd indicated.

Carrying the war into the enemy's camp, she held out her wrist to Jos and asked, 'Please won't you fasten it for me, darling?'

For a moment she thought he was going to refuse and insist on her having something better, but, his jaw set, he did as she asked.

When she said, 'Yes, that's much more me,' without a word he drew out his wallet to pay for it.

'Shall I put it in a case for you?' the salesman queried politely.

Clare shook her head. 'There's no need, thank you. I'll keep it on.'

Once outside, as though trying to find an outlet for his anger, Jos walked so fast that she had to almost trot to keep up with him.

When they reached the relative quiet of a small park he stopped beneath the shade of a tree. With a swift movement she was unprepared for he pushed her against the smooth trunk, trapping her there.

She started to protest, but his expression had hardened into a merciless mask which effectively frightened her into silence. Looking up at the hard, ruthless lines and planes of his face, the cool blaze in his green eyes, she froze.

He bent his head so that his face was only inches from hers, and demanded with soft violence, 'What the *hell* were you playing at just now?'

CHAPTER FOUR

'I WANTED—' She broke off abruptly as his hand came up to encircle her throat lightly.

'You wanted to make me look a fool.' His fingers began to stroke gently up and down.

She swallowed convulsively. 'If I'd wanted to make you look a fool I'd have walked out of the shop.'

'You managed quite well as it was.' Then in exasperated fury he went on, 'I've a damned good mind to take that cheap thing off your wrist and throw it away.'

'As you like.' She managed to sound indifferent. 'I never wanted you to buy me a watch in the first place.'

She heard the breath hiss through his teeth. At the same instant she became aware of approaching footsteps, and out of the corner of her eye saw an elderly couple walking slowly towards them.

Jos gave no sign that he'd either heard or seen them, but his hand moved to cup her face and his mouth swooped to cover hers.

His kiss seemed to obliterate time and space, to go on for ever. At first it was cold, punitive, a means of venting his anger, then it became heated and hungry, an ardent demand that she was unable to refuse.

When he finally lifted his head, every bone in her body felt as though it had turned to water, and if it hadn't been for the support of the tree she would have slid into a heap.

She opened heavy violet eyes to find he was staring

down at her, and momentarily he looked as dazed by passion as she was.

A second later his face was wiped clear of all emotion and he said thinly, 'Don't ever do anything like that to me again, Clare.'

'I won't if you don't try to buy me any more expensive presents,' she retorted jerkily.

He looked genuinely surprised. Then he smiled sardonically. 'Not wanting to take the perks without coming up with the goods?'

'That aspect hadn't crossed my mind.'

'In that case why the objection to me buying you something?'

'Until I *know* why I married you, I prefer to think it wasn't for your money.'

'Ah... So that hit a nerve, did it? But then truth often does. Don't look so upset. I don't mind.' He smiled mirthlessly. 'Knowing why you married me salves my conscience.'

She was still worrying over the implications of that last remark when he said, 'Look, I don't want to upset what is supposed to be a therapeutic period by quarrelling. It's up to you whether you keep the watch or throw it away.'

In a small voice, she said, 'I'd like to keep it.'

'Very well.' He brushed a strand of dark silky hair away from her cheek. 'And if it's going to upset you, I won't spend money on costly presents, but I reserve the right to buy my wife candy or flowers or any inexpensive gift that takes my fancy.'

'But I've nothing to give you in return.'

His smile was crooked. 'Oh, I wouldn't say that.'

'I don't even know if I've got any money,' she ploughed on desperately.

'I'll give you whatever you need, and as soon as we get back to New York I have every intention of opening a bank account for you.'

'But that would be *your* money. I couldn't spend that on you.'

'Then just give me a kiss.'

'It would seem as though you were buying my kisses,' she said stiffly.

He sighed with exasperation. 'All right, *don't* give me a kiss. You don't even need to say thanks.'

Suddenly weary of arguing, wanting to defuse the situation and get back on the friendly footing they'd achieved over the past few days, she widened her eyes and said in mock-horror, 'I'm sure that posh finishing-school you once mentioned would be shocked to think I'd learnt no better manners than that.'

His face relaxed into a smile of genuine amusement. With his wide forehead, high cheekbones and straight, bony nose, he had an inordinately handsome face that gave the impression of stark, uncompromising strength. Smiling, he was even more attractive, the harshness overlaid with humour.

'OK, so thank me. Now, come on—' reaching for her hand, he tucked it through his arm ' —let's forget the past half-hour and start enjoying ourselves again.' Then he added with a slight bite, 'And just so you don't get uptight about what I'm spending on you, I'll try to find a cheap café to buy you a coffee.'

After that conversation he made a point of buying her a cheap gift almost every time they went out.

On the first occasion it was a large, cross-eyed teddy bear—so ugly, he said mournfully, that it needed someone to love it.

'I love it already,' she assured him. Adding serenely,

'But it's a bit cumbersome, so I'm sure you'll carry it back to the car for me.'

After that he stuck to flowers or candy.

On what was to be the last weekend of their honeymoon, Jos was planning to take her to see Niagara Falls. On the Saturday morning, after breakfasting early on the sunny terrace, Clare was feeding crumbs of toast to the sparrows when he surprised her by saying, 'You'll need to pack an overnight bag before we go.'

'I thought we weren't very far away.'

'We're not. But when we first discussed our honeymoon you expressed a desire to stay near the falls. I wasn't keen. Hotels there can be noisy and crowded... However, so you won't miss out totally, I've managed to book at the Luna Towers for tonight and tomorrow night.'

Having gathered from various tourist brochures that the Luna Towers had one of the most spectacular views of the falls, Clare exclaimed, 'Oh, thank you! How nice of you.'

To her surprise he looked disconcerted, a faint wash of colour appearing along his hard cheekbones. Curtly, he said, 'You'd better save your eulogies until I tell you that the best I could manage was one double room.' As she took in the implications of that, he added, 'Of course, if you'd rather, we could always come back here.'

Knowing what trouble he must have gone to to secure even one room at the Luna Towers at the height of the season and at such short notice, she shook her head. 'I'd like to stay at the falls.'

But what if the room had a double bed? She could hardly expect him to go on sleeping on the floor...

That thought was followed by an even more disturbing one.

Suppose Jos was banking on that very thing? He'd been extremely patient, but what if he'd decided to take this opportunity to strip off the kid gloves?

Watching her expressive face, he asked sardonically, 'Changed your mind?'

Lifting her chin, she met the challenge of his brilliant gaze, and, though all manner of warning bells were sounding, said calmly, 'No, I haven't changed my mind.'

After a good run through to Niagara they checked in at the busy hotel, and then, having been provided with a picnic lunch, left the car there and set off on foot to take a closer look at the falls.

Their stroll took them through a pleasant, lightly wooded area, which was alive both with tourists and squirrels.

The fact that their large, comfortable room was furnished with twin beds had done a lot to ease Clare's worries, and she walked with a little smile on her lips, prompting Jos to remark sardonically, 'You look happy...or should I say relieved?'

Flushing a little, she said mendaciously, 'I was just thinking how tame the squirrels are.'

'They're used to being fed.'

As though to prove his point, a black squirrel made a short rush and stopped right in their path, his plume of a tail arched over his back, pointed ears pricked, bright eyes hopeful.

'Oh, isn't he sweet?' she exclaimed. 'I don't think I've ever seen a black one before... Oh, I'm sorry I've nothing suitable to give you.'

Feeling in the brown paper carrier bag that held their lunch, Jos produced a bag of nuts. 'Try one of these.' Smiling at her astonishment, he said, 'I asked for them specially. You have a penchant for feeding things. In Meredith it was the ducks.'

Opening the bag, she asked, 'But how did you know about the squirrels?'

'I've been here before.'

When she crouched down, the animal took the proffered nut from her fingers, and in the twinkling of an eye they were surrounded by a dozen or more of the appealing rodents, who ranged in colour from pale cream through to chocolate and jet-black.

As soon as the last of the nuts had been distributed Jos put the empty bag into the pocket of his cotton jacket, and, while they carried on to the falls, the furry gang went off to mug the next willing tourist.

Clare could hear the thunder of the falls well before they reached them, and felt a growing excitement. Up close, she found the smooth rush of water plummeting over the edge disorienting, and instinctively reached for Jos's hand.

It closed around hers and squeezed, the warmth of the little gesture making her heart sing with a sudden gladness. For the first time since waking in hospital she felt optimistic about the future—hopeful that, whether she regained her memory or not, things might turn out well after all.

'So what do you think?' he asked. 'Worth the trip?'

'They're magnificent,' she breathed in awe.

'To get the best view, I suggest that after lunch we walk over Rainbow Bridge to the Canadian side...'

Sitting in the sun by the fast-flowing Niagara, talking companionably, they unpacked their picnic of ham and sourdough bread and fruit.

A bedraggled-looking water bird appeared and watched them with black, shoe-button eyes.

'Poor thing, it looks hungry,' Clare exclaimed, and threw it a chunk of bread.

After studying her for a moment or two, Jos remarked, 'I'm continually surprised by how tender-hearted you've grown up to be.'

'You sound as if you knew me when I was young, and I was a heartless little monster.' Then with a puzzled frown she asked, '*Did* you know me?'

After a split second's hesitation, he said, 'I didn't need to know you. In my experience a lot of children can be heartless little monsters, and usually the females stay that way.'

Which only echoed his poor opinion of women.

She shook her head. 'You're a cynic.'

'I'm a realist. Though I must admit that at times you're so soft-hearted you tend to confound me.' Though he spoke teasingly, there was an underlying current of seriousness.

Having finished her ham sandwich, Clare fished in the carrier and offered him a tin of cola.

He shook his head. 'I must be one of the few people in the States who doesn't like it. Probably because I wasn't brought up with it.'

'What *were* you brought up with? Good old British lemonade?'

'I guess you could say that,' he answered lightly.

Passing him a peach, Clare pursued the subject. 'I don't really know anything about you…the names of your parents…where you lived…which school you went to…if you have any brothers or sisters…'

He bit into the peach with care. 'I thought we'd agreed not to worry about the past.'

'*My* past. It can't do any harm to tell me about *yours*.'

Glancing up, Clare saw that all the warmth had vanished from his face, leaving it curiously bleak and empty.

Judging by his expression, his childhood had been anything but happy, and, wishing she'd never asked, she said hurriedly, 'Of course, if you'd rather not talk about it…'

'Why not?' His tone was brittle. 'You'll need to know some time.'

She was just thinking that that seemed an odd way to phrase it, when he went on in a curiously formal way, 'I was the only child of Charles and Rebecca Saunders. We lived in a rural area fairly close to London. The house, our family's home for generations, had belonged to my grandfather, but after my grandmother's death, he couldn't stay. He gave Foxton Priory to my father, and travelled a great deal before eventually reaching the States. After crossing from the eastern seaboard to the west, and making money in various ventures, he went up to Alaska and joined a mining consortium.

'My father was a businessman turned politician. My mother, who adored him, gave up everything to support his political ambitions. She entertained his colleagues and constituents, sat on committees and attended endless charity functions…

'If *you* were a mistake, so was I.' Just for a moment his bitterness was searing. 'I always felt rejected. My father had no time to bother with me, and my mother was too busy taking care of him. Her husband's career and interests came first. Oh, I don't mean to say I was *neglected*—they appeared to be wealthy, able to provide every material thing I could have wished for.

'My mother hired a nanny to take care of me until I could be sent away to boarding-school, but I loved Foxton Priory and didn't want to go. Nanny kept assuring me I was too young at seven, but she was wrong…'

His voice was flat, hard as polished granite. 'You know what they say about hope springing eternal? Well, each time I came home for the school holidays I hoped my mother wouldn't send me back. I told myself that things might alter and improve, that she might have more time for me.

'Finally things did change, but not for the better. I discovered that all my mother's devotion had been for nothing. My parents' marriage was crumbling, on the point of breaking up. My father was embroiled in an affair. I overheard them quarrelling, talking about a divorce…'

'Quite a few of the other boys' parents were separated or divorced, but I'd never thought of it happening to mine.

'In the event it didn't. My mother died and a few weeks later my father was killed when his car careered off the road and hit a tree head-on. It said in all the papers that he was hopelessly drunk at the time.'

Glimpsing the pain and futile anger beneath the dispassionate words, Clare caught her breath.

'My parents' *appearance* of wealth turned out to be just that. The house I loved was mortgaged up to the hilt and there was no money to pay my next term's school fees.'

Without a trace of self-pity, he continued, 'All that was left, the solicitors informed me, was a heap of worthless mining stock that my grandfather, who had died in Alaska the previous year, had left me, and a load of debts. I was thirteen at the time. An awkward age. I had no close relatives, no one who wanted me…'

He was watching her face closely, almost as if he was waiting for some reaction.

Knowing instinctively that it wasn't pity he was looking for, she remained still and silent.

'I was put into council care, then sent to foster-parents. I didn't fit in, and their own son hated me. The boys at school made fun of me, and I was frequently in trouble for fighting.

'My foster-parents did their best to tame me—Mary Kelly with secret bribes, her husband, John, by leathering the daylights out of me. He was a heavily built six-footer, and a bully by nature. I was almost sixteen when he accused me of stealing money out of his pocket to go to the local cinema. Mary had given me the money, and I told him that. But when he asked her, she swore she hadn't...'

No wonder Jos had no liking for women, Clare thought bleakly. Every woman in his life appeared to have failed him in some way.

'It was only later that I realised she was probably too scared to admit it. Anyway, he called me a lying, thieving bastard and laid into me with a strap. By that time I was getting some muscles of my own. I knocked him down and walked out. I never went back.

'With what was left of the money I took a train up to London. I slept rough for a night or two before managing to find a bed in a hostel. After a few days I was lucky enough to get a live-in job in a pub, humping barrels of beer and doing the heavy work. With the money I earned I took a business course and set out to better myself. I found I had a flair for the stock market, and by the time I was twenty, though far from rich, I was making a healthy profit.

'I wanted to make a clean break with the past, so I contacted my father's solicitors, and, with a view to paying off the debts he'd left, arranged to go in to see them.

'There was a surprise waiting for me. They had been advertising, trying to contact me. The "worthless stock" my grandfather had left me had, almost overnight, become worth millions with the Alaskan mining company's discovery of huge deposits of gold.'

So that was the source of his wealth.

Sounding cool and detached, he went on, 'I found that money breeds money. I bought out a small merchant bank and turned it into a big one, and during the next five or six years acquired property and various businesses that put me securely in the wealthy class.'

Wealth that had come too late to save what must have been years of hell. 'It's a pity the mining company didn't strike lucky sooner,' Clare commented with a sigh.

To her surprise, he shook his head. 'Those years taught me a lot. They taught me to be tough, to be ruthless. Taught me to hate. Taught me that money buys power—'

'But not necessarily happiness,' she broke in swiftly, appalled by such black bitterness.

'It buys what I want,' he told her with savage satisfaction. 'It bought you.'

Bending her head, she looked down, all her new-found hope and optimism dying in the grass at her feet.

He rose, uncoiling his length in one swift movement, and held out his hand. Just for an instant she had the strangest feeling that he was regretting his words, but, his voice curt, all he said was, 'About ready to move?'

She nodded, and, putting her hand into his, let him haul her to her feet.

Unable to look at him, scared he'd see just how badly he'd wounded her, she stopped and began collecting their litter to drop into the nearest bin.

Money didn't make a successful marriage any more than a wedding ring made a happy wife, she thought sadly, as, hand in hand, they set off to walk to Rainbow Bridge. But at least she was coming to understand him a little better and to know something of her own feelings.

What he'd gone through had hardened him, warped him, destroyed his ability to love and trust, made it difficult for him to accept, or even recognise love.

For she had loved him. It hadn't been merely a physical attraction that had drawn her to him. Remembering the snapshot that had been taken on the day they'd got engaged, she *knew* she had loved him. It had been implicit in her look, her smile, her whole bearing.

That was why she'd married him. Not for his money or the lifestyle he could give her, but for the oldest and most bitter-sweet of reasons.

Only he'd never known, and if she told him now he wouldn't believe her... But why hadn't she told him *then*?

Perhaps, aware that he didn't love her, she'd been too proud to. Maybe she had kept silent, hoping she could *show* him she cared, hoping eventually to strike an answering spark. Though surely knowing about his loveless childhood...

But *had* she known? He'd said, 'You'll need to know some time', but had he meant *know* or *remember*?

'Jos...?'

He glanced down at her enquiringly, green eyes gleaming between thick dark lashes.

'Did I know about your childhood? I mean, before I lost my memory.'

His face suddenly inscrutable, he said, 'I'd never mentioned it to you. Why do you ask?'

'I just wondered.'

So, not knowing about his childhood, she wouldn't have been aware of how necessary it was to tell him she

cared, to make him believe she loved him. She'd kept it
hidden, and in doing so had convinced him that she was
marrying him for what he could give her. No wonder he
was so bitter and cynical…

Reaching the bridge, mingling with a small throng of
sunburnt tourists, they crossed into Canada—Jos produc-
ing their passports for Canadian Customs—and followed
the crowd along a bustling thoroughfare, with the Niagara
Gorge on one side and the other lined with shops and
cafés and amusements.

'Ah, just what we need!' he exclaimed suddenly, and,
stopping at a kiosk, proceeded to buy a couple of plastic-
hooded yellow capes.

'Expecting rain?' she queried.

He grinned with a flash of white teeth. 'Believe me it
pays to wear a mac. Here—' he shook one out '—put it
round you.'

A little dubious, she asked, 'Are you sure it's necessary?'

'Unless you want to end up drenched to the skin by
spray.'

Before they'd gone more than a hundred yards or so
she discovered that Jos had been right. The pavement and
the roadway were wet and the air was full of a fine mist.

Some people wore raincoats, one or two carried umbrellas, but quite a few were unprepared. A group of
youths swaggered along, getting wet with macho pride,
while girls in summer frocks shrieked and giggled as they
tried to stay out of range of the blown spray.

When they got to the viewing-point, the roar of the
falls and the sheer spectacle took Clare's breath away.
She gazed entranced at the never-ending avalanche of
water thundering onto the rocks, and the flashing rain-
bows made by the sun slanting through the spray.

Turning shining eyes on her companion, she exclaimed, 'Aren't they *wonderful*? I heard someone mention the Bridal Veil Falls—which are they?'

'The Bridal Veil Falls are the smallest. Tomorrow, if you'd like to take a closer look, we'll go across the footbridge to Luna Island, where you can get a bird's-eye view... But perhaps the most exhilarating way to see the whole panorama is to take a boat trip on the *Maid of the Mist*...'

'That sounds like fun, but a bit scary.'

'Afraid of being on the water?'

'I don't think so... But there's only one way to find out.'

He saluted her spirit before saying, 'The *Maid* leaves from Prospect Point on the American side, so we'll be nice and handy. But now time's getting on and you must be tired, so I suggest we make our way back to the hotel and have Buffalo Wings for dinner.'

'What on earth are they?'

His grin made him suddenly boyish. 'Wait and see.'

Once back they took it in turns to shower and change— Clare into a silky, blue and mauve evening skirt and matching camisole top fastened with tiny self-buttons, Jos into a white lawn shirt left open at the throat.

They ate the spicy Buffalo Wings, which turned out to be chicken, on their balcony. There was a marvellous view of the falls and the scented air was balmy. In the gathering blue dusk a flock of small birds wheeled about overhead before settling in the trees like black snow.

On the table the candle flame flickered in the faint breeze, casting shadows on Jos's strong face and making his eyes gleam silver.

It couldn't have been a more romantic setting.

Beneath her lashes she watched him move the tip of his tongue across his lower lip and shivered slightly, wanting to follow it with her own tongue. Wanting to touch him.

As if he'd read her mind, he reached across the small table and lifted her hand to his lips. She gave a little gasp as, turning it slightly, he kissed the palm, his tongue tracing the heart line.

The deliberately sensual act turned the violet of her eyes almost to purple, and tore a rent a yard wide in her composure. When he released her hand she hid it in her lap, nursing it as though it was wounded, feeling a sharp pang of regret for what might have been.

Their holiday was almost over and she still hadn't regained her memory, nor did she know what had made her leave him. If only things had been different and this had been a real honeymoon...

But it *was* a real honeymoon. The fact that she had lost her memory didn't make it any less real, only a great deal more difficult.

As difficult as facing the future would be if she didn't get her memory back.

Without her past—her emotions, her awareness, her experience—she was incomplete, like a one-dimensional cardboard cut-out.

No, that made her seem lifeless, without feelings. She was more like a shadow who had lost its substance and was left alone and scared and bewildered.

Though she was sure now that she had married Jos for the right reasons, she was equally sure that he had married her for the wrong ones.

She sighed. There was still so much she didn't understand. Strange undercurrents, nuances she could almost but not quite catch, the way he often seemed to use words

to conceal thoughts rather than express them, a feeling
that at times he regarded her as an enemy.

And always at the back of her mind that lingering feeling of unease and apprehension, as though subconsciously she knew something dark and deep and terrible
that she was unable to bring into the open and face
squarely.

Suppose she'd done something awful? Something that
Jos wouldn't tell her. Something, that with very mixed
feelings, he was waiting for her to remember.

But what if she never did? She gave another short,
sharp sigh.

'I'd like to think those were contented, languorous
sighs, but I rather feel they're anxious ones.'

She tried to keep her head bent but his will dragged
her glance upwards.

He was watching her, his brilliant eyes boring into her.
'What's wrong, Clare?'

The words came in a rush. 'It's over two weeks now
and there's still no sign of my memory coming back.
Surely the more days that pass, the less chance there
is…?' Agitation bringing her to her feet, she cried
hoarsely, 'Suppose I *never* get it back?'

He rose in one swift movement and came round the
table to take her upper arms in a firm grip. 'That's a
possibility we may have to face. But if there's no *physical* reason, and Dr Hauser assured me there isn't, it's
much more likely that you *will* get it back. Though he
did stress that pressure of any kind could have adverse
effects…that the past should be allowed to come back in
its own good time.'

'So what do I do while I'm waiting?' she asked
bleakly.

'Just what we have been doing. No effort of will can

bring it back, so all we can do is carry on with our lives as if—'

All the tensions that she had managed to ignore for the past fortnight suddenly surfaced like sharks. 'As if I'm normal instead of some kind of freak?'

'Don't be silly, Clare,' he said shortly.

'Well, that's what I feel like. Someone who's only half alive, with no past and no future, on honeymoon with a man I don't remember marrying, a husband who is to all intents and purposes a stranger…'

Just for an instant his fingers bit painfully into her soft flesh, then they released her, and, his smile as slow and premeditated as a striptease, he said, 'Well, tonight I think we should remedy that state of affairs.'

CHAPTER FIVE

SHE caught her breath in shock. 'No, no I won't—'

A single finger touched her lips, effectively cutting off her instinctive protest. 'Oh, but you will, my darling wife,' he told her with icy determination. 'I've waited long enough. Too long. There would have been a lot less tension if I'd made love to you that first night at the International, instead of sleeping on the floor. I held back to give you time to adjust, to get used to the idea of being married to me, but it doesn't seem to have worked.'

'If you mean I still don't want to sleep with you, then you're right.'

'Why this show of reluctance? It's quite out of character.'

She flushed a little. 'Even if I'm the kind of woman you say I am, I'm sure I've always wanted to *choose* who I slept with.'

'I'm your husband. You *chose* to marry me; I didn't force you.'

But she felt oddly convinced that, if necessary, he would have been prepared to.

'So why shouldn't I have what I'm convinced you've dispensed with…shall we say…abundant generosity…?'

Though her heart felt as if it was being squeezed in a giant nutcracker, she fought back. 'Are you sure you're not mixing me up with my mother?'

'I doubt it. Any woman with your looks and sex appeal must have had plenty of propositions.'

'That doesn't mean to say I accepted any of them.'

His laugh was almost a sneer. 'In a minute you'll be trying to tell me you're still a virgin.'

'And you think that's impossible?'

She was waiting for him to say, I *know* it's impossible, but he said, 'I certainly think it's *improbable*. You're nearly twenty-five. There can't be too many twenty-five-year-old virgins about.'

'Especially *married* ones.'

'Ah!' he murmured softly. 'So now you know what you didn't want to ask.'

'And what you didn't want to tell me. *Why* didn't you want to admit that our marriage hadn't been consummated?'

'Because I thought it would make things easier to let you believe that we'd already crossed the Rubicon.'

'Easier for *you*!'

'For both of us.'

Everything he'd said and done pointed to the fact that though he might not love her he certainly *wanted* her, so why hadn't their marriage been consummated?

Smiling a little, once again reading her mind, he drawled, 'I'm more then willing to prove I'm not impotent, if that's what's worrying you...?'

The idea laughable, she half shook her head. At that instant a thought struck her, and she asked sharply, 'How long were we engaged?'

His eyes narrowed a little. 'Six weeks.'

'And we were never lovers...' It was a statement rather than a question. Lifting her head, she met his eyes. 'Why?'

He shrugged. 'You held back.'

She found that difficult to believe.

'Why did I hold back? If I'm as free with my... er...favours as you seem to think...'

'Perhaps you were making sure of the wedding ring first. But now you have one—' he picked up her hand and twisted the broad band of chased gold round her slim finger '—so the time for excuses and holding back is over.'

Before she had guessed his intention, he'd stooped and swept her into his arms. Suddenly unnerved by his arrogant self-confidence, his undoubted strength, she began to fight.

Holding her easily, despite her struggles, he carried her inside the room and tossed her onto the nearest bed.

Switching on the bedside lamp, he sat beside her, his hip touching hers, and, gripping her wrists, pressed her hands into the pillow, one each side of her head.

Her hair was a dark cloud around her heart-shaped face, her violet eyes almost black with fear and anger.

'Let me go,' she whispered fiercely. 'I don't want to sleep with you.'

'You will.' He bent his head until his mouth was only inches from hers. 'Your breathing has quickened, and there's a telltale pulse hammering away in your throat. When I kiss you you'll start to respond, and five minutes later you'll be begging me to make love to you.'

'Like I did on our wedding night?' she taunted.

'You have a sharp tongue, my darling. But then I like a little spirit.'

Hating her own defencelessness, she begged, 'Please, Jos… I don't want to make this marriage a real one— not until I get my memory back, until I *know* how things were between us.'

'As I've said before, you *chose* to marry me…'

'But on our wedding night it seems I didn't choose to sleep with you.'

'All right, so we quarrelled. But there's no call to let

your imagination run riot. I didn't suddenly grow horns and a forked tail and turn into the devil himself...'

He was doing his best to play things down, but the instinct that had warned her of danger was still there, sharp and insistent.

'All I'm asking is to wait until I get my memory back,' she pleaded.

'And suppose you never do?' His voice was suddenly harsh. 'You're a passionate woman with needs. What do you intend to do? Sleep with every man who comes along rather than with your own husband? No, Clare, I've been patient long enough.' A set purpose hardened his dark face into ruthlessness. 'If you won't give me what I want, then I'll have to take it.'

He swooped and covered her mouth with his own. It wasn't the brutal assault she was expecting, but a light brush of lips and tongue, a startling sensation made all the more sensual by the lightness, the delicacy of his touch.

She tried to keep her mouth closed against him, but his tongue-tip parted her lips and brushed the sensitive inner skin, making her gasp and quiver. He caught her lower lip between his teeth and began to suck and tug gently.

It was the most erotic thing she had ever experienced, and her stomach clenched and contracted at each pull.

What he was doing to her was so mind-bending that she scarcely noticed that he'd released her wrists and that his fingers were unfastening the buttons of her silky top and the front clip of her bra.

Her nipples were firm, waiting for his touch, and as his mouth followed his teasing fingers she began to make little whimpering sounds deep in her throat, trapped in a web of sensual enchantment.

As though he found her exquisite, and beautiful, he undressed her slowly, carefully, touching and stroking, unerringly finding and stimulating every erogenous zone.

She made no move to escape, lying in a pool of lamplight, helpless, dazed, her mind drugged with sensations so meltingly sweet that she was held in thrall.

Her body was slim yet curvaceous, with firm, beautifully shaped breasts, flaring hips and long, slender legs. Against the thin white sheet her skin was the palest gold, fine and flawless.

When she was naked, he turned her onto her stomach and kissed and caressed a leisurely path from her nape to the soles of her narrow feet, following the bumps and indentations of her spine, smoothing her buttocks, seeking the unexpectedly sensitive skin behind her knees with a warm tongue, making her wriggle and squirm, before turning her onto her back again.

Her breath was coming in quick shallow gasps between parted lips and her eyes were tightly closed, long lashes lying like black fans against her flushed cheeks.

He studied her for a long moment before bending his head to kiss her again. His mouth was gentle, yet with a hint of violence held strictly in check.

This time, at the mercy of sensations she couldn't remember ever experiencing before, she let her lips part helplessly, and he deepened the kiss, exploring her mouth like a conqueror.

When finally he lifted his head she put her arms around his neck, on fire for him, and tried to draw him back to her.

He laughed softly, triumphantly, and pulled away to strip off his own clothes.

In those few seconds of anticipation she knew instinctively how his weight would feel, what shape his body would take as it enclosed hers...

Then he was back, naked flesh against naked flesh, his hard legs parting her soft thighs, his lean hands stroking her breasts, his mouth on hers.

As he drew her down into the heated, erotic depths of passion, mingled with her breathless excitement was a sudden feeling of certainty, of *rightness*. All her doubts and fears belonged to a bad dream. This was reality. She and this tough, complex man belonged together. He was hers. Her husband. Her love...

'Oh!' A sudden tearing pain made her cry out.

She felt him freeze in shock, and, fearing he might be going to pull away and leave her bereft, she said hoarsely, 'It's all right... It's all *right*...' and held him to her, her arms across his broad back.

Still he hesitated, and with an instinct as old as time she pressed the lower half of her body against his and moved her hips enticingly.

With an inarticulate sound he began to move again, slowly, carefully, building up a spiralling core of tension until, passion riding him, he gave a kind of growl and drove hard and fast as she shuddered beneath him in convulsive ecstasy.

When, a second or two later, he groaned her name, she barely heard him, lost in a world of pure sensation. And them, with his head heavy against her breast, she slept.

When she awoke to instant and complete remembrance the room was dark, and cool air wafted softly in from the French windows. Still euphoric, she sighed and stretched like a satisfied cat.

If she'd dreamt it could be like this, she would never have held out against him for an instant, she thought, and turned to look at the other bed.

It was empty.

Feeling a sudden chill that had nothing to do with the night breeze, she sat up. At the same instant she caught sight of the dark silhouette standing still and silent on the terrace.

Slipping out of bed, she pulled on the satin robe that she'd tossed over a chair earlier and, tying the belt as she went, padded out to him.

Though she guessed he'd heard her coming, he made no move. Not until she touched his arm did he turn his head to look at her.

He might have been looking at a total stranger.

Her heart sank. He'd believed her to be experienced and clearly she wasn't... Perhaps he preferred a more sophisticated woman?

'Jos...? What's wrong?'

'What should be wrong?' he asked shortly.

She bit her lip, then persevered, '*Something* is. Did I...? I mean, were you...disappointed?'

'Because you were a virgin?'

There was such bitterness in his voice that she found herself stammering, 'I—I'm sorry...'

'What in heaven's name are you apologising for?' he burst out.

'You sounded as if you thought I was to blame for misleading you.'

'No, I'm the one to blame.' He turned away, his hands gripping the balustrade until his knuckles gleamed white. 'Before we got married we discussed contraception—I knew you were already taking the pill.'

'Yes, I found them. But some women take them for other reasons...'

As though she hadn't spoken, he went on, 'And because you *look* like your mother, without any concrete proof I somehow convinced myself that you must *be* like her.'

Every time he mentioned her mother his voice held the same sharp edge of contempt and animosity that conveyed much more than mere disapproval...

The thought crystallising, Clare said slowly, 'You *hated* her.'

He didn't answer. But then he didn't need to.

She wanted to ask him why, how he could hate a woman he hadn't even known. But an instinctive feeling that this wasn't the time or place held her back. And there were more important considerations—things she needed to know now she had committed herself.

Taking a deep breath, she broke the tense silence to ask, 'The fact that I'm not experienced...does it make any difference?'

'In what respect?'

'Well, if you'd prefer a woman who knows how to please you...' She faltered into silence.

'I won't be looking elsewhere, if that's what you're thinking. One woman is all I need. And, contrary to what you seem to imagine, I haven't had endless affairs. In fact I'm rather fastidious in my choice of lovers. When no one matches up to what I'm looking for, I've even been known to be celibate for months at a time.'

Though she felt halfway towards being reassured, it wasn't precisely what she'd been asking. Gathering her courage, she said, 'I meant would you have married me if you'd known?'

'Oh, yes.' His voice was pure polished steel. 'Though at first I was thrown, it doesn't really alter anything...'

Without knowing why, she shivered.

'In some ways it makes things easier. Now I can teach

you everything I want you to know, and you'll be mine in a way I never expected you to be.'

He turned and took her chin, lifting her face to his. It was too dark to read his expression but his desire beat against her like black wings.

When he led her back into the bedroom she went with undisguised eagerness, not to say abandon, breathless and trembling a little.

Jos made love to her again, and this time there was no pain, only a wild explosion of excitement and delight, and while she lay with her head on his shoulder she felt a gradual slide into a warm sea of mindless oblivion.

When she awoke it was to daylight and to shuddering sensation. He'd pushed the sheet away and his lips and tongue were travelling over her stomach, making a sensuous exploration of the warm flesh he'd laid bare.

As his mouth moved lover she gasped, 'No, Jos,' and made an instinctive attempt to reject such intimacy. His hands tightened on her thighs, his fingers biting painfully.

'You're hurting me,' she protested.

He lifted his head and she saw the hard, clear-cut lines and planes of his face, the blaze in his green eyes, the arrogance.

'Then lie still.'

A moment later his mouth was warm against her flesh again and his tongue was flicking and probing, insisting that she yield to the erotic pleasure he was giving her.

Only when she gave a little cry and arched towards him did he release his grip and cover her body with his own. 'Now relax. I'm going to show you the difference in sensations, make love to you until I've made you feel what it's like to...' His lips brushing her ear, he whispered his intentions.

'I *can't*...' she breathed.

He laughed softly. 'Of course you can. A twenty-five-year-old virgin bride has a lot of catching up to do.'

But she couldn't *stand* any more, she thought a shade wildly, before all thought was washed away and sensation after sensation began to flood through her body in slow waves of pleasure and delight...

After they'd showered and eaten a late breakfast on the balcony, his green eyes gleaming, Jos queried, 'Do you want to go out?'

She had begun to shake her head when, wondering if even his magnificent virility was starting to flag, she said hastily, 'Unless you do?'

Laughing under his breath, he hung a 'Do not disturb' notice on the door, and they went back to share the single bed.

Jos made no attempt to hide his satisfaction at the way things had turned out, and when they returned to the Lakeside International he made arrangements to stay on for a further week.

Having bulldozed down the barriers, he proved to be an exciting, inventive lover, with what a blushing Clare told him was an almost insatiable appetite.

He only laughed, and with consummate skill proceeded to prove that he could make her just as hungry for him.

She might have been a virgin, but he seemed to have tapped a latent spring of desire and need, and she was startled and somewhat alarmed to realise what a warm, sensual woman had been lying hidden beneath the cool surface.

So much so that she wondered how she had managed to remain a virgin for so long. Unless, scared by her mother's excesses, her own passionate nature had been deliberately suppressed?

Perhaps that was why she had been able to hold out against Jos? That and the uncomfortable knowledge that he hadn't loved her.

And he still didn't, she admitted sadly. He didn't even *like* her.

There was no doubt that he *desired* her, but his coolness was only melted by the heat of passion, never by the gentle warmth of affection. And though he gave free rein to his passion, her suspicion that he regarded his need for her as a weakness, and despised himself accordingly, added an extra and disturbing dimension to an already fraught relationship.

Each time she lay in his arms she hoped that things would change, that one day he would look at her with tenderness in his eyes. But always she was conscious of a fundamental hostility, usually carefully hidden, but present nevertheless.

Neither of them mentioned her loss of memory but as the days passed, instead of easing, her need to know and understand him and their complex and puzzling relationship became more urgent.

On the last night of their honeymoon, her thoughts restless, she lay beside him in the big double bed. After a while, aware that he too was wakeful, she said quietly, 'Jos, won't you talk to me?'

'About what?'

'About us. If I only knew what you *wanted*…'

He answered sardonically, 'I thought I'd made that abundantly clear.'

She sighed. 'Yet I feel you resent me and despise yourself for wanting me…'

A barely perceptible stiffening told her she'd hit gold,

but his voice was smooth as he mocked, 'Don't feminists assert that most men resent women?'

'So far as I know I'm not a feminist,' she said evenly.

When he stayed silent she pushed herself up on one elbow, and, peering down into his dark face in the half-light, said helplessly, 'I just don't understand you...'

His eyes gleamed between thick dark lashes as he stonewalled. 'How many people do understand their partners?'

She gritted her teeth. 'All I'm trying to do is make sense of our relationship. Without knowing or understanding, how can I have any faith in it?'

'Even relationships that are started with the best intentions sometimes become a test of blind faith.'

'But I don't even know what our intentions were...'

'Yours was to have a rich husband.'

Though she knew he was wrong, his words still had the power to hurt and agitate.

Taking a calming breath, she asked evenly, 'And *yours*?'

With a kind of bleak mockery that made her shiver, he said, 'I have very few scruples, and it's always been my intention to enslave you, to tie you to me with bonds of passion that would make it impossible for you to leave me.'

She found herself saying, 'Bonds of love would be stronger.' Again she sensed his lean body tense, and, knowing she was getting to him, she went on with growing confidence. 'Passion is relatively easy to come by, and therefore expendable.'

'But at least it exists.' He sounded angry.

'And you don't believe love does?'

'I have no reason to believe it.'

'Just because you missed out as a child, it doesn't

mean...' She stopped and tried again. 'If you knew how love can—'

'But I don't. The only thing I know about love is how to live without it.'

She heard the desolation, the pain. Putting her palm against his cheek, she said softly, 'Jos, I've never told you what I feel for you—'

'Don't try and kid me you feel anything for me beyond desire and the gratification of knowing I can provide what you want.'

He rolled over suddenly, pinning her down with the weight of his body. 'The last thing I want from you is any pretence of love. Even if you hate me I'll make sure you enjoy my wealth and the kind of lifestyle you married me for.'

Filled with a kind of cold anguish, she asked bleakly, 'And what will you enjoy?'

But she already knew the answer to that. A sensual exploitation, a cynical ownership without respect or even liking...

He laughed harshly, and settled his lean hips into the cradle of hers. 'Surely you don't have to ask.'

Afterwards, lying listening to his even breathing, she found her mind rerunning the tape of their conversation, heard him saying again, '...it's always been my intention to enslave you, to tie you to me with bonds of passion that would make it impossible for you to leave me.'

But before he could start to weave those bonds she had left him...

Then she heard herself averring that bonds of love would be stronger.

But even with those bonds already in place she had still left him...

Why...? *Why?*

*   *   *

They set off for home the following day—Jos with his usual air of cool assurance, Clare with a feeling of anxiety that lay like a dark cloud over her spirits. Apart from any other consideration, what was she to *do* with herself all day in a penthouse flat that was already perfectly run?

As their plane headed for La Guardia she was aware of Jos's eyes fixed on her half averted face, before he leaned towards her and asked quietly, 'Something bothering you?'

Everything. 'Not really.'

'So tell me about it.' There was a look in his eyes that convinced her he meant to know.

She chose the simplest problem. 'I was just wondering how I was going to fill my time…I mean when you go back to work. I have no friends in New York, and you pay Roberts to take care of everything…'

He lifted a dark brow. 'You don't like the idea of being a lady of leisure?'

'No.'

'But you've never had what you might call a career,' he pointed out. 'In any case—'

'I'm useless until I get my memory back,' she broke in bitterly.

'That wasn't what I was going to say.'

'But it's the truth.'

'I hardly think so.' Though soft, his voice had an edge to it. 'In fact the last thing I'd call you is *useless*… And you show so much enthusiasm, such a willingness to learn.'

He watched the colour flood into her cheeks before going on, 'Of course, if you fancy yourself in the role of a shop assistant or a waitress, and you don't mind waiting in line for a job that someone else is going to need a great deal more than you do…'

The words hung sharp and hurtful in the air.

But though she accepted the justness of the latter half of his sentence, she fought back, low-voiced. 'Rather than have to sit alone in an empty apartment all day with nothing to do, I'd prefer it if I *was* a shop assistant or a waitress.'

'Well, I wouldn't,' he said shortly. 'And though you won't remember, when we first discussed it I made no secret of the fact that I didn't want a working wife, I wanted a full-time companion, someone who's there when I get home, who's free to travel with me at a moment's notice...'

'And what did *I* want?' Then she added bleakly, 'Apart from a rich husband, that is...'

'What *do* you want?'

A real home and a family, a husband who loves me, my memory back... She shook her head helplessly. 'If I just had a home to look after...'

'Do you want me to fire Roberts?'

'No, of course not. Even if you did—' She broke off abruptly.

'Even if I did...?'

Bracing herself, she spoke the truth. 'I couldn't think of the penthouse as home.'

Surprising her, he said, 'I've never thought of it as home either... But to return to the point you were making, you won't be sitting in the apartment alone all day with nothing to do. I've no intention of going straight back to work. In fact I plan to take an extended honeymoon while I show you around New York and introduce you to my friends.'

Had that been on the cards *before* her loss of memory? she wondered. Aloud, she asked, 'But are you able to take more time off?'

'One good point about being the boss is that you get to call the shots. I have an excellent staff. An occasional phone call or an hour at my desk should be enough to keep my affairs running smoothly...'

When she said nothing, he queried a shade sarcastically, 'Does that make you feel any better?'

Though well aware that what he'd outlined was a short-term solution—it didn't actually *solve* anything—perforce she nodded.

Seeming to know what she was thinking, he took her hand and went on, 'And I intend to make changes to our lifestyle in the not too distant future.'

'What kind of changes?' she asked uncertainly.

He lifted the hand he was holding and touched his lips to the delicate blue veins on the inside of her wrist. 'Sweeping ones.'

A passing stewardess, seeing the intimate little caress, sighed audibly, and gave Clare a quick, envious glance.

They arrived to find New York baking and airless, heat and humidity gripping the city like a sweaty fist. The smell of melting tar and hot metal mingled with dust and exhaust fumes. Perspiring pedestrians mopped their brows. Bus doors hissed open, sucked in limp passengers and hissed shut again. Even the bright yellow cabs had lost their briskness and assumed a lethargic air.

When they reached the penthouse, Roberts, balding and benign, was waiting to welcome them with glasses of fruit juice chinking with ice.

After expressing a polite hope that they'd had a good journey, he continued, 'Ms Dwyer has rung several times, sir.'

'What did she want?' Jos sounded far from pleased.

'Merely to enquire when you would be home,' Roberts said blandly. 'I told her you were expected back today, and she asked if you would call her as soon as you got in.'

Jos gave a curt nod.

Having announced that an evening meal would be ready shortly, the manservant deferred to Clare. 'Would madam prefer to eat in the dining room or on the terrace?'

It might be hot and muggy on the terrace, but she favoured the idea of eating in the open air rather than the air-conditioned sterility of the dining room.

'Oh, on the terrace, I think.' She glanced at Jos. 'If that's all right with you?'

'Of course,' he answered smoothly. Then he went on, 'If you'd like to go ahead and shower... I've a couple of business calls to make first.'

Did Ms Dwyer come under the heading of business? Clare wondered a shade waspishly as she made her way to the bedroom, then told herself not to be a fool. How could she feel jealous of some unknown woman who might even be married?

As though to emphasise the fact that they would now be sharing a room, Jos had carried both sets of luggage straight through to the bedroom and placed them side by side on a long chest.

The cross-eyed teddy bear he'd bought her, and which she'd refused to leave behind, was sitting a little drunkenly on her case.

Lifting him off, she imitated his expression before dropping a kiss on his black felt nose and putting him in the nearest chair.

As she did so Clare noticed that the light jacket Jos had taken off and slung casually over the chair-back had slipped to the floor.

It was the same one he'd worn the day they'd picnicked by the Niagara and crossed Rainbow Bridge into Canada.

All at once that seemed a long time ago.

Stooping, she picked up the jacket, and as she did so their passports slid out of one of the pockets and dropped onto the carpet. Jos's fell open, and a fleeting glimpse of something as the pages turned arrested her.

A frown marring her smooth forehead, Clare picked it up and took a closer look. The pictured face, with its handsome eyes and chiselled mouth, was familiar. But the accompanying name was strange.

Yet not strange.

Clave.

It seemed to jump out from the page at her. Staring down at it, she began to shake.

Clave...

A roaring sound filled her ears and she felt as though her head was bursting with the knowledge that somewhere, some time, way back in her childhood, perhaps, she had known a boy named Clave.

CHAPTER SIX

SHE was sure she hadn't liked him. She'd been afraid of him… But suddenly she was racked by a terrible feeling of guilt and regret.

Sinking into the chair, she covered her face with trembling hands and tried to think, but already the crack in the door was closing relentlessly, shutting out that tiny glimmer of light.

It took several minutes and a lot of will-power to pull herself together. When she felt calmer, she picked up her own passport and returned both of them to his pocket, before going into the bathroom on legs that still shook a little.

She was back in the bedroom, wearing a blue silk button-through dress but still barefoot, when Jos came in.

Careful not to look directly at him, she began to brush her hair, the dark, glossy cloud settling round a face that, despite its light tan, looked drained of colour and taut.

He'd taken off his shirt and footwear and was opening a drawer to find a change of clothing when, catching sight of her reflection in the mirror, he paused.

Turning, he put a hand beneath her chin and tilted her face up to his. Green eyes looked deep into violet and assessed the lingering agitation she was unable to hide. 'What's wrong?'

Some instinct warned her not to say anything until she'd had more time to think.

'Nothing.' She strove to look unconcerned.

His glance shadowed, yet intent, he ordered, 'Don't lie to me, Clare.'

'What makes you think I'm lying to you?'

When she would have turned away, he caught her arm and swung her back, holding her by the elbows. A little smile twisting his lips, he warned, 'If necessary I'm prepared to beat it out of you.'

It was a threat in spite of that smile, and she had a feeling he meant every word.

'Well?'

'Your jacket was lying on the floor. When I picked it up the passports slipped out of the pocket. Yours fell open…'

'And?' A dark brow lifted in interrogation.

Flustered, she said, 'Though I couldn't actually *remember*, I felt almost certain I'd once known someone with the same name…'

His face wiped clean of all expression, he remarked, 'Saunders is a fairly common name.'

'*Clave* isn't.'

His green eyes narrowed, leaving just a gleam of colour between the thick lashes, but he said nothing, merely watched her.

She went on haltingly, 'It seemed familiar… I associated it with my childhood…'

When he still said nothing, she asked, 'Why didn't you tell me your name was Clave?'

'Because I don't use that name.'

'Why not?'

He answered indirectly, 'I was christened Clave Joseph, after my grandfather. As you remarked, it isn't too common. After my parents died and I was sent to a state school, with a name like Clave and a "posh" accent you can imagine what kind of fun was poked at me.'

Almost wearily, he added, 'After I'd tried to fight half the school for chanting "Clavie" after me, I started to call myself Jos in self-defence. I've been Jos ever since.'

She felt a great sadness, a compassion that brought a lump to her throat.

His green eyes flared. Curtly, he said, 'I can do without your pity.'

Flushing, she told him briskly, 'That's good, because I wasn't going to give you any.'

He smiled with savage self-mockery. 'Don't tell me you weren't feeling sorry for me, thinking—'

'Shall I tell you what I *was* thinking?' Though thoroughly hot and bothered now, she lifted her chin and looked him in the eye, trying to meet the impact of his stare without flinching.

'Please do,' he invited, silkily sarcastic.

She took a deep breath while adrenalin pumped into her veins. 'I was thinking that at six foot three you're too big to carry a chip on your shoulder.'

The instant the words were spoken, she wished them unsaid.

For what seemed an age he stood quite still, his gaze heated and furious. Then, his anger masked, his tone as smoothly abrasive as pumice-stone, he said, 'I take great exception to that remark.'

'Because you think I'm wrong about the chip?'

'Because I think you're right.'

'Then you're not *too* angry?' She held her breath.

'Let's say that though I recognise the basic truth of your words, I still intend to make you pay for them.'

Before she could take evasive action, he swooped and threw her over his shoulder in a fireman's lift. 'There, that should dislodge any chip. Now I think we both need to cool off.'

He was opening the bathroom door before she guessed his intention. 'No, Jos.' She began to struggle. 'I've already showered.'

Grimly jocular, he said, 'Not with me, you haven't.'

He turned the powerful jet full on, and, stepping beneath it, set her on her feet, hands gripping her shoulders, cold water pouring over them both.

Making no attempt to struggle now, she stood quietly, her hair a dark tangled mass of wet curls, her clothes plastered to her.

His eyes dropping to where her nipples were clearly visible through the thin material of her bodice, he enquired with mock solicitude, 'Not too cold?'

'Not at all,' she lied spiritedly, and, trying to stop her teeth chattering, added, 'I'm finding it quite refreshing.'

The effect was somewhat spoiled when a moment or two later she began to shiver.

He bent his head, and she felt his warm mouth close over a silk-clad nipple.

She continued to shiver, but for a different reason.

Reaching for the shower control, he turned it to comfortably hot, and with deft fingers began to unfasten the buttons that ran down the front of her dress. Then, slipping it from her shoulders, he tossed it aside before undoing her bra.

He claimed her mouth, deepening the kiss while he slid her clinging panties down over her hips and his fingers combed through the tangle of wet curls to find their goal and explore and stimulate with slow, rhythmic movements.

Steam began to swirl round them while those long, skilful fingers built a spiralling core of sensation.

Just as she felt herself arching helplessly towards him

he lifted his head and withdrew his hand, leaving her on the brink.

She bit her lip hard, determined not to show her feelings, not to let him manipulate her as though she was some puppet.

'Now it's your turn.' He took her hands and guided them to the waistband of his trousers.

Instead of immediately unfastening the clip, she ran her fingers over his chest, the golden skin smooth and slick except for the light sprinkling of wet black hair that arrowed in a V towards his stomach.

While the hot water continued to cascade over them she leaned forward and took one of the small flat nipples between her lips, stroking it with her tongue, tugging slightly, learning its resilience, its leathery texture, before closing her teeth on it with erotic delicacy.

He gave a kind of shudder.

Eyes closed, nuzzling her face across his chest, she searched for and found its twin while her fingers undid the clip and zipper and pushed the soaking trousers over lean hips.

As though the steamy heat had unfrozen the last of her inhibitions, with great deliberation she smoothed her palms down his flat stomach and her thumbs sketched slow arcs over the clinging silk shorts, before she sent them to follow the trousers.

When he'd stepped out of the garments and tossed them aside, her hand returned to caress the firm flesh she had freed.

When she heard his breath hiss sharply through his teeth, she smiled a small, triumphant smile. Now who was calling the tune?

Her satisfaction was short-lived.

Seizing her hand, he held it away from him, then, capturing the other, placed them both round his neck. A moment later he was lifting her, and, with his hands supporting her buttocks, urging, 'Wrap your legs around me, darling.'

When she did so, he smiled and guided her into position, his eyes glittering with a male triumph that even the pouring water and the wreathing steam couldn't conceal, before they went out of focus as he leaned forward to kiss her.

Afterwards they dried each other.

By the time they were both dressed they were late for the meal, and Clare tried not to dwell on what Roberts was bound to think when he found their saturated clothing.

Though out on the terrace it was warm, it was blessedly free from the dust and fumes encountered at street level. An electric fan whirred quietly, moving the still air, and the fountain, a delightful bronze of a pair of geese landing on the water with outstretched feet, was playing.

The splash and gurgle added to the impression of coolness, but, recalling the shower, Clare decided wryly that much more water and she'd develop webbed feet along with the geese.

Glancing up, she saw Jos's eyes were fixed on her, irony in their depths, as though he was reading her thoughts.

His face was too strong, too tough to be called conventionally handsome, but his mouth and his eyes, the arrangement of his features, his bone structure, made him compellingly attractive.

Even as an old man he would still be incredibly good to look at, she realised. But it was his eyes, brilliant, habitually mocking eyes, that never ceased to fascinate her.

Although she couldn't remember it, she could imagine the impact when he had first looked at her with that cool, ironic gaze.

She must have been intrigued from the start, in fact he had remarked on it. But he'd described her response as 'cool reserve' so she must have also been instinctively scared, or at least *cautious* about getting involved with such a man.

Though now she could see clearly that she wouldn't have stood a chance when once he'd started to stalk her...

When once he'd started to stalk her...

Suddenly she shivered. The idea was so uncomfortable, so emotive, that she wondered what had made her subconsciously phrase the thought in such a way.

Something that had happened in the past? Something her subconscious knew that her conscious self couldn't remember? Something he was taking care not to tell her? Something to do with a boy named Clave?

After the shower, while Jos had dried her glowing body, he'd remarked teasingly, 'As a cooling off operation, this hasn't been a notable success...'

But as a diversionary tactic it had been highly successful.

Though if they *had* known each other as children why wouldn't he admit it? Unless there was something he wanted to keep hidden? Something that the name Clave Saunders might have recalled and that Jos Saunders didn't.

While she ate Clare struggled to get her thoughts in order, to find some answers, but all that emerged were more questions.

Had she known his name was Clave before she'd lost her memory? Had she recognised him as someone from her childhood? If she had, would she still have gone ahead and married him? Or had she only known him as Jos, and recollected nothing of any past involvement?

As he reached to refill her wine glass, she asked abruptly, 'Did I know your name was Clave before I lost my memory?'

The green eyes regarded her coolly. 'As I told you earlier, I haven't used the name since I was thirteen.'

She gritted her teeth and persisted, 'Then I only knew you as Jos?'

He answered obliquely, 'Our full names were used during the marriage service.'

Though if she had recognised it then, realised she had known him, she would have been already committed…

But that day at Niagara, when she had asked him if they had known each other as children, he had denied it. Or had he?

She thought back. After he'd remarked that he was surprised by how tender-hearted she'd grown up to be, she had asked, *Did* you know me?

There had been a short, but marked hesitation before he'd answered, 'I didn't need to know you. In my experience a lot of children can be heartless little monsters, and usually the females stay that way.'

So he hadn't actually denied it.

And now a growing conviction made her almost certain that they *had* known each other, that their paths had crossed in some disturbing way.

But *when* and *how*?

Summoning up all her courage and determination, more than tired of half-truths and evasions, Clare had opened her mouth to demand an unequivocal answer when, with a discreet cough, Roberts appeared.

'I'm sorry to disturb you, sir, but Ms Dwyer is on the phone asking to speak to you. I told her you had barely finished eating, but she was most insistent.'

Tossing down his napkin in a way that clearly indicated he wasn't too pleased at the interruption, Jos pushed back his chair and, saying curtly, 'You can serve the coffee,' preceded the manservant indoors.

The moment was irretrievably lost. Clare sighed. Now she would have to wait, screw up her courage all over again, before she could ask Jos what she wanted to know.

And even then there was no guarantee that he'd tell her. If, for whatever reason, he didn't want her to know the truth, he was quite capable of lying…

A minute or so later Roberts returned, grave and deferential, carrying a round silver tray with a pot of coffee and a dish of Turkish delight.

'This confection is Mr Saunders favourite, but if madam would prefer mints…?'

'No, I love Turkish delight.' *I love Turkish delight…I love Turkish delight…* As though spoken into an empty biscuit tin the words echoed hollowly inside her head, while, as if she was looking through the unfocused lens of a camera, her brain produced a blurred picture of a boy with dark hair and a thin face holding out a brightly coloured octagonal box.

Gripped by a kind of sick excitement, she strove to hold onto the picture, to bring it into focus, but abruptly it was gone.

She stifled a groan, but something of her mental turmoil must have been evident, because Roberts was asking with concern, 'Is anything wrong, madam?'

'No, I'm fine, thank you.' She managed a smile. 'Just a slight headache.'

Having filled her small cup, he placed the pot and the silver dish within reach and departed noiselessly.

Hoping that it would retrigger the memory, Clare helped herself to a piece of the delectable sweetmeat and chewed slowly, but while her saliva glands sprang into operation her brain stubbornly refused to co-operate.

Disappointed, she was licking the fine sugar from her fingers when Jos came back. His handsome face expressionless, he told her, 'We've been invited to a party.'

'Oh…'

He picked up the coffee-pot and filled his cup. 'I've accepted for us both. I hope you don't mind?'

Though well aware that the 'I hope you don't mind' had been added out of politeness, she nevertheless answered, 'No…' Then, appreciating that she'd sounded a little doubtful, she said more positively, 'No, of course I don't mind. When?'

'As soon as we've finished our coffee.'

Feeling a sudden flutter of panic, she objected, 'But I can't go to a party looking like this.'

His gaze lingered on the heart-shaped face that was free of make-up, on the cloud of dark curly hair and the winged brows, the violet eyes and flawless skin, the short, straight nose, high, slanting cheekbones and the disproportionately wide mouth, before travelling assessingly over the slender figure in a grey chiffon dress with a simple cross-over bodice and a full skirt.

A flame leapt in his green eyes. 'Every man there will envy me.'

Feeling a little flush of heat, she persisted even so, 'But I'm not dressed for a party.'

'What you have on looks fine to me. It's a fairly laid-back affair. I'm going as I am.'

Wearing well-cut casual trousers and a dark green silk shirt open at the neck, his cool elegance was enhanced by the kind of magnetism that was only partly sexual. It was his basic self-confidence, Clare decided, his aura of strength and authority that rounded off his powerful attraction.

'I thought it was about time I introduced my wife to some of my friends and acquaintances, and this is a perfect opportunity.'

Reaching for the coffee-pot once more, he raised an enquiring brow.

Playing for time, she nodded. 'Please.'

When he'd poured them both another cup, he went on, 'Tom Dwyer is a merchant banker; he lives in this same building a few floors down. He's both a friend and a business associate, so we know many of the same people.'

'And Ms Dwyer is his wife?'

'Tom's a widower. Andrea is his daughter.'

'And your mistress?' The words popped out without her conscious volition.

'Ex-mistress,' Jos corrected coolly.

Remembering the phone calls, Clare asked sweetly, 'Does *she* know that?'

'Jealous?'

Yes! 'No. I was just wondering if you'd got round to telling her.'

His face cold, almost disdainful, he said, 'I played by the rules. I told her it was finished before I went over to England.'

Repelled by what she saw as his heartlessness, Clare felt sorry for the other woman.

'There's no need to look so outraged.'

Aware that they shared no common ground, that he was a sophisticated man who held cynical views on relationships between the sexes, she said stiffly, 'That's a matter of opinion.'

A muscle tightened in his jaw. 'It was agreed from the start that there should be no commitments, and that either one of us could end the association without recriminations.'

Except that Andrea hadn't wanted to. Clare knew that as surely as if he'd admitted it aloud.

'To reinforce the fact that it *was* ended, and so there should be not the slightest doubt about my intentions, I told her as soon as we got engaged.'

'Over the phone?'

'Do you think I should have travelled all the way back to New York to break the news?'

'No, but… Well, it seems so *unfeeling*.'

He laughed derisively. 'Don't get it into your head that *feelings* were involved. She's a pretty cool lady, and it was a convenient arrangement that suited us both. Nothing more or less.'

Watching Clare's expressive face, he said, 'Look, let me put things into perspective for you. Andrea's only about your age and she's already had two husbands and a string of lovers. As far as I know she hasn't cared a jot for any of them, so I shouldn't waste too much sympathy on her.'

'I wasn't… But I don't like the idea of going to a party in her apartment.'

'Andrea has her own place when she cares to use it. This is her father's apartment.'

'I still find it hard to believe that she'd want me there,' Clare objected doggedly.

'*I* want you there.' His handsome face was hard, un-compromising, and his eyes held a steely glitter. 'When Andrea first mentioned a party, I told her that if I came I'd be bringing my wife.'

Her voice accusing, Clare said, 'You just want to use me to get her off your back.'

'Would you rather I allotted you alternate nights?'

'You're a brute!' she muttered hoarsely.

Appearing unmoved, he said, 'I may be a brute, but you're quite wrong about me wanting to use you. I'm more than capable of discouraging any woman who looks like becoming a nuisance. The problem I have with Andrea is that her father is a good friend of mine, and I don't want him to be hurt.'

'Then perhaps you shouldn't have chased after her in the first place.'

'At the risk of sounding ungallant, I must tell you that it was Andrea who did all the chasing…'

'Oh…' Clare said a little blankly.

'In case you hadn't realised,' he added sardonically, 'females are often more predatory than males. Your own mother was a prime example.'

She flushed painfully.

Watching her face grow hot, he swallowed the last of his coffee and rose to his feet. 'Ready?'

She shook her head. 'I won't go.'

'You will.'

His determination beat against her like an iron fist.

'I have no intention of going without you, so we can do this the easy way or the hard way… Whichever, the end result will be the same.'

'Please, Jos…'

Ignoring her plea, his face implacable, he held out his

hand. 'Now, are you going on your own two feet or do I have to throw you over my shoulder?'

'I abhor caveman tactics,' she muttered mutinously. But, knowing he was quite capable of carrying out his threat, and unwilling to be humiliated, she rose and let him take her hand.

Tucking it through his arm, he glanced down at her set face and offered, 'We needn't stay long if you don't want to.' She was just breathing a sigh of relief, when he added ironically, 'They'll no doubt put our eagerness for an early night down to the fact that we're newly married.'

They were stepping out of the lift outside the Dwyers' apartment when Clare voiced the question that had been bothering her. 'Do they…do any of them know I've lost my memory?'

His finger on the door-bell, Jos said, 'Tom does. No one else, unless he's told them.'

The door was opened by a casually dressed, pleasant-looking man with a thick thatch of grey-blond hair. He seemed startled when he saw Clare, and she wondered with a sinking heart if she hadn't really been expected.

Switching his gaze to Jos, he exclaimed, 'Hi! Glad you folks could make it at such short notice. Come on in.'

Inside the opulent apartment there was a crowd of people and the talk and laughter of a party in full swing.

Clapping Jos on the shoulder, he went on, 'I understand Andrea's been trying to get hold of you…'

Clare noticed the faintest shadow of unease flit across his face as he mentioned Andrea.

'We've been away on honeymoon,' Jos told him easily. 'Just got back a couple of hours ago.'

His arm around Clare's waist, he made the introductions. 'Darling, this is our host… Tom, my wife, Clare…'

Tom Dwyer was a lean, rangy man in his early fifties, Clare judged, with level blue eyes and a firm handshake.

'It's nice to meet you,' he said, sounding as if he wanted to mean it. Then, glancing up, 'Ah, here's Andrea.'

'Darling!' A tall, slender woman with shining blonde hair and a dress like blue lightning appeared from the throng and made as if to throw her arms around Jos's neck and kiss him full on the lips.

He was took quick for her. Catching her wrists, he held her away, and when, after a second or two, mortified colour began to creep into her face, bent his dark head to give her a chaste peck on the cheek.

'How are you, Andrea? You're looking very well…'

That was a blatant understatement.

Andrea was dazzling and glamorous, blessed with a marvellous figure, and only a certain hardness detracted from what was still a stunning beauty.

'This is my wife, Clare…'

The blonde carried off the snub admirably. 'Having a new wife has made you very formal,' she rebuked Jos gaily, and for the first time took her attention from him and transferred it to Clare.

As she did so the pale blue eyes widened and gazed almost in disbelief, before the bright lips twisted into a smile as false as her greeting. 'I'm so pleased you could come. Do forgive me for staring, but you remind me of someone…'

A waiter appeared with a loaded tray.

'Champagne?' Tom Dwyer put a glass in Clare's hand and one in Joe's, before serving his daughter and himself.

'What are we celebrating?' Jos enquired idly as they stood sipping the sparkling wine.

Andrea answered. 'My divorce, darling. The decree absolute has just come through.'

She gave Clare another smile which, though brilliant, left her eyes as cold as chips of blue ice. 'I hope you don't mind me calling your husband darling, but you see, we're old friends.'

'Yes, I know,' Clare said quietly.

'Oh, really?' Though not excessively loud, Andrea's voice was pitched to carry. 'I thought your mind had gone funny, that you couldn't remember anything…'

Several people glanced furtively in their direction.

Feeling like some freak, but determined not to show she was upset, Clare had just schooled her face into careful blandness when Tom said hurriedly, 'Jos told me you hit your head when you were knocked down by a cab?'

'That's right.' She smiled at him, trying to ease his obvious embarrassment. 'I can't remember anything that happened *before* the accident, but hopefully the amnesia will pass.'

'There's nothing you can do?'

'Nothing but wait.' Her voice was level. 'No effort of will seems able to bring my memory back, so I've just got to make the best of things.'

'Suppose it never comes back?' Andrea gave a mock shudder. 'Poor you. I've always had a dread of being *abnormal*… I really don't know how you'll cope…'

Sensing that the blonde was trying to get at Jos through her rather than making a personal attack, Clare said mildly, 'Oh, I think I'll manage to struggle along. I just won't have any recollection of my childhood or growing up.'

'How awful. And no memories of your wedding day—'

'There's a lot of people who would be only too pleased to forget *that*,' Tom broke in, clearly uncomfortable.

Turning to Jos, Andrea persisted, 'You must find it terribly upsetting, having a wife who's not quite... I mean, who's lost her memory.'

Smiling down at Clare, Jos dropped a light kiss on the corner of her mouth and drawled, 'Not at all. You see, it makes her mine in a very special way.'

Andrea's tinkling laugh sounded forced. 'I don't quite follow...'

'There are no memories of any other men to come between us.'

The pale blue eyes bright with malice, Andrea said smoothly, 'I expect Clare wishes that would work in reverse.'

Just as smoothly, Jos murmured, 'I have to say that none of the women in my past have been memorable enough to intrude.'

Little coins of colour appeared on Andrea's beautifully made-up face.

Wishing the floor would open and swallow her up, Clare tried to think of something innocuous to say—and failed miserably.

Though inwardly admitting that Andrea should have had more sense than to goad him, she felt sorry for the other woman, and regretted Jos's deliberate cruelty.

The doorbell enabled Tom to rescue the situation. Turning to his daughter, he said hastily, 'While I see who that is, can you go and be nice to the congressman's wife? She doesn't know many people here and she's looking a bit out of things.'

'Certainly.' A smile pinned to her lips, and ignoring Jos completely, Andrea suggested to Clare, 'When you've had a chance to mix a bit, perhaps we could get together for a chat?'

Wondering why the blonde wanted to talk to her, and her heart sinking at the prospect, Clare nevertheless said, 'Of course,' and managed to return the smile.

When the other two had gone, Jos slanted her a glance. 'Do you really want a tête-à-tête with Andrea?'

'No. But as she seems to be our hostess, what else could I say?'

'Those good manners will be the death of you.' He sounded half-amused, half-irritated. 'And she's such a bitch, I don't know why you feel the need to be kind.'

'It's better than being cruel.'

'Andrea won't appreciate it. In her book, kindness equates with weakness.'

'But not in mine,' Clare said firmly.

Jos sighed, and, having disposed of their glasses on an occasional table, said, 'As soon as we've said hello to a few people, we can leave.'

'And let her think I'm running away?'

He half shook his head. 'She's out to hurt you.'

'Why should *you* care, when—?' Clare broke off.

'When I'm not always kind to you myself?' He hesitated, then said slowly, 'Perhaps I prefer to be the one to hurt you, to make you bleed.' Watching a shiver run through her, he added flatly, 'If you stay and fight, she'll rout you.'

'Do you think so?'

He looked down at her, at the steady violet eyes, the firm mouth and stubborn chin. 'No, I don't. I'm underrating you. Despite your gentleness, your softheartedness, you have plenty of courage and strength.

'Come no, then.' He tucked her hand through his arm

and, looking cool, slightly formidable, said, 'Let's go and circulate.'

At the end of perhaps an hour, Clare had met nearly all the people there. Though she had made an effort, she was ashamed to admit that she'd already forgotten most of their names.

Many of them had looked surprised when Jos had introduced her as his wife, and several of the females had said how unexpected it all was, and tried to hide their regret that he was no longer an eligible bachelor.

He had just presented Clare to a small group of financiers from Wall Street, when Scott Wendell, a young man with a weak chin and the beginnings of a paunch, burst out, 'Do you know, I thought for a minute—'

Catching Jos's eye, he stopped abruptly, before continuing a shade awkwardly, 'Well, I must say you kept that very quiet, you sly fox.' Then he turned to Clare. 'And he tried to tell us that his visit to England was a business trip.'

She smiled, 'Well, I gather it was.'

Clearly a ladies' man, Wendell said gallantly, 'Speaking as someone who makes similar trips, I wish *I* could do that well for myself during the course of business… Oh, and with regard to business,' he went on, just as Andrea joined the little group, 'had you heard that Clemensons's Bank is—?'

'If you men are going to talk business,' the blonde broke in, 'we'll leave you to it.' Slipping a hand through Clare's arm, she added with a smile that was about as friendly as a clenched fist, 'There's something I'd like to show you…'

As they moved away Wendell could be heard to say succinctly, 'Her claws, no doubt.'

CHAPTER SEVEN

APART from a tightening of the carmine lips, Andrea gave no sign that she'd heard as she led Clare away from the noise and laughter of the party and into a small library-cum-study.

A tray of drinks stood at one side. After splashing bourbon into a couple of glasses, she added ice and handed one to Clare, waving her to a brocade-covered couch.

Dropping into the chair opposite, the blonde took a long swallow of her drink and said without preamble, 'I suppose you know that I was going to marry Jos when he came back to the States?'

'No, I didn't,' Clare said quietly.

'I was only waiting for my divorce to go through.'

'Did *he* know that?'

Almost defiantly, Andrea said, 'At that time there was no other woman in his life and I understood his needs.'

'I take it you're referring to his sexual needs?'

'Don't kid yourself he has any others.'

'Doesn't everyone?'

'He's as tough and impervious as they come, with no room for softer feelings or emotional commitments. I don't pretend that he loved me—I doubt if he's loved any woman—and he can be a cruel swine, but he's the only man I've ever gone overboard for, and we could have made a go of it if it hadn't been for you.'

Feeling an unwilling sympathy for the woman, Clare said, 'He told me the affair was over before he left for England.'

114

Her nails crimson talons against the glass, the blonde tossed back her drink and reached to pour herself another. 'I could have changed his mind if you hadn't set out to hook him.'

'But I didn't set out to hook him.'

'I thought you couldn't remember.'

'Jos told me. He said I hadn't used my wiles to catch him.'

'And he's some catch. Even if he wasn't filthy rich he'd still be every woman's dream. I take it you didn't marry him for his money?'

'He thinks I did.'

Andrea raised a beautifully plucked brow. 'So when you stuck out for a wedding ring he was ready to buy you... How did you manage it so he thought you hadn't used your wiles? Did you hold back? Play hard to get? Make him believe you were an untouched English rose? Jos is the kind of man who would enjoy a challenge, and perhaps the idea of breaking new ground held a special appeal for him. Did he think you were a virgin and—?'

'Hardly,' Clare said drily.

'Then why do you suppose he married you?'

'He wanted me.'

'Well, that makes us equal. So when the bloom has worn off we might end up sharing him for a while, before you get your final marching orders.'

'I doubt it.'

Her lip curling, Andrea said almost pityingly, 'You don't believe he'll tire of you?'

Clare shook her head. 'I mean I wouldn't share him.' With sudden passionate intensity, she added, 'I *couldn't*.'

The blonde's eyes narrowed. 'Anyone would think you loved him.'

'I do.'

'Then I'm sorry for you. He won't want your love.

He's a hard-as-nails, self-sufficient bastard, and if you imagine for one minute that he cares about you…'

All at once weary, sick to death of this futile tête-à-tête, Clare said, 'I don't imagine he cares about me.' She put her untouched drink on the table, slopping it a little, clumsy in her agitation. 'Now, if you'll excuse me, I think I'll go back to the party.'

'But we haven't finished our conversation, and I still have something to show you.' Andrea's voice was light, almost friendly, but her face looked cold and tight.

Shaking her head, Clare rose to her feet. 'All this is pointless…'

'Far from it.' The pale blue eyes glittered with triumph. 'Shall I tell you the *real* reason Jos married you?'

Suddenly aware that this was the whole purpose of the get-together, what the other woman had been leading up to, Clare asked with studied calmness, 'Are you sure you know it?'

'Oh, I know it all right. Though I didn't fully realise until I *saw* you and discovered just how like her you are. Of course, you haven't got her kind of glamour, her stunning sexual aura—in fact it's like comparing a watercolour to an oil painting—but still the likeness is strong, wouldn't you say?'

'I haven't the faintest idea what you're talking about…'

As though Clare hadn't spoken, Andrea went on, 'While she was visiting New York he became infatuated with her, and I think it must have come as a real shock when she died…'

'Died?' Clare echoed, dry-mouthed. Beginning to understand. Not wanting to understand. 'How did she die? When did she die?'

'A few months ago in a plane crash in Panama.'

Clare's palms grew clammy and her stomach tied itself into a knot of tension as Andrea went on.

'I knew Jos needed a woman, and that was when I went to him. With the opposition out of the way, I thought he'd be mine.' Bitterly, she added, 'But his obsession obviously hadn't been cured, and he must have decided that if he wasn't able to have the mother, he'd have the daughter...'

Her knees turning to jelly, Clare sank back onto the couch. Scarcely above a whisper, she said, 'I don't believe you. He didn't even know my mother—at least not personally.'

'He knew her, believe me. When he first saw her picture in the papers he couldn't hide his interest, and, though she must have been a good twelve years older than he was, as soon as they met he became her lover. He was so fascinated by her that for weeks he scarcely let her out of his sight...'

The blood pounded in Clare's ears and sweat broke out on her forehead. So she had been just a substitute. Was that why Jos sometimes appeared to hate and resent her? Because she was alive while her mother was dead?

No, surely not. If he seemed at times to hate *her*, he'd almost certainly hated her mother more. It had been implicit in his look and his voice every time he'd mentioned her.

'I don't believe you,' Clare repeated more firmly, certain now that the blonde was just out to make trouble. 'He didn't even like her.'

'Perhaps that's what he wanted you to believe. But does this look as though he didn't like her?' Taking a glossy magazine from one of the drawers in the bureau, Andrea tossed it onto the couch. 'Have a look at the society gossip pages.'

Trying to keep her hand steady, Clare opened *Jet Set*

and flicked through it until she found what she was looking for.

Staring up at her from the shiny double-page spread
was a full-length picture of a slender dark-haired woman
with a Sophia Loren type of face.

A face that was familiar to her...

But was her sudden shock of recognition due to the
fact that the face, apart from its hollow-cheeked gaunt-
ness and the age difference, which was evident even
through the make-up, could have been her own?

Wearing an ankle-length black sheath, slashed almost
to the thigh, the woman was clinging to Jos's arm while
he, devastatingly handsome in impeccable evening dress,
was looking down at her.

Clare read the caption.

Wealthy banker Jos Saunders is seen here escorting
Lady Isobel Berkeley, the wife of diplomat Sir Roger
Berkeley, to Culpeppers. Later in the evening they
were spotted dancing cheek to cheek at the Pelican
Club...and, in the early hours of the morning, engaged
in cementing Anglo-American relations...

The accompanying photographs showed the pair first
entwined on the dance floor and then sitting at a table,
their dark heads close together, their mouths clinging.

Feeling as though she was slowly bleeding to death,
Clare read on.

It has been rumoured that Lady Berkeley, previously
known for her somewhat wild lifestyle, has ditched all
her former admirers in favour of the handsome
banker...

She stared at the caption, re-reading it until the print
danced before her eyes, before returning her gaze to the

damning photographs and marvelling at how alike her mother and she had been...

No wonder Andrea had done a double-take on meeting her for the first time, and so many other people had looked surprised!

It was a miracle no one had said anything... But of course, Scott Wendell had started to blurt it out, and had been stopped by Jos's cool, repressive glance...

So now she knew why Jos had married her, and Andrea was right. Still obsessed by a woman he could no longer have, he'd settled for her daughter because of a strong physical resemblance.

Could that have been what she'd discovered after their wedding? Was that why she had left him?

Closing the magazine, feeling oddly numb, detached, as though she was herself a bloodless corpse, she got to her feet and, vaguely surprised that her legs would support her, heard herself saying stiffly, 'If you don't mind, I'll go now.'

At the same instant there was a rap on the door and it opened.

Jos glanced from one woman to the other, then his narrowed green gaze returned to rest on Clare's taut white face. 'Ready to leave, darling?'

'Yes, I'm ready.' In her own ears her voice sounded thin and strained.

She allowed him to put his arm around her waist and lead her out and through the throng, walking by his side like a zombie.

One or two people said goodnight as they passed, and she answered automatically.

Tom, his blue eyes showing a marked anxiety, popped up from nowhere to escort them to the door. 'Pity you have to go so soon. Hope to see you before too long.'

'Yes, of course,' she answered meaninglessly, and, taking his proffered hand, even managed a smile.

Not until they reached the penthouse did Jos say almost curtly, 'I'm sorry you found the tête-à-tête with Andrea distressing, but I did warn you what to expect.'

Clare looked up at him, her gaze curiously dark and blind, and all at once the false calm deserted her and she began to tremble uncontrollably.

With a muttered oath, Jos picked her up in his arms and carried her through to their bedroom. He laid her down on the bed. Her eyes were tightly closed, her whole body shaking.

Having slipped off her sandals, he started to undress her. Despite the heat, her skin felt cold, and he pulled the lightweight duvet over her before stripping off his own clothes and getting in beside her.

She had stopped shaking now, and was lying quiet and still as a corpse, her face turned away from him.

When he attempted to draw her close and warm her cold flesh with his own, she suddenly came to life and began to fight like a tigress, crying fiercely, 'Get out and leave me alone... Leave me alone... I won't sleep in the same bed with you.'

Without loosening his hold on her upper arms, he demanded roughly, 'What is it? What did that bitch say to you?'

'Take your hands off me.' Beside herself, she struck at him repeatedly, savagely. 'I don't want you to touch me. I hate you! I hate you!'

Her clenched fist caught him a glancing blow high on his cheekbone and he released his grip, but only to catch hold of her wrists and pin them to the pillow.

'Let me go!' she spat at him.

'Not until you're through acting like a wild cat.'

When she continued to struggle and thrash about he

held her, using one muscular leg to trap hers, so that she could hurt neither of them until, totally exhausted, her breath coming in harsh gasps, she lay still.

He looked down at her in the half-light, his own breath coming quickly, a lock of dark hair falling over his forehead. 'Now, suppose you tell me what all that was about?'

'Please let go of me.' Her voice was hoarse, rasping; her throat felt sore.

His expression wary, as though he was half expecting another onslaught, he let her go and sat up.

Moving as far away from him as the bed would allow, she pushed herself up against the pillows and turned to look at him, her eyes brilliant with anger.

'Well?' He raised a dark brow.

'You lied to me. If not directly, then by omission. When I asked if you knew my mother, you said you knew *of* her. You pretended to hate her.'

'That was no pretence. I *did* hate her.'

'You can save yourself the trouble of lying any more. I know that while she was in New York you became infatuated with her.'

'You're quite wrong.'

'You were her lover.'

His voice like ice, he said, 'I was *never* her lover.'

Furiously, she cried, 'It's no use trying to deny it. I *know*.'

He gave an elaborate sigh. 'I hope you didn't believe everything Andrea told you?'

'I believe the evidence of my own eyes. I read the society gossip and saw the pictures of you and my mother in *Jet Set*.'

She saw him stiffen. 'So that rubbish was what Andrea wanted to show you.'

'But it isn't rubbish, is it? And now I know why you married me.'

He looked at her, his eyes narrowed to green slits. 'Then perhaps you'd like to tell me?'

'Because my mother was dead and I look like her. That was why I left you, wasn't it? I found out that I was just a substitute…'

'That wasn't the reason at all.'

Ignoring his denial, she rushed on, 'Well, I won't be *used*. I won't be a stand-in for any woman, let alone my own mother. I'm leaving you.'

There was a moment of ominous silence before he said mildly, 'Don't be foolish, Clare.'

'I mean it.'

'Where would you go?'

'I don't know… Anywhere would be better than staying here.'

'You have no money. No means of supporting yourself.'

'I'll get a job—manage somehow.'

He shook his head. 'I've no intention of letting you leave. And you know you don't really want to.'

His arrogant confidence infuriated her. 'I do want to. I'm going first thing in the morning.'

'I think not.'

'You can't stop me.'

'Oh, yes I can.' His absolute certainty made her blood run cold.

Trying not to shiver, she asked defiantly, 'Wouldn't Roberts think it strange if you kept me locked in?'

'If necessary I'll have you restrained in a private clinic. All I need to do is contact Dr Hauser and tell him that as well as leaving you with amnesia, the blow to your head has made you…shall we say…unstable. That you refuse to stay with me and you're not able to take care of yourself.'

She looked at him in horror. 'You *wouldn't*...'

'I'd rather not. But unless you're willing to see sense...'

'You're a swine,' she said jerkily.

'I'm your husband.'

She stiffened. 'Well, you might be able to make me stay—' at least for the time being, she qualified silently '—but I've no intention of sleeping with you.'

His smile was mocking, reminiscent. 'I don't think I'll have too much trouble changing you mind. Last time—'

'That was before I knew I was merely an understudy for my mother.'

'Jealous?'

'No, I'm not jealous!' Her voice shook. 'But it's...it's disgusting and degrading.'

'It might be if it were true. But you're nothing of the kind.'

Ignoring the denial, she demanded, her voice rising, 'Do you think of *her*, see *her* face while you're making love to me?'

'I haven't so far.' His voice had an edge that should have warned her. 'But we'll try again, shall we?'

'No! I don't want you.'

'You know perfectly well that's a lie. You *do* want me.'

She felt an urge to fly at him, to rake her nails down that hard, arrogant face. 'Well, if you think I'm going to fight my mother's ghost for a place in your bed...'

'We're in my bed now, and I'll be happy to prove that if your mother's ghost does share it, it's not in the role of ex-mistress...'

Hands gripping her waist, he pulled her further down the bed and held her with steely fingers.

'And just to give you confidence that her features aren't superimposed on yours, I won't even look at your face and I'll keep saying your name.'

With a sudden movement she was unprepared for, he rolled her onto her stomach and used the weight of his body to pin her there.

Disregarding her muffled protest, he brushed aside the cloud of dark silky hair and put his lips to her nape, his breath warm against her skin.

Clare lay rigid, such intimate contact with the full length of his body making the blood rush through her veins. She could feel his heart thudding into her back, his crisp body hair against the smoothness of her skin, the roughness of his legs along hers, and the ripple of each muscle whenever he moved.

Her response was immediate and electric.

At first his mouth roving over the back of her neck remained gentle, his tongue exploring the hollow behind her ear with sensuous appreciation, but soon the kisses were interspersed with little bites and nibbles.

As she gasped, and tried to evade such erotic torment, he slid his hands beneath her to cup her breasts and tease the nipples while he moved rhythmically, mimicking the thrust of possession.

Fire flashed through her and a core of molten heat began to form low in her abdomen. She gave a little moan.

'Let me know when you're ready for the real thing,' he whispered.

'No,' she gasped hoarsely. 'I don't…I won't…'

'Ah, but you *do*, and you *will*, my darling wife.'

He was ruthless in his mastery, and even when she was almost sobbing, a victim of the dark sensuality he'd unleashed, he made her beg for release from the exquisite torture he was so good at inflicting.

Then, sliding his hands down to lift her body a little, and repeating her name as he'd promised, he made love to her with maddening slowness until she was finally engulfed by such a torment of delight that her whole body felt boneless, just a shuddering mass of sensations.

When he moved away from her she lay quite still, her face buried in the pillow. Hating him for his arrogant domination. Hating herself for her own humiliating lack of will-power where he was concerned.

'Turn over and look at me.'

She wanted to ignore the order, but somehow she found herself obeying. Turning over stiffly, reluctantly, she sat up, and, drawing her knees close to her chest, hugged them defensively beneath the duvet while her violet eyes met and clashed with Jos's green.

Studying her through half-closed lids, he said, 'I hope I've established that you *do* want me, and that I don't think of any other woman while I'm making love to you?'

'As far as I'm concerned, the only thing you have established—apart from the fact that you're utterly ruthless—is that in some form or other my mother's ghost *does* share the bed. Even if it isn't as your ex-mistress… Though after seeing that magazine I find it almost impossible to believe you weren't lovers.'

'It happens to be the truth.'

'How can I credit anything you tell me?' she cried helplessly. 'You lead me to believe you didn't know her, then I see a picture of you kissing her passionately…'

'Not to put too fine a point on it, *she* was kissing *me*.'

'I don't see what difference it makes,' Clare said wearily.

'A great deal of difference.'

'That's just sophism. You said you hated her, but those photographs and what Andrea told me prove otherwise.'

'What exactly did she tell you?'

'That when you first saw my mother's picture in the paper you couldn't hide your interest, and that despite the age difference as soon as the pair of you met you became lovers—'

'As I don't go in for three in a bed, how could Andrea know a thing like that? At best it's mere supposition.'

Ignoring the interruption, Clare ploughed on, 'She said you were so fascinated by her that you scarcely let her out of your sight. And even though that gossip column goes to prove it, I suppose you're going to try and tell me that it's not the truth.'

'Part of it is,' he admitted flatly. 'I was more than interested when I first saw your mother's picture in the paper. It aroused the kind of feelings that might have been best left buried. Telling myself she'd go to the devil anyway, I tried to put her out of my mind, but without much success.' He sounded grim. 'In fact she became almost an obsession.

'I made certain that our paths crossed. I wanted to take a closer look at the woman I'd loathed for years, to find out for sure if she really was the kind of tramp I'd always thought her.'

He paused for so long that Clare was forced to ask, 'And was she?'

'Oh, yes.' His teeth gleamed in a smile that was more like a snarl. 'If I hadn't hated her so much, I could almost have felt sorry for her, for what she'd become.'

'But you must have had some *reason* to feel so strongly about her. I can't believe it was just because you disapproved of her lifestyle.'

'Oh, I certainly had a reason.'

'Then don't you think it's time you told me what it was? Told me what she'd done to make you hate her so much?'

Clare held her breath until he said abruptly, 'Yes, perhaps you should know exactly what kind of bitch your mother was... We'd scarcely been introduced when, despite the fact that her husband was looking on, she made a dead set at me. It was so blatant it was sickening.

'She wanted me to take her to bed that first night, but I refused on the grounds that I didn't fancy being one of a string of lovers, and I had grave reservations about accepting what she offered while her husband was on the scene.

'She said, "If the thought of me having other lovers bothers you, I'll give them up, and as for my *husband*, so long as there's no *open* scandal, believe me, he wouldn't care a damn."'

'Oddly enough, I *did* believe her. I suppose, over the years, he must have become inured to her goings-on. But I told her that in the circumstance I wasn't prepared to cuckold him. Though, God forgive me, I was tempted. She had the kind of beauty that can drive a man out of his mind. I knew only too well how immoral and unscrupulous she was, but I still had to fight the pull of her physical attraction when she tried to seduce me.'

Through stiff lips, Clare asked, 'Then why did you keep on seeing her?'

His face hardened into a ruthless mask. 'Because knowing I'd been right about her all along had revived all my old desire for revenge. But I needed time to decide on the best way to make her pay, in some small way, for what she'd done. And by then, possibly because I'd refrained from taking her to bed, she seemed to be besotted with me...'

Oh, yes, Clare thought, and knew a kind of bleak empathy. She could imagine the hunger that must have clawed at a woman of her mother's temperament.

'She said she had to accompany her husband on a diplomatic mission to Panama, but that after they returned, while Sir Roger went to Washington, she would come and join me in New York… I made up my mind that when she did, after I'd told her exactly what I thought of her, I would drop her as publicly as possible. But, as you know, fate stepped in…'

And if it hadn't he would no doubt have carried out his plan to publicly humiliate a woman he admitted he'd hated.

A woman she couldn't remember; a woman of whom she'd heard nothing but ill; a woman for whom, she was shaken to realise, she suddenly felt a strong compassion, even a wish to defend.

Trying to hide her agitation, Clare said, 'You still haven't told me why you hated her so much.'

If only he would tell her that, she would have the key to his behaviour, would know what all these dark undercurrents meant.

Jos's eyes were thoughtful as they watched her hand, slender and restless, repeatedly smoothing the duvet over her knees.

He answered with a question of his own. 'Seeing a picture of your mother didn't bring anything back?'

'No.'

'You've had no flashes of memory?'

'When I first saw the name Clave in your passport it was familiar, and I felt as if I was on the brink of recalling something important. But all I could think was that somewhere, some time—in my childhood, perhaps— I'd know a boy named Clave.'

'That's *all* you remembered?' Jos's question was sharp.

'I… I was sure I hadn't liked him. I'd been afraid of him… Then suddenly I had an awful feeling of guilt and regret…'

Just for an instant Jos's dark face seemed to be full of pain and anguish, but the look vanished so swiftly that she wondered if she'd only imagined it.

'Nothing else?' he asked, more gently.

'When Roberts brought in some Turkish delight with the coffee he asked if I would prefer mints, and I said, No, I love Turkish delight. The words seemed to echo inside my head, and I half remembered a boy with dark hair and a thin face offering me a box... I tried to keep a hold on the memory but I couldn't...' All the frustration she felt was there in her sigh.

'And you think that boy was me?'

'Don't *you* know?' Her eyes and voice beseeched him.

'Yes, it was,' he admitted abruptly. 'I gave you a box of Turkish delight on your eighth birthday.'

'Then we *did* know each other as children?'

'Our families were neighbours.'

A thought struck her, and she asked, 'My mother didn't know who you were? Didn't recognise you?'

'She was hardly likely to. I was only thirteen at the time, and she'd known me as Clave.'

'The same as I did.'

'Yes.'

'Were we friends?'

'No. I was five years older than you. That kind of age gap is too wide for friendship, even had we been so inclined. But I remember you as a quiet, skinny little thing, with a mop of dark hair, huge violet eyes and a kind of infuriating self-sufficiency... Even then it was clear you'd grow up to be a beauty. Like your mother.

'We lived just outside Meredith, at Foxton Priory. Your family lived at Stratton Place, about a quarter of a mile away. As well as neighbours, our families were good friends—' his voice now held a glacial coldness '—your mother and mine were particularly close...'

Clare began to shiver, chilled by a sudden nameless dread, a premonition of disaster.

Jos looked at her, his gaze hard and inimical, and at that moment she knew he was seeing her mother's face rather than her own.

Through stiff lips, she asked, 'What happened? What did my mother do?'

He answered slowly, 'She was my father's lover and the direct cause of my own mother committing suicide…'

'Suicide?' Clare whispered, aghast. This was worse than anything she might have envisaged.

Jos drew a harsh breath. 'Though somehow they managed to hush things up and get a verdict of accidental death, I knew it was suicide. She hadn't been able to bear to lose the man she'd devoted all her adult life to.'

While one part of Clare's mind struggled to take in the implications, another part remained curiously detached, isolated from the shock and horror.

She heard the faint, musical splash of the fountain on the terrace, and through the open window smelt the tubs of night-scented stock. The curtains hadn't been closed, and beyond the trees in Central Park she saw that the squares and rectangles of the lighted windows of Upper West Side formed geometrical patterns against the dark buildings.

'Your mother betrayed and caused the death of the woman who was her best friend.' Jos's biting accusation broke the lengthening silence. 'But though she shed tears at the funeral, and said how sorry she was, she never appeared to feel any real guilt or shame…'

No! No! Clare cried silently. She couldn't believe it. Some instinct insisted that though her mother might have been weak, she hadn't been *wicked*.

But with her memory gone, how could she be sure?

Clutching at straws, Clare asked, scarcely above a whisper, 'Was she *truly* so cruel and heartless?'

As though striving to be fair, Jos answered evenly, 'When she set out to seduce my father I don't suppose she anticipated quite such tragic results.'

'You seem to be laying all the responsibility at her door... Remember it takes two to tango.'

'Reduced to quoting clichés?' he sneered, apparently angered by her attempt to defend the indefensible.

'It may be a cliché, but like most clichés it contains more than a grain of truth.'

Irritably, he said, 'I'm not trying to pretend my father was entirely blameless, but if Isobel had set out to seduce the Archangel Gabriel he would have had a struggle to resist her...'

In her mind Clare heard the echo of Jos's earlier words, 'I knew only too well how immoral and unscrupulous she was, but I still had to fight the pull of her physical attraction...'

Trying desperately to find some small excuse, some shred of evidence in mitigation, Clare found herself asking, 'You don't think they...my mother and your father...might have loved each other?'

Flatly, he answered, 'I very much doubt it. If they were in love it didn't survive my mother's death...at least not on Isobel's side. Immediately afterwards she dropped him, and he started drinking heavily. So you see, she was also, indirectly, the cause of *his* death.'

CHAPTER EIGHT

'IT SEEMS she had a great deal to answer for,' Clare said quietly.

'Indeed she had, but it wasn't until after he was dead and buried that she showed the slightest trace of remorse…'

Remorse… Written in letters of fire, the word seemed to be burning into her brain. *Remorse*… With a little half-stifled moan she closed her eyes, trying to shut out the pain, but it was still there inside her head and she moaned again.

Gripping her upper arms, Jos demanded, 'What is it? What can you remember?'

His obvious concern, his urgency got through, and after a moment she pulled herself together and answered a shade unsteadily, 'Nothing really. It was just that word…' As he released his grip she went on, 'You once said it would spoil all your plans if I didn't remember. What did you mean, exactly?'

For an instant he seemed discomposed, then he said evenly, 'What do you think I meant?'

She drew a deep breath and, applying her new-found knowledge, said, 'I think you meant that for you to enjoy your revenge to the full I would need to remember *why* you married me, need to remember what I was being punished for.'

'You think I married you to punish you for your mother's sins?'

'Didn't you?'

He turned his head to look at her. 'It was rather more complicated than that.'

Her mouth dry, she asked, 'Before I lost my memory, had you meant to tell me the truth?'

'Yes, but not straight away.'

'Didn't it occur to you that when you did I might leave you?'

'I judged you would have enough spirit to stay.'

'You must have thought I was some kind of masochist.'

His bare shoulders moved in a slight shrug. 'There would still have been the things you'd married me for. Wealth. Lifestyle. The way our tastes and minds are in accord... And, as I mentioned previously, the bonds of passion to tie you to me... But before those bonds were in place—'

'I ran away and got knocked down by a cab. Why did I go?'

'Our full names were used during the marriage service, and you realised, rather belatedly, who I was...'

And even though she couldn't have known the whole story, Clare thought, it must have come as a shock, made her wonder why he'd kept his true identity a secret.

With sudden clarity she recalled the two snapshots he had shown her. In the first, taken on the day they'd become engaged, she had been happy and smiling, a woman in love.

In the second, taken after their wedding, there had been no smile on her face and she'd looked tense and nervous.

'During the journey back to the States,' Jos went on, 'you were very quiet and withdrawn. In the lift on the way up to the apartment you remarked that you were scared of heights—'

'Just as I did that night you brought me home from hospital. And both times you said, "Then perhaps you shouldn't have chosen to marry a man who lives in a penthouse"…'

'How do you know?' Jos demanded sharply.

'I had a feeling of *déjà vu*—only I realise now the feeling wasn't illusory. Please go on…'

'Well, after that, you seemed even more uneasy, and while we ate supper and Roberts unpacked you asked me point-blank why I'd married you…'

'And you told me the truth?'

'Some of it. Too much, apparently. You refused to sleep with me, said you needed time to think things over. It was late and you were very tired. There seemed no point in forcing the issue just then, so I slept in the guest room.

'Next morning I was forced to go into the office, just briefly. I'd been in England for quite a while, and they needed my signature on some papers. You appeared to be still asleep, so I didn't waken you.

'When I got home I found you'd gone. I must confess I hadn't expected such a violent reaction. It took me completely by surprise…'

Well, it would have, because he'd got his calculations all wrong. She hadn't married him for any of the reasons he'd listed. And the thing she *had* married him for was the one thing that must have made her unable to stay.

'I knew you hadn't taken your passport—as luck would have it I'd slipped both passports into the pocket of the jacket I was wearing—so you couldn't leave the States. Nor had you taken any clothes. That meant one of two things: either you intended to come back, or you'd been afraid to stay and pack.

'You hadn't any dollars, or much English money, so if your idea had been to lie low for a while, I couldn't understand why you'd left valuable rings behind…'

She could, Clare thought trenchantly.

'Though I was very glad you had—for more than one reason.'

As though recalling that morning was a far from pleasant experience, Jos's jaw tightened. 'I wasn't sure what to do for the best. New York can be a dangerous place if you don't know which areas to avoid…'

'I wasn't sure what to do for the best…' Assured, assertive, self-confident Jos? It was so out of character that Clare was staggered.

Like someone in a dream, she found herself asking, 'What did you do?'

'I called a top private detective agency and hired all the good people they could spare. Within an hour they were out, armed with photographs of you, making enquiries, checking guest houses and hotels… But it was a mammoth task…

'Of course, there was still a chance that you'd return of your own accord, but I didn't want to lose any time. All I could think of was getting you back safely and as soon as possible…

'When evening came, and they'd drawn a blank, I started to ring round the hospitals—there are more than one hundred and fifty in New York City—all the while terrified of what I might discover…' His face was rigid, his lean body taut as a drawn bowstring.

A tremor running through her, she realised that though he might not love her, his feelings for her had a dark depth she had never envisaged.

Trying for casualness, she observed, 'So it must have come as a relief when you found out I'd only had a trifling accident.'

'If you'd cracked your skull,' he said grimly, 'that "trifling accident" could have been fatal…'

In a sense it *had* been fatal. Losing her memory had

put her back in his power, given him a chance to form those bonds of passion he had talked about.

'And if anything had happened to you...' His voice was harsh, ragged, full of raw emotion.

Putting out his hand, he touched her cheek. There was something fiercely possessive in the gesture, but nothing of the tenderness she yearned for. His index finger traced the line of her lips before moving to find a linger on the pulse hammering away at the base of her throat.

'That first day I saw you in Ashleigh Kent's office, I couldn't take my eyes off you. You were so beautiful, so—'

'Like my mother?' she interrupted jerkily.

When he didn't answer, she said in a strangled voice, 'And because I *looked* like her, you thought I *was* like her.'

'Yes, for a while.' He drew back with a sigh. 'But nothing seemed to add up properly. So many things didn't fit.'

'I wonder why I didn't recognise you.'

'Seventeen years is a long time.'

'Did we meet entirely by chance?' Even as she asked she knew that that would have been too much of a co-incidence.

'No.'

'You knew I worked there?'

'Isobel mentioned it.' Abruptly, he added, 'Though she said for the most part you'd lived separate lives, she seemed fond of you.'

A little warmth crept into Clare's cold heart, only to be immediately frozen over. 'Then your "business trip" was made simply to get to know me?'

'If necessary I would have made the trip solely for that purpose, but, to use a hackneyed phrase, fortune took a hand...'

He sounded relaxed now, self-assured, once more master of himself and his emotions.

'I'd been notified that a house I was interested in buying had come on the market. The sale was being handled by Ashleigh Kent. That simplified matters and enabled me to kill two birds with one stone. All I had to do was tell them I was looking for a property and ask for you to show me round.'

'And the rest was easy,' she said with some bitterness.

'Not as easy as I'd envisaged,' he corrected smoothly. 'Though you didn't seem to remember me on any conscious level, I sometimes wondered if your subconscious knew me. I could tell you had an interest in me as a man, as well as in my money, but you were so cool, so wary, I was forced to move very carefully...'

A chill ran through her as she recalled her own half-formed suspicion that he'd *stalked* her...

'How soon did you decide to marry me?'

'That very first day. I wanted you the moment I set eyes on you.'

So the bitter, unwilling sexual attraction he'd felt for her mother had been transferred to herself, along with his unsatisfied desire for revenge.

Hotly, she said, 'Then I was right the first time. I *am* just a stand-in for my mother.'

'I've already told you, you're no such thing.'

Ignoring his curt denial, she rushed on, 'You just see me as a body you can use to get rid of urges you despise and want to be purged of because fate got in first and you lost the chance to take your revenge, as a scapegoat to be punished for my mother's sins.'

'That might have been so originally,' he admitted. 'Now it's no longer the case. My views have started to change. I can even feel a kind of sneaking pity for *her*, for what she became...'

'I don't believe you!'

She *knew* he was lying. He hated her mother, held her responsible for the loss of his home and his parents, and for his subsequent years of misery,

But had it been all Isobel's fault?

There were two sides to everything, and until she got her memory back there was no real way of knowing whether so much hatred was justified.

Until she got her memory back... *If* she got her memory back... And what would she do if she didn't?

Living in a world of shadows and half-truths, knowing he would never feel any warmth or affection for her, her spirit trapped in the shell of an empty mind, her body trapped in the gilded cage of an empty marriage, she would eventually be destroyed, her heart and her spirit broken. That might sound melodramatic, but nevertheless it was so...

'I can't bear it!' she choked despairingly. 'You've got to let me go.'

Suddenly she was crying, hot tears rolling down her cheeks in a steady, silent stream. She turned her head away, pressing her lips tightly together, trying not to make a sound, trying to stem the flow.

But he saw, and said gently, 'Don't cry, my love.'

The endearment was her undoing. It opened the floodgates, releasing all the tensions of the past weeks. She began to sob, harsh, gasping sobs that hurt her throat and took more breath than she'd got.

Jos drew her close, one hand cradling her head against his chest, the other moving up and down her spine in a curiously soothing gesture until she began to quieten and the sobs died away.

When she was all cried out, he slid down the bed, taking her with him. Switching out the light, he settled her head against his shoulder and held her until she slept.

*   *   *

Clare awoke to bright sunlight and a feeling almost of well-being. As she sighed and stretched remembrance came swiftly. Just as swiftly the feeling of well-being vanished.

A quick glance showed the other side of the bed was empty, and the faint sound of running water told her Jos was in the shower.

She shivered. Since the night he had picked her up from the hospital she had been sure there was something dark and bitter in their relationship. Now, thanks to Andrea's jealousy, she knew what it was…

And it was worse than anything she might have suspected. She couldn't, *wouldn't* stay to become a whipping-boy. If he refused to let her go freely, at the first opportunity she would retrieve her passport and fly back to England, even if it meant selling her rings.

Once there, if she chose a big enough city, it should be easy to disappear without trace. She could find a bedsitter, a job of some kind, start a new life. She would never have to set eyes on Jos again…

At the thought of never seeing him again she felt as though she was being shut in an iron maiden. Yet she couldn't stay with him; it would be too hard, too cruelly painful.

Loving him as she did, knowing how he felt about her would be more than she could bear. Her mind would be always in a turmoil…

But what about Jos?

All at once she felt deeply ashamed. How blindly selfish to be thinking only of herself. Her mother, however unintentionally, had wrecked his life, made him the kind of man he was.

A man who used women and despised them, who lived in a luxurious prison rather than a home. A man who had grown up to be hard and bitter and was, in spite of all his wealth, *lonely*.

He had always been alone, and if she left him now, unable to give love or receive it, he was likely to remain alone—except for women like Andrea, who believed he had no needs apart from purely sexual ones.

But surely he needed other things as well? Warmth, laughter, companionship, that rapport of minds and tastes he'd talked about...? All things she could give him.

She was sure that he wanted her, and if he also wanted some kind of retribution then she couldn't find it in her heart to blame him. Surely she owed him that much?

If she stayed freely, willingly, without him having to force her, if she gave him all she had to give, including love, surely her mind would be at rest?

Andrea had said he wouldn't want her love, and, remembering his own comments on the subject, Clare had no doubt that the blonde was right. But it would be her secret gift to him, her way of making reparation for the harm her mother had done...

'Awake?'

Clare jumped. She had been so deep in thought she hadn't heard him emerge from the bathroom, and now he was standing by the bed looking down at her.

Her pulse began to race with alarming speed, and she felt a heated surge of desire.

He was naked apart from a white towel slung around his neck, and his hair was still damp and mussed from its towelling. Freshly shaved, his olive skin clear and healthy, fuzzed on the chest and arms by a light sprinkling of crisp body hair, his green eyes brilliant between thick dark lashes, he looked disturbingly virile and attractive.

Perhaps something of what she was thinking showed in her face, because he said, 'If you look at me like that

I might be tempted to come back to bed, and I dare say you wouldn't like that.'

'You'd be wrong,' she said boldly.

He raised a dark winged brow. 'Well, well, well…'

To her annoyance, Clare felt herself starting to blush.

Sitting on the edge of the bed, his eyes ironic, he watched the colour mount in her cheeks. 'Is this sudden compliance…enthusiasm…whichever…designed to put me off my guard?'

'I don't know what you mean,' she said stiffly.

'I mean are you planning to run off again the minute I turn my back?'

'No.' Taking a deep breath, she announced firmly, 'I have every intention of staying.'

'For how long?'

'For as long as you want me.'

He looked at her thoughtfully. 'Does that mean you've changed your mind about not believing me?'

As she hesitated he said incisively, 'No, I can see you haven't.' Then, with that lightning perception that was so unnerving, he went on, 'So you've decided you owe me something and you're going to make reparation? Well, isn't that nice?'

She hadn't been prepared for such a sardonic reaction, and, infuriated by his open mockery, she cried fiercely, 'Oh, go to hell!'

Green eyes gleaming, he clicked his tongue reprovingly. 'If you're planning to be a tractable wife, that's no way to speak to your husband.'

She fought back. 'I don't recall saying I was going to be *tractable*.'

'That's just as well. Too much docility would bore me. I'd much prefer you to be fiery and passionate, maybe even a little rebellious at times…'

'So you can have the fun of taming me?'

He laughed, showing white, even teeth. 'How did you guess?'

With an air of calm deliberation, he tossed the towel aside, drew back the lightweight duvet and got in beside her.

Repressing an instinctive urge to move away from so much overpowering maleness, she made herself lie quite still while he propped himself up on one elbow and smiled down into her wary violet eyes.

'Well?'

'Well, what?' she snapped, flustered by his manner.

'Now you've enticed me back to bed, what are you going to do with me?'

Her heart sank. Plainly he was out to tease and taunt her.

When she didn't answer, he sighed theatrically. 'Surely you can think of something to…shall we say amuse me?'

His smile was devilish, derisory, and her insides knotted with tension as she realised that beneath his cool veneer of lazy mockery he was furiously angry with her.

The last trace of desire fled with the realisation, leaving her feeling chilled and frightened.

But why was he so furious? Had she hurt his pride in some way? Did he think she was presuming to offer him pity? Or was he angry that she hadn't believed his assurance that he no longer wanted to punish her for her mother's sins?

'Jos, I…' She faltered to a halt.

'Perhaps you could begin by kissing me?' he suggested blandly. 'And see what that leads to?'

'I haven't cleaned my teeth,' she muttered, 'and I need a shower.'

'Chickening out?' he queried, interestedly.

'No, I'm not,' she snarled.

'Then I'll wait.'

Scrambling out of the opposite side of the bed, she grabbed her satin robe and fled into the bathroom.

Having showered, cleaned her teeth and brushed her shoulder-length dark hair, she pulled on her robe and stood irresolute. Could she bring herself to go back and face his biting scorn and fury?

But it wasn't a case of whether she *could* or not; really she had no choice.

Perhaps if she waited a while he might get impatient and come and fetch her. It would make things so much easier if *he* took the initiative.

Even as the thought crossed her mind she knew that he wouldn't. He was a ruthless, sadistic devil, and he had no intention of making things easier for her.

So was she going to let him rout her completely?

Was she hell!

Squaring her shoulders, she tightened her belt and headed for the door. Her hand was on the knob when she paused... Making up her mind, she untied the belt, discarded the robe, and with the light of battle in her eyes sallied forth.

He was lying on top of the duvet now, stretched full-length, relaxed and indolent, eyes closed, hands clasped behind his dark head.

Though he must have known she'd returned he kept his eyes closed, obviously waiting for her to make the first move.

Well, she would surprise him by doing just that, by taking the initiative. Nerving herself, she stretched out beside him and, propped on one elbow, studied his face.

His hair was rumpled and his mocking eyes hidden. The closed lids and long dark lashes lying on his hard cheekbones gave him a boyish, vulnerable look.

Her resentment faded, leaving only love. The intention

to boldly caress and arouse him forgotten, with a little murmur of tenderness, she leaned over to kiss his cheek.

At the touch of her lips his eyes flew open, and with a smothered oath he pushed her roughly away and leapt out of bed.

'Jos, what is it?' she whispered. 'What's the matter?'

'You can save the play-acting,' he told her savagely. 'It's enough to have you in my bed. I don't need any pretence of love.'

A second later the door into the dressing room slammed behind him.

Staring at the white panels, her eyes filled with stinging tears.

She had set out to make him lose his calm, and had succeeded in a way she had never envisaged.

Over the next two or three weeks, while the heatwave continued unrelentingly, Jos took her out and about, showing her New York from the Bronx to Battery Park.

The city was hot and airless and dusty, but Clare found she loved the thrill and excitement of the place, and the supposition, not to say conviction of most native New Yorkers that it was the hub of the universe.

Together, almost making a game of it, they did all the touristy things. They visited SoHo and Chinatown, crossed Brooklyn Bridge, climbed the Statue of Liberty and went to the top of the great pointing needle of the Empire State Building.

Making an effort at least to come to terms with her fear of heights, Clare had gritted her teeth and forced herself to tackle the latter two.

Climbing the spiralling metal stairway up to Liberty's crown had been just bearable so long as she didn't look down. But in the Empire State lift her ears had popped uncomfortably, making her wonder if she would ever get used to New York skyscrapers. And when they'd reached the top she'd found herself trembling, gripped by a kind of nausea, and had been only too pleased to have the comfort of Jos's arm around her.

Though she still couldn't think of the penthouse as home, she became more used to it, and was quite happy on the terrace so long as she kept away from the balustrade.

As if by tacit consent they never talked about the past or Clare's loss of memory, but sometimes she caught him looking at her oddly, and one day, when she'd asked him why, he'd said, 'You still have that lost look... I thought it might go away, but it hasn't.'

In the evenings they went out to dine and dance in the top nightspots, to shows and concerts and sometimes, though less frequently after she admitted how much it bothered her, to parties to meet more of his friends and acquaintances.

For the most part they were nice people, whom she felt she should have been comfortable with, but her memory loss made her sensitive to casual queries, such as, 'What a beautiful ring! Where did Jos take you to buy it?'

That time she'd stammered, 'Well, I—I...'

Squeezing her hand, smiling down at her, Jos had responded quickly. 'We got it in London's Bond Street, didn't we, darling?'

And though he made a point of never leaving her side, and was always ready to field any awkward questions, she felt foolish and embarrassed when he had to answer for her.

'I almost feel I could cope better with some physical disability,' she'd said to Jos late one night. 'At least that would be visible, something people could see and accept without needing explanations. As it is, I'm frightened to even try and explain in case they think I'm...well...not all there.'

'No one would think that,' he'd said brusquely.

'Andrea did.'

'Andrea didn't. She was just being bitchy.'

To Clare's great relief they'd seen nothing more of the blonde, and until that moment neither of them had referred to that traumatic evening.

Though, at times, the thought of it made her shiver, she never for an instant regretted her decision to stay with Jos. He was everything, and more, that she could have dared hope for, and every day she fell steadily deeper in love.

With him she found a kind of poignant, bitter-sweet pleasure, an ephemeral happiness that left her only too aware that any lasting happiness and contentment depended on two things: Jos loving her enough to want *her* love, and her getting her memory back.

Both seemed unattainable.

Yet just being with him was precious to her, and each day she found herself eagerly looking forward to all the pleasures the nights brought: going to bed together hand in hand, making love—slow, delectable love, fierce, passionate love—sometimes just lying quietly in his arms while they talked over their day.

It was a serene interlude, a time of peace, yet a peace that was oddly fragile, as if they were waiting for some kind of explosion that they both sensed was inevitable.

Towards the end of the third week, it came.

They were just finishing breakfast on the terrace when Roberts carried out the morning post. Amongst the small pile of envelopes were two letters that bore English stamps.

Jos tore open the first, and as he glanced through it Clare caught a look of blazing excitement and triumph.

It was gone almost immediately, leaving his green eyes cool, his face expressionless.

The second, from a firm of solicitors, was addressed to *Mrs* J. Saunders. Jos passed it to her, and with a strange feeling of trepidation that amounted almost to foreboding, Clare unfolded the single sheet of headed paper and read it.

Dear Mrs Saunders,

As you are aware, we act in the administration of the estate of Sir Roger and Lady Isobel Berkeley. In furtherance of this we should be grateful if you would advise us as soon as possible if you still wish to proceed with the sale of Stratton Place, willed to you by your late parents.

Ashleigh Kent, the estate agents you nominated, now have several parties interested. Though, as we pointed out before you left for the United States, the property market is still somewhat depressed, the proceeds from the sale of the house and contents, should you wish to part with them, should prove adequate to clear any outstanding debts.

We await your instructions.

Yours sincerely,
YORK, THOMAS & WILDGOOSE

Clare looked up to find Jos watching her intently. Without a word she handed him the letter.

When he'd read it, she asked, 'Did you know about the house?'

'Yes, I knew.' His green eyes hooded, he queried carefully, 'So what do you intend to do?'

Heart thumping, she asked, 'What do you think I should do?'

As though he knew what half-formed thought lay behind her question, he answered indirectly, 'I have to go to England myself soon.'

'And you think I should go with you?'

'I think you should make up your own mind.'

'The very idea makes me feel on-edge and nervous,' she admitted.

'You could be taking a risk, disturbing the status quo. It depends, surely, on how much you want your memory back.'

She sighed. 'I can't *tell* you how much. There's only one thing in the world I want more.' The fateful words were out before she could prevent them.

His face growing suddenly taut, he asked, 'And what might that be?'

Flushing hotly, knowing she couldn't bring herself to sit and beg for love he was incapable of giving her, she stammered, 'W-well, I—'

'There's no need to tell me,' he interrupted, his voice curt. 'I can guess. You'd like your freedom and a substantial divorce settlement.'

As, startled, she began to shake her head he went on grimly, 'Well, I've no intention of giving you either.'

Before she could try to undo the damage her unthinking stupidity had caused, he rose to his feet, tall and dark, icily composed. 'If getting your memory back means that much to you, then I think you *should* go to England.' Tossing down his napkin, he headed for the sliding glass doors.

'Jos, please wait…I need to talk to you.'

'We can talk later.'

'But where are you going?'

'I've some things to do, some arrangements to make. Then I propose to go into the office.'

'How long will you be gone?'

'I don't know. Most of the day, probably.'

He left without another word, and without kissing her. Sitting at the table, Clare had to struggle to hold back her tears.

CHAPTER NINE

WITHOUT JOS, the morning dragged endlessly, the book she was trying to read completely failing to hold her attention.

As though to match her mood, the weather was breaking up, becoming gloomy and overcast, with heavy spots of rain plopping onto the terrace and rumbles of thunder in the distance.

Having resisted Roberts' efforts to serve lunch in the dining room, Clare ate a solitary salad in the kitchen which, in spite of all its shining gadgetry, seemed to her to be the most homely room in the apartment.

Lunch over, a glance at her watch showed it was barely one o'clock. With a sinking heart, she realised that the afternoon threatened to drag even more than the morning had.

Rebelling against the boredom, deciding to pass some time by going down to the foyer and having a wander round the shops, Clare collected her shoulder-bag and donned a light jacket.

Roberts was hovering in the hall looking somewhat uncomfortable. 'Madam wasn't planning to go out? A thunderstorm appears to be imminent.'

'I'm not afraid of storms,' she said briskly, and wondered how she could be so sure. 'And anyway, I'm not actually going *out*. I'm just planning to do a spot of window-shopping.'

Looking even more uncomfortable, the manservant observed, 'Mr Saunders was most anxious that after what happened last time madam shouldn't venture anywhere alone.'

Clare bit her lip. Clearly Roberts had received instructions not to let her go out. But what if she insisted? Had he been ordered to restrain her physically?

He was a nice man, and, unwilling to put them both in an embarrassing situation, she decided not to risk it.

Lightly, she said, 'In that case, though I'm quite sure Mr Saunders is fussing unnecessarily, I'll wait until he gets home.' And she watched the relief spread across the manservant's usually impassive face.

Taking off the jacket, she handed it to him, and then, feeling frustrated and rebellious, asked on a sudden impulse, 'Roberts, do you know how to play poker?'

If he was surprised, he hid it well, merely answering, 'Yes, madam.'

'Have we got any cards in the house?'

'I believe so, madam.'

'Then perhaps you'd be kind enough to bring them to the kitchen and teach me how to play poker.'

'The *kitchen*, madam?' He seemed more distressed by the location than any other consideration.

'The kitchen,' she said firmly. 'Oh, and Roberts, have we any bourbon?'

'Would madam not prefer a little wine, perhaps?'

Shaking her head, she said seriously, 'Bourbon seems much more appropriate.'

She was sitting at the kitchen table waiting when the manservant appeared with a new pack of cards, a bottle of bourbon and two small bags of what looked remarkably like dried beans.

Having opened the whisky, he produced a tray of ice cubes and a single glass.

'You drink bourbon, don't you?' Clare queried.

'Indeed, madam, but not during working hours.'

'Then you'd better have the afternoon off. I can't drink alone... Now, just run through the game for me...'

When the manservant had carefully explained the intricacies of poker, she said, 'Yes, I'm sure I must have played it. Let's make a start and see how I get on...' Then she asked curiously, 'Roberts, what are the beans for?'

'I thought madam might wish to place a bet...'

The evening finally brought the threatened storm, but there was still no sign of Jos. After asking Roberts to delay dinner for more than an hour, and getting angrier by the minute, Clare had finally eaten alone and then gone straight to bed.

If Jos thought he could treat her like this, walking out and leaving her a virtual prisoner, then he had another think coming!

But where *was* he? It didn't seem feasible that he would still be working. She pushed away a sudden mental picture of Andrea's cold blonde beauty. No, she couldn't believe he was with another woman.

Or was it just that she didn't *want* to believe it?

Her anger was turning to a sick fear that something must have happened to him when finally, lying in the dark, awake and unsettled, Clare heard his voice as he spoke to Roberts and then, a short time later, the click of the bedroom door.

Without putting on the light, he crossed to the bathroom, and a few seconds later she heard the shower running.

When finally he emerged and, still without speaking, got into bed beside her and turned his broad back, she could have wept with frustration.

Too uptight to try and sleep, and determined to have

things out, she pushed herself up and reached to switch
on her bedside lamp, bathing them both in a pool of light.

Her voice carefully moderated, she said, 'I'd like to
talk to you.'

He turned to look at her, pushing himself up on one
elbow, tension etched sharply on his dark face. Coldly,
he informed her, 'I'm in no mood to talk. I've had a long,
frustrating day.'

Her breathing quickening to match her temper, she
threw caution to the winds and said, just as coldly, 'So
have I. That's one of the things I want to talk to you
about. As you're so fond of telling me, I *chose* to marry
you. Even after I discovered why you married me, I *chose*
to stay with you, and I *intend* to stay with you. I don't
want a divorce and I don't want your money.'

His expression was shuttered and it was impossible to
tell whether or not he believed her.

'But I *do* want some freedom. Don't think you can just
stalk out and stay out, and then keep me here like a
prisoner.'

When he remained silent, merely looking at her with
glittering green eyes, her anger boiled over. 'I refuse to
be treated like something of no consequence—a…a sex-
object with no will of my own. I *won't* just be used whenever it suits you…'

The words ended in a throaty gasp as he rolled over,
pinning her beneath him. With a kind of raging calm, he
said, 'You'll be treated exactly as I want to treat you,
used whenever I want to use you…'

She began to struggle then, striking out at him, wanting
to hurt him. But with a cruel disregard for her feelings
as a woman he used his superior strength to force her to
compliance, and for the first time took her brutally, without any preliminaries.

She should have been scared by the violence she'd

aroused, but her anger rose to meet and match his, and in that instant it changed to a searing, white-hot passion that sent them both up in flames.

He was kissing her mouth now, and his hands were beneath her buttocks, lifting her. She felt intense pleasure, a fierce concentration that wasn't just physical but emotional, a longing for release, a desperate wish for his love.

Her release came with a brilliant flash of light, an explosion of ecstasy that sent her mind reeling and made her cry out again and again.

The weight of his dark head against her breast was a pleasurable burden while their breathing and heartbeats slowed to a more normal rate.

It wasn't until he lifted his head and said with sudden urgency, 'Don't cry... For God's sake don't cry...' that she realised tears were running down her cheeks.

'I'm sorry.' He sounded anguished. 'I didn't mean to hurt you.'

'You didn't hurt me,' she assured him as he brushed the tears away with his fingertips. 'It was *wonderful*.' Smiling at him, hearing his indrawn breath of relief, she added with a throaty chuckle, 'Perhaps I should make you angry more often...'

Observing sternly, 'Perhaps you shouldn't push your luck,' he reached to switch off the light, and, stretching out beside her, pulled her close against him so that her head was on his shoulder, her body half supported by his.

'Jos...' She had to ask. 'Where have you been all evening?'

'You're beginning to sound like a wife.'

'Of course, if you don't want to tell me...'

He sighed. 'Earlier I went to talk to Dr Hauser about your amnesia. He suggested that I got in touch with a Paul Gregson, who's a specialist in the field. After an afternoon spent trying, I finally tracked Gregson down at a West Side clinic. He already had an early evening appointment, so I invited him to dine with me later…'

'And?'

'He wasn't a great deal of help. All he would say was that amnesia can sometimes be a functional disturbance of the nervous system—a defence mechanism, if you like.

'I asked if remembering anything unpleasant could harm you. He hedged a bit, and then said that so long as you *want* to remember, you'll probably be able to cope if and when you do.'

Jos sounded anxious, dissatisfied, far from reassured. She found herself wondering what unpleasant things he'd omitted to tell her, but knew it was no use asking.

'I'm sure I will,' she said, with more conviction than she felt. Then, nestling against him, she went on, 'It was kind of you to go to all that trouble, but, Jos…' Her fingers traced slow circles in the crisp dark hair on his chest. 'Don't leave me again like that.'

Half humorously, he said, 'I wouldn't dare! I don't know what I might find when I get home. Already you've been leading Roberts astray. Encouraging him to drink and play poker…giving him the afternoon off…and worst of all hurting his feelings.'

'Hurting his feelings?' she echoed.

'He tells me you won all his beans.'

Still oddly restive, unable to sleep, Clare lay for what seemed an age, uneasily aware that Jos was also lying wakeful.

Though on the surface things appeared to be all right between them, she knew that the calm of the preceding few weeks was over. Not only had the letter from the solicitors disturbed their tranquillity, but her unthinking words had torn a rent in the delicate fabric of their almost-happiness that she wasn't certain was mended.

Perhaps her restlessness communicated itself to Jos, because, though it was long past midnight before she finally fell asleep, he was still lying wide awake staring into the darkness.

Next morning, even though it was early when she stirred and opened her eyes, Jos had already showered and breakfasted.

Wearing a smart lightweight suit and silk shirt, he was standing in front of the dressing table knotting his tie. His handsome face looked grim and preoccupied.

Sitting up in bed, Clare met his eyes in the mirror and smiled tentatively at him.

He didn't return her smile.

'You're looking very businesslike,' she remarked, with what lightness she could muster. 'Are you going into the office?'

'Only for ten minutes. I have a couple more things to attend to before we start for JFK.'

'We're flying to England today?'

'Yes. We're booked on Concorde. I'm sorry I didn't get round to telling you last night.'

But she guessed the omission had been a deliberate one, designed to give her less time to worry.

He turned to face her, saying evenly, 'I hope you agree that there's no point in delay, that it's better to get things over with?'

'Yes.' Clare sighed inwardly, finding his cool civility more off-putting than anger.

'We could no doubt get a room at the Barley Mow— that's where I stayed last time—but it might make more sense to stay at Lamb Cottage.'

'That's the cottage I rented?'

'Yes. I understand the leave still has a couple of

months to run. You didn't give it up because some of
your belongings were being left there until you'd decided
whether or not to have them shipped over.'

Pushing back her cloud of dark hair, she asked, 'Do I
still have the keys?'

'They were left with Mrs Carter, the lady who lives
next door. I gather she's the niece of the man who actually owns it, and she acts as caretaker. I'll get in touch
with her and tell her to expect us.'

'You think staying at the cottage might trigger my
memory?'

'It's possible.'

His voice was casual, non-committal, but she guessed
that he was still worried, far from happy at the prospect.

The flight on the beautiful, graceful plane was smooth
and fast and incident-free. Jos appeared withdrawn, deep
in thought, and for the greater part of the journey a silence hung between them, sheer and impenetrable as a
glass wall.

Formalities over, they got into the hired car that was
waiting for them and, leaving the bustle of the airport
behind them, drove down to Meredith through quiet
county lanes and pleasant, rolling countryside.

They had left the bad weather over the Atlantic, and
the evening was calm and slightly hazy. It was just starting to get dusk, and as they approached the outskirts of
the old, carefully preserved village Clare could see the
bats were out, flittering around the period streetlamps and
the lighted sign of the Barley Mow.

Lamb Cottage was one of a row of six rose- and
creeper-covered stone cottages facing the village green
and duck pond. Though they were joined, each of the
roofs had a slightly different pitch and the chimneys were
at various angles, giving them a look of slightly rakish

individuality. At each end the outer cottages leaned in a little, like amiable drunks supporting their neighbours.

At the end of the little road that fronted them was a neatly paved area, partly screened by trees and bushes, that served as a car park.

Mrs Carter, a plump, round-faced woman with frizzy fair hair, opened her door to Jos's knock, spilling yellow light into the porch, and handed him two bunches of keys. 'I've given you the spare set as well, in case you want one each. The place is aired, I've made up the bed and lit the water-heater, and I've got the groceries you asked for.'

When Jos had thanked her, and given her a smile that visibly melted her, with an effort she transferred her attention to Clare. 'It's nice to see you again, Miss Berkeley...I should say Mrs Saunders. Are you liking New York?'

Breathing in the scent of roses and honeysuckle, Clare smiled at the woman who was a total stranger to her and said, 'Loving it.'

'It must be very different to village life?'

'Yes, it is.'

'I've often wondered what it must be like to live in one of those skyscrapers...'

Mrs Carter seemed set for a long chat, and Clare was wondering how best to cut it short without hurting her feelings when Jos, who had moved away to unlock the door to Lamb Cottage, called, 'Darling, could you make some coffee while I park the car and bring in the cases?'

'Yes, of course,' she agreed thankfully.

'Americans and their coffee!' Mrs Carter exclaimed archly.

Clare smiled, and, having said, 'Well, goodnight, then, and thank you again,' lost no time in escaping.

The two-up, two-down cottage, with its tiny low-ceilinged rooms and chintz-covered furniture, was quite charming but totally unfamiliar.

At the front, casement windows looked out across the green to the old village school, and at the back the kitchen overlooked a picket-fenced garden bright with snapdragons and lupins and hollyhocks.

A cardboard box full of groceries stood on the draining board, and several packing cases took up most of the available floor space.

When she'd found the cafetière and plugged in the kettle, Clare opened the door to the staircase and climbed the narrow, cramped stairs, which creaked at every step.

The front bedroom, with its polished floorboards and black-grated fireplace, its faded rugs and flowered counterpane, was ready for occupation. The back bedroom had at some time been converted into a nicely equipped bathroom and, as Mrs Carter had promised, the pilot light on the water-heater had been lit.

Tired from lack of sleep the previous night and a day spent travelling, Clare was thinking longingly of bed when Jos brought up their cases.

His eyes resting on her thoughtfully, he said, 'I take it nothing looks familiar?'

Realising now why he'd let her walk through the cottage alone, she shook her head. 'No, I might never have been here before.' After a moment, she added with a sigh, 'I don't know about you, but I'm ready for bed.'

'Do you want anything to eat, or perhaps a milky drink before you turn in?' he queried, with that cool, disconcerting politeness that she sensed masked real concern and anxiety.

'I don't think so.'

'Then if you'd like to use the bathroom first while I get a cup of coffee...?'

Clare had been in bed for almost half an hour when

Jos finally joined her. Though she had put the light out and tried to sleep she was unable to settle, her mind restless and uneasy.

Lying in the semi-darkness, she found herself thinking about her parents, and the house she had come to England to look at. But if the cottage she'd lived in until just a few weeks ago had failed to spark off any memories, what chance would Strattan Place stand?

At the moment it was just a name to her, and a not very familiar name at that. She had no recollection of what it was like or where it stood…

She turned to look at Jos, who was stretched on his back beside her. His handsome profile appeared aloof and unapproachable, but, suddenly determined to break through the barrier he'd erected, she blew softly on his bare shoulder before resting her cheek there and asking, 'Jos, how well do you know Stratton Place? Did you go there much as a child?'

'Yes.' With a kind of bleak humour, he added, 'I almost got to live there.'

Afraid he was going to leave it at that, she begged quickly, 'Please, darling, won't you tell me about it?'

There was a long silence, as though he was debating the advisability of it, and she was just beginning to think he'd decided against telling her when he said flatly, 'I believe I told you that it wasn't until after my father was dead and buried that your mother showed the slightest trace of remorse…?'

Clare's 'Yes' was just a sigh, a thread of sound.

'Your father, who was an extraordinarily good-looking man, tended to stay in the background and say very little, but I'm certain he must have known the score, because he at least had the grace to look ashamed and harassed…'

Poor Father, Clare found herself thinking. He was the

one person no one seemed to have felt any sympathy for, yet he too had been a victim of a sort...

But Jos was going on. 'While my parents' solicitors tried to sort out the unholy mess that had been left, I was staying at Stratton Place. When it became obvious that I would have to be put into care, your mother, apparently in a fit of conscience, suggested that they should give me a permanent home, and your father agreed...'

'Then, why...?'

'They asked you what you thought about having me as a brother, but you shook your head and mumbled, "No, I don't want him here." When they pressed you, you cried, "I don't want him to live with us. I don't want him! I hate him!" It was like being rejected all over again.'

'Dear God,' Clare breathed. 'I see now why that day at Niagara you implied that I used to be a heartless little monster...'

As though she hadn't spoken Jos went on, his voice full of black bitterness, 'I didn't really want to live at Stratton Place, for more than one reason, but my life had been turned upside down and your home and family seemed to be the only familiar things left.'

And because of her even they had been lost to him. Desperately, she said, 'But if I was only eight, surely they shouldn't have taken any notice of me?'

'Well, you were pretty vehement about it—almost distraught. Though in retrospect I have to admit it was my fault you felt as you did.'

'Why was it your fault?'

'Because I hadn't always been nice to you. I thought you were a self-righteous little prig. I disliked your haughtiness, your air of superiority, and during the school holidays, behind our parents' backs, I used to tease you unmercifully, try to make you cry… When I said children were heartless little monsters, I was including myself.'

'Did you succeed in making me cry?' she asked curiously.

'No. You had extraordinary composure for a child of that age. You used to look at me with those huge violet eyes and make me feel ashamed—which, of course, only made me want to persecute you more.'

Clare sighed. 'I sound unbearable.'

'There was one thing in your favour, one thing I admired about you—your spirit. You took everything I handed out without begging or whining, and you never split on me…

'I was beginning, reluctantly, to like and respect you— I bought you that box of Turkish delight as a peace offering—when you did something I thought was cruel and unforgivable…' He hesitated, as though wondering whether to go on.

After a moment, she asked uneasily, 'What did I do that was so terrible?'

'You laughed when my mother died.'

Feeling as though she'd been kicked in the solar-plexus, Clare lay frozen, unwilling to believe it but unable to move or protest.

'When I heard that half-stifled giggle I lost my head. I lashed out and hit you as hard as I could, knocking you down… So, you see, after I'd been so cruel to you, I couldn't blame you for not wanting me for a brother.'

Somehow she found her voice. 'But why…*why* did I laugh when you told me your mother had died?'

There was a pause before he said carefully, 'It was only later I saw your response for what it was…a young child's shocked, unbelieving, half-hysterical reaction…'

A shadowy image loomed in her mind, wraithlike but insistent. She seemed to be on the brink of understanding, of remembering… But there was something he wasn't telling her, something she needed to know to get the full picture.

'What happened after you'd hit me?' Her voice was hoarse.

'You picked yourself up without a word. Your face had gone absolutely white, and I could see the mark of my fist on your cheek. But even then you didn't cry, and when, some time later, your mother asked about the bruise, you said you'd bumped into a door…'

His words were fairly graphic, but they didn't tell her what she needed to know. She sat up in bed and pressed her fingers to her temples in sudden frustration. The knowledge was hovering there, practically within her grasp.

If only she could *remember*…

'What is it?' Jos sat up to peer at her face in the gloom.

As she strove to catch and hold the elusive image it was suddenly blotted out by a black, almost tangible cloud of fear—fear that made her moan and cover her face with her hands.

Taking her wrists, Jos pulled her hands away, trying to read her expression, demanding, 'What do you remember?'

'Nothing. Nothing! Yet it's all there at the back of my mind… If only I *could* remember I think I'd be able to bear things better…'

Then, as she began to tremble, he said, his voice suddenly sharp with anxiety, 'Don't try too hard. Let it go.'

No, she wanted to face the fear and *know*…

But as though her bold decision had put it to flight the blackness began to recede and the knowledge dispersed with it, leaving only a grey emptiness. She stifled a groan.

Gripping her upper arms, his fingers biting in, Jos demanded, 'Clare, are you all right?'

'Yes… Yes, I'm all right,' she assured him shakily.

But she was more than pleased when instead of letting her go and turning away, as she'd half expected, he settled down with her in his arms and held her closely until sleep finally claimed her.

Next morning she opened her eyes to bright sunshine and a sense of complete disorientation. As she blinked at the strange room Jos appeared in the doorway, with a cup and saucer in one hand and a plate of toast in the other, and, as if she'd shaken a kaleidoscope, yesterday's pattern of events fell into place.

He was dressed in smart but casual trousers and a black cotton polo-necked shirt, his jaw was clean-shaven and his dark hair was brushed smoothly back from his high forehead. Though his expression was studiedly calm, relaxed, she sensed a certain tension in his long, lean body.

She hoped he would kiss her, but he didn't. Stifling her disappointment, she accepted the tea and toast and asked, 'Why are you up and about at the crack of dawn?'

'Crack of dawn, nothing. It's gone ten! I've been into the solicitors on your behalf, and into Ashleigh Kent to pick up the keys to Stratton Place and the Priory.'

'Foxton Priory? Your old home?'

He sat down on the edge of the bed. 'After my parents died it had to be disposed of. As I told you, it had been in the family for generations, and I swore I'd get it back as soon as I had the money.

'When the money was available, however, the new owners didn't want to sell. But they promised to let me know if it was ever put on the market…which they did, some months ago.

'That's when I got in touch with Ashleigh Kent and told them I was coming over to England to buy a house in this area.' He smiled a shade grimly. 'They gave me first option on a couple, one of which was the Priory.'

'Showing you round was something I half remembered that day in Central Park...'

She shivered, suddenly excited and afraid, convinced now that somehow Foxton Priory held the key that would unlock both her memory and the past.

Seeing that uncontrollable shiver, Jos asked soberly, 'Are you sure you still want to go through with it?'

'Yes.' There was no hesitation. 'I have to.'

'Then eat your toast and let's get started.'

Less than half an hour later they turned between stone gateposts topped by miniature unicorns and followed the drive through a pretty walled garden to draw up outside Foxton Priory, a charming, seventeenth-century manor-house built in honey-coloured stone.

To the best of her knowledge Clare had never seen it before in her life. Shaking her head at Jos's questioning glance, she commented, 'It's smaller than I'd expected.'

'There's a living-room, a morning-room, a library, a dining-room, a kitchen and six bedrooms. The others have been made into bathrooms.'

'It looks empty,' she observed.

'It is. The previous owners have gone abroad to live.'

She wrinkled her brow. 'I'm surprised the estate agents didn't feel they should send someone with us.'

'That's no longer necessary. I own it. I received confirmation the same day you heard from your solicitors.'

Yes, she could visualise his look of fierce satisfaction and triumph as he'd read the letter. Clearly having it back meant a great deal to him.

Recalling other things—his mention of sweeping changes, his assertion that he'd never considered the penthouse home—she asked slowly, 'Do you intend to live in it?'

'That was my original intention, but now it's up to you.'

Why was it up to her? she wondered.

But all at once she *knew*. Though the house nestled and slept innocent as a babe in the sunshine, there must be something about it that Jos knew would frighten and upset her. Black memories of something that had happened there in the past.

Jumping out of the car, Jos came round to help her out. His hand beneath her elbow, they crossed the old flagstone paving and walked over to the black-studded door. While he produced a heavy bunch of keys and opened both the ordinary and the security locks, Clare held her breath.

The door swung open and, still holding her breath, she walked into a long, wood-panelled hall with a graceful horseshoe staircase rising to the second floor. Despite the dark panelling, polished oak floorboards and double windows at each end gave an overall impression of lightness.

She had no recollection of ever having been here before, and if the house had any bad memories for her they were certainly not apparent. The atmosphere felt calm and friendly; it was impossible to believe that any traces of past unhappiness still lingered here.

Releasing her breath in a sigh, she smiled shakily at Jos who, his face studiously blank, was watching her.

'All right?' he queried.

Relief and frustration mingling, she said, 'I don't recognise it, and it's not at all what I...at least my *subconscious*...expected.'

'What did you subconscious expect?'

'I'm not sure... Something frightening...'

As they walked through the big, sunny, empty rooms

Clare's impression of it as a beautiful, tranquil house strengthened. Though it had been altered and modernised, it still kept a feeling of rightness, a harmonious blend of past and present.

No wonder Jos loved it and had wanted it back so much. Though as a child he'd found little real happiness here himself, it seemed to be a house made for fun and laughter, for a big, happy family.

The thought was an oddly poignant one.

When they'd completed their tour, without a word Jos locked up and led the way back to the car.

When they were both seated, their safety belts fastened, he glanced at his watch, and with a frown drawing his dark brows together suggested, 'As it's almost lunchtime, suppose we leave Stratton Place until this afternoon?'

But, all psyched up, Clare said, 'No, I'd rather go now, if you don't mind.'

After a marked hesitation, Jos shrugged and agreed, 'Very well.'

She found herself wondering at his strange reluctance. If it was simply that he was hungry, why hadn't he said so?

Stratton Place was less than half a mile to the east. It was a stone-built three-storey house, much older than she'd envisaged—late sixteenth century, perhaps—with a shallow flight of steps leading up to a porticoed entrance.

Jos drew up on the gravel by the steps and came round to help Clare out.

So this was her childhood home. She had no recollection of living here, yet it seemed vaguely familiar, like something she might have glimpsed in a magazine.

The house lay in a dip, with the lower rooms looking out onto lawns and gardens and high beech hedges, but she guessed that the upper rooms would have marvellous views over the surrounding countryside.

Standing to one side of the steps, she stared up at the house. Though small by country house standards, it was larger than she'd expected. At one time the rooms on the top floor would no doubt have been used as servants' quarters. Now they were probably attics. From a purely practical point of view, she found herself hoping that they weren't full of accumulated junk.

Having produced another large bunch of keys and opened the door, Jos stood quietly to one side, making no effort to hurry her.

Fairly sure now that she was to be disappointed, her memory, that essential part of herself, to be locked away for ever, she mounted the steps and pushed open the door.

CHAPTER TEN

CLARE found herself looking at a rectangular hall of unusual design. It was high and white, soaring to open rafters. On each side a curving staircase led up to two dark-oak galleries which ran round three sides of the hall.

On both upper and lower galleries were doors leading off to various rooms. High, narrow windows, set in the end wall of the upper gallery, threw lozenges of light onto the dusty stone flags three floors below.

As she looked up everything whirled hideously round her head, and icy cold all over, assailed by a sudden nausea, Clare covered her face with her hands. But, as though some old, silent film were being run in slow motion, she saw in her mind's eye a woman, tall and slim and dark-haired, hurry from one of the doors on the upper balcony, stumble against the balustrade and fall, her body hitting the flags with a sickening thud. There was a roaring in her ears, and a second later the scene was blotted out by a merciful blackness...

When Clare regained consciousness she was slumped in the passenger seat of the car, and with the door wide open Jos was crouching beside her, chafing her cold hands.

Lifting her head, which felt too heavy for her slender neck, she looked at him, and, her voice sounding oddly thin and high, like the voice of someone who had been very ill for a longer time, said, 'We'd been told to stay in the playroom that day, but you complained it was too much like a nursery. We were in the hall together when your mother fell. That was when you hit me...'

He gripped her hands hard. 'Don't try and remember any more.'

'I don't need to *try*.' Seeing the tension, the barely hidden fear on his face, she added, more hardily, 'It's all right, really. Nothing could be worse than not knowing…'

Lifting her hands to his lips, he saluted her courage. 'Do you feel well enough to go? You look as if you could use a brandy.'

'Yes, I do. And yes, I could.' She answered as lightly as possible.

He closed her door, and a moment later slid behind the wheel and reached over to fasten her seat belt.

Though he glanced at her from time to time, as if to reassure himself, Jos didn't speak until they were drawing up in the car park at the Barley Mow.

'Would you prefer to sit inside or outside?'

Normally Clare would have preferred to sit outside, but the garden, where wooden tables and benches jostled for a place in the sun, appeared to be crowded with tourists.

'Inside, I think.'

His arm firmly around her waist, they went into the comparative gloom of the lounge, which was practically empty except for a small group of men clustered by the bar exchanging banter with the bartender.

The place smelled of coffee, bitter beer and the lemon-scented geraniums that stood in pots on the deep window sills.

Having seated Clare at a small corner table, Jos went to the bar. She noticed that, though he made no effort to attract attention, even in the casual trousers and cotton polo-neck he had presence enough to make the bartender immediately leave the group and hurry over.

Carrying a double brandy for her and a half-pint of bitter for himself, he returned quite quickly. He still looked taut, she thought, the planes and angles of his face sharp beneath the tanned skin.

Eyeing the brandy he'd placed in front of her, Clare remarked ruefully, 'If I drink all that on an empty stomach I'll have to be carried to the car a second time.'

Jos grinned briefly, as she'd hoped he would, and told her, 'There's a plate of beef sandwiches coming.'

She was still sipping the brandy when they arrived.

They ate in silence—Jos like a man with a great deal on his mind, Clare with an appetite that surprised her.

They were each drinking coffee before he remarked, 'You look better. You're starting to get a trace of colour back.'

'I feel better, and I'm glad I finally know the worst...' she said, and in a low voice she added, 'But why did your mother commit suicide in *our* house?'

'Do you remember which room she came out of?'

'Yes...' Clare whispered. 'My mother had had two bedrooms converted into a sitting room-cum-study on the top floor. She loved the view from the windows and said she didn't get disturbed up there when she settled down to write letters. In those days she was an avid correspondent. But why should your mother...?'

'I can only presume she'd been to have it out with Isobel, to ask her to give Charles up. When Isobel refused, I suppose my mother couldn't bear the thought of losing the man she was devoted to. Perhaps, on the spur of the moment, it seemed preferable to end it...'

Clare shuddered. 'That's *never* the way. Things change, situations alter. There's no sense in deliberately throwing your life away...'

'I agree.'

'Are you *sure* she did?'

'You were there.'

'But I'd never heard any mention of divorce, and I just

thought your mother's fall was a dreadful accident... As surely it *must* have been? Those balustrades are very low...'

'They're at least waist-high,' he corrected.

'I thought they were a good foot lower than that... and it seemed to me she stumbled...' Clare shuddered again at the memory. 'The first time I showed you round Stratton Place—I relived everything then, though I didn't appreciate you were Clave. I was horrified...'

'Yes, I know. Your face turned as white as paper and I thought you were going to faint. But it was obvious you didn't recognise me, and when I asked what was wrong, you just said you weren't feeling well.'

'That day in Central Park... when you were talking about looking round houses... it was that half-remembered recollection that frightened me so much. And I suppose that's what scared me today. But for some reason I wasn't expecting it to be Stratton Place...'

'You thought it was the Priory?'

'Yes. Even though you said you'd looked at *two* houses, it didn't occur to me that Stratton Place was the other one...'

A thought struck her, and she asked, 'Jos, why did you want to leave going there until the afternoon?'

'The first time we looked at the houses it was in the same order, and at about the same time of day, with the sun coming through those high windows...'

'And you wanted the conditions to be different?'

'I was afraid of what the shock of remembering might do to you. I wanted you to get your memory back—you seemed only half alive without it—but I didn't want you to remember that particular incident. I got the impression that you'd managed to block it out of your mind until that first time you took me round.'

'I had. You see, after that awful day I could hardly

bear to be in the house. For a long time I had bad dreams and waking nightmares. The doctor called it some kind of neurosis… You obviously didn't know, but until then I'd secretly hero-worshipped you, and longed for your approval. Then afterwards, when I thought you might be going to live with us, I couldn't bear it. You were so much part of that terrible memory—a memory I *had* to get away from somehow… That's why I behaved as I did. When it was too late, and I realised what I'd done, I felt ashamed, bitterly sorry…

'You once told me my parents pushed me off to boarding-school. But that wasn't so. I *asked* to go… After I went, gradually the nightmares and the feelings of guilt stopped, and I was able to bury the memory in my subconscious. The only thing that remained was my fear of heights…

'I never went back home after that, not even for holidays. My parents had a flat in town, and if they were going to be there I joined them. If not, I made arrangements to stay with one or other of my friends. And when the time came to finally leave school, I could have lived at Stratton Place but I knew I didn't want to. I told myself it was because I liked the idea of being totally independent.

'Though I prefer the country, I'd half decided to try and find a job and a bedsit in London when Graham Ashleigh offered me a job with his firm. He also made arrangements for me to rent Mr Drury's cottage…'

Jos's mouth moved in a smile that was more of a sneer. 'He sounds like a Mr Fix-it.'

Stiffly, she said, 'Graham was an old family friend.'

'And a would-be lover? Despite the fact that he was a widower and lot older than you?'

With touch of malice, she informed him, 'He's only four years older than you are.'

'Would you have become Mrs Ashleigh the second if I hadn't come along?' Again there was that curl of the lip.

'I don't know,' she admitted truthfully. 'I might have done…'

Judging by the glitter in Jos's green eyes, that wasn't what he'd wanted to hear.

'We'd been out together quite a lot and we were fond of each other.'

'*Fond!*' Jos echoed derisively. 'The man was besotted; he could barely keep his hands off you.'

For a moment or two the realisation that Jos was jealous gave Clare a lift, but common sense soon pointed out that you didn't have to be in love to be jealous, only possessive.

Suddenly, unexpectedly, she yawned.

Jos's eyes narrowed. 'It's time we got you back to bed.'

'Bed? But it's only two-thirty.' Despite her protestation, she yawned again.

'Come on.' With an arm around her, he half lifted her. 'Tiredness can be one of the signs of delayed shock.'

'It's more likely to be the brandy.'

Whatever the cause, half an hour later she was in bed. Jos drew the flowered curtains across the open window to shut out most of the brightness and stooped to kiss her lightly. 'Try to get some sleep.'

For a moment the kiss and his obvious concern warmed her, and spun a thread of hope for the future. But what chance had they of finding any kind of happiness together when he was convinced that *her* mother was responsible for *his* mother's suicide?

If it had been suicide. Somehow she couldn't believe it.

Eyes closed, mentally bracing herself, she deliberately relived those few seconds, seeing again that slim hurrying figure, the stumble, the thigh-height balustrade…

The *thigh-height* balustrade…

But Jos had said *waist-height*. One of them had to be wrong… Her thoughts were getting blurred and she was too tired to decide which…

A second later she was fast asleep.

Jos stood gazing down at her, on his lean face a look of such tenderness that Clare would have been transfixed had she seen it.

She looked childishly innocent, he thought, and frighteningly vulnerable. One hand was lying on the pillow beside her dark head, palm up, fingers slightly curled, showing the oval nails with their natural shine.

Her heart-shaped face was still wan, and the long lashes, spread like fans, failed to disguise the mauve shadows beneath her eyes. Her lips were pale and her flawless skin looked almost translucent.

But, fragile as she seemed, he knew now that she had grown up with strength and courage, an inner core of steel that made her a fighter. Made her able to face life, to look tragedy in the face and then put it behind her.

He touched her cheek in a gentle caress, before going quietly out.

Clare awoke to immediate and complete remembrance, her mind oddly clear and lucid. A glance at her watch showed she'd slept for almost two hours.

While she'd slept her subconscious had been busy. Knowing now what she had to do, she jumped out of bed and, pulling on the cotton skirt and button-through top and the sandals she'd taken off earlier, hurried downstairs.

There was no sign of Jos. Opening the window, Clare stuck her head out and looked towards the parking area. The hired car was missing.

Jos had obviously gone somewhere, but the keys to both the houses—probably because they'd weighed his pocket down—had been left on the coffee-table, along with the spare keys to Lamb Cottage.

Dropping the keys to Stratton Place and Lamb Cottage into her shoulder-bag, Clare let herself out and walked the two hundred yards to where George Hammet, who drove the village taxi, lived.

There was no sign of either George or his vehicle.

She was wondering whether to set off on the two-mile walk to Stratton Place when the obvious solution struck her. Before her marriage, often needing to take clients to view properties, she'd had the use of one or other of Ashleigh Kent's cars, and she had no doubt that Graham would lend her one now, if one was available.

Crossing the green, abstractedly enjoying the smell of the newly mown grass, she made her way up Yeoman Street and pushed open the door to the estate agents.

Graham, impeccably dressed as usual, his fair hair neatly brushed, was coming the opposite way and they met in the doorway. He was a big man, almost as tall as Jos and considerably heavier. He'd been a Rugby Union forward in his younger days.

'Clare!' His good-looking, somewhat heavy face lit up. 'How nice to see you…' Then, 'Oh, hell! I'm just on my way out; I've an urgent appointment.'

'That's all right.' She smiled up at him. 'I only came to ask if I could borrow a car for an hour. Jos has taken ours.'

'I'm afraid all the cars are out. Where did you want to get to?'

'Stratton Place. I…I went there this morning, but I need to go again…'

He beamed his relief. 'My appointment's at Copthorn. I can easily drop you at the house and pick you up on the way back, if that will suit you?'

'That's ideal.'

When they were in the sleek Jaguar, heading out of the village, he glanced at her, his blue eyes troubled. 'Is everything working out all right? I mean…well, you do love Saunders, don't you?'

'Everything's fine. And, yes, I do love him.'

'I suppose I shouldn't have asked, only you're not looking too well.'

'I think it must be the heat.' Then, realising he knew quite well that she could stand any amount of heat, she asked hurriedly, 'So how are things at this end? How's the real estate business?'

'Could be worse. Buyers are still a bit cautious, but we've several parties interested in Stratton Place…'

Graham had always been an enthusiastic talker, and while he launched into an account of the various possibilities Clare allowed part of her mind to wander, listening with one ear.

When she'd first taken Jos to view Foxton Priory and Stratton Place, some four months previously, it had been in this self-same car.

Remembering that drive now, she could recall how much just sitting beside him had affected her. Overwhelmingly conscious of that powerfully attractive face, that lean, muscular body, that potent sexuality, her pulse had raced and her cheeks had been unusually flushed.

Aware that Jos had turned a little in his seat and was studying her profile with great deliberation, she'd stared

resolutely ahead, doing her best to keep her attention on
the road but feeling the betraying flush deepen.

'Warm?' he'd teased.

She'd given him an angry glance and, seeing the
amusement gleaming in his green eyes, inviting her to
laugh with him, had succumbed then and there to his
charm.

He'd been irresistible, and every instinct she'd possessed had been warning her that he was also *dangerous*.
The knowledge had scared her half to death.

Instead of laughing with him, she'd armoured herself
with that cool composure he'd talked about. But, against
what she now recognised as a determined assault, it had
proved as ineffectual as glass armour…

'And the contract could be signed as soon as you've
decided whether or not you want to part with the contents,' Graham wound up as they stopped by the steps at
Stratton Place.

Anxious not to make him late, Clare scrambled out and
thanked him with a smile.

'I'll pick you up in about an hour,' he told her, and as
soon as she'd closed the car door accelerated away down
the tree-lined drive.

Overcoming her nervous qualms, her sudden fear of
going in alone, Clare opened the door and forced herself
to walk over the threshold.

Expecting to be met by dark memories and ghosts of
the past, she found neither. Facing them had apparently
put them to flight.

The hall was bare and beautiful, the air a little musty,
the atmosphere innocuous. Its only furnishings were a
long oak table, a matching settle and several heavy metal-
bound chests that Clare knew had always stood there.

Bracing herself, she looked up at the galleries. Jos had

been right; the balustrades were at least waist-height. But her conviction that they had been a lot lower was so strong that her mind would scarcely believe the evidence of her own eyes.

Of course, it was still possible that his mother's fall had been accidental. Though less likely.

Her footsteps sounding loud in the silence, Clare took the right-hand staircase up to the second gallery and opened the door into what had been her mother's sitting-room-cum-study.

It was light and spacious, furnished with carefully chosen antiques. Only the comfortable armchairs and the curtains looked modern. Between the two windows stood a beautiful walnut bureau, and she had a sudden vivid picture of her mother, wearing something blue, sitting writing at that desk.

She couldn't have been much more than four at the time, and Nanny had brought her in to say goodnight. She'd asked, What are you writing? She could almost hear her own childish treble, and her mother's slightly husky voice answering, 'My diary. I always write down everything that happens to me and then I don't forget.'

Sitting down at the bureau, feeling a kind of silent communication with her, Clare thought about her mother. They had never been close, but she still felt sure in her own mind that though Isobel might have been weak and amoral she hadn't been wicked.

Obeying an impulse, Clare began to look through the drawers, searching for something, anything, that might back up that certainty.

One was full of letters and personal papers, another packed with a jumble of household bills and receipts. A third held several piles of leather-bound diaries.

Surely a diary, that most intimate confidant, would reveal a person's true character...

Hands a little unsteady, Clare went through them. Finding the year she was looking for, and unaware of the shock that was in store for her, she started to read.

She'd almost reached the end when the sound of a car horn jolted her back to the present. Stumbling to the window, she looked down and saw Graham's Jaguar waiting for her.

Putting the diary into her bag, she walked along the gallery, careful not to look over, and down the stairs, holding onto the handrail. She felt sick and agitated, stomach churning, thoughts in a whirl.

Graham got out of the car to open her door. 'I hope you don't think I'm rushing you, but I've got another early evening appointment and—'

He broke off at the sight of her strained white face and exclaimed, 'God, you look terrible! Are you sure you're not ill?'

It seemed easier not to explain, just to say, 'Perhaps I'm coming down with summer flu. I'll have a cup of tea and a lie-down when I get back.'

Once settled in the car, reluctant to talk, she rested her head against the back of the seat and closed her eyes.

When they reached Lamb Cottage there was still no sign of the hired car. 'Jos isn't back yet.' She voiced the thought aloud.

Graham frowned, and, clearly concerned about her, said, 'I'll see you in.'

She made no demur, and with an arm about her waist he walked with her to the door and opened it for her.

'If you'd like to go straight to bed, I'll bring you up a cup of tea before I dash off.'

Without waiting for an answer, he followed her in and went through to the kitchen.

Feeling ashamed that all she really wanted was for him to go and leave her to think, Clare tossed her bag aside and took off her sandals.

The door had been left ajar and the scent of roses and honeysuckle drifted in, their combined scent filling the air.

Graham returned to say, 'The kettle's on. Do you want an aspirin or anything?'

'No, I'll be fine, thank you.' Grateful for his kindness, she raised herself on tiptoe to kiss his cheek and, standing on one of the discarded sandals, wobbled a little.

Putting an arm around her waist to steady her, he asked, 'Would you like me to help you upstairs…?'

'No, she wouldn't, Ashleigh! Or rather, *she* might, but *I* wouldn't.'

'Jos!' Clare exclaimed as they sprang apart.

Tall and dark, his face taut above the black polo-neck, an angry glitter in his green eyes, Jos seemed to dominate the small room.

Thrown, because she knew they must have looked guilty, Clare stammered, 'I—I didn't hear you come in.'

'That's quite obvious.' Jos's voice was icy. Turning to Graham, he ordered with quiet menace, 'Get the hell out of here! If I catch you within a mile of my wife again, I'll break your neck.'

'You don't understand,' Clare cried desperately. 'Graham was only trying to help…'

As though she hadn't spoken, his eyes fixed on the other man, Jos went on, 'In fact, if you don't move fast I might be tempted to do it right now.'

Standing his ground, Graham began, 'Now, you just listen to me, Saunders, you've got it all wrong…'

At the same instant Clare begged, 'Jos, please don't do anything you might regret...'

But with a dangerous gleam in his eyes Jos was advancing on the other man, while Graham, recovered from being startled, was now looking distinctly belligerent, his heavy face darkly flushed.

Realising she had no chance of physically stopping the pair, Clare put a hand to her head and with a low moan pitched forward into Jos's arms.

He gave a little grunt as he caught and supported her weight.

In the split second that followed both men glared at each other. Then, muttering, 'Oh, hell!' Graham headed for the door.

In the doorway he turned. 'Everything was completely innocent, so for God's sake don't take it out on Clare.' A second later the door banged behind him.

Supporting Clare's inert figure with one arm, Jos pulled open the door to the stairs and carried her up to the bedroom. Then, setting her on her feet, gripping her upper arms, he said grimly, 'Right, you can quit the play-acting. I know a genuine faint from a phoney.'

Lifting her head, Clare opened her eyes and sighed. 'It wouldn't have been necessary if you hadn't jumped to conclusions. You know you were quite mistaken—'

'Mistaken be damed! When I find my wife in another man's arms, kissing him, and hear that the next move is upstairs...' He ground his teeth. 'Obviously I'm not keeping you satisfied. Well, if it's sex you're in need of...'

'Jos, I—'

'Take your clothes off.'

'Don't talk to me like that,' she flared.

'Think yourself lucky I'm only talking.'

'Perhaps you'd like to beat me?'

'I'm tempted. But I haven't struck a female since I was thirteen and I don't intend to start again now. There are other ways of reinforcing my ownership.'

As he spoke he was stripping off his clothes.

Her eyes were riveted to the masculine perfection of his naked body, the broad chest with its plates of muscle layering the ribcage, the bunched power of shoulders and biceps, the narrow waist and lean hips, the long, straight legs.

He was beautiful...

Her soft mouth firmed. But that didn't mean she was going to allow him to ride roughshod over her.

His hands moved suddenly, and she gasped as her cotton top was wrenched apart, the buttons torn forcibly through the buttonholes.

'I said, take your clothes off. Unless you want me to do it for you.'

Her expression mutinous, she stood silently, making no move to obey.

He smiled sardonically. 'You do like playing with fire, don't you?'

As soon as he touched her she started to fight, kicking and scratching, striking out at him fiercely. But despite her struggles, using swift, decisive movements, bothering with neither buttons nor hooks, he tore off the rest of her clothing.

The next instant she found herself spread-eagled on the bed and Jos bending over her, his hands and knees trapping her there.

For a while his mouth roved over her breasts, playing with the sensitive nipples, then, to give himself more scope, he brought her hands down, pinning them by her sides.

'I hate you!' she muttered fiercely.

He laughed while his mouth moved over her flat stomach and the silken skin of her inner thighs and drove her slowly wild.

Eyes closed, turning her head restlessly from side to side, hands clenching and unclenching, she groaned as his lips and teeth and tongue wrung from her an intensity of stimulation that was akin to torture.

It was almost a relief when she felt the weight of his body settle on hers. Despite his threats he was gentle with her until, showing one last spark of defiance, she sank her teeth into his shoulder, then, with fire and arrogance, a fierce, driving passion, his body made itself master of hers.

Engulfed by a rapture so pure and intense that it was almost pain, she cried silently, I love you. Oh, I love you…

Then Jos's hands gripping her, Jos's voice demanding fiercely, '*Who* do you love?' cut short the bliss.

'What?' she asked dazedly.

'*Who do you love?*'

'You. I love you.'

Looking shaken, he said, 'You sound as if you mean it.'

She turned her head so that her face was pressed against the brown column of his throat. 'I *do* mean it. I've loved you from the first moment I saw you. Even when I couldn't *remember*, I knew I loved you.'

'In spite of everything?' He sounded stunned.

'In spite of everything.'

'Then what was Ashleigh doing here? Why were you kissing him?'

Briefly, she explained.

'You went back to Stratton Place *alone*? But why?'

'I wanted to take another look at the balustrades. I

found they were waist-high, as you said, but I *remem-bered* them as being lower—the kind they used to have in minstrels' galleries…'

'And you were right.'

'How do you know that?'

'I went into town, to the *Gazette* offices, and asked to see back copies of the paper. I found the one with the story of what they called THE FATAL PLUNGE.

'The coroner's verdict was accidental death, and it was suggested that the low balustrade and the fact that the victim had been drinking heavily prior to the accident had been the main contributory factors. He further suggested that to prevent any further tragedies the balustrades should be replaced by higher ones…'

'And they were. My mother recorded it in her diary.'

'She kept a personal diary?' Jos asked sharply.

Clare nodded.

'Did she go into detail about what happened and why?'

'Yes, it's all there. But it might be better not to read it, just to let the past go.'

His face tight, he said, 'If you're trying to protect her—'

'I'm not.'

'In any case, I think I have a right to know.'

'Very well. The diary's in my bag, downstairs. I'll get it.'

When he'd been reading for some ten minutes, his face pale beneath the tan, Jos looked up to say slowly, 'So it was *me* you were trying to protect.' Then, 'God! All these years I've been hating the wrong woman…' His knuckles gleamed white as he clenched his hands.

'There's no need to hate anyone,' Clare said urgently. 'Especially not yourself.'

'How could I have been so wrong?' He sounded agonised.

She touched his cheek. 'You were young when you overheard your parents quarrelling, talking about a divorce. It wasn't your fault that you misinterpreted what you heard…'

'I didn't misinterpret it so much as turn the whole thing back to front… But even as a child I could see how bewitching Isobel was, and my own mother had always seemed such a devoted wife…'

There was a long pause before he went on, 'I'd never dreamt of my mother falling so deeply in love with another man that she'd want a divorce…'

Clare sighed. 'Neither had my father, apparently. As far as *he* was concerned, your mother was just another one of his affairs. The last thing he wanted was a divorce, in case it ruined his career. Strange how two women could have kept loving a man like that.

'Though it's clear no one doubted that your mother's death was an accident, it must have been the realisation of what kind of man my father really was, how he'd just *used* her, that made her drink too much. And you saw what it did to my own mother… So if anyone's responsible for wrecking so many lives, it's my father…'

'You once remarked that it takes two to tango,' Jos said quietly, 'and I've since realised you were right. My mother must at least share the responsibility.'

After a moment, Clare said, 'The only thing I can be happy about is that despite everything our mothers stayed friends until the end.'

Jos sighed. 'Can you ever forgive me for laying all the blame at Isobel's door?'

'If you hadn't, we wouldn't be where we are now,' Clare pointed out.

'And where are we now?' He sounded weary.

Ignoring the deeper meaning, she answered, 'In bed together.'

'Is that where you want to be?'

'It is.'

She saw the flare of hope in his green eyes as he asked, 'Then, generally speaking, you're happy with the way things are?'

'They're *almost* perfect.'

'So what do you need to make them *absolutely* perfect?'

'A marriage that will last until we're old.'

'I've always intended it to. Anything else?'

'A real home in the country.'

'Could you bring yourself to like the Priory?'

'I already do. In fact it was love at first sight.'

'Then we'll make that our home. Anything else?'

A shade hesitantly, she suggested, 'It's a house that cries out for a big, happy family…'

'Children?' He raised a dark brow. 'How many were you thinking of?'

'Three or four.'

'I guess we could manage that. Anything else?'

'Perhaps—for when we visit New York—a penthouse with a butler who plays poker and drinks bourbon.'

'That you already have. Anything else?'

For a moment she was silent, then she admitted, 'Most of all, I'd like you to like me.'

He said, as he'd said once before, 'Liking is such a bloodless, insipid emotion. Would you settle for enough deep, passionate love to last a lifetime?'

Violet eyes brimming with tears, she whispered, 'I might.'

'Then it's yours.' Holding her close, he kissed away the tears. 'It always has been.'

MILLS & BOON®

*M*akes
any time
special

Enjoy a romantic novel from
Mills & Boon®

Presents...™   *Enchanted*™   TEMPTATION.

Historical Romance™   ✚ MEDICAL ROMANCE™

MAT1

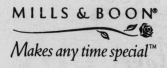

MILLS & BOON®

Makes any time special™

By Request™

Seduction GUARANTEED

THE MORNING AFTER *by Michelle Reid*

César DeSanquez wants revenge on Annie Lacey for tearing his family apart. Sweeping her off to his family island, he ruthlessly seduces her, only to discover she is innocent…

A WOMAN OF PASSION *by Anne Mather*

In the heat of Barbados, cool Helen Gregory's inhibitions are melted by Matthew Aitken's hot seduction. But Matthew seems to be already involved—with Helen's glamorous mother!

RENDEZVOUS WITH REVENGE
by Miranda Lee

Ethan Grant was Abby's boss—so why had he asked her to pose as his lover at a weekend conference? Ethan hadn't let Abby in on his plans, but, once he seduced her into becoming his real lover, would he tell her the truth?

**Look out for Seduction Guaranteed
in June 2000**

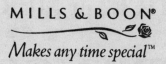

MILLS & BOON®

Makes any time special™

COMING SOON

St. Elizabeth's Children's Hospital

A limited collection of 12 books. Where affairs of
the heart are entwined with the everyday dealings
of this warm and friendly children's hospital.

Book 1
A Winter Bride by Meredith Webber
Published 5th May

SECH/RTL/2

JUSTICE? or MURDER?

Men are dying unexpectedly—all victims of
bizarre accidents. Policewoman Melanie May
sees the pattern of a serial killer
targeting men who have slipped through the
fingers of justice.

Melanie risks her career to convince
Connor Parks that she is right and finds
herself in the limelight…and a target of a killer
who will not stop until…

ALL FALL DOWN

ERICA
SPINDLER

MIRA

Published 21st April 2000
1-55166-551-4

LINDA HOWARD

LOVING EVANGELINE

LOVER, VICTIM…SPY?

It wasn't just a case of theft or corporate espionage—it was treason! And the trail led straight to Evangeline Shaw.

When Robert Cannon meets Evie he begins to have doubts about her guilt.

Is he being duped by a professional or is she just an innocent pawn caught up in a deadly game?

Available from 19 May 2000
ISBN: 1-55166-457-7

M180

NAN
RYAN

Wanting you

Heiress…
She has no memory before her kidnapping.
Then suddenly Anna Regent Wright is given a
past and most of all, a future beyond her
wildest dreams.

Or Impostor?
There is no doubt in Brit Caruth's mind that
Anna is a fake. But this beautiful stranger
has a hold on his body. Will he risk the
inheritance he's always believed to be his?

Available 19 May 2000
ISBN: 1-55166-521-2

M181

MIRA®